# BRIGHT MONTANA HOME

## CYNTHIA BRUNER

Montana Inspired Arts

# CHAPTER 1

$\mathcal{T}$he pink and ice-blue sunset had faded on the long trip to Moose Hollow until just traces of blue lingered and stars blinked in the darkened sky. With the passing miles, Avery had found it harder to keep her hopes up. She had wanted to find something magical. A sign of some sort. Something that could salvage this day—her wedding day.

She'd seen online pictures of Moose Hollow: a colorful little town of Victorian houses and quaint storefronts, old-fashioned lampposts lining Broadway Avenue, smiling tourists everywhere. Even the town's trash cans had looked artistic. But in the last of the evening light, the town she drove through looked dreary. A wall of snow sat between the road and the sidewalk on either side of the narrow main street, the road was nearly empty, and the only people she saw were milling around in front of a bar.

Her destination was on the left. In person, it looked stranger and smaller. The brick building abutted much nicer buildings on either side, one in refurbished brick with a balcony and a fancy patio, the other a rustic combination of stone, wood, and hand-stripped log work. Between them, her building looked plain and worn. The upstairs windows were dark and dirty looking, the downstairs storefront even darker.

The left half of the front of her building was parallel to the street, and the right half angled back in. It appeared as though the two adjacent buildings had been built different distances from the road, and the middle one was an attempt to link the two together. Its peeling front door was set back into the building, shadowed and half hidden, with no lamp to light the way.

Avery drove behind the building and down an alley. As Tabitha had promised, there were two parking spaces and a dumpster there. A half-open bag of garbage was blocking the first space, so she parked in the second and hoped her little rental trailer didn't block the alley. She looked around nervously for anyone creeping through the alley, saw no one, and climbed out of her little SUV, stretching her stiff legs.

The air in Montana felt thin and sharp. She'd noticed it down on the eastern plains, and it was even more so here in the mountains. She tipped her face up. Something tinier than snow was falling on her face—icy fairy wings, here and then gone just as fast. She could see the sparkle of it in the yellow halo of the light next door.

There was no light in the back of her building. She pulled the key out of her pocket, the one she had strung on a lovely apricot ribbon, the color of spring and new beginnings. It looked sickly in the yellow light, and at first, it didn't fit the lock. For a moment Avery thought she was going to freeze to death in this lonely little town. But then she wriggled the key in and wrestled the lock into a creaking, crunching half-turn that ended with a hopeful click. She pulled.

The sound of metal on metal was like nails on a chalkboard. She winced and pulled again, and this time the door swung free. She found a light switch, hit it, and a couple of old fluorescent fixtures buzzed to life.

She was in the "back room" Tabitha had talked about.

Once she made it past the tunnel of boxes stacked by the back door, it looked much bigger than she'd expected. She knew it would be a mess, so that was no surprise. She would clean it and fill that dumpster out back a couple times, and then it would be useful. Avery sniffed the air. Musty, not a good smell. And the wooden boards beneath her feet creaked as she walked.

Well, the store would be better. Avery would save that for last. Right now she needed to head upstairs to the apartments and find out where she'd be living. The stairway was to her left; the boxes and garbage bags full of heaven-knows-what had nearly hidden it.

It was her wedding night. She had planned to spend her honeymoon camping in a van. She shook her head. *Not now.* Memories of what she had done and what it had cost him threatened to drown her. She had to keep moving. She owed him her life.

The smell upstairs was even worse than she'd imagined. In the first room there was a stained and burned carpet covered in cigarette butts, fast food wrappers, and what appeared to be a wad of clothing in the corner. She closed the door and moved on. Next door was another small bedroom, its floor covered in garbage bags and empty cardboard boxes.

Next to that was the bathroom. The door was ajar, so she peeked inside. But the dark stains on the floor, not to mention the smell, drove her back.

She stood in the hallway a moment, trying to fight off the feeling of dread that threatened to overwhelm her. So the bathroom was a disaster. She could handle it, little by little. Surely it would be less intimidating in the morning, after a good night's sleep. She moved on to the next open door, the kitchen. She'd seen the photographs—piles of dishes in a dirty kitchen—but she hadn't appreciated the backed-up sink and garbage tossed on the floor.

Had someone actually lived this way? Or was it a dozen people?

The final door was also open. Avery reached in, found a light switch, and then quickly wiped her hand on her pants. Blankets and more clothes, including a filthy bra, lay at one end of the room. There were burns on this rug as well. The room reeked of vinegar and something sweet, like a mixture of garbage and butterscotch. She rushed over to the windows and slid one open, then ran out and closed the door before she had to take another breath.

Where she was going to sleep?

What had she done?

Her back pocket started playing "Ode to Joy." She pulled out her phone. "Hello, Mom. I was just about to call you." There was a window here, too, at the end of the long hallway. It was angled to face up the road, but with the lights on inside and darkness outside, she couldn't see very much. She leaned forward and shielded her eyes with one hand, looking down. A couple was hurrying by below her, hunched over and half frozen. "Yes, as a matter of fact, I just got here," she said brightly. "It's so quaint!"

She backed away from the window, noting how filthy it looked and wiping her hand on her pants again. All she could see now was her own reflection in the window. When her mother was done admonishing her for not calling to say she'd arrived, she plastered a smile on her face. "Well, I'm excited. In a small town like this, it won't take any time at all to make friends." Her mom didn't say much to that, so Avery added, "In fact, tomorrow I'll start sampling some of the churches around here."

Her mother had a lot of questions. Avery pressed the heel of her hand to her forehead. "Yes. Yes. I know, Mom. But I need to go because I need to bring some things in from the car, and it's snowing, it's quite warm inside." Well, not quite warm. But probably warmer than camping in a van in Utah. "I've got to go, Mom. I love you. Yes. Me too. Bye."

She disconnected the call and closed her eyes. The store. She still had the store itself. She took a minute to work up her courage. Then she heard a sound below where there shouldn't be any sound, especially one like a door opening.

Tabitha had moved to California. Who would be in this awful place? *No one with good intentions*, she thought. And she was alone.

She looked around, spotting—of all things in the mess of a kitchen—a broom. It was as good a weapon as she could find unless just the smell of the place made the intruder pass out. She quietly hurried toward safety, down the stairs and toward the door to the alley, but when she reached for it, the handle spun freely in her hand. She pushed. It didn't budge.

She didn't have time to think. The intruder was between her and the only other door, and he would have heard her by now. She held the broom up and charged forward, hoping that the closer she got to the front door before the intruder caught her, the better her chances were of getting help from a passerby.

There was a tall, hooded figure near the front door, hunched over by some shelves. At the sound of her approach, the figure straightened with a loud gasp and pressed one hand to his chest. The hood slipped back a little, and by the faint light through the front windows, Avery saw tendrils of pale hair, wide eyes, and parted lips. Lipstick?

Avery froze. "Tabitha?"

They faced each other, unmoving. Then Avery saw another figure hurtle through the front door.

# CHAPTER 2

*A*nother hour, another pile of papers. The entire filing cabinet held piles of receipts, handwritten notes, and overstuffed folders that were organized vaguely chronologically. Liam's best guess was that his uncle had, one by one, stuffed a file folder with everything that had crossed his desk until it couldn't hold any more, then shoved it into a drawer and started a new one. This folder held articles of incorporation, inspection certificates of some sort, bills of sale, and invoices numbered randomly between 0001 and 10,000. He didn't even know if any of them had been printed out and mailed, let alone paid.

After one day of reconnaissance, Liam was getting a pretty good idea of the mess he'd gotten himself into. And this was only the beginning. Once he had the new brokerage under control, he'd have to address the parent company, Gunnerson Landholdings, Inc. It could be a month before he even got close to work worthy of his pay grade.

He'd suggested his uncle Cash hire a bookkeeper to organize things before getting Liam involved, but that wasn't how Cash worked. He was the kind of guy who cleaned his house before the maid came over. He trusted Liam only because he was family. But once this mess was cleaned up, Liam would force his uncle to find a good bookkeeper and then keep a close eye on him.

Knowing Cash, he had better not hire a pretty girl, either, or nothing would ever get done.

Liam stretched his arms high over his head. He'd been sitting too long. He was going to be at this job long enough that he'd need to add a standing desk to his bill, then leave it behind for Cash to use. Not that Cash needed it. The man was always in motion, and almost never at his desk. Good thing, since his ornate desk was so overcome by paperwork that there wasn't room to set a water bottle down. Liam spun the fancy, old-fashioned office chair around and looked out over Broadway. It was a weirdly quiet night for a Saturday, which made him think something big was going on in Billings.

It was a great view. The ceilings in Cash's new office building were higher than even the old Victorian buildings, which meant that his second floor looked down on the second floors across the street. And over them, beyond the old mining abutments and the ridge trailhead, the moon was about to rise and shine down on Moose Hollow.

He had a lot to do. The sooner he finished, the sooner he could leave town again. For good.

A light came on across the dark road, illuminating a narrow, dingy window. It was on the right side of the vacant building across the street. Cash had mentioned the place, and that it was empty, hadn't he? Liam did a quick scan of the road and the rooftops and then focused. He could just make out a hallway and a line of painted doorways down one side of it. And there was someone inside, edging closer to the window.

He saw shiny brown hair and a lavender jacket. A woman. She looked unsure, as if she wasn't supposed to be there. Was she there to steal something? Cash had hinted something shady had gone on in that building. Liam turned off the desk lamp to better hide from view. As he watched, the woman held one hand over her nose and peeked inside a door, then backed away as if there was a wild animal inside. Then she edged down the hall, peeking and backing away again. By now her arms were wrapped tightly around her middle, except when she reached out a tentative hand to open a door.

She didn't even peek behind the next door. But she spent about a minute inside the room after that.

Then she came closer still. A light came on so that now the whole second-floor row of windows was lit, and Liam took in the view in an instant. Flophouse. Drugs. *She doesn't look the type, not that most people do,* he thought. At least in the beginning. But it wasn't just her nice clothes that convinced him. It was that she seemed disturbed by what she saw. She hurried forward and opened a window, and he resisted the urge to duck out of sight. Then she ran out and slammed the door.

Next she reached into a pocket. Had drugs brought her there? Whether or not she was a user, that building wasn't a safe place for her. He contemplated calling the Moose Hollow Police. He'd heard there had been a change in leadership, but what he knew of the police didn't bode well for them getting involved, especially since he didn't own that building. They seemed to prefer to let their residents solve their own problems.

Liam knew not all of Moose Hollow's problems got solved.

The woman made a phone call. She leaned forward to look out the window, and Liam held still, knowing that movement was the one thing that would make him most visible. But rather than spotting him, she leaned back, and for the first time, he got a clear view of her. Was she smiling? Liam's chin dropped a little as he studied her. Pretty, with a narrow chin and large eyes. Probably younger than himself, maybe just out of college. At least it seemed so. She touched the phone screen, and at that moment he saw her entire body slump in defeat.

Her smile had been an act. She was in trouble and didn't want anyone to know it. Or perhaps she was inviting her drug-using friends over and now she regretted it.

Movement on the street below caught his attention. A figure —tall, broad-shouldered, and thin, wearing a dark, long coat with a hood—was hunched over in front of the iron gate that barred the way to the front door. The hooded coat was overly dramatic, but maybe it was someone's idea of camouflage. The figure turned, looked surreptitiously up and down the street, then went back to work. Was he picking the lock?

Liam sat forward, his hands on the arms of the chair. The young woman was still standing there, hugging herself. Waiting for what?

The iron door below pushed open. Liam stood. The woman across the way turned suddenly as if she had heard it. He flicked on the desk lamp, stood, and waved his arms, but she didn't see him. She disappeared into one of the rooms and reemerged with a broom in one hand, wielding the handle like a sword, and started running down the hall and away from the window.

She was expecting a fight, and that was all he needed to know. Liam crossed the room, took the stairs down in three steps, and flipped the deadbolt as his shoulder hit the door, hardly breaking stride as he burst across the street. The front door to her building gave way, and in an instant he registered the young woman's open mouth and the broom held high—not a very practical attack pose—before he tackled the hooded figure to the ground. His target made an awful, choking squeal.

A boy? There was hardly anything to the person beneath him. As he flipped him over, the young woman holding the broom cried, "Don't hurt her!"

*Her.* Liam froze for a moment but didn't let go. Attackers could be male or female. A threat was a threat.

But then the hood fell back, and he found himself staring into the face of an old woman. To make matters worse, the young woman rushed behind him and turned on the lights, making it even more clear that he'd attacked someone who looked far too frail for the hit she'd just endured. He was so distracted that he didn't see the next blow coming.

The broom handle crashed across his shoulder blade.

"Leave her alone!"

More irritated than hurt, Liam scrambled to his feet. He crouched down to take the older woman's hands. "Do you think you can stand?" he asked softly. Then said over his shoulder, "Do you mind holding off your assault for a moment?"

The young woman's gaze flicked from him to the older woman and back to his outstretched hands. She pressed her lips tight and raised the broom handle inches higher in what appeared to be a threat. Ignoring her, Liam put one hand around the older woman's waist and helped her to her feet.

He shifted his assessment. She was old, but maybe not as old as he'd thought. Her shocked expression and tangle of gray hair had influenced him.

"Are you all right, Tabitha?" the young woman asked.

"I'm not Tabitha," the older woman said. She pulled her hands away from Liam and brushed her hair back. Then she took off her coat and handed it to Liam as if she expected him to hold it. And he did.

"You're not…who are you?" the younger woman said.

The older woman carefully rearranged her outfit, an orange turtleneck over a pleated lime green skirt, and said, "I'm the maid."

The look of incredulity that passed the younger woman's face made a smile twitch across Liam's face, but he kept his expression neutral. At least he wasn't the only confused person here.

The older woman put bony fists on her hips and glared over her shoulder. "And who are you?"

"Who am I?" Her lips remained parted. They were a shiny,

pale pink, he noticed. "I'm the one who just saved you from being mugged by this...this..."

"Liam Gunnerson," he supplied.

The older woman reached out her hand, and the tips of her cold fingers slipped loosely into his grasp. "Pleasure to meet you, young man," she said. "Next time we wrestle on the floor, it really should be away from prying eyes, don't you think?" She winked at him.

Liam's eyebrows rose. "Yes, ma'am. I mean, no. Ma'am."

The woman laughed and turned her back on him. "What is your name, young lady?"

"I'm the new owner," she said.

"I didn't ask that, Miss."

The younger woman bit her lip. "Avery Maier."

"I'm Melanie," the older woman said, reaching for Avery's hand. Avery had to finally lower the broom to accept the handshake.

*Not that the two were shaking hands,* Liam thought. It was more as if Melanie was accepting accolades. She held out her fingertips like a princess.

"I suppose this means Tabitha's building sold." Melanie looked around. "I work on Monday and Friday nights, dear."

"It's Saturday," Avery said. She looked as confused as Liam felt.

"Is it?" Melanie shrugged. "Ah, well, that happens. I guess I'll be on my way, then. See you Monday." She stepped closer to Liam and held out one thin arm. She expected him to put her coat on, and he did. It was wool, well worn, and looked to have been made for a large man. She put both arms through it, gave him another wink, then headed for the door.

"Wait," Avery said, propping the broom up against the wall. "I don't need a—"

*A maid,* Liam finished in his mind. At that moment Melanie turned around, her eyes narrow with anger.

Avery balked. "We'll talk about it on Monday," she said.

Melanie smiled and waved one hand through the air, then left, closing the door behind her.

Avery stood still so long that Liam was sure she had forgotten he was standing there, and sure enough, when she turned around, she jumped a little and stared at him, backing closer to the door. "You need to go."

"I certainly do," he said. "Unless you'd like to take another whack at me. You seemed to enjoy it well enough the first time."

A tiny flush of color appeared on her cheeks. Mad looked good on her. Liam would've loved to tweak her a little more, but there was business to attend to. "You're the new owner of this building, correct? If Melanie has a key, it's very likely that others do as well. You should probably get your locks changed."

She nodded in a quick, tiny movement.

"You just got here, right? If you don't mind, I'd like to check the place to make sure no one else is around."

"No."

"I insist. Or we could call the police and let them search."

She blew air out of her nose so sharply he heard it. "Fine."

He looked around the store, at the overstuffed racks and the 1980s cash register, and out of the corner of his eye, he noticed Avery doing the same thing, as curious as if she'd never seen it before.

There wasn't any good place to hide, other than the curtained-off corner that passed as a dressing room. Liam walked through the back of the shop to another room.

This place was a disaster. It was like a police obstacle course. Anyone could be hiding anywhere. He searched as quickly as possible, including a nearly hidden bathroom, and then headed upstairs.

"You don't need to check there, I already did," she called.

He ignored her. He knew there was at least one room she

hadn't checked. She hadn't opened that door enough to stick her head inside.

"I said—"

"It will only take a minute, and then I'll be out of your hair." Silky, chocolate-colored hair and smooth skin. She looked too healthy to be a drug addict. Was she really the landlord? She didn't look old enough to be able to afford a building like this, let alone the renovation costs it would require.

Liam looked in every room. The toilet was beyond functioning but had been used nonetheless. The kitchen floor was covered in mouse feces and thick brown stains.

Avery followed behind him, staying a few steps away, not saying a word.

The last room, the one with the light on and the window open, was the worst.

"What is that smell?" she said.

"Heroin. Pretty recent." He turned off the light and closed the door. "This is a flophouse. You can't stay here until you know no one can come in here anymore. It isn't safe."

Her shoulders straightened, her narrow chin lifted and jutted out a tiny bit, and she frowned until a single line was etched between her eyebrows, just off center. "You can go now."

He crossed his arms. "I know a hotel where you could stay. Plus my uncle owns quite a few rental properties. Chances are that something is vacant and you—"

"I'm fine."

"You have another place to stay tonight?"

She stepped back a little, turning to the side, and shrugged. "I have a place."

*Very well*, Liam thought. He walked past her, making sure to give her a wide berth since she still looked jumpy. She followed him down the stairs, then trailed him all the way to the front door and out onto the sidewalk.

"Are you going to follow me home?" he asked.

"My things are out back," she said.

That made no sense at all.

"The back door..." Avery stopped there.

It didn't work. He would have bet his aching shoulder blade on it. "Would you like some help moving things inside?" he asked.

"No," she said sharply, and off she went down the street, passing the shoulder-width alley between where the Red Fox restaurant used to be and the fishing gear store still was. *She probably didn't know that shortcut was there*, he thought. For a new property owner, she didn't seem to know much about her building.

But he had an office to close, and down the road, a beautiful little room in his family's hotel. He put all thoughts of the stubborn young woman out of his mind.

# CHAPTER 3

*F*irst thing Monday morning, Liam saw Avery march to the realty agent next door to her building. She was wearing a skirt, boots, and tights, and the same puffy lavender jacket he'd seen before, and she looked like she was on the fight. Curious, he set the papers in his hand on Cash's desk. Avery stormed inside the office. A couple minutes went by. Then she came out and headed down the street, still stomping all the way. He had caught a glimpse of her expression: dark eyes looking fierce, lips pursed. He wondered if she was wearing that light pink lip gloss again. It was hard to tell from where he stood.

She went down a block and a half and then ducked inside another door. If Liam had to guess, she was inside another one of the half-dozen or so realty offices in Moose Hollow.

He shook his head and turned back to his paperwork, losing himself there until he heard Cash coming up the stairs. There was no mistaking it was him, since Cash liked to step in the rhythm of whatever song was playing in his head. Liam glanced at his watch. Nine forty-five, earlier than usual. He started gathering up his papers. Cash came through the door, looking extremely cheerful for someone who had probably been out drinking until midnight the night before.

"Let me give you your desk back, Uncle Cash."

Cash shook his head. "Naw." He came over and handed a hot coffee cup to Liam. "I don't want to interrupt your work. I can actually see part of the desk for a change." He put a hand on the bare brick between the floor-to-ceiling windows. "What a beautiful day." He took a drink of his own coffee. Regular coffee with more sugar than cream, Liam knew.

"Have you been out in the sunshine yet?" Cash asked.

"Nope."

"What time did you get here?"

"Sometime around seven." Six forty, actually.

Cash whistled. "Did you see Lynn called again? And again?"

"Yes, thank you." He saw his chance to change the subject. "Do you know anything about the new owner over there?" He gestured across the street.

"Not much," Cash said. "I tried to get it myself, but it was crazy overpriced. Plus it's a gut job. Electric is old, plumbing is shot. And it's been a flophouse for the last three years. Poor old Tabitha Vaber just lost control of the place. She moved out after you moved to Chicago. Dementia, I think, and some other health issues."

"So you put in an offer?"

"Of course I did. So did the Hallowells, and I thought they won, but the sale fell through. Rumor was Tabitha refused to sell to them. Why so interested? Is the new owner cute?"

Liam shook his head. Of course Cash would go there. Liam didn't give him the pleasure of saying it was true. "I thought I saw a break-in last night, that's all. Turned out to be the maid."

Cash laughed. "You mean Mad Mel." He looked back over the street. "Yeah. She and Tabitha were close. Crazy as bats, both of them. I think Melanie was the one who opened up a boarding house," he said, marking those words with air quotes, "on the top floor." He stood up straighter. "Well, now. This is interesting."

Liam followed Cash's gaze down to the street below and caught a flash of lavender. Then he heard the door open at the bottom of the stairs.

"My lucky day," Cash grinned.

Liam jumped up. "You'll need your desk," he said, grabbing papers to his chest. "I'll get out of your way."

"You don't have to..." Cash's words faded away as the sharp stomping of feet marked Avery's imminent approach.

Liam was glad he'd put his temporary desk at the other end of the long office, under a clerestory window and half hidden by the big wooden filing cabinets that had yet to be moved into place and properly filled. He kept his back to her and slid into his seat and out of sight.

"Hi, my name is Cash Gunnerson." Without looking, Liam knew his uncle's words had filtered through a wide smile, as usual. For some reason, it set him on edge. "What can I do for you?"

"My name is Avery Maier. I'm trying to find the broker who handled the sale of that building across the street." Her words came at the same fast clip as her steps.

Liam's curiosity got the best of him. He pushed the chair back a couple inches and looked through the crack between the filing cabinets. He could only see Cash, not the woman.

"I see. Here, have a seat. I have a fresh cup of coffee here if you're interested."

Cash handed her Liam's cup. Liam rolled his eyes.

"I'm interested in finding the broker who cheated me."

The cup of coffee went back to the desk untouched. Liam leaned farther back to get a view of Cash's face. Eyebrows raised, Cash nodded slowly. "I see. Have a seat." He waited for her to sit, and no doubt won the war of wills. "You won't find the broker around here, Miss Maier. Or should I call you Missus?"

"I—no. No. You can call me Avery." She sounded flustered.

Liam frowned. Was the famous Gunnerson charm working? Not that any of that charm had been passed on to him.

"Avery, I have only a little information about that piece of property. It was owned by Tabitha Vaber, who became ill several years ago. She tried to keep the store running, but from what I heard, it was a losing battle. About six months ago her family took legal responsibility for her. I believe the broker you are looking for is in California. That's where her family is, and now her, too, I bet."

Liam heard Avery sigh from across the room. "The agency listed on the contracts was from San Bernardino. I just assumed someone local handled the sale."

Cash sat down on the edge of his desk and shook his head slowly in sympathy. "You might be able to get more information from the public records. I'm sorry I couldn't help you, Avery. But if they cheated you, maybe you could bring suit against them."

"I don't know if they did. To be honest, I had a hard time understanding the contract. I had an agent, but it turns out he wasn't as helpful as I thought he was."

The agent probably hadn't received anything more than a token fee, Liam guessed. But whoever it was hadn't done his job, and now this woman was paying for it. Liam could imagine what the contract looked like. It was probably half disclaimers, and the other half indemnities.

"Making things clear is your agent's job," Cash said, echoing Liam's thoughts. "Shame on him. But don't give up hope just yet. Have you had the contract reviewed since the sale?"

"No. To be honest, I've been spending my time on the store. I can't make heads or tails of what's going on. I don't think Tabitha has done inventory for, well, at least three years."

"I think I know someone who can help you," Cash said, and he glanced in Liam's direction. Liam jumped and his chair squeaked. He shook his head at his uncle.

But Cash's eyes had already moved on. "My CPA, besides being a terrific accountant, has a good sense of legal mumbo-jumbo. I think I could spare him for a little while to help you sort things out with the contract, taxes, inventory, even your business plan. And he'll do it because I'm his uncle and he loves me." Then, louder, "Did you hear that, Liam?"

He had, and he certainly wished he hadn't. With no place to run, and nowhere left to hide, he stood up and came out from his desk. "Are you calling...oh, hi. Sorry, I had my headphones on and—" Of course now that he'd lied about hearing them, he couldn't correct Cash for representing him as a CPA. He wasn't. He could be, he should be, but he wasn't.

Avery stood up and said, "You." There was nothing nice about the way she said it. Cash covered a smile with his hand, and once it was under control, he took his hand away and said, "Have the two of you met?"

"He broke into my building and attacked one of my workers," Avery said. She stared him down with chocolate-colored eyes and a firm set to her jaw.

"And she hit me with a broom," Liam said, closing the gap between them. He folded his arms across his chest.

"Oh, that can't be right," Cash said. His voice was conciliatory, but his eyes had activated all the laugh lines around them. "Why, I know I've only just met you, Avery, but you are perfectly lovely. And Liam, well, he's a good boy. It must have just been a misunderstanding. Whatever happened, the two of you just need to get to know one another better. Liam, I'm sure you didn't hear us talking because of your *headphones*—"

Liam didn't take the bait.

"—but Miss Avery Maier here needs a little guidance in examining the store's books and the contract she signed to purchase the building across the street."

Again Liam shook his head no, but he had to stop when Avery looked his way. Her eyes narrowed. He probably hadn't stopped soon enough.

Cash continued. "You see, Liam isn't the type to stand on the sidelines when he can help. Right, Liam?"

Liam silently plotted ways to get his uncle back for this. There weren't many. And besides, his was the only job offer Liam had received in the past month, and he couldn't afford to alienate him.

Avery gave Liam a smirk. It was a perfect smirk, as if she'd practiced it often. Somehow it was vaguely insulting but also so cute it was difficult to feel insulted by it. Then she turned back to face Cash. "I don't think so."

"Please, Avery, consider it a welcome present for your new business. Let me do this for you. It really would be a pleasure. For me, and for Liam, of course."

"Well." Cash could see her considering her options. "If Liam is interested, I suppose we could take a few minutes to review the contract. Before I hire a *real* lawyer, of course."

Liam took the barb without comment. It was nothing compared to the grilling Cash was going to give him shortly. "What time would be good for you?" he asked her.

"I close the store at five," she said.

"Excellent," Cash said. "Dinner is on me. I'll make the two of you a reservation for six-thirty at the Third Street Inn."

Liam had seen that coming. Cash was a runaway freight train. A happy one. But Avery's jaw dropped.

Cash ushered her out, talking all the way until she had no other move but to go down the stairs and out the door without getting a word in edgewise.

Cash waited until the door to the street opened and shut.

Then he retrieved Liam's coffee cup and handed it back to him. "Oh, buddy," he said with a laugh, "I think you're about to make my morning. Tell me everything."

It was going to be a very long day of work at Gunnerson Landholdings.

# CHAPTER 4

*A*very had trudged upstairs to the living area of her building first thing Sunday morning, hoping it would look better with a little light on it. But it had looked much the same, especially in the middle rooms, where the only sunlight came through dingy, leaking windows on the roof. Still, the light of day had chased away some of the ghosts, and she was no longer worried about anyone breaking through her barricaded back door.

But Sunday night had felt just as bad as her first night in the building. At least no one had burst inside and tackled her. Liam never had apologized for that.

The man talked as if he knew everything. The night he broke into her building, he'd made it clear he thought she was an idiot. That from a man who had just tackled an old lady. And she never had figured out how he'd arrived so quickly. Had he just happened to be walking by? How had he known that Melanie had entered the building?

By Monday morning, she had decided he wasn't worth thinking about, other than to make a point of avoiding him if she saw him again. Yet here she was, thinking about him still.

And worse, she would be having dinner with him at the end of the day. Avery tapped her pen on the checkout desk and stared at the front door of the Moose on the Loose, which had swung open exactly once this morning. She had few options, and turning down free assistance wasn't one of them. She had spent every cent of her insurance money on this building, and it clearly wasn't worth what she'd paid. But here she was. Up the creek, irrevocably. Unless there was a loophole Liam could find, of course.

But that wasn't the way things worked for her. "I made the bed, I'll sleep in it," she said out loud. The irony of that metaphor wasn't lost on her.

She had phone calls to make—utilities, plumber, locksmith. The search results on her phone began to overwhelm her. And then, somewhere in the middle of searching "is heroin dangerous to clean up" and "who provides electricity to Moose Hollow," she saw an ad for a "disaster restoration" company.

She hadn't even known there was such a thing. And the company was located in Billings—a town name she recognized from the highway signs and the city lights she'd seen Saturday night. Without thinking, she called.

A woman named Bella answered the phone, asked a few questions, and said she'd be there in an hour and a half. And that was that.

Avery wondered what on earth she had just gotten herself into. After thinking herself in circles, nearly working herself into an anxiety attack, she got busy.

Yesterday she'd cleared the wall-to-ceiling garbage bags out of the downstairs bathroom and cleaned it as well as it could be cleaned, short of the new floor, toilet, and sink it needed. The job had taken nearly all day, filled what empty space remained in the dumpster, and given her the opportunity to discover a good local pizzeria across the street. Then she'd cleared out the checkout desk in the front of the store, which left her with a confusing mass of papers, notes, invoices, and receipts. After that, she'd crawled into the hidden spot she'd constructed out of boxes and slept, finding some rest between nightmares, all of which starred her ex-fiancé, Eli, in one form or another. Then she'd woken up angry.

No wonder no one would enter the store. The place was a mess. A large, round sale rack was just inside the front door, which was a bad first impression. She walked around it, fingers trailing the sleeves of clothing. The tags read 50 percent off. Despite the name brands, the clothing didn't look familiar to her, even though she'd done some research to prepare for running the store. She looked more closely at the tags. The first was three years old. She grabbed another. Four.

With yet another feeling of dread pouring over her, she walked over to the first full-price rack. The clothing on it was four years old.

There was nothing new in the store. She wandered from rack to rack. What about the new inventory mentioned in the contract?

On a hunch she went into the back room. She reached up onto a stack of boxes and pulled one down to the ground, where it fell with a thud. Curling back from the seams was what looked like the original packing tape. It had never been cut. She tore it away and opened the box to find shirts in their original plastic bags. She examined the packing slip on the top. It had been sent in March—two years ago.

She stood up with a sigh. There were other unopened boxes as well, though if last night's attempt at box rearranging was any indication, many were filled with odds and ends. And there was no more room in the dumpster.

She would need to open an online store through one of the auction sites. "New with tags" stuff sold well. And she had to find a way to make the store look more attractive, because if she didn't start selling things immediately, the small amount of cash she had left would be gone. Cash that might already be earmarked for plumbers and the like.

But first she needed to tackle the appearance of Moose on the Loose. There were so many items, strewn everywhere, including clothes for every season. She decided that since she'd always been drawn to color, other people might be as well. She picked up all the orange items first—orange being a happy color—and put them on one rack. To sort through them, she put some of the clothes on the floor, which was fairly clean. Maybe Melanie had been cleaning after all. Not that Avery could afford a janitor. Then she made a sign that read, "20% off today's color: ORANGE" and hung it on the door.

Avery had made a fair dent in rearranging things by the time Bella Smith arrived. In her thirties, she wore a black polo with the company logo on it and khakis, both of which were ironed, and her makeup was subtle but precise. *Attention to detail*, Avery thought. And a kind smile. That was important, because the thought of showing yet another person the mess that was upstairs made her feel embarrassed. Guilty, even. After all, it was her mess. Her sight-unseen purchase. After a brief intro-duction, Avery led Bella to the back stairs.

It was different, walking up the stairs with someone else. She noticed more, like the tears in the carpet and the awful stain that spanned three steps. The cigarette burns in the hall. And the pervasive smell. If it made Bella want to gag, the way it did Avery, the woman hid it well.

Bella looked in each room, wandered around a bit, and then wrote something on a tablet. She even leaned into the bath-room, although the floor was obviously not worth stepping on. The last room was no better or worse. The vinegar smell was gone, leaving the scent of bile behind it. Through it all, Bella's calm expression never wavered. "What's a flophouse?" Avery asked out loud, thinking of what Liam had said.

"It has a few meanings. A free, usually illegal place to stay, like an abandoned building. Or the place where heroin or meth addicts go to shoot up."

Avery felt tears welling in her eyes. "This had to have taken longer than a couple weeks to get this bad, right?" she said softly.

Bella looked her in the eye and spoke clearly but gently. "Months at least. Probably years."

If Avery had seen the place in person before buying it, just like everyone had told her to, she would have known.

But they hadn't understood how badly she needed to leave and to come here. And she never would have imagined someone lying about something like this.

"And you just purchased the place so your insurance won't cover it."

Avery nodded her head. Then she hugged her arms over her stomach.

"Let's go back downstairs," Bella said, and Avery followed after her. Just as expected, there were still no customers in the store. They returned to the front desk. "It'll take me a little while to get an estimate together, but I can tell you from what I've seen, we will need to do a hazardous waste removal and a thorough chemical cleaning. Each of the skylights is leaking. That probably means that the roof needs to be resealed as well. The drywall will need to be replaced around the skylights, and several places on the walls.

"Because of the water damage, the floor in the bathroom will most likely need to be replaced, and possibly the tub. We won't know what the other floors are like until we get things cleared out, but the kitchen floor didn't look promising. In buildings this age, this almost certainly includes a new subfloor and, depending on how they're doing, some work on the joists."

Avery bit her lips back into her mouth and tried not to cry.

"This is where you planned to live, right?" Bella asked.

Avery nodded.

"I suggest we start with the room that faces the street. It's got a lot of yucky stuff in it, but it actually seems sound to me. Besides, you'd have fresh air and sunlight. We could make that our priority and get you moved in, and then start in on the rest of the project."

The bell that hung from the front door rang and three young men walked in. Except for one of them, she recognized the type —clothed in stylish gear made from high-tech fabrics that cost as much as a mortgage payment. They were her customers. She knew she should greet them, but she didn't feel up to it. "How much?" she asked Bella.

"As I said, I need to get an estimate—"

"Ballpark."

Bella's smile pulled sideways into a wry look. Then she spoke a number that would require Avery to use up every last bit of money she possessed, including the money earmarked for new inventory. There were places near her old hometown where she could have bought a house and land for the same amount.

The figure left her so shocked she couldn't speak. She tried to wrap her mind around what it would mean for her financial status. She couldn't walk away—no one would be foolish enough to purchase this property for what Avery had paid, even at the big discount she thought she had gotten. And of course, she could never sell the property or the business without telling the truth about the shape it was in.

"Okay," she said at last.

"I'm sure you want time to think about this. It isn't a small sum."

"And I don't have many choices." *Besides,* she added silently, *I'm apparently not good at thinking about things before I do them.*

The three young men were congregating around the rack of orange clothing, holding up a fleece jacket and laughing.

Bella was watching her. "I can have a team come in

tomorrow morning to clear out the room and rip the carpet in the west room. And I will get the estimate together so we can make decisions about what gets done and when." She took a breath. "And I'll pray for wisdom for you and my team, okay, Avery? I'm sorry that you're going through this. And I hope this doesn't offend you, but I think God has a plan for you. Either you'll find a way out of this or you'll find a way through."

Avery was startled by Bella's remarks, but she nodded. It was a little strange, hearing those words from a complete stranger. It sounded so much like something her mother would say. But it didn't mean the same thing to her anymore. *He has a plan.* She'd heard nearly every version of that line in the emergency room in Salt Lake City. The place where all the good things she had planned for her life had been taken away.

One of the men, the one with his back to her, pulled his hat from his head. She felt such a jolt it left her heart hurting. The same height, the same tall, gangly build, the same light brown hair with a hint of red, the same cowlick in the back.

*Just like Eli.*

Bella put a hand on her arm. "I'll call you with a quote and a schedule first thing in the morning. If anything comes up between now and then, just call me. The emergency service will find me any time of day."

Avery made an effort at being in the here and now. "Thank you for coming all the way to Moose Hollow, Bella."

"My pleasure."

Avery's gaze drifted back over to the man who had seemed so familiar. His face was not as angular as Eli's, and he wasn't as thin as she'd thought. Even his hair color looked darker now. Suddenly, the similarity that had seemed so convincing a moment ago vanished.

He glanced up and caught her staring. She looked away, but not quite in time. When he strode toward her, she felt her heart race. He probably thought she was flirting. If so, he couldn't be more wrong. She looked up again as he approached.

He was good looking in the most universal way. Square jaw, narrow nose, perfect teeth. "Are you certain this counts as orange?" he asked, holding up a gray fleece jacket with an orange half zipper.

"Good enough for me," she said.

"Me too." He put one elbow on the desk and leaned over it. "What's tomorrow's color?"

"I wouldn't want to ruin the surprise."

"I like surprises." Perfect white teeth. And a dimple in the middle of his chin. "I suppose I'll have to come back tomorrow."

*Or you could just look in the window*, she thought. "That would be the thing to do," she said in what she hoped was a cheerfully neutral voice. But when she met his eye, she saw the flirtation there, and she looked away quickly.

"In the meantime, I'll take this jacket. I wouldn't want to wait for Gray Day and find out it doesn't qualify."

That made her smile. But she kept her eyes on the jacket as she wrote a receipt. "Nine dollars and ninety-seven cents," she said. Nine dollars for a fleece that had probably cost Tabitha forty dollars. And nine dollars was a pathetic drop in the bucket of money the restoration company would want from her.

"It's a steal. I'd better stuff it and run."

She tensed. There it was again, the feeling that Eli could be standing right beside her. *Stuff it and run.* It had been Eli's standard phrase when he found a great deal—a reference to shoplifting, something he would never have done. She fumbled as she put the jacket in a plain paper bag.

"See you tomorrow," he said with a grin, and he turned to join his friends.

*Stuff it and run.* Avery had never heard anyone else say that, except a couple of Eli's friends, who had picked it up from him.

She was in one of Eli's many hometowns, the one he'd liked the best. "I'm sorry," she said.

The man turned with an expectant look.

"I know this sounds crazy, but do you know someone named Elijah Canten?"

His eyebrows shot up. "Elijah? Yeah. Of course I do. Do you know him? How's he doing?"

A wave crashed over her. A feeling of homecoming, of comfort, and of incredible dread. She didn't want to tell him about Eli, and she wasn't sure if she could get the words out. She felt as if she should just let it go. But she couldn't help but grasp at any trace of Eli now. "He was my fiancé. He died in a climbing accident a few weeks ago."

*Twenty-seven days ago*, she thought. At eight o'clock tonight, it would be twenty-eight.

The man's mouth opened. She saw shock, real shock. She felt terrible for springing this on a stranger, but it also felt good to not carry the grief alone for just a moment.

"You said stuff it and run," she explained. "It sounded like something Eli would say."

His eyelids lowered. "Yeah. He says that all the time." He opened his eyes, walked over to the desk, and reached for her hand. "I'm so sorry. What happened? He's the best. He's always so careful."

She nodded. "They were just fooling around on the boulders around the campsite, nothing technical. Something broke free, and he took a weird fall. I don't know much more than that."

He searched her eyes, his eyebrows arched in concern, then he walked back to his buddies. "I'll meet you guys back at the Combine, okay?"

One winked at him. "Gotta do what you gotta do, Griff."

Eli's friend came over and sat on the half wall that separated the display windows from the rest of the store and leaned onto the desk. He introduced himself as Griffin Hallowell, and she told him her name was Avery Maier. By now she should have been Avery Canten.

"Tell me about it," Griffin asked.

She told him in the fewest words she could manage about the fall, the coma, his death days later. She told him about the vigil his friends held outside the hospital, and he said he wished he could have been there. He said he would have flown out in a heartbeat if he'd only known.

"How did you know Eli?" she asked.

"High school. I hated his guts when he showed up. It only took one day on the slopes, and after that, we pretty much spent all our time together." One corner of his mouth drew back in a wry smile. "He got me in so much trouble. But it was worth it. I have to say I'm surprised he got engaged, I didn't think he was the type. But I guess he always did know a good thing when he saw it."

She glanced up, but he was looking down at the desk. He didn't act like a guy trying to hit on her. She didn't know why she kept getting that itchy feeling as though he were. "Becoming a Christian changed Eli."

Griffin gave Avery a sideways look. "Christian?"

"Yes. He got in with a pretty radical house church." She breathed out half a laugh. "He always had to do things the hard way. Other people would just start going to church on Sundays. Eli made it a lifestyle."

"Wow. I didn't know."

"Most of the people in his church were climbers."

That made Griffin smile. "Now that part makes sense. So how did you meet?"

"We had a class together."

He had pursued her, and hard. By the time she'd finally agreed to have coffee with him, he'd told her he knew they belonged together. Two weeks later, he was talking about marriage. But she didn't tell Griffin about any of that. She'd never told anyone. They would have called her gullible. But she wasn't. She was right to believe him. Her name had been the last one on his lips.

She breathed in, out, and in again, trying to make room in her constricting chest for fresh air until the threat of crying passed. Luckily Griffin didn't seem to notice.

"So you own this place now?" he asked.

She nodded.

"Why did you move to Montana?"

"It seemed like the right thing to do." Eli said he loved living here. He thought maybe someday he'd come back. And he'd always wanted to open a store for climbers, get free stuff, share his knowledge. And to be honest, to preach. For him, people through the door meant opportunities to share the gospel.

The bells on the door jangled.

Griffin turned to see a woman enter, and then looked back at Avery. "I know you have to work, but I would really love to get together tonight. To talk about Elijah."

She remembered the conversation with Cash at Gunnerson Landholdings. "Actually, I have a business meeting at six-thirty."

"What time do you close?"

"Five."

"Great. We have time to grab a quick beer before your meeting. I know a place. I can meet you here and walk there with you." He searched her face and frowned. "Unless you don't feel up to it. Or maybe we could have dinner tomorrow."

"No. I'm fine." She wasn't interested in the beer, but it would be a lot easier to find the energy for a quick soda at the bar than spend a long dinner trying not to cry as they talked about Eli. "I'll see you tonight."

He reached over to squeeze her hand again. "Thank you so much, Avery. It means a lot to me. I still can't believe he's gone."

She nodded numbly, and he let go. When Griffin walked out the door, she struggled to paste a smile on her face. "Welcome," she said to her newest customer. "Everything orange is an additional twenty percent off today." Her voice sounded thin and strange, swallowed up by all the clothing. She wondered if anyone could hear her at all. Not that it mattered. She was part of the crowded backdrop, and that was just as well.

# CHAPTER 5

*L*iam stared at the untouched place setting across from him, irrefutable evidence that he was being stood up. At first, he thought she was late, which was itself a measure of her respect for him. He understood that some people, including a few he loved, just couldn't get out from under their own cluttered lives to arrive on time. But Liam worked hard never to be late. He didn't want to send the message that whatever else he'd been doing was more important than the person waiting for him.

Which was why he'd arrived ten minutes early at the restaurant on the first floor of the Third Street Inn. Five minutes to make sure he had time to find his mom and say hello, and five to demonstrate to his "client" that he took her store and building problems seriously. Now it was 6:45. There was something about that fifteen-minute barrier that said, "I have no intention of showing up."

Or more accurately, she had no intention of walking the few blocks between the Lantern Bar and the Third Street Inn restaurant.

The "Closed" sign had been hung on the door of Avery's

store for about ten minutes when he'd seen Avery let Griff Hallowell in. A moment later the door had opened, and she'd left the building in her lavender jacket. Liam had watched as Griff followed and put his arm around her shoulder. They'd walked a block uphill to the Lantern and gone inside.

Liam took a sip of the Malbec he'd ordered. It wasn't any of his business. Although it did seem strange how familiar she was with Griff. No, not strange. Griff didn't have any trouble meeting women here in town, or anywhere else the Hallowells had real estate interests. What women found attractive about him—other than his beefy build—had often confused him. He was more beef than build these days, but there it was. If she was the kind of girl who liked Griff and his miscreant friends, it was one more piece in the puzzle that was Avery Maier.

Not that he intended to spend a lot of time on that puzzle. It was just that when he got bogged down in the confusion of Cash's business dealings, he liked to turn his uncle's fancy chair around to look out over the snowy hills and the sunshine or watch the brooding clouds rise and dip across the big Montana sky. Situated in the middle, just below the view, was Avery's building. The cashier's desk was close enough to the window that he could see her there, working on her computer and phone at the same time, like a multitasking teenager who was unable to survive without constant electronic contact. It wasn't that he wanted to watch her, it was just that she was always in his line of sight. And from time to time, he noticed.

A waiter came over. "Would you like to order an appetizer?" he asked. It was more diplomatic than asking if he'd like to have the second place setting removed and give up.

"In just a couple minutes, thank you," Liam said. He'd make it an even twenty. Then he'd be free of his obligation to Avery and, even better, another step away from Griff Hallowell.

He pulled some papers out of his laptop case. Tomorrow he'd drag his uncle to the bank to get a separate account for the realty company, possibly two or three, and he'd read him the riot act about using funds from one branch of the business to fund the other. It was something Cash already knew but hadn't taken seriously. A little talk about his tax position might drive home how serious this was. Cash's business wasn't a hobby anymore. It was a massive endeavor, so profitable he doubted even Cash realized it. And it had a tax load to match.

Liam heard a staccato march of heels in a short, fast stride and shifted his gaze up over the papers he held. Snowflakes were still clinging to her brown hair, but there was no trace of them on her lavender jacket. It looked too slick for the snow to gain purchase.

He stood up to pull out her chair, but she did it herself and beat him to a sitting position. "I am so sorry," she said. "Have you been waiting long?"

"That's fine," he said, answering only the first question. "Did you bring the contract?" He was half hoping she hadn't.

"I did, and some other things, but I'm afraid Tabitha's accounting system was made up of receipts, several tablets of paper, and some sticky notes."

"I've dealt with that before," he said. "Today, as a matter of fact."

She smiled, sort of. It was a small thing, with one side turned up and the other straight, like a gentler version of the smirk he'd seen before. The smile didn't seem to make it all the way up to her dark eyes, either. He put his own papers back into the messenger bag as she slipped off her jacket and looked around. "I'm underdressed," she said softly. "And you look so nice."

Nice. *Not exactly a compliment*, Liam thought. He glanced up and agreed she looked very casual in her shirt and cardigan, but with a fancy, light scarf like some women wore these days. Casual but stylish. He looked away so he wouldn't give the impression that he was staring. "You look good," he said. "Don't worry. Most people don't dress up for this restaurant. Or much of anything in Moose Hollow."

Liam was about to reach for another sip of wine, but he figured that would be rude since she had none. "Would you like a glass of wine?"

"What are you drinking?"

"It's a Malbec. I don't remember the label."

"What's a Malbec?"

"It's a pretty strong-flavored red. You're welcome to try mine."

She frowned. "No thank you. I'm not a fan of red wine."

The waiter—Liam had seen him before and was almost certain his name was Sam—spotted Liam's companion and came over to hand them menus and take her drink order. But instead of ordering white wine, as he'd expected, she asked for a ginger ale. Liam assumed she'd already had a couple drinks at the Lantern. He took the contract from her outstretched hand. "I promised to ask you to dinner Thursday night."

Her eyes widened.

"That didn't come out right. Let me try this again. My friend Poppy—actually, she's almost family—has a standing Thursday night dinner. She's new to cooking, sort of, and she invites family and a few friends over to try out recipes. When she found out there was someone new in town, she made me swear to ask you to join her."

"Are you going?" Avery asked.

Liam balked. He really hadn't thought this through. "I wasn't planning..."

Her eyebrows dropped the slightest bit, and he realized how rude he sounded. "I wasn't planning on going, but Poppy insisted. I'd be happy to give you a ride."

"I'll think about it," Avery said.

What? A simple no would have done. Intractable, that's what she was. He turned his attention to the sales contract. The preamble was four pages long. He was pretty sure what he was getting into just by looking at that, but he took his time to read it just the same. He was aware of her sitting across from him, thanking the waiter, taking a sip of her drink, her hands crossed primly on the white tablecloth.

When it was time to order, Liam set the contract down. Avery ordered a beef dish, pronouncing the French words effortlessly. He ordered a pasta dish that hit all the same comfort notes as macaroni and cheese but without the cardboard box. Grilled steak on top finished it off. Just ordering made him realize how hungry he was.

Then he saw the expectant look in her eyes as she stared at the papers in front of him, and his appetite waned.

"Avery, at first glance this looks to be a watertight contract. There's nothing unusual in it, it's just that they've included every single indemnity they possibly could. They cut ties with every aspect of the building and the business. However, I still think it's worth having a lawyer review it." He didn't, really. "But I wouldn't get my hopes up."

"Well, then."

He wished he had something better to say. But the silence stretched on.

Avery took a sip of her ginger ale and looked at him over the rim of her glass. "This is awkward. I suppose it would be less awkward if I hadn't hit you with a broom."

Liam rotated his shoulder and winced dramatically. "Oh, that? I almost forgot."

"Oh, you don't want to forget that." There it was again, the smirk, this time coupled with a devilish look in her eyes. It was a very good look on her. "I have a brown belt in Broom Chi."

Okay, that was cute, he admitted. So she had a sense of humor too. "That explains it. Where does one learn the ancient art of Broom Chi?"

"At college. From the janitors. But don't tell anyone—it's a secret society. They don't let just anyone in."

"How did you convince them to let you in?"

"I can't tell you." She looked up under long eyelashes. "But the initiation may or may not have involved hitting someone with a broom."

He smiled. "Then I consider myself lucky."

"Maybe not, after you take a look at these." She reached down into her bag and handed him some papers. "This is just the beginning. Although I don't want to ruin your appetite, especially since the food here looks delish."

"You brought me tax documents."

"Yup. And I can't find a single sheet of paper to back up the numbers Tabitha submitted."

He winced. "I see. And an inventory?"

"Remember all the boxes in the back of the store? About a third of them are clothing, most a year or more old. And about half the boxes have been opened. Let's just say that shrinkage is an issue. I don't think that her inventory has much relation to reality at all."

"You'll have to do your own inventory."

She sighed.

He rifled through the papers. "How can I help?" He couldn't believe those words had slipped past his lips.

"I'm not sure, to be honest. But I might need a loan. To get a loan, I'm going to need to have something that looks like business records, right?"

Liam nodded thoughtfully. "You can give Tabitha's tax records to represent past years. I realize they aren't accurate, but that's between her and the IRS. I'm guessing they're going to want to have a five-year business plan from you. Unless..." His mind finally caught up with his mouth, and he regretted saying that last word.

"Unless what?"

"I was going to say unless they think it's too much of a risk."

For a moment her dark eyes met his again. *Sad puppy eyes*, he thought. Deadly. He shouldn't say anything to her since Cash's speculation about that building was just that, speculation. Being the bearer of bad news wasn't his favorite part of his job. But it bothered him that she seemed to have little knowledge of her own property, and he didn't see how she could make sound financial decisions without the facts. "A lot of the buildings in downtown Moose Hollow are of a similar age. In some, the plumbing and electric have been updated. But it's a rare building that has been completely renovated. A bank will want an appraisal—"

"I had one done," she said.

He tried not to frown. No reputable appraiser would have approved a loan for that building at that sale price. He rifled through the papers, searching for a settlement statement.

"They'll want their own. I'm just saying, getting a loan might require additional renovations. That might be worth it to you, or it might not."

A blink. Then another. Then Avery lifted her narrow chin. "It's worth it."

She couldn't know that. The purchase price of the building had been both too low and too high to be a reasonable purchase. Well below the going rate, but crazy expensive nonetheless. Someone had known the building, and the business it housed, was a disaster. He opened his mouth to speak, then shut it.

He found the settlement statement. There was no appraisal, just a market analysis. Avery had gotten away with it because there was no loan involved. Had she paid cash? The idea startled him. A woman her age with that much money on hand? If it was family money, why didn't someone in her family give her better financial guidance? He flipped through the other pages and cleared his throat. She was still looking at him with that deter-mined expression. The whole thing was a mess. There was nothing he could do for her. But he couldn't manage to spit those words out. Instead, he said, "There might be other things in Tabitha's records that are useful to you. If you still want me to look at the other papers—"

"Yes, I do," she said. "If you have time."

"Sure. When could I come by to pick them up?"

"How about as soon as we're done here?" She lifted her glass and took another sip of ginger ale.

Liam smiled weakly. Another night of overtime, this time for no pay. With Griff's new girlfriend. What could go wrong?

# CHAPTER 6

*A*very had only picked at her dinner, but Liam knew by the way she looked at the tray of decadent treats that she had room for dessert. She insisted she didn't. So he asked a few questions to see which of the treats she would like best, and when the waiter returned, he asked for the triple chocolate cake to go. It made her smile—a real smile that made her eyes glitter—then she looked down as if she'd done something wrong.

Having already memorized the way her fingers danced when she talked and the way she tugged at her scarf where the seam touched her neck, he now found himself wondering about her hair. In the dim light of the restaurant, it was nearly black. She had it pulled back and up, and somehow it seemed to poof out into loose curls and then back again so that the ends were invisible, and so was the mechanism holding it all up there. He couldn't even guess how long her hair really was. He wondered how she would look with her hair down and then pushed that thought aside. It was none of his business.

She was pretty, that was all. There were traces of tomboy in her, including what seemed like a general reluctance to use her utensils when her fingers would do, but the rest was all girl. No

"BRIGHT MONTANA HOME 43

wonder Griff had sniffed her out. Every single man in Moose Hollow would know about her in a week or two. And a few men that weren't single.

As he suspected, the check had indeed been covered by his uncle. He left a substantial tip, pulled on his wool coat and scarf, and gathered up the two leftover food boxes and his own satchel. "I can carry those," she said.

"I know." Of course she could, but that wasn't the way Gunnerson men did things. He held on to the boxes.

His mother was at the front desk as they emerged. Normally he would have introduced them, but he didn't want his mother to get the wrong idea. This was not a date. It was a setup by Cash, who liked to make connections wherever he could, especially with the cute owner of a piece of property he wanted to own someday. He smiled at his mom, and she gave him a grin back. She'd raised three boys, and she was adept at showing love without being too "Mom," especially in public places.

He opened the door and a blast of cold air rushed by. March in Montana was still winter, although the longer days made it all seem more bearable. But tonight the sky was clear and the stars were sparkling, and there wasn't even a hint of snow in the air. It was a good night for a long walk. But it was just a few blocks uphill to her building.

He noticed the light shining out over the sidewalk before they arrived. "Do you leave the store lights on all night?"

She shook her head, looked at her store windows, and stopped in her tracks. "No. I left all but one bank of lights off."

"I'll check it out," he said, increasing his pace.

"Melanie. It's got to be Melanie," Avery called. "She said she'd be back on Monday."

His heart rate slowed again, and so did he. Sure enough, he caught sight of Mad Mel through the window, and she appeared to be mopping the floor near the back of the store. "I'll go in with you."

She flashed him a suspicious look.

"To get the papers, not to attack your employee."

Avery fumbled with her keys. "She's not really my employee. But thank you for not attacking her. This time."

The store was bright and warm, especially after the cold night air. He followed behind Avery, keeping a little distance between them. Mel was hunched over the mop as she wrung it out over an ancient-looking wheeled bucket. At first, Avery was the only person Mel noticed. But when she saw Liam, her entire demeanor changed. She tossed her gray hair back from her face, crossed one leg in front of the other, and leaned jauntily on the mop handle. "Well, hello, handsome. Have you come to clean or wrestle?"

His face heated up. Mel was much older than his mother, and flirting was the last thing he'd expected. But there was something about her smile that made him grin. "Neither, I'm afraid."

"Such a shame." Mel leaned over to Avery and in a conspiratorial but loud voice said, "The Gunnerson men are pretty well known around here. If I were you, I'd snatch him up before the other girls find out he's back in town."

He didn't know Mel, and he was certain she didn't know him. She was probably talking about his cousin Colton, a former rodeo star. Or his father. Since they owned the nicest hotel in town, his parents got to know a lot of people. Mel couldn't have been talking about him. It was true that most of the Gunnerson men stood out in many ways, but Liam was the exception. He always had been.

The color of Avery's face pulled him out of his own thoughts. She looked even redder than he had felt. She spoke up. "Mel, thank you so much for coming to clean tonight. But I have to let you know that—"

"It's a good workout," Mel said, interrupting. "Better than that nasty old Jane Fonda thing. Remember those leotards? No, of course you don't, dear." She snickered to herself. "It amazes me what passes for fashion sometimes. Then and now."

Avery smiled kindly. "Yes, well, I need to speak to you about your job."

"I also help check on things. Make sure everything is okay. My therapist said it's important I get out and around other people. Therapist! Isn't that a strange way to make a living? I think they're just busybodies. Mine wants all the juicy details." She winked at Liam.

*Avery is lost*, Liam thought. She'd begun to waver the moment Mel mentioned the word "therapist." He tried to throw her a lifeline. "You'll need to sign a new contract if you stay on with Avery. I'm assuming you're an independent contractor. Because I'm sure Avery isn't in a position to hire you as an employee. There's social security, insurance, workman's comp, all that."

Avery's eyes widened. Her business knowledge might be tinier than he had imagined.

"Nonsense," Mel said, putting bony knuckles on her hip. "It's just a little cash here and there."

"How little?" Liam asked. He noticed the way Avery frowned at him. She wasn't happy that he was butting into her business again. She certainly sent mixed signals. After all, he'd been invited here to get her financial papers.

Mel lifted her head and looked down her nose at Liam. "Two hundred dollars a month. Hardly worth involving the government. And barely enough to cover my prescriptions, I'll have you know."

*She might change her mind when Avery submitted a 1099*, he thought.

"And what business is it of yours?" Mel asked him.

Avery spoke up. "He's a CNA. He's here to look over Tabitha's old business documents."

He wasn't a CNA—he was pretty sure that was a medical

assistant. Neither was he a CPA, a certified public accountant, no matter what Cash had said. But he figured this wasn't the best time to correct her.

Mel looked from one of them to the other and then gave an overly dramatic sigh, as if she was giving up on both of them. "My dears, Tabitha's most important documents were in her head, and what was there is now lost in the wind. And that..." Her voice softened, and a swallow stretched the cords of her thin neck. "...is not always a bad thing. However, that a young woman who looks like you, and a young man who looks like"— she examined him from top to bottom—"*you*, would prefer to spend a starlit evening talking about accounting, demonstrates everything that is wrong with the world today. For heaven's sake, Liam, take the girl to a movie."

"We are not on a date," Avery said.

It was the most confident she'd sounded all night, and that chafed. If Avery Maier knew anything, it seemed, it was that she wouldn't go out with someone like Liam Gunnerson. Griff, however, was just her style.

"True," Liam agreed.

Her lips parted, and she turned her back to him. "Everything I've found is back here. Follow me." She led him back to the box-filled room.

"You've gotten rid of some of this."

"I have. I have it piled out there." She gestured toward the back door.

"In the dumpster?"

"No. The dumpster's full. The restoration people are going to bring a new one tomorrow."

He took a breath. "You might want to bring it back in for the night."

She had stopped at what might be a desk, underneath the papers, magazines, and newspapers. "You think I should bring a bunch of rotting trash inside the building?"

"One of the things you'll find out about Moose Hollow is that there are all kinds of regulations about trash. Everything has to be in a bear-resistant container."

"Bears are hibernating right now," Avery said, gathering up papers.

"Not necessarily. And it's not just the bears. There are deer and moose and—"

"Moose want my trash? Really?"

A hint of that smirk again. Avery looked like a librarian hushing a child. No matter how cute, Liam didn't appreciate the condescension. "I'm just letting you know. It's very likely someone has called you in already, and the fines are high. Let me just take a look."

He started to walk over to the back door and realized she had an old folding chair propped up under the doorknob.

"You can't go out," she said. Her tone of voice snapped. "The knob is broken. You can come in, but you can't go out."

He reconsidered the chair. "What do you mean you can come in?"

"Just what I said."

So the flimsy chair was her idea of protection. As she tossed her way through the papers, he noticed the large stack of boxes to his left. That was new. He walked around it until he found the opening and caught a glimpse of a flashlight and a floral bedspread. When he looked back at her, she quickly turned away, but not before he saw the embarrassment on her face.

She wasn't safe. She knew it, too, or she wouldn't have made a box fort to hide in. Part of him thought it was smart—he could see the box she must use to slide over the entrance, turning her "bedroom" into just another pile of boxes. But all of the rest of him thought it was ridiculously dangerous, and dangerously stubborn, to stay in this building.

"You should know my parents own the Third Street Inn, the

hotel where we ate tonight. They would be happy to get you a room there, at least until the door is fixed."

"It will be fixed tomorrow," she said. She shoved a wrinkled mess of papers into Liam's hand. "This is all I can find right now."

She was breathing fast. He could see the tension in her face as well. He knew there was nothing he could say that wouldn't be taken as an unwelcome intrusion. "Thank you," he said. He took the papers from her and tucked them into his satchel.

"I appreciate your time," she said. Then she added, as if she was convincing herself, "I really do."

*Not enough*, he thought. "I'll let myself out the front."

He walked fast enough to avoid any more conversations with Mel. He strode across the street to drop off the papers. But after he'd unlocked the door and walked up to Cash's office, he dropped the satchel on his desk and walked in the dark to Cash's chair.

Avery was in the store window, hanging some pieces of cardboard by a string. He stared at the dark windows above her. The mess there was hidden in the dark, but he remembered it well enough, including his conclusion about it. Those rooms had been used very recently. Knowing the history of the place, whoever used them might still have a key. And if not, they could just push their way through the back door. Avery wasn't safe.

Mel left, cloaked in her coat, face down and long hair tucked into her hood. In that getup she looked like a man. She was tall enough, too, nearly six feet from what he could tell. About his own height. He wondered if she dressed that way for self-defense or just to be left alone.

The pieces of cardboard took shape, becoming two stick figures. Avery dressed them entirely in shades of purple, throwing purple snowballs at each other made of mittens or something like it. All out of nothing but cardboard and string hanging from the ceiling. He could have been given a month to plan and still not come up with something so eye-catching and clever.

She left, and the lights went out. Liam spent a little time trying to talk himself out of his plan, but he wasn't the type to walk away from trouble. The accounting firm had proved that. And the mess his professional life was now in was proof that his real problem was learning to avoid trouble in the first place. He hadn't managed to do that at the firm, or in high school. And here he was, on the edge of another mess. He went home to his hotel room to change into warmer clothes and then he got in his blue FJ Cruiser and quietly and slowly drove to the back of Avery Maier's building and parked.

The light near the back door was off. He shook his head at that.

He let the heat run on high, then turned the car off, reclined his seat, and settled in for the night watch. No reason to leave the car running, it would only draw attention. If he sorted through her papers and did his research quickly—and God willing, if she didn't come out and see him sitting here—he might be done with Avery Maier in a week or so. It couldn't be soon enough.

# CHAPTER 7

*C*ustomers were gathered around the rack of pink clothes. Avery never would have guessed there was so much pink in the sporting world, or that so many people would be interested in it at a quarter to five in the afternoon. She checked her watch. Most of the shops in Moose Hollow stayed open until five. But she'd been told by Lettie the Chamber of Commerce woman that some stayed open as late as ten during the summer. But Avery was exhausted, and she would have liked to have closed forty-five minutes ago.

In addition to that useful if unwelcome information, Lettie had delivered a basket of goodies and an application form. The cost of admittance to the association was enough to make Avery choke on her tea. And her stomach, which had been aching all day, made the goodies unwelcome too. Most annoying of all, Lettie had informed her that the large dumpster out back was not in compliance with "bear-resistance restrictions." Luckily, Bella had dropped by just then to review the progress her team was making upstairs. Bella handled Lettie gracefully and firmly, explaining that their work fell under emergency restoration policies and was exempt, at least for a time. She assured her the dumpster would be gone soon. Lettie seemed assuaged.

Avery chose not to point out that bears hibernate in the winter and, although it was March, there was plenty of snow and cold weather in Moose Hollow.

Leaving the welcome but unwelcome customers to their searching, Avery checked her new Moose on the Loose online store for sales and reviewed the numbers for the day.

Then she did her own math. This was the nine-day anniversary of her arrival in Moose Hollow. Thirty-four days since the night she and Eli had broken their vows to each other. Thirty-one days since he'd died in that hospital bed. Five days since what should have been her wedding day. Seven days since her period was late.

Thinking about everything that had transpired didn't make her feel as sad today. Instead, she felt hollow.

She focused on the renovations upstairs. She'd seen the west-facing room yesterday, and that was progress enough for her. By now the paint she had picked out would be dry, and tomorrow she could move in. She could unlock the little rental trailer parked in the alley and get rid of it. But that was tomorrow, and she couldn't ever remember wishing so much that a job was finished for the day. Except perhaps when she'd babysat the Hanser kids—four children who expressed all emotion, no matter what emotion, by hitting.

Her exhaustion didn't bode well for her.

She focused on the way the front bedroom had looked: the drywall repaired and newly primed, the clean, wide expanse of windows overlooking the ridges and distant peaks to the west. But the last of her cash was almost gone. The business had to start carrying its own weight, and it wasn't even close to doing that. The truth was, when she'd put almost all of the insurance money into the Moose on the Loose and the building that housed it, she'd figured it would look like the Taj Mahal. She'd been sure of it. How else could it look, if it cost so much? And she had been able to close so fast because the title company had already been preparing for a sale, which had fallen through. She'd never asked why. She'd overlooked all the warning signs. *So gullible.*

The heavy feeling in her stomach distracted her, along with the dull ache in her lower back. It had been an uncomfortable day.

She pressed her hand to her stomach as if that would make the ache go away. She didn't know for sure she was pregnant, but all the signs were there. She'd been late before, but not for this long. It might be the stress of Eli's death, the move, or anything else, but she didn't think so.

Today something about her body felt different—whether from the good night's sleep she'd had or the good cry she'd had before that, there was no way to be certain. But she felt as if she could skirt the edges of the thought, if not face the implications of it head-on. She was carrying his child. Eli's baby.

Something like a smile touched her lips. That was okay, too. There were enough rooms in her house. And she couldn't beat the commute. She would practically be a work-at-home mom. Here in the town Eli had loved, with people who had known and loved him close by, she could risk believing it would all work out. It was the next best thing to seeing the sweet, fun father Eli would have been.

She could make so many mistakes right for this child. Even if there was no forgiveness left for her.

She looked at the young women huddled around the pink clothes, half mocking and half adoring them. Were they visitors or residents? Judging by the expensive gear they wore, they were visitors. The residents of Moose Hollow looked less polished. They were about her age, just out of college or maybe a little younger. She'd had a group of friends like that once, but she'd left them behind when she'd started dating Eli in earnest.

He'd always been on the move, and following him had been the only way to spend time with him. She missed the feeling of having a band of sisters and inside jokes to giggle over. But those days were in the past.

She'd come to terms with Eli's lifestyle, mostly. And she would adjust to this life as well. She'd always wanted kids, she reminded herself. She just hadn't thought it would happen so soon. Here. By herself.

The bell on the door clanged, and she couldn't help but glance at her watch before looking up. Five minutes until closing time. When she saw who had arrived, the first thing she thought was that Liam looked like a tourist, too. He had on an awesome wool coat that hit him mid-thigh, something that was half Old West and half 1940s couture. Beneath that was his usual—a thin cashmere sweater over a perfectly tailored dress shirt, tailored slacks, and a dressy leather version of old-fashioned sneakers.

Even his build didn't seem local. He had the sculpted form that men paid trainers a lot of money to get. Not the bulky, weight-lifting kind, but more like a model. Square shoulders, narrow through the hips. Definitely like a model.

She realized she was staring, and frowning, so she gave him a quick grin and then gazed back at the computer screen. But she was still thinking. His parents owned the hotel, he'd said. And hadn't he mentioned staying at a hotel once? No doubt the same place. When he walked right up to her, she asked, "Are you from Moose Hollow?"

"Born and raised," he answered. "Why?"

"You just don't look it."

He blinked his eyes slowly, and she got the feeling he was shutting her out. "I think I've deciphered some of Tabitha's bookkeeping." His voice was flat. She had insulted him somehow.

"Really?"

"If you have a minute, I can go over it with you."

"I do," she said, glancing at the girls. They weren't going to buy anything, even though some items were seventy percent off. She couldn't really blame them. She'd been through the store from top to bottom, and all she'd liked were a couple hand-knit sweaters. Then again, she wasn't exactly the target audience for a store like this. She wasn't anyone's target audience, as far as she knew. She watched Liam pull papers out of his satchel and set them to one side.

"As far as I can tell," he said, "Tabitha stopped placing orders about three years ago. However, she had a standing order system with a distributor. Tabitha wasn't actually picking out which items to carry in the store, and the distributor had her on a plan according to gross sales. Because she didn't do inventory, she sent him the same numbers every year, so the boxes kept arriving and she kept paying the bills. Late, usually, but she paid them."

Avery tried to imagine the poor woman, overwhelmed as the bills and boxes kept coming. With her memory problems, she must have felt so trapped and confused. Not to mention whatever had been going on in the upstairs rooms.

"I took the liberty of calling the distributor and asking them to suspend all future shipments. They're waiting for a call from you to see what you want to do next."

Avery's lips parted. The shipments could have kept coming? "Thank you."

"I couldn't find a complete list of vendors anywhere." He pulled a flash drive out of his satchel. "I assembled what I could, with phone numbers and business IDs where available. Although I didn't find any evidence of it, you might want to call them all to make sure she didn't have similar deals with any of them."

Avery stared at the stack of papers, all of which had been straightened out and clipped together in an organized way.

"One more thing. I think you're free and in the clear. I don't think you have any payables outstanding, and it looks as if all utilities and taxes were paid up as part of the closing statement. As far as your inventory goes, you might want to consider opening up an online store."

"I did."

His eyebrows raised slightly. That irritated her. It was as if every sensible thing she did surprised him. But she had said something to hurt him, too, and she hadn't fixed that. "Portland?" she asked.

His forehead wrinkled a little, and the corners of his mouth tipped up. "Excuse me?"

"When I said that you didn't look like you were from around here, it was because of your fashion sense."

"Fashion sense," he repeated, looking as if she'd just said he had three eyeballs.

"Yes. Your clothes. Business chic, but with a western sensibility. I'm guessing you worked in Portland. Maybe Seattle."

A crooked sort of smile spread across his face, and suddenly Liam Gunnerson looked a lot younger than she had pegged him to be. "I've been told that before."

"Really?"

"At my last job. My boss told me to buy a suit, that I looked like I'd transferred from the Portland office. Maybe I should be looking for a job there."

"You mean a gig like you have with your uncle?"

"No, more like a real job. Like the one I just lost."

"Laid off?"

"Fired," he said.

Avery wrinkled her nose. "I find that hard to believe."

"I didn't find it hard to believe at all."

Avery waited for more information, but it didn't come. There was something like a growl in his voice, and it made her think there was a lot more to the story. Maybe she'd find out someday, but for now, the conversation seemed closed. "Thank you, Liam. You've really helped me out."

"I have a few more—" His mouth shut.

She knew he'd been about to say something else but had changed his mind. She could guess what it was. "You have more suggestions for me?" The look on his face was so hesitant it made her smile. "I'm open to suggestions. More or less."

He gave a slight shrug and looked down at the floor.

He didn't think she was? Avery splayed her hand over her heart and opened her mouth to speak, but the door jangled again, and she looked up to see a woman enter the store.

"Liam!"

The young woman waved as she hurried over toward them. She was cute, with shining black hair and dark red lipstick. In fact, all of her makeup trended a little too dramatic for Avery's taste, but it was stylish and it seemed to suit her. Liam dropped his satchel and walked forward to meet her, arms outstretched.

Avery's mind raced ahead. So this was Liam's taste in women. She'd expected a little older. Someone a little more like...*someone like me*, she thought, *but beautiful.*

The woman made her way around the racks, and a moment before she ended up in Liam's arms, Avery saw the rest of her.

"Mara!" he said. He squeezed her in a hug, leaning over her large belly to do it. "I can hardly get my arms around you."

"That is so not good to say," Mara said. She looked at Avery, down to the satchel on the floor, and back at Liam. "I haven't seen you in a week. You haven't come out to the ranch. Or to church, you loser."

"The time change is still getting to me," he said.

"Poppy invited you to this week's dinner, right? The results are mixed, but the food is free. It's awfully nice to have her around since all I can cook is mac and cheese."

"Wait, is Poppy living there?" Liam asked.

Mara punched him in the arm, hard, although Liam didn't

budge. "Not until the wedding, butthead. But she's on the ranch a lot when she's not at work." Mara leaned her head back and groaned. "Work. I can't find a job. Even a little part-time thing."

"Why not? No one hiring?"

Mara gestured to her stomach with both hands. "Not pregnant girls."

"You've got school anyway."

"But I have very important baby things I need to buy. I found a baby motorcycle jacket. Can you imagine how cute that is?"

Avery smiled.

Liam shook his head. "Nope. I can't imagine."

"Come tomorrow." She stretched one arm out toward Avery. "And bring your girlfriend."

Liam looked at Avery and gaped. "No, she's...not..."

Mara ignored him and walked over to the checkout desk. She had an awesome pair of high-heeled boots on, and she wore them as easily as tennis shoes on a not-pregnant woman. But even with the boots, she was only about Avery's height. "My name is Mara Gunnerson."

Gunnerson. Same last name as Liam. Sister? Avery didn't think so. "Avery Maier."

"And you just moved here. Liam was supposed to tell you about dinner tomorrow."

"I did," Liam said, looking perturbed.

Mara pointed at her own large belly. "And this is baby Veronica."

Liam laughed out loud. "Veronica is slightly better than Leticia Lou."

Avery was shocked until Mara grinned at her. "Oh, he's not being rude, he's just in on the joke. Veronica's not the baby's real name. Only Zane and I know what that is going to be. You know, everyone has an opinion about names, and if the baby hasn't been born yet, they have no problem telling you how much they don't like your choice. So every morning Zane and I come up with a new name, and that's what we tell everyone that day. It should be a riot the first year when everyone calls the baby little Veronica-Leticia-Rudolph-Lakeshore-Jasper-whatever."

"That's brilliant," Avery said.

"I know, right? So you're coming to dinner tomorrow."

Avery faltered. Pregnant friends would be hard to come by. She could hardly turn down the opportunity, *if* she was pregnant, of course. And even if she wasn't, hadn't she just been lamenting the loss of girlfriends? Mom would call this a God Thing, but she called a lot of things that.

"She isn't coming," Liam said.

"Of course I am," Avery said. She shouldn't let him get to her, but the way Liam told her what to do was irksome. Like he was so sure he knew better than her. The fact that he did know more about loans and contracts and stuff didn't matter. He didn't have to *sound* like it.

"Great. You should have Liam drive you. It's a little hard to find until you've been there once or twice." She added with more volume, "Besides, he's the guy. He should always drive his girlfriend."

"She's not my girlfriend." He picked up his satchel and faced the other way.

"It's so fun to rattle his cage," Mara said softly. "I'm glad you're coming."

After watching her play Liam, Avery was too. "I'm looking forward to it," Avery said.

Mara said good-bye, walked over to the rack of pink clothes, and said something just out of earshot that made all the women laugh. Then she grabbed something off the rack and handed it to one of them. Did she know them? They seemed older than her. Mara walked out, but the customer held on to the short tennis-style dress.

"I'll pick you up tomorrow at closing time," Liam said before leaving abruptly.

Avery stared after him. He was just plain difficult. But she wasn't about to let him come between her and people who just might turn out to be friends.

"I'm ready to check out," someone said as she approached Avery. It was the young woman with the pink dress.

# CHAPTER 8

*L*iam had never liked nights when he was the odd man out in the company of happy couples, although he'd had plenty of opportunities to get used to the feeling. But now he realized that was better than being seated next to Avery in the Gunnerson farmhouse. She was certainly not his date. No one thought she was, of course. But he was here, she was there, and it was painfully awkward that she wasn't his date.

At least it was awkward for him. Avery seemed fine with it. A little tired, perhaps, but fine. She cracked a few well-timed jokes, said the right things about Poppy's much-improved cooking, and asked all the right questions about Zane and Mara's wedding. That had been the last time he'd been in town, Thanksgiving, for his younger brother's shotgun wedding. That's what Zane called it. He liked to say that it took a shotgun to get all four parents to let them get married.

When they'd first sat down, Avery had discreetly slid her chair a few inches farther away, so he was enjoying plenty of personal space. Her perfume, if it was perfume and not shampoo, was faint and didn't interfere with his meal. She didn't talk too loudly, didn't sulk in silence, and never hogged the conversation.

So why did he feel her next to him so strongly? It was like being seated next to a seething pit of lava. He couldn't get his mind off her or shake the feeling that she was trouble. He never looked her in the eye, but he saw her just the same, every perfect dark-eyed smirk, every flutter of her hands. He also heard every word she said and turned each one over and over, looking for multiple meanings. But he couldn't find any. In fact, she didn't seem to have a single thing to say about him. She seemed to have forgotten he was there at all.

And just when it looked like the whole friendly ordeal was over, it became the very first night Poppy served dessert. Cheesecake, no less. "Oh wow," Avery said. "I've never dared to make real cheesecake. With chocolate drizzled on top? This looks so good!"

"You never know what I've done wrong until we taste it," Poppy said.

"It will be great, no matter what," Colton said, and he seemed to mean it.

Poppy shook her head. "Your unreasonable faith in my cooking is one more reason to marry you, Colton."

Liam was happy for Colton, he really was. In fact, he was growing to like Poppy just as much as he liked his cousin, the young man he'd idolized in high school. But sometimes he wished they'd just get married and get it all over with so they could go on being people rather than a Hallmark movie.

A slice of cheesecake arrived in front of Liam, but he waited politely for the host and hostess to try it first. Avery beat them all to it. And with a full mouth, she moaned and said, "Diss is so guhd!"

Poppy positively lit up. Then she took a bite of her own, and she and Colton exchanged a glance and a laugh. "Definitely doing this again," she said.

Mara was next. "Oh, my word. I get two slices, right? For little Toblerone and me?"

Liam almost spit out his first bite when she said that. After tasting it, he was glad he hadn't. Cheesecake wasn't usually his thing, but he'd be a fool to turn this down.

"No! Did anyone believe you today?" Avery asked Mara.

"The librarian. She almost didn't, but then I very seriously told her we were looking for a name that sounded rich and sophisticated, but a little sweet."

Colton laughed out loud. "Poor woman."

"I know. But think about the excitement we're bringing to town," Zane said. Liam was pretty sure the whole baby-naming fiasco had been his idea. His brother had a sense of humor all his own.

"Well, people are going to talk," Mara said. "I figure I might as well make it an interesting conversation." He could feel Avery staring at him. He tried to ignore it, lava and all.

"Yesterday Griff believed we were naming our baby Zephaniah."

"Griff?" Colton asked. "Griff Hallowell?"

Liam felt like the lava was beginning to boil. He knew he was on dangerous ground. He kept his head down and picked at the cheesecake.

"Aren't you two seeing each other?" Mara asked Avery. "When we were talking he kind of made it seem that way."

"No," Avery said smoothly. "Griffin and I are just friends."

"Nobody's just friends with Griff."

The words just spat right out of Liam's mouth. Four sets of eyes locked on him, everyone's except Avery's. She politely acted as if he didn't exist. Colton's eyes widened, and he jutted his chin forward, the universal body language for "What were you thinking?"

"I'm sorry, that sounded bad. What I meant was—" He meant

that Griff manipulated people to get what he wanted. Liam doubted Griff had any true friends. But he couldn't say that, at least not now that he'd implied that Avery was a foolish girl who couldn't resist Griff's charm. He tried to shift gears. "Girls find Griff to be an attractive guy." Bad start. "Most girls. Usually."

Avery didn't move at all, except for taking tiny, mouse-like chews of her cheesecake.

Colton's lips parted, and his head slumped forward. That was universally translated as "You've blown it now." But he mercifully rode to his cousin's rescue. "Well, back in high school they might have. Nowadays I've heard Griff is very busy with work."

"Yes," Avery agreed. "From what I know, he's working hard trying to keep the local office going while his father is in Bozeman getting a new branch set up."

"That's great," Liam said lamely.

"I always thought he was kind of a jerk," Mara said. "No offense."

Liam made a mental note to get her something very special when the baby was born.

Instead of giving her the polite silent treatment Liam had received, Avery actually smiled. "None taken. I'm not sure he always knows when to turn the sales pitch off and just be himself."

Just be himself. *She said it as if that could be a good thing*, Liam thought.

The conversation thankfully switched to dogs, since it seemed Colton and Poppy were thinking about getting one and couldn't decide which breed. Colton wanted a working dog, and Poppy wanted a hiking companion. Avery seemed to know a lot about working dogs, and she joined right in. Then the conversation dissolved into which breeds had the most adorable puppies. By then, Liam had had just about enough.

Avery refused coffee, and so he did as well, and to his relief, she said she had something to take care of at the store and needed to leave. Liam retrieved their coats from the stairwell. Maybe he could get Colton and Poppy a coat tree for their wedding present. Mara could help him pick it out. She seemed to know Poppy's tastes better than Poppy did. Everyone said their thanks and goodbyes, and he found himself out in the cold mountain air.

"They still have Christmas lights on the house," Avery said as they walked over to Liam's FJ Cruiser. "I meant to ask about that."

"Colton said Poppy likes them. The way he said it, I'd be surprised if they ever took them down again."

He opened the door for her, but instead of climbing in, she turned to face him. "Do you have something against Griffin?"

Yes. Liam could have screamed the word. But instead, he chose his words carefully. "I've had difficulty with him in the past."

"Anything that pertains to me?"

Yes, potentially. She was a woman, and he knew how Griff treated women. But that wouldn't be enough to convince her. "Not particularly."

She just stood there looking at him, brown eyes glittering in the starlight, waiting.

"I'm sorry, Avery. I was out of line."

She looked back over toward the homestead and its colorful lights. It occurred to him that if this had been a date, and she hadn't been angry with him, he would have kissed her right then. But it wasn't a date. And Liam had insulted Griff, and she was clearly loyal enough to him to resent it.

She sighed. "Griffin and my fiancé were friends."

He felt as if he'd been struck right over the sternum. He couldn't manage to draw in breath. But he pulled it together as fast as he could. "You're engaged," he said, hoping he sounded happy for her.

She looked down now, so that all he could see was a faint sheen of light over her dark hair. "No. He died. Before I moved to Montana."

This strike hit lower, deeper in his gut. It was worse than the disappointment he'd felt a second before. The tone of her voice pulled at him. He wanted to reach out to her, to draw her close, but it wasn't his place to do something like that. All he could do was say, "I'm sorry, Avery. I didn't know."

She climbed into the car seat, and Liam shut the door, walking stiffly over to the driver's side. He was still making sense of what she'd said when they pulled down the long drive to the main road and headed toward Moose Hollow. "Do you mind if I ask what happened?"

"It was an accident. He was climbing."

"Were you with him when it happened?"

"No." She looked away, out the window. "I was never any good at climbing."

There was something darker in her voice now. It sounded like guilt. Liam sighed. There was nothing he could think of to say, or to do, to ease her sadness. He said a silent prayer.

"I had fun tonight," she said. "Your family is great."

To him, the statement sounded a little like "I forgive you for being an idiot." So he said, "Thank you."

He pulled into the alley to drop her off in the back. "You fixed the light."

"I just screwed it back in," she said. "Thanks for the ride."

He waited for her to open the back door, which appeared to be functioning. It felt rude to stay in his car, but it would have been even more awkward to walk her to the door. It wasn't a date.

He drove away feeling as if he should have done or said

something to help, but he had no idea what. It felt a lot like being a teenager, which was something he'd worked hard to shed. He drove across the road, parked in the alley, and walked back to the office. His phone vibrated. It was his old roommate Maccus Fortner texting to say he'd finally sent the papers. The package, an envelope from Chicago, was already sitting on his desk, and on top of it was a sticky note that read, "Lynn again. CALL HER."

Liam sat and pondered that a moment. Lynn's phone number had a Billings prefix. Was she living in Billings? He hadn't thought of her in ages. He peeled off the note, and after looking around for a moment, he found some duct tape. Then he opened the bottom drawer in one of Cash's filing cabinets. It was tricky to remove, but he found a catch lever near the back of the slide. Then he stuck the envelope firmly to the bottom of the drawer, closed the drawer, and hoped he could get it back out without dismantling the whole thing.

He had good reason to avoid Lynn. She was a reminder of the worst night of his life. All his other bad days faded into a miserable blur compared to that one. All the times he was knocked into the lockers, perpetually slammed by passing shoulders, or found his belongings missing...or on public display.

He'd almost mastered the art of seeing while not being seen. That was how he'd noticed Lynn. She was beautiful, and she had once been bright and popular. Then she'd become Griff's girlfriend.

He tossed and caught his cell phone a couple times. Why not? He dialed the number, and Lynn answered. He still remembered her voice.

"Hello?"

"Hi, Lynn. This is Liam Gunnerson."

"Liam. I didn't think you were going to call me back."

"I just stopped by the office and found a message that you'd called."

"You're at the office? Now?"

"Yes."

"Would you like to go get a drink? Your choice. I'll buy."

Well, this was new. And it would go a long way toward washing away the generally awful aftertaste of the dinner party. "Certainly."

CHAPTER 9

he stick-figure mannequins were gone from Avery's window, and a light was on in the store. Liam figured she was changing the color or item of the day. He liked the one she'd just taken down. The female figure had been gracefully draped in scarves, and the male figure, apparently shivering, had worn one scarf around his neck and one as a makeshift kilt. It was one of his favorite scenes so far.

But he really didn't want her to see him with Lynn. Dinner with Avery hadn't been a date, but it would be awkward to meet another woman on the same night. So he waited by the window, and when a car pulled up in front of the office, he jogged down the steps and met her on the sidewalk.

She was a sight. Long legs over stiletto shoes, and above that, a coat he guessed was cashmere. Her once-black hair had lighter lines in it. Highlights of some sort he supposed, although they looked red. It wasn't unattractive.

"Liam." She looked surprised, as if she hadn't actually expected him to be there. "It's good to see you."

He glanced up at the empty window display. He had to think fast. He'd been planning on the Combine, the well-lit brewpub, but Lynn wasn't dressed for that. There were only a few places fancy enough for her. One was in his mother's hotel, and he didn't relish the questions that would follow that appearance. "How about the wine bar at Zoe's?"

"That sounds great," she said. "I suppose we could just walk."

In those heels? Maybe. "It's at least three blocks."

"That's okay." She smiled. Liam remembered that smile. It was sweet and just a little shy. It wasn't the smile you would expect to see on what appeared to be a model's face. He held out his arm for her, and they started down the sidewalk.

Lynn told him she was living in Billings now, although she had been in town tonight to have dinner with her mom. She was a loan officer for a new branch bank. He knew the bank and knew all the offices were big and ostentatious, and the work paid well. The bank's specialty was ranching, but Lynn worked mainly on home loans.

She reminded him that they'd been in math club together their freshman year of high school. Liam laughed and changed the subject back to her. High school memories weren't his forte.

As it turned out, Lynn had just leased a chic new apartment in a renovated downtown building. He had already noted the little Lexus she drove. She was gorgeous and successful. So why had she called?

They walked into the quiet, gold ambiance of Zoe's, past the hostess desk to the bar in the back, and chose a table in the corner. He took her coat from her and pulled out her chair, then draped both coats over the empty seat on his other side. The bartender arrived with an appetizer and the dessert and wine menus, and the conversation stopped for a while as they ordered. He preferred wines with teeth, so he chose the Malbec from a winery he hadn't tried before and eyed the menu. "Are you hungry?" he asked. He certainly wasn't.

"I suppose I could order something sweet if you'd be willing to share," she said. She was looking shy again, almost uncomfortable.

"Anything you'd like," he said. He set his menu aside, and for a moment he could actually watch her.

It wasn't a trick of the light: the highlights were scarlet. The color matched her nails. She was beautiful but more angular than he remembered. Definitely model material. But she wasn't pretty like she'd been in high school. She looked more like the racks of bones many designers liked to drape their clothes over. He preferred women who filled out their clothes. In fact, Lynn looked like she needed a little less stress and a little more food. Maybe with the makeup gone and her hair back in a ponytail... yes, he could just imagine it. She'd be a stunner, like she used to be.

The bartender came back and Lynn greeted him with a wide, confident smile. "I'm finally ready," Lynn said. Liam glanced up at the man. He was smiling back, and he missed a beat before asking her for her order. Liam couldn't blame him.

She ordered a pinot grigio and a slice of cheesecake. *Maybe he could offend Lynn over her cheesecake as he had done to Avery*, Liam thought wryly.

As soon as the bartender left, Lynn turned to face Liam. Her gaze slid over his shoulder and back up again. "You really look great, Liam."

At least she didn't say how different he looked, like most high school acquaintances did. It never quite sounded like a compliment when they said it that way.

"What's your workout plan?" she asked.

He noticed the taut muscles in her arms as she lifted her water glass. No doubt she had a plan.

"It's pretty old school. Pushups, situps, that sort of thing." And more, but he didn't like to talk about that. Almost all the dojos he'd studied at advised against advertising that kind of knowledge.

Her forehead wrinkled. "Really? I would have guessed running."

"I hate running," he said. "Seems like a lot of wasted time."

She grinned and shook her head, and when she did, perfect curls slid over the silky burgundy shirt she was wearing. "So what are you doing these days?"

When he mentioned he was working toward his CPA, she looked genuinely impressed rather than bored to the edge of dread like most people. Then again, since she was in banking, she knew the value of what he did. He didn't tell her that he should have had his license by now, and a swanky Chicago apartment of his own.

She asked great questions and understood what he meant when he said he preferred management consulting to assurance work. They talked a little about the finance industry, which had been taking a hit of late. Her eyes never once glazed over. In fact, she held that glass of wine just below her red lips and watched him with real intensity. Even admiration, now and then.

"Are you going to open up your own shop in Montana when you get your license? Because if you do, I'd love to send some business your way. It's hard to find a CPA who knows what he's doing and is still easy to talk to."

He shook his head. "I don't know." He'd liked his job in Chicago, before it had all gone so ridiculously wrong.

He pictured himself walking into his old office and felt a twinge. A constriction. It had been so long since he'd felt it he'd almost forgotten the feeling. He had liked the work, hadn't he? The excitement? But that tightness in the center of his back, running all the way up his spine, said otherwise. He'd lived with that feeling for just over a year, and the truth was, he didn't miss it at all.

"I understand," Lynn said, but she looked disappointed. "But if you decide to stay, I'd like to be the first to know."

He raised his eyebrows. "You don't know if I'm any good."

"I know you were the smartest guy in high school," she said seriously. "And the nicest." She looked down and rotated her wine glass by its stem. "I was thinking—"

"You said something about painting," he said. "What do you like to paint?" He knew he was interrupting her.

She told him about a little shop in Billings that offered classes in silk painting. She said it was a great way to unwind and make friends. "It's good to meet people who have real lives, you know? Kids and spouses and yards and stuff. People who work forty hours and then go home and forget it for a while."

"I know what you mean. It's tax season. I'm only in town to work on my uncle's finances, and already some of his friends are trying to get me to do their taxes."

"Oh," she said with a small smile. "Hiding out in Montana hasn't kept them away?"

"No. And bachelor ranchers with shoeboxes full of receipts are worth hiding from."

She laughed softly, and he felt a little rush of ego. She thought he was funny, too. "But you aren't getting your CPA license just to do taxes," she said.

It was good to hear someone say that to him. It didn't hurt that it was a beautiful woman who hadn't taken her eyes off him, not even as other men walked by the table and openly stared at her.

"You're so easy to talk to," she said.

"You're easy to talk to, as well."

Lynn smiled and reached out to touch his arm as she did. It sent a jolt through him. He kept his gaze lowered and took a sip of his wine to cover any trace of surprise on his face.

It wasn't a surprise that a beautiful woman would find him attractive. Once he'd left Moose Hollow, it had been easy to get dates, although with his busy schedule, it had been hard to keep them. But it was jarring to experience this here, in his hometown. He had been someone very different in high school, and most everyone from Moose Hollow still saw him as that high school boy.

But he wasn't that person. The one with his eyes down— secretly watchful, ever avoiding. He didn't do that anymore. Which was ironic. If he'd kept his head down, maybe he'd still be employed and, in a handful of years, rich.

Lynn flirted with him over the cheesecake, and she ordered a second glass of wine. He didn't flirt—it wasn't something he admired in a man—but he was attentive. That was easy enough. She was beautiful and elegant, and they had a lot in common.

He couldn't help but compare her to Avery. Lynn was a sort of anti-Avery. The fact that Avery had been nothing but trouble, and had caused him a couple sleepless nights, surely meant that he should steer clear of her. Liam wished he hadn't mentioned he had business advice for her. He just needed to type up a few recommendations and hand them to her, then be done with it. The sooner he turned his full attention to Cash's business, the sooner he'd be leaving town.

The beautiful woman across from him understood the value of what he had to offer. Maybe in more ways than just being a CPA. But it was getting late, he had an early morning meeting, and she had work to do as well. He finished his glass of wine, paid the bill, and helped her into her coat. She smelled like a complex but elegant perfume, and he breathed it in as she walked beside him to the door.

The air outside was as cold as winter. After only one block of walking, he noticed how chilled she seemed. He took off his coat and draped it over her shoulders. She protested, but not for long. A couple blocks of Montana air wasn't enough to make him cold, just a little uncomfortable. Although he would have picked up the pace if Lynn hadn't slowed down.

"I haven't said why I wanted to meet with you," she said.

Liam gave her a dubious look, but she didn't meet his eye.

"I've been seeing a life coach. He's great, he's really been helping me get things in order. He gave me an assignment. He said I needed to make a list of people I need to apologize to and do it. And make a list of people I needed to thank, and do that too."

He didn't put a lot of stock in life coaches, or any nonfriend or nonfamily member who felt comfortable running another person's life. But he walked slowly alongside her, waiting for the other shoe to drop.

"You were on both lists, Liam."

Was that a good thing? He looked up ahead. Two more blocks to go. March in Montana was volatile, and it was a little colder than he'd counted on.

Lynn was looking at him, waiting for a response. "Why would I be on either list?" he asked.

"The night Griff broke up with me."

There it was, the very last thing he wanted to talk about in the whole world. He'd hoped she would take pity on the coatless man and make it a short. "You don't owe me anything."

"It was the worst night of my life, Liam."

He was a little surprised by that declaration. After all, no one had jumped Lynn or destroyed her car.

"Griff meant everything to me. When he dumped me, I didn't know how I was going to make it. When you found me in the gym, I was thinking I just didn't know how to get over him. And that maybe I didn't want to. Do you know what I mean? I know it was just high school, but for me, it was the worst. I couldn't stand it."

Liam reconsidered. Love was real enough for his little brother and his wife, and they'd fallen in love in high school. Maybe it had been real for Lynn, too.

"You said all the right things, you know?" she said softly.

*That would be a first*, he thought.

"You made me feel smart and pretty." She glanced up at him,

and he was startled to see a sparkle of tears in her eyes. "And if I remember right, you were a good kisser, too."

She stopped. He was surprised to find that they were standing in front of her car, and Cash's office, already.

"And I owe you an apology, Liam. I know what Griff did, him and his stupid friends. I know you wouldn't tell Officer Mike who it was. I've always known you did that for me. So I wouldn't have to go through it all, at least publicly."

No. Liam hadn't had noble intentions at all. He had been a seventeen-year-old boy who had nearly died. He'd kept his mouth shut out of fear, that's all. He hadn't had enough faith in the police, or anyone, that they could keep Griff from killing him if he told. The police surely knew it had been Griff, but they had never pressed charges. Besides, Griff had possessed two alibis: his stupid friends, Chris and Eli. It had been their word against his.

"I'm sorry, Liam." She was standing close to him, right in front of him, so traces of her perfume drifted past him again. Her expression was full of regret.

"I don't want you to feel bad," he said. "You didn't do anything wrong." Everything had changed after that night— changed him irrevocably, shaping him into the man he was today. What those young men had done in an act of evil, God had used to build him up. *God does that a lot*, Liam thought. He wanted to tell her that. He was almost sure she wasn't a believer, so he tried to choose his words carefully. While he was thinking of what to say, she leaned into him and kissed him.

He was stunned. He could feel her hand on his chest, her lips against his, and the sudden warmth of her body pressing against him, but it just didn't compute. Then it didn't matter. He pulled her even closer and ran the fingers of one hand up her neck and through her red-streaked hair.

And that's what brought him back down to earth. Her perfect hair was full of some sort of styling substance, and it tangled over his fingers. He carefully extracted his hand and drew back from her. Her eyes were still closed, and a half smile was on her parted lips.

It had taken about one and a half seconds to go from wanting to give his testimony to her to kissing her as if he cared for her a lot more than he really did. Obviously, she was wrong. He wasn't some sort of protector. The high he'd been on for the last couple hours crashed, and the cold returned.

"Even better than I remember," she murmured. "Does it have to end so soon?"

"I think it's best."

"Always the gentleman." She handed him his own coat, shivered, and hurried over to the driver's side of her sleek car. "You have my number," she said with a smile before getting in.

He stepped back and waited until her car started and she pulled from the curb. He plastered a smile on his face and waved goodbye.

Liam glanced up. Had a light just gone off in the Moose on the Loose? He scanned the inside of the store, at least what he could see in the few lights Avery had left on, but saw nothing. Upstairs, he could only see the ceiling and an old-fashioned chandelier glowing hazily through sheer curtains.

Good. That woman wasn't around. The last thing he wanted right now was to know Avery had watched him make yet another mistake.

# CHAPTER 10

*S*tanding outside her trailer, ready to unpack it, Avery caught sight of someone in the alley and jumped. She couldn't have been more relieved to see Griffin's smiling face. "I scared you, didn't I?"

"You did," she admitted.

"What's all this?" He peeked into the trailer. "You haven't moved your stuff inside yet?"

"No, I had to get some...redecorating done."

"I saw you had some contractors working the last couple days. I didn't recognize their name. But if they don't do right by you, just let me know. I know somebody. Which reminds me..." He pulled out his phone and tapped and swiped it for half a minute. She waited, unsure if it would be rude to turn away. "There. That should do it."

"Do what?"

"My crew is on the way. So what do you have in here? What're all the boxes that say 'fabric' about?"

"It's fabric," she chuckled.

"Ah. Inventory."

"Inventory in the making, maybe." That's what it had been at one time, but not anymore. She just couldn't bear to part with all her hard-won treasures. She didn't know when she'd have time to tinker again. Anyway, it all seemed like a waste of time. It had been a failed business, and her life was going to be far too busy for such a time-consuming hobby. She hoped, just a little bit, that Griffin would move on. She didn't want to have to explain the five dress forms she had crammed in the trailer.

Griffin leaned against the door to the trailer, which made it about impossible for her to start unpacking. She hugged her arms around her. Her pretty down jacket wasn't quite up to Montana in the spring. "So how was dinner?" he asked.

"It was nice. I like Poppy and Colton."

"Yeah, Colton's quite a character. A little odd. Word is he landed on his head a few too many times, but that's rodeo."

But Colton hadn't said a word about rodeo.

"And he hasn't been in trouble with the law for a while. Did you find your way there okay?"

"Liam Gunnerson drove me. He was going there anyway." Griffin's forehead wrinkled. *So there is something between the men,* she thought. At least Griffin didn't make a snarky comment.

Instead, he nodded thoughtfully. "You know, he and I aren't close."

"Really?" She hoped she sounded convincing. She was beginning to wish the conversation would end so she could go inside and get warm. The ache in her back had returned, and it was getting worse. She was spending too much time on her feet.

"I don't know exactly why, but somewhere along the way, I offended him. I think he has me confused with someone else. And I'm sure you've figured out by now that Liam can be a little…intense."

That was one word for it.

"So I wasn't going to tell you, but now that I know you're spending time with him, there's something you should know."

"I'm not spending time with him. He was just looking over the books. He's going to give me some business advice."

Griffin gave her another thoughtful nod. "Still. The other night I was out pretty late. Clients, you know how it goes. It was a big deal, and they wanted to celebrate. But I left my car keys in the office, so I had to go back in to get them. This must have been around one, maybe two. I just happened to look out my office window, and I saw his car parked back here. And someone was in the car."

She frowned. "That doesn't seem right. Maybe it was someone else."

Griffin looked truly sad to disagree. "There aren't a lot of blue FJ cruisers around, and only one with an Illinois license plate. I recognized it right away."

She couldn't believe it. Then again, gullibility was one of her downfalls. "I don't know why Liam would have been here."

"I'm sure there's a perfectly logical explanation. Either way, you have a right to know. I'm just saying that it might be in your best interest to keep a little space between you and Liam Gunnerson."

She heard footsteps behind her, and Griffin's face broke into a wide smile. "What took you guys so long?"

She recognized two of the men approaching as Griffin's friends, but there was another who didn't seem familiar. After two "happy hours" with him, she was pretty sure he knew everyone in town. Griffin swung the trailer doors wide. "Your moving crew has arrived, Miss Maier."

It took almost no time at all. Avery could smell the alcohol on their breath, and they were a little reckless getting the big items up the stairs, but in no time, a bed, a dresser, and the two wooden filing cabinets and huge wooden door that formed her desk were in her new room. And the dress forms were stacked in a corner, looking like headless rejects. They needed clothes. And hats.

She made sure Griffin carried the two sewing machines up, because she trusted him. He was so busy joking with his friends he never even asked what was inside the bulky cases. When the job was finished, she thanked them all. Griffin promised them a pitcher of beer at the Combine, but he lingered by the back door.

"I can't thank you enough," she said. "I had no idea how I was going to get that stuff up the stairs." Especially with the ache in her back.

"You can always count on me," he said. He looked up toward the top of the stairs, where the old chandelier was lighting the hallway. "You'll have to show me the renovations."

She got the feeling he meant now. "I will, I promise. But it's my bedtime, and thanks to you, I get to sleep in my own bed for a change."

"Anytime, Avery." Griff turned to go but looked back over his shoulder. "You know, I just live a couple miles away, by the ski hill. If you ever need anything, just let me know."

She smiled. "I will." Then she closed the door.

She really didn't feel well, but the window display hadn't been changed yet. She walked to the front of the store and turned on a single light. *Gray would be good*, she thought, massaging her lower spine. And that was when she saw them.

She saw the whole thing in one flash. The long, thin fingers with long, red nails at the back of his head, her dark hair shining in the light of the old-fashioned lanterns on the street, and the streaks of scarlet in her hair. The oversized wool dress coat she was wearing, the sky-high heels—all of it faded when his hands reached for her and he kissed her in a way rarely seen in public.

Then the man leaned back, and with a gasp, she realized it was Liam. *Liam*. And she was standing there staring at him. With the light on. She jumped, fell off balance, and landed hard on her rear end. She clenched her teeth to keep from crying out. Then she realized she could still see them, and therefore they could see her, and so she crawled on all fours to the light switch and flicked off the lights.

But the lights in the back were still on, still drawing attention to her. She sat still with her back against the wall, waiting. Who knew how long a kiss like that might go on? And no wonder Liam had been so reluctant to invite her to Poppy's dinner. He had someone else in his life, and he'd probably wanted to bring her instead. But still, it was bad form, wasn't it? Even though dinner at Poppy's hadn't been a date, wasn't it weird to go to dinner with him and then have him mash with some other woman a couple hours later? She tried not to feel offended. But she did.

And then the back pain returned. Though it was different now. It didn't feel like a pulled muscle anymore. Forgetting Liam and being seen, she hurried to the bathroom and found just what she had feared the most. She was bleeding.

Avery panicked. The baby—she had to save it. She would drive to the hospital. Was there even a hospital in Moose Hollow? Should she call an ambulance?

But what if there was no baby? Had she just made it all up in her mind?

She found her phone and searched for hospitals. She saw Moose Hollow Clinic and the name of two hospitals in Billings, each with at least a dozen more sublistings. But one thing stood out in big black letters. "Ask a Nurse," the listing said.

She called. At first, she could hardly get the words out. She felt like she was going to be sick, and her heart was racing crazily. The woman on the other end was patient and kind, but she had a lot of questions. And after she'd answered the nurse's questions, it was time for the nurse to answer hers.

No, falling down a few minutes before had probably not

caused the miscarriage. It had been underway for some time. No, there was no way to stop it at this early stage in the pregnancy. No, she didn't need to come in unless she felt ill or the bleeding was unusual, but she should see her doctor very soon. And no, it would be difficult to find out now if she had been pregnant.

The nurse suspected a chemical pregnancy, something Avery had never even heard of. She said the embryo had probably never implanted. That if she had tested earlier, Avery might have gotten a positive test, but that now it was unlikely she still would.

The nurse even answered the hardest question Avery asked. If she had miscarried, the baby would probably look no different than a blood clot, she said. It seemed wrong to Avery, but there was nothing special to be done. No way to mark the passing of a child she wasn't sure she'd ever had. No small body to honor or bury. She didn't know whether to feel relieved or horrified.

The nurse asked a few more questions aimed at Avery's mental health. Yes, she had a family to call. Yes, she had friends to call, she lied. No, the father was out of the picture, Avery said. There was no use saying more than that. She wasn't a widow; she had never earned that title. She was just a woman who had made terrible decisions.

She dug through the boxes labeled "bathroom" until she found the supplies she needed, and then dealt with the bleeding as if it was nothing unusual. Then she walked upstairs to her new room. The bed was supposed to go on that wall, the sewing table by the windows, and near her bed, the crib she had planned to buy. Standing in the middle of the room, Avery thought she should feel relieved.

She didn't want to be a single mother. This was good, right?

But instead, she felt the loss of a baby she didn't know she'd ever carried. If she'd only talked Eli out of that last trip. But the truth was, she'd been relieved to see him go that day. Her feelings for him had been so conflicted. She hadn't deserved to have his child. Without a child, no trace of Eli remained now, except this building and the dreams it represented. Everything was gone. She sank down to the floor and pulled her knees up to her chest, wrapped her arms around them, and began to cry.

# CHAPTER 11

*L*iam hadn't set the office alarm. He went upstairs just to make sure things were in order so he could leave that one thing off his troubled mind. In the dark, the windows across the street glowed. He knew he shouldn't, but he looked for Avery anyway, just to make sure she was all right. That no one was breaking in.

Just one quick look and he'd be gone.

He saw Avery downstairs, talking on the phone, pacing in and out of sight until she stumbled toward the front of the store. She put her back to the checkout desk and slid down onto the floor. As she did, he saw tears shining on her face.

Was this his fault? Had he bothered her so much? He chided himself for how self-centered he was. It was grief for her fiancé, he was sure. He'd never been through pain like that. He couldn't imagine how her grief must ebb and flow. And it was none of his business.

But there she was, and he couldn't just walk away. But she wasn't alone, she was on the phone with someone. Probably family or a close friend. He was the last person she needed. He paced to the back of the office and then forward again. She was gone.

What had happened? Had he imagined it, or had she looked ill, pale even? Was it more than grief? Maybe she had the flu. It could be drugs or drink, but he doubted it. Had someone broken in, hurt her, or threatened her? He couldn't imagine how she'd gone from healthy and beautiful at dinner to looking so lost she could hardly walk.

He paced again and again, but he couldn't shake the feeling. He had to do something. And just when he felt as if he would crawl right out of his own skin, he saw the store lights darken. Seeing nothing, he waited until time and more time ticked by. He reasoned with himself, saying that the moment he saw Avery again and knew she was okay, he would leave. He hunted for a glimpse of her in the upstairs hall, which was still well-lit. It took forever for her to appear.

She was trailing her fingertips down the wall of the hallway, head hanging down, her other arm clasped tight across her stomach. She walked into the newly remodeled bedroom. There were no curtains—he'd have to remind her to fix that.

To protect her from people like him.

He drove the heels of his hands into his temples to chase away the headache growing there. Avery was up and walking. She'd talked to someone. She didn't need him, he told himself. How arrogant did he have to be to assume that he was the one who should be helping her? She didn't even like him, let alone trust him. And if she found out he was looking through her window, she never would. Avery turned around slowly, and for a moment her gaze swept the spot where he stood. His heart nearly stopped.

This was ridiculous. What he was doing was so, so wrong. He'd let it go too far.

Avery sank to the floor, wrapping herself up like a child, until she melted onto her side in the fetal position. He couldn't see her face. But the random placement of boxes and furniture still left him a perfect view of the way her shoulders shook. She cried so violently that she looked as though she were coughing or screaming. He saw her hands clinging tight to her own belly, holding on to herself.

Liam sat on his heels. There was something he could do— the only thing he had a right to do. He prayed for Avery, for peace, for healing, and for loving friends to circle around her. He prayed that if he was given the opportunity to help, he would, but in the right way. And when he was finally done praying, he gathered his things and made a promise. Unless she called him, she was out of his hands. No more night shifts, no more watching. It was time to go home.

# CHAPTER 12

oday was the last day. The dumpster would be hauled away, and with it the last of the trash and pallets in the back alley. The paint and trim would be retouched, and the floors cleaned so that all would be shiny and new. Not fancy, but clean, and that was all Avery had ever wanted. And in Bella's opinion, the renovation would add twice its cost to the value of her building. But looking back now, what it had really done was force her out of bed each morning before the workers arrived. And as miserable as that had been, that was what she'd needed the most.

It hadn't been easy. The morning was the only time Avery felt like she could sleep. The evenings were for TV, her phone, and whatever silly thing could distract her. She would stay up until she was exhausted. Then, in the middle of the night, night after night, the fear would jolt her awake. Sometimes it was her own dreams that woke her, but usually, it was the strange sounds around her—the creaking, the pinging, and what sounded like footsteps. She stared at her open door, at the light in the hall, watching and imagining someone bursting through to harm her. Sometimes she imagined a drug addict. Sometimes she pictured Eli, half dead and angry at her. At other times, when she was tired out of her mind, it was some sort of monster crawling up from beneath the building. And always there were the real monsters, too: the roof that needed resealing, the electrical trouble, the old pipes, the customers who weren't coming, the new inventory she didn't have money to buy.

Avery didn't know what it was about the first trace of blue light in the morning, but it chased away the anxiety like sunlight dissolved snow in the springtime. Then she would sleep soundly, at least for an hour. Then it was time to get up and go to work.

Maybe she was strong enough now to get up on her own. Perhaps she would tackle that pile of unopened mail. Or go for a walk at lunchtime. Or answer some of the phone messages she hadn't listened to. Just thinking about it made her feel as if she was sinking and drowning. But the workers wouldn't be arriving tomorrow to chase her out of bed, so she had to start doing it herself. She had no choice.

She took a fast shower, put her hair in a bun, dressed in one of her favorite skirts and a light sweater, and headed downstairs. The back room looked the same. She had thought she'd have it cleared out by now. And the store looked the same. Behind her, she heard someone approaching the back door. The workers were here to close out the job site. She slipped through to the main store.

She was thinking she should move the coffee maker downstairs, for herself and customers, when she heard a knock on the front door. She walked over to it, plastering a polite smile on her face, ready to shoo someone away because it was too early. But the face at the glass was familiar: straight blonde hair, a kind smile, shining eyes. She unlocked the door. "Am I interrupting something?" Poppy asked.

"No, not at all."

"Good." She had a paper cup of coffee in each hand and held one out for her. "I haven't seen you in forever."

"I know. I actually meant to call and thank you for dinner last…" Not last week, she realized. About three weeks ago.

"Did you get my message?"

"I did. But I didn't listen to it. I'm sorry, it's not you. It's been…" Avery let that sentence trail off, too. She had absolutely no idea what to say. *I was tired*, she thought. That's what she wanted to say. But tired didn't even cover it. "It's been…" she began again, hoping the perfect word would pop into her head.

"Sounds like things have been hard," Poppy said.

Avery blinked. It would be stupid to cry. She took a deep breath and nodded.

"Well, you don't owe me any explanation. I just wanted to drop by to see how you were doing. If now isn't a good time, I'll leave you alone."

Avery shook her head and gestured over to where wooden stools now stood by the checkout counter. "Want to have a seat?"

"I do."

There was something confident about Poppy's walk. In fact, all of her just sort of oozed confidence. Or was it competence? Either way, Avery was jealous. "I like your belt," she said lamely.

Poppy smiled. "Oh, you like conchos? They aren't that big of a thing in Montana."

"Iowa either," Avery smiled. "Unfortunately."

Poppy asked her about Iowa, and before she knew it, they were talking about the farm, her family, and her little brothers. And even laughing. She tried to find out a little bit more about Poppy. She had a younger sister named Sierra—tall, red-haired, and gorgeous, Poppy said. But unlike Avery, Poppy and Sierra didn't have one hometown, they had many. Their parents sounded a little bit like gypsies. But Poppy carefully shifted the subject away from them to the here and now. She had been planning to visit Avery, she said, but the last of the calving, and now trying to fix up the barn, was taking all her time. It took a minute for Avery to realize the barn was where the wedding was going to take place.

"We're not sending out invitations. You're invited. Anyone who hasn't got something better to do can come. We're going to feed you and make you dance if you do come, though."

Around the time Avery was finishing the last of her coffee, and not feeling bad at all that she hadn't tackled the growing pile of mail yet, she somehow let it slip that she liked sewing. Poppy looked as surprised as if she'd said she liked bungee jumping.

"It's always been a mystery to me," Poppy said. "But then again, clothing is a mystery to me. Can you show me something you've done?"

Avery balked. Her new room was a mess. She had set up the dress forms in an attempt to feel better, but the rest of it definitely wasn't company worthy.

"I made the skirt I wore to dinner."

"Oh, the ribbon and velvet thing? It did that thing when you walked." She waved her hands through the air. "I loved that skirt. You made that? Really?"

Avery had to chuckle. "It's just sewing."

"Show me something else."

Avery took a deep breath. "Okay. It's back through the construction zone."

"You have room for another store," Poppy said as they entered the back room.

*And no money to fill it with things to sell,* Avery thought. She led Poppy up the staircase to her "home," past the kitchen where a few people were cleaning up. They'd already cleaned out the two vacant rooms, and without money to make something else happen, vacant was how they would stay.

"This room is so cool," Poppy said, stopping in the first

empty room. "Look at this window. You're up so high. You could rent this out too, you know. Although I'm not one for roommates. Maybe as another office space?"

"They said I'd have to put fire sprinklers up here if it was an office so I can't rent it out now." As it was, the sprinklers only extended down the hallway. It wouldn't be too difficult to extend them into the rooms...just expensive.

"Too bad. Love the high ceilings. And the skylights are great. Did you find any secret chambers as you renovated?"

Avery's heart did a little jump. Just the thought of that was enough to fuel another night of anxiety. "No, why do you ask?"

Poppy laughed. "Liam. He's convinced there's a secret passage underneath your building. Well, not just your building, all the ones in this area. I guess when he was in high school he tried to get the Hallowells next door to let him search the basement, but they never would. As much as he mentions it, I'm surprised he hasn't said something to you."

That surprised Avery, too. And not in a good way.

They made it past the kitchen, which was clean but ugly. Simple, clean appliances and one wall of cabinets were at one end of the room, and the rest was empty space. They had stripped everything down to the wood floors. She had no idea what to do with the place. She didn't need a living room, her bedroom was big enough. "My room is the last one," she said, and Poppy continued down the hall. "Please don't expect much. I barely moved in."

Poppy was in the bedroom, looking at each of the dress forms in turn. Avery had dressed them with her favorite creations, complicated combinations of antique lace and other lovely fabrics that she'd worked hard to form into one coherent, flowing piece of clothing. A long time passed without Poppy making a comment, and Avery began to feel nervous. Poppy wasn't one to hold back her opinion.

"This is just what I wanted," Poppy said at last. She threw a look back over her shoulder. "For my wedding."

"Wedding decorations?"

"No, my dress, silly. I've had so much trouble finding what I want. I don't know, it has a Stevie Nicks vibe."

Avery rolled her eyes. She had heard that before, and it wasn't her favorite compliment. Her clothes were far more structured and shape conscious. That was half the magic in her creations. She was most proud of mixing the fabrics so that the seams were flat and the movement was just right. She used stronger fabrics where the dress should fit a certain way, softer where it should flow. "I don't make wedding dresses."

"You could make mine."

"Oh, no. I don't make wedding dresses. It's just too much stress. They're difficult."

"Not for me it won't be, because we're friends," she said, coming back to one of the dress forms. "I want it to be off-white or cream. I want yellow somewhere, just because that's the ranch color, but I don't want a whole yellow dress. I want it to feel like a T-shirt and not be fussy or need one of those ruffly slips they wear underneath. And I want it to feel exactly like this." She pointed at the dress beside her. "Or this. Or this, this, or this." She pointed at the others. "Not old, not modern, but a little of both."

"Poppy, really. I can't."

Poppy crossed her arms. "Tell me you aren't interested in trying."

She was. She had an old lace with tiny yellow flowers in it, vintage curtains waiting for the right project, and she'd thought of it the moment Poppy mentioned the color. "You're talking about your wedding, for heaven's sake. And photos that last forever." She hadn't even made a dress for her own wedding. Not really. She had planned to wear one of the hippie tank dresses she'd made to sell at fairs because Eli thought wedding dresses were too formal.

"Tell me you'll think about it. Please tell me you will. This might be stressful for you, but it would take a world of worry off me."

*Because we're friends.* That had sounded good. "I'll think about it."

A huge smile spread across Poppy's face, and Avery felt sunk. And a little excited. Maybe...no. It was ridiculous. She was a hobbyist at best, not a designer.

"One more thing," Poppy said.

Avery slumped. "No. Whatever it is, no."

"I just want to know why your store looks like that," she said, gesturing to the floor below her feet, "instead of this." She used both arms to include the clothing on the dress forms.

Avery didn't answer.

"You can tell me why after you tell me you'll make my dress," Poppy said. "I should go. I'm late to meet Colton. I'll text you tonight."

Avery moved to the window and watched through the sheer curtains as Poppy ran across the street and into the door that led upstairs to Cash's real estate office.

Poppy had wanted to know why she was selling outdoor clothing. *Because,* she answered in her mind. Because her dreams became forfeit the day she stole Eli's dreams from him.

# CHAPTER 13

*S*itting in the back of the office kept him focused, Liam knew, but time was moving so slowly today that it just made him feel claustrophobic. He needed to finish his work. He also needed to refuse to take on another last-minute tax client just because Cash wanted the man to owe him a favor. But here he was, treading water. It was the time of day most people went home. He decided a little break and some Moose Hollow comfort food was in order.

As his shoes hit the sidewalk, he felt better. It was warmer than he'd expected after yesterday's snow shower. He felt a little sad for having missed the day, but that was what being a grown-up was all about, right?

"Liam?"

He glanced down to find Avery looking up at him. He'd missed her entirely. She was crouched down, petting a dog tied up to a bike rack. Liam hadn't spoken to her in weeks, which wasn't an accident. He'd done a good job of avoiding her, but bits of her leaked into his thoughts. He'd wanted to talk to her. To tell her how relieved he was when the window display finally changed again five days after he'd seen her crying. He wanted to tell her he was praying for her and for her business. But other than a few whispered wishes, he wasn't praying often enough. He hadn't prayed much since leaving Chicago. And now there she was, decked out for a chilly Montana spring day in boots and a skirt that looked like it had come from a gypsy caravan, and a neatly tailored sweater and blouse on top of it. Who wore that? It wasn't casual or dressy. It was Avery. He definitely thought she was cute, and that wasn't good. He already knew he was better off not getting involved in her life. But he felt guilty about not having done what he said he would do, and the words just poured out. "I wrote down some things that I think might help your business, as I said I would. I have them with me now. Do you have time to grab a quick bite to eat?"

She glanced up the hill. "I was going to meet some friends for a drink." She thought about it. "But I don't think they'll miss me."

She was looking toward the Lantern, which meant she was meeting Griff, of course. Liam was secretly pleased Griff would be getting stood up. "Have you been to Annie's?"

She shook her head and looked uncertain. "Let me get my coat." She disappeared and then came back out, locking the shop door behind her.

Annie's Asian Ciao was located in a little old house. It was from the same era as the town's stately Victorians, but it was just a plain and tiny house, narrow and tall. He jogged up the steps to open the door for her and saw the doubt in her eyes. As luck would have it, Annie was in the front room talking up a couple who didn't look familiar. She had her hair up in a sort of crocheted hair net and was wearing a frilly floral apron, jeans, and the muck boots she always wore when she was cooking. She looked at Avery, looked at Liam, and then said, "Gotta go" to the couple she had been talking to.

She grabbed Avery by both hands. "You must be Avery Maier. It's about time someone brought you here. I can't believe you went to that uppity Jet restaurant first. I bet you went away hungry."

Avery smiled, although she looked as if she was trying not to. "Maybe. Do you have spies in all the other restaurants?"

Annie snorted. She pointed at Avery and looked at Liam. "This one I like."

Liam tried to ignore the comment about Jet, the most expensive restaurant in town. No doubt Griff had taken her there. Griff Hallowell was one more reason he wanted to be clear of this town. Liam needed to start over, no matter how unfair it felt. And worse, Dad had almost finished the renovations to the room where he was staying, so if he hung around any longer, he'd be interfering with their business.

Annie took them upstairs. *She is up to something*, he thought.

No matter how he approached it, the truth was that Liam had failed at his job. He'd known the risks and taken them anyway, and now he had to pay the price. Starting over wasn't the end of the world. He'd done it once, and he could do it again. He needed to leave. Griff could have Avery. And she could have *him* if she was foolish enough to want him.

Annie sat them in the front of the house on the top floor, in the treasured two-seated table with its white Christmas lights strung around the window frame, fully a third of them not functioning. On the table sat white plastic apple blossoms in a replica Chinese vase, circa 1970, he guessed. There was no cloth tablecloth—it wasn't Annie's style—but there was her usual white butcher paper and a new set of crayons. It was the most romantic thing Annie had to offer, which meant she had entirely the wrong idea about why he had brought Avery here.

"It's the warmest place in the house," Annie said. "All the heat from the kitchen goes up here. If it gets too hot, just ask Liam to crack open the window." Annie retreated. That's when Liam saw she was wearing a Green Bay jersey under her apron. He didn't know how he'd missed seeing that before. Liam wondered if either of her exes had liked, or hated, the Packers. And if she secretly missed any of them.

Avery was already looking at the menu and didn't seem to have noticed the matchmaking Annie was attempting. He wasn't surprised she'd missed it. Jet was much more of a date-night place if you liked that sort of thing. The liquid nitrogen and whipped cream "dragon eggs" that made you breathe smoke sounded interesting, at least on the right night and in the right company, but that wasn't worth the forty dollars Jet charged for them. He gave the new chef a few months until he was freed to move on to more pretentious digs than Moose Hollow had to offer.

"Thai pizza? How does that taste?" she asked.

"Weird. And delicious." And to his surprise, when Annie returned, that's what Avery ordered. He asked for the dubiously named Moose Rut calzone. Despite what everyone said about Chicago cuisine, he'd missed Annie's cooking over the past year.

He pulled his phone out of his pocket. "I'm not making a call," he said. "I have my notes on here. I will send this to you in an email, but I wanted to ask a couple of questions and talk to you about a few things."

"Sounds ominous," Avery said, putting her paper napkin on her lap. "You first."

First? Was she going to go next? "I was wondering if you've ordered for summer and autumn yet. I know you've been over-whelmed with the old inventory, but while you make a dent in that, you need new inventory."

She said a lot of words that ended up meaning no, she had not.

"My turn for questions," she said as he jotted down a couple words with a stylus. "What does a person have to do to become a CNA?"

"CPA," he said. "Certified Public Accountant. And it varies. Generally you need a degree in a related field, plus 150 hours of additional classes. About five years of college total. There's a big exam. And 2,000 hours of related work under the supervision of a CPA in good standing." *Good standing.* His bosses had that, ironically. A lot of good it had done Liam. "So after the classwork, you work for about a year until someone can vouch for you."

"That's a lot of work," she said.

She seemed surprised. "Next question," he said. "Have you raised your insurance since you found out about all the additional inventory?"

"No, but I will." She looked a little annoyed. Then she stared at him with narrowed eyes. "Why did you come back to Moose Hollow?"

"I was fired from my job and Cash needed work done. Now about the upstairs room in the back, the one facing the alley—"

"That was half an answer," she interrupted.

"It was a complete answer to the question you asked." He didn't want to think about getting fired now. "You could rent it out."

She frowned. "It would need sprinklers." She took a drink of water, and he waited for the inevitable. "Why were you fired?"

"My employer didn't like the work I was doing."

She smirked. "That wasn't even half an answer. Here you are digging through the intimate details of my financial life—"

"As a favor." Traces of the smirk seem to have taken up residence on her pretty face. It was deviously cute.

"Fine. I considered something at my firm to be a conflict of interest." That was a nice way to put it. "My supervisor's supervisor disagreed, and he fired me for having what he called questionable judgment."

For just a moment a look of real concern crossed her face. It was enough to make Liam feel things he wasn't ready to feel, so he looked back down at his phone. He asked her about a business plan. She said she didn't have one and immediately asked, "Is that going to make it hard for you to get a job now?"

"Now, yes. Eventually, it will blow over." As long as he never tried to get a job in Chicago. Or New York. Or Portland, or anywhere else Ackerman, Jones & Fetterman had connections. "It does make it more difficult for me to get my CPA license." He would have to go through the entire internship again, if he could find someone to take him on. A whole year of his life had washed down the drain.

Her lips parted, and she leaned back. Of course, she'd thought he already had one, and he'd passed up the chance to clarify his standing. Now he sounded like a liar. "I've completed everything required. Other than the internship."

"When are you going to do that?"

"Me first," he said, grateful to dodge that question. "If you need a line of credit, you'll need to provide a good business plan. A five-year plan at least. Do you know how to write one?"

"No."

Well, then. Annie came up the stairs with their food. She set the pizza down in front of Avery. "Try it," she ordered.

Avery didn't seem taken aback by Annie at all. She used her fork to cut a bite-sized piece out of the pie.

"You eat pizza with a fork?" Annie said. She was still holding Liam's calzone, evidently as a hostage.

"When it's this hot I do," Avery said. The smirk was back. It made Liam smile. She blew on the piece and took a bite. Surprise and something else crossed her face. "This is awesome," she said. "Oh my gosh. I get the Thai thing. It sounded kind of strange on the menu, but it tastes so good."

"Exactly," Annie agreed, and she set Liam's calzone on the table. Then she raised her chin, looking triumphant, and strolled back downstairs.

A less stressful conversation took over as they talked about the food, the view, the lengthening days, and more. Then Avery gave him a guilty look. "I'm sorry. We came here to discuss work. I don't want to waste this time."

*So I'm a waste of your time*, he thought.

"That sounded unappreciative," Avery said.

He wondered if his thoughts had been evident in his expression. "Not at all," he said. "I'm just relieved you haven't gotten the wrong idea about my intentions."

She blinked. Smiled. Nodded and went back to her pizza, with a little less enthusiasm. Liam inwardly kicked himself.

He made it through the rest of his questions and noticed she'd stopped asking hers. They talked about the essential elements of a business plan, and why she needed one, and soon she was typing notes of her own into her phone. It had seemed a little harder than it should be to get her interested in her own business, but once she'd settled down, she'd come up with some very good ideas. And she had the work ethic, too. As far as he could tell from her online site and walking by her store, she was always working.

When she wasn't with Griff, of course.

When Annie returned, Avery made an effort to reach for the bill, but there was no way Annie was going to give it to her. It came to him, and he immediately handed it back with a debit card.

"Thank you," Avery said. "But you should really let me pay."

"I couldn't do that," he said. His mother hadn't raised him that way. Or his father, for that matter. Some rules were more important than business.

On the walk back to her building, Avery gazed up at the sky and asked, "When does it stop snowing?"

He laughed. "You can get snow every month of the year."

"August?" she asked.

"Yes. But it doesn't stay cold. Believe me, it'll get hot enough. And the sun at this altitude is fierce."

Avery stopped in front of the Moose on the Loose. "I have

another question. What does it mean when an insurance company says they're opening an investigation?"

That had come out of the blue. And it gave him a sick feeling in the pit of his stomach. "It probably means they suspect there has been some fraud and they aren't willing to pay out the insured amount."

She frowned. "What if they already paid the money?"

"They'd have to have some pretty substantial evidence."

"Okay," she whispered.

"Do you mind me asking what insurance you're talking about?"

"My fiancé's life insurance."

"Do you want me to take a look at whatever document they sent you?"

"Maybe." Her frown deepened. "No one said anything about a basement."

Liam was trying to keep up, but all he could be sure of was that Avery looked genuinely troubled, and it was striking all kinds of notes in him, none of which were pleasant. "You didn't know the building had a basement."

"It doesn't."

His eyebrows raised. "Well, there's one way to find out. Mind if I come in?"

She looked at him like a creeper, which was absolutely what he deserved. He needed to shut his mouth and keep it shut. But she ruined his plans to do the right thing when she said, "Sure."

# CHAPTER 14

*L*iam found the access to the basement. It was easy enough since there were concrete steps in the back of the building leading down to a door with a padlock. There had been pallets covering the entrance when he spent the night in the alley, but they must have been hauled away. He saw the look on her face when he discovered the door, but he couldn't read it. No doubt there was some real tension there. Maybe she didn't like being proved wrong.

Then, when he gave her some excellent reasons to believe there was an additional entrance to the basement hidden somewhere on the ground floor, her expression wasn't hard to read at all. She was furious. And he'd blundered right through it, asking if she wanted him to find it. He wasn't trying to be funny or rude, he was trying to help her, and she'd practically thrown him out.

Though to be honest, it wasn't only about helping her.

He'd grown up underground, in the smallest room in the basement of the Third Street Inn. There wasn't even a window in that room, and his parents had drilled him regularly that in case of fire, he had to use the living room window to escape.

There had been advantages to being out of the normal flow of traffic in their crowded apartment. Mostly, it had been a space of his own when the alternative would have been sharing a bedroom with his younger brother, Zane.

But then he'd found the closed-off entrance behind the utility closet, and after prying that off while his parents were working, he'd discovered the sidewalk vault in front of the Third Street Inn.

His parents hadn't appreciated his excavation.

None of the adults in his life seemed to have grasped the mystery and magic of the hidden passages beneath the town's sidewalks. They saw them in terms of structural engineering, liabilities, and money. Always the money. Just like he'd been trained to see the world since then. But he'd never been good at putting numbers ahead of his restless mind. If he had been, he wouldn't be out of a job now. Or under scrutiny with the national board that licensed CPAs, and with a year of his life—and maybe his whole career—up in smoke.

He shoved his hands deep in his pockets, hunched his shoulders against the cold, and headed around the block to the alley where his Cruiser was parked. Back in high school he'd researched. He'd done proposals. He'd created a presentation on the hidden world under the nearby towns of Livingston and Bozeman. The Hallowells' realty building had that telltale grate in its sidewalk, a grid of tiny glass blocks designed to let light through to a space beneath, all purplish from nearly a hundred years of sunlight. He'd known it was the best place in Moose Hollow to search. What if the sidewalk vaults extended all the way to the hotel? Who wouldn't want to discover a secret passageway like that?

But the Hallowells had refused to give him access to their basement. In fact, Hallowell Sr. had threatened him, telling him to leave him and his property alone. Like father, like son. But Avery's building was right next door, and of a similar age. If there was a vault under the Hallowells' sidewalk, there was probably one under Avery's.

"Living on the streets now, Gunnerson?"

*Perfect timing,* he thought. The voice was as familiar to Liam as any in Moose Hollow. Every muscle in his body tensed. He breathed deep and low to force himself to relax before turning around.

"Out on the street? Even your mom's had enough of you now, huh?" Griff Hallowell's building, and his favorite bar, were on the other side of the street. There was no reason for the man to be in this alley. His presence here wasn't an accident. Liam scanned the area for Griff's usual associates but saw no one. That was a miscalculation on Griff's part.

Griff stepped closer to Liam and raised his chin so he could look further down his nose at him. The sweet scent of alcohol was mixed with spicy food. No matter what Avery thought, he wasn't wrong about the fact that Griff was a dangerous man. What could she possibly see in him? "We like to keep the streets clean of beggars around here," Griff said with a grin.

Liam saw Griff's meaty hand come up.

"Shove off," Griff said as he thrust his hand forward toward Liam's chest. But Liam was already moving, a measured movement away and to the side as his right foot swept backward. Griff stumbled forward under the momentum of his own strike and turned around with an expression that was half confusion and half frustration.

So many images of Griff flashed in Liam's mind at that moment, but one stood out. His shining wet face, swollen and otherworldly under the greenish field lights, inches away as he sat on Liam's chest and rained down fist after fist into Liam's face. And he felt his own anger, years of it, welling up in him as hot and sharp as if he'd swallowed a dragon.

Liam knew that when Griff gained his feet, the man was going to strike. But things were different now. With one blow,

Liam could drop Griff. He could be seriously injured, or he could land in the hospital for days, just like Liam had. Liam could finish Griff's endless malice and probably stop him from hurting someone else. All at once thoughts crowded his mind, a constellation of fire and ice, all of them pointing to his next move. Griff turned to face him.

But what would Avery think? What would his parents think? Not to mention God. Would one strike be enough to calm Liam's anger? Would it take a hundred? Then what?

Liam's hands flew up. "Whoa. Lay off, Griff. Pick on someone your own size."

"Get moving, slacker," Griff said. He looked unsteady on his feet.

Liam turned his back on Griff. He listened to his laughter, hearing him until he rounded the corner and the laughter faded. It had sounded forced. He wondered if Griff suspected that he wasn't the same kid he'd ambushed years ago. Liam shook his head. No, muscle-bound thugs usually only respected other thugs, and no matter what skills he'd gained, he didn't look like someone to be taken seriously. He didn't have the height or girth to intimidate that kind of guy.

Someday Griff was going to pick a fight with the wrong person, but it couldn't be him. He imagined what Griff would say to Avery if Griff was injured, and imagined her wide brown eyes wet with tears, grasping his hand with her slender fingers. Then they'd call Officer Mike, who had changed jobs in the intervening years. He was another person Liam could do without ever seeing again. What a mess that would be. What a mess it had all been before.

Liam put the duffel bag in the back of his FJ Cruiser and tried without success to relax. He wasn't sure what it would take to calm the storm of emotions running through his veins.

Except leaving Moose Hollow.

# CHAPTER 15

*A* very watched Griff walk away across the street, catching the toe of one shoe on the pavement, veering sideways once. Maybe he was just tired. Or distracted. But he didn't notice her watching.

The lights were off in her room, and she was sitting on the floor, her arms perched on the windowsill. She'd been having an imaginary conversation with Liam, at times berating him for his snotty attitude, at other times apologizing for overreacting. And after all that practice, she still had no idea what to say to him.

He'd left his black sweater by the back door when he came back inside and offered to search for some sort of hidden entrance to the basement. He'd forgotten to take it when he left. Or rather, he hadn't had time to put it back on when she kicked him out.

Avery had folded it neatly and tucked it under her chin on the windowsill, waiting. But enough time had passed that she realized he wasn't coming back for it. She had wanted him to, maybe. It was hard to tell as her mood shifted. She did want to make peace. He must think she was a moody, volatile person. She didn't like moody people; they were so difficult to please.

BRIGHT MONTANA HOME 107

So she had held on to his sweater, but he hadn't returned. Apparently he didn't care if she was mad or offended. Or scared.

And she *was* scared. The sun had barely gone down, and already shadows were creeping and shifting all around her. She knew what lay ahead. A night of sounds that might mean a secret door opening to a basement filled with mold, or pooled water, dead mice, or a secret passageway to a haunted vault. Isn't that what a vault was—a place where they put dead bodies? Or maybe she wanted Liam to come back because she just didn't want to be alone.

And that said nothing good about her. Other adults didn't act this way. She felt ten again, afraid of the dark, fearful of being alone as her overactive mind created monsters that reassurances from her parents couldn't banish.

Just when she was sure she was grown up enough to be over her fears, something would trigger them all over again. It got bad when she moved to the dorm, no longer living within a couple steps of her parents and brothers. Then bad again when she moved out of the dorm, although she had apartment neighbors who were equal parts comfort and annoyance. But this tall, shadow-filled building was her home alone now. Griff's office next door was vacant at night, and the cafe on the other side still seemed to be closed for the season. There would be no husband or child to share the space, and that was her fault.

What had the pastor called the unforgivable sin? There was a particular name for it. She didn't even remember what the sin was, but she was pretty sure she'd committed it. What she remembered perfectly was the realization that God could turn his back on a person. That was the most important thing. It made everything else she'd been told at church suspect.

There were days, when she was little, she had imagined Jesus as a kind of imaginary friend when she was lonely. He loved kids, they had pounded that into her head, so she figured he wanted to hang out with her, at least when she was behaving. But as a woman, Jesus seemed remote at best. But how else could it be? She was the dangerous woman who had driven her fiancé away to a trip that had cost him his life. The trip he'd gone on to "get right with God."

She hoped he had reconciled with God before the fall, but she was still here, still alive, and she still had a price to pay. She was the woman who broke vows. She put her forehead down on the sweater. It was softer than she'd expected, and for one selfish moment, she lost herself in that comfort.

She had done a lot of things right, hadn't she? Not all the little things, of course, but she hadn't made any horrible mistakes. Until that night with Eli. *Adultery.* She had gotten him to do what he'd said he would never do: sleep with her before marriage. And now none of the things she had done right mattered anymore. She stared at the street below for a long time. No cars came by, and no one was out walking. If she hadn't known better, she would've thought she was the only person in Moose Hollow.

Avery still had work to do, though she knew she wouldn't sleep much. She would get up tomorrow and try to make things right, even if she didn't think it was possible. And there was one thing she *could* do to make the night bearable. She turned on the lights, every single one of them, and undressed one of the dress forms. *When you feel like something is missing, find someone else's missing thing,* her mom had said. In other words, do unto others.

The pity party had to end sometime, didn't it? And the only way she knew how to stop it was to start making a wedding dress.

# CHAPTER 16

"*I* keep hoping you're going to change your mind and come home to Iowa, honey." Her father's voice echoed from the speaker on her phone into the empty store.

"I know, Dad." Avery closed her eyes tight. He had no idea how good that sounded to her right now.

"But your mother keeps me up to date, and she said things are going well for you. She said you've gotten so big you're even selling clothes online."

"Well, there was some old inventory. It's not that I've gotten big, really."

"Honey, I don't know much about insurance for a business like that, other than to buy lots of it. And you said you have enough to cover the building and the business, right?"

"I do." Purchased online from a company with good reviews. That move had probably been as naive as any of her other business decisions, but the truth was, the purchase had required more research than she'd done before buying the Moose on the Loose. But that wasn't her concern now. "It isn't really about that, Dad. I think I have good coverage. It's that I don't really understand...I got a couple letters from an insurance company, and I'm trying to figure it out."

"Maybe you need some of that other insurance, like if you get sick or something. I'd tell you to talk to Frank, but I don't think he knows much outside of agriculture. Is there someone there you can trust? Someone who knows insurance? Or another business owner, someone who could direct you to a person who could help? It's probably time to start lining up a team, honey. Accountant, insurance agent, lawyer. Just some people you can trust when you have a question or two."

"I trust you," she said weakly.

He chuckled. "Thanks, but you know what I mean. There's lots of new stuff going on in your life, and you shouldn't expect to do it alone. I'll help any way I can, but I'm no insurance agent. Isn't there someone you can trust?"

She sighed. "There's a know-it-all accountant across the street."

He laughed again. Avery loved her dad's laugh. Mom had said it was why she'd married him, that he could find the bright side in just about anything. Avery used to think she was like that, too. "A know-it-all might be just what you need, Avery. What's his name?"

"Liam."

"Is he Irish?"

"I don't know. His last name sounds German."

He laughed again. "So then he's both hot-tempered and methodical. He must be one heck of an accountant."

That was enough to make her laugh, too. "I think you're giving him too much credit, Dad."

"Maybe. But I'm not giving you too much credit. You can figure this out, Avery. Just don't try to do it all alone. Look at everything you've accomplished, my girl. I'm so proud of you."

She stared at the phone where it sat on the counter of her

empty store, bowed her head, and rubbed at her temples. Was it pride that kept her from telling him the truth?

Maybe. But what bothered Avery the most was the thought of disappointing the two people who had stood by her every day of her life, and then some. Swallowing her pride and calling Liam was nothing compared to destroying the confidence her parents had placed in her. She couldn't tell them what a mess she'd gotten into. She had to find a way to make it right. "Thank you, Dad."

"I'll tell your mom you called. She'll be disappointed she didn't get to talk to you."

"Tell her I'll call Sunday when the store is closed."

"Will do. Love you, little girl."

"Love you, too." She tapped the phone and sat with her head in her hands. Then a minute later, she sat upright and straightened her shirt. Well, she couldn't call Liam, since she didn't have his number. But she knew where he might be. She didn't even bother to close the store or put on a jacket to protect herself from the freezing rain. It was just a few steps across one narrow street to the office where Liam worked.

Cash was in the office, but Liam was nowhere in sight. "Hello, Avery Maier! What brings you all the way over to my neck of the woods?" Cash gave her a big smile, one that crinkled into sun-etched lines all over his face. He obviously did two things a lot—smile and spend time outside.

"I was wondering if Liam was around, but—"

"Oh yeah. He's back with a client right now."

She looked toward the back where Cash gestured. All she could see was a wall of wooden filing cabinets. "I thought tax season ended last week."

"That's what he thought, too. But word got around. Or I should say I got word around that he was helping me and he was excellent. And they wanted him to work on tax planning. I didn't even know there was such a thing. But I guess he's pretty good at it, because people keep calling. And he's still helping me. Look at this place." Cash held his arms out and turned around.

It did look different. Avery hadn't paid a lot of attention to how it had looked before, but she seemed to recall boxes and endless stacks of papers, scattered furniture, and open drawers. She could hear the murmur of voices at the other end of the room. "It looks nice," she agreed.

"It looks nice, but on the inside, it's nothing short of miraculous. You know, it's amazing the amount of knowledge his brain holds. Crazy things. Numbers and rules and all sorts of stuff I could never keep straight. All in that head. You know, I saw him the day he was born, the very day. I looked at that squirming, loud thing with a mess of black hair and red skin—I mean blotchy, with this white stuff, like for a minute there I was afraid I was going to catch something if I touched him—oh hey, Ole. How did my nephew do?"

Avery turned to see a middle-aged man in dark jeans and a light denim shirt. "Better with numbers than you, you old swindler. If I'd talked to Liam first, I might not have bought that apartment building from you."

"You'll thank me in five years," Cash said.

"If the tenants don't kill me."

Liam was right behind him, looking at Cash with a long-suffering expression. He didn't seem to notice her.

"Lucky for you Liam's got a plan," the client said. He shook Liam's hand. "Talk to my man, right? I know a few things about bucking the system."

"Thank you," Liam said. The denim man gave Cash a wave and headed down the stairs to the street.

"We were just talking about you," Cash said.

"I heard."

Cash turned back to Avery. "I didn't have time to ask. Is there something I can help you with instead?"

She lifted her chin. "I have an insurance letter."

"Oh, I know all about insurance," Cash said.

"No, he doesn't," Liam said. "But as I said, I don't know a lot either. Not about insurance, or basements."

So that was it. Avery felt her face growing hot. "Of course." *Of course* he was still mad at her for kicking him out. And now she was mad at him for being a jerk, so they were even. She didn't need him. Dad said to seek out a business owner. "Do you know anyone in town who could help me understand an insurance issue?" She looked at Cash to make it clear she was asking him, not Liam. But Cash was busy glaring at Liam. And she was pretty sure Liam was glaring back. They were having some sort of silent argument, and that actually made her feel a little better.

"I do, Avery Maier." Cash's face lit up again. "Mrs. Ullman. And lucky for you, Liam was just on the phone with her answering a few questions for free. So she owes you a favor, right, Liam?"

Back at the store, Avery retrieved the letter and stuck it back in its overnight delivery envelope for the hundredth time. She flipped the sign on the door and locked it behind her. Liam seemed to appear out of thin air behind her, and she jumped a little when she saw him. But she straightened her spine until she was almost as tall as him. She was all business, and he'd better realize it. And she was grateful for the high heels on her boots.

They walked two blocks in silence before Liam said, "I'm sorry I was so pushy about the basement."

It irritated her that he'd apologized because that meant she should do the same thing. "I'm sorry too. It was a lot to process." It still was, but she didn't say so.

He didn't answer, which set her on edge even more than she already was. She was surprised to feel Liam's hand at her elbow as he stopped and reached out with his other hand to open a door for her.

"Liam! It's about time you actually dropped by!" A middle-aged woman in khaki slacks and a blue oxford shirt hurried out of a back office and gave him a back-thumping hug. "Solid," she said, leaning away and thumping him once more on the shoulders. "You've been busy."

He shook his head and grinned a little, just for a moment. "I need a favor."

"You got it."

They followed her into a back office, where the woman held out her hand for a firm shake of Avery's hand. "Name's Renay. R-e-n-a-y, good American spelling. What's yours?"

"Avery."

"You own Tabitha's old shop, right?"

Avery nodded.

"The shop is why we're here," Liam supplied.

"Well, I knew it wasn't about you," she said, moving papers from her desk to a little table behind her. "You'd rather chew your own leg off than ask for help." She held a hand to the side of her mouth and spoke to Avery. "Some men are weak that way."

Avery held the cardboard envelope out, and Renay took it. She put on her reading glasses and read slowly, without expression. When she was done, she handed it back to Avery. Over her glasses, Renay gave her a look. "Elijah Canten. That name seems familiar. Who was he to you, sweetie?"

"He was my fiancé."

"I'm sorry for your loss." Renay re-read the letter and sighed. "What did Elijah do for a living?"

"Not much," she said. She didn't mean it to sound bad, but it did. "He did some roofing jobs and odds and ends. But that's okay because he didn't spend any money. He was very frugal."

"Did he get climbing equipment for free?"

"Sometimes, I guess. A few things here and there."

"And endorsements?"

Avery frowned.

"Say, T-shirts? Backpacks? Anything with company logos on it?"

"Yeah. Everyone wanted to have Eli wear their stuff."

Renay leaned back in her chair, and it creaked. "So it's possible. It doesn't take that much in-kind payment to push him over into the category of a professional climber. And that would invalidate the insurance policy as it was written."

Avery's stomach soured. "I don't know what you mean."

"They have opened an investigation into his life insurance, which means they think there may be some fraud at play."

"But they already paid it," Liam said.

"Yes, it looks that way. And I'm guessing it was a lot of money?"

"A million dollars," Avery whispered. She felt Liam stare at her, but she ignored him.

"Well," Renay said, "that explains part of what's going on. A million bucks is a lot of money, even for a big insurance company. But on a policy that big, the investigation happens before they pay out. After it's paid, it's done. It's really very unusual to take another look after the investigation."

"Then why would they investigate now?" Liam asked.

Renay put her fingertips together and frowned. "Usually they investigate repeat offenders, which obviously Elijah can't be. No offense, Avery, I'm just thinking out loud. So the only other thing that comes to mind is that someone brought them evidence they couldn't ignore."

"Evidence of what?" Avery asked.

Renay explained that if Eli hadn't smoked and he'd passed a physical, which he certainly would have, they wouldn't have liked the fact that he was a rock climber.

"He didn't lie," Avery said. Her eyes started to sting. "He wasn't that kind of guy. He would have told them."

"I'm not saying he lied. What I'm saying is that they agreed to insure a hobbyist, not a professional climber. The money he made is an indication of how much time he spent climbing and how difficult his routes were. So this company set the limit at five thousand dollars. If he made that much, then he's a professional and that would break the insurance contract. And getting paid can be in the form of cash or even free gifts in return for the climbing he did. If he wasn't that into money, maybe he just didn't realize the value of some of the climbing equipment he'd gotten."

Avery thought of the ropes, the shoes, all the hardware that Elijah had. And more: gas and park passes, meals, energy drinks, hotel rooms at a couple climbing events. He never could have made enough to pay for all of that. Why hadn't she realized it before? But she didn't know about the specification in the insurance policy that he was an amateur climber, a hobbyist rather than a professional climber. She hadn't even known about the policy while he was alive. He could have made more than five thousand in gifts. For all she knew, he'd made a lot more than that.

She felt sick. "But I spent the insurance money, all of it, on the Moose on the Loose."

She was grateful that Renay didn't look shocked or tell her what a ridiculous thing that had been to do.

"They haven't made a decision yet," Renay said. "Nothing is written in stone."

"So the next step is for Avery to get a lawyer, right?" Liam asked.

Renay sighed. "You can do that. And maybe it's a good idea. But I gotta say, they've put their necks out with this letter. Investigations, not to mention a team of lawyers, are expensive. I hate to say it, but they probably have all the evidence they need to win a case. Do whatever you need to do to protect yourself, but if money is an issue, be careful of how deep you're willing to go. Lawyers are scum, they'll take your last cent if you let them. Like insurance agents." Nothing about her expression said she was joking.

"And what if they do have evidence?" Liam said. "I'm guessing she'll have to pay it all back. Or maybe declare bankruptcy, whatever good that would do her. Will she be able to come up with some sort of payment plan instead?"

"Maybe. And that's actually worth hiring a lawyer for. But if they believe they were deliberately tricked, they won't be in the mood to play fair. Then it'll be up to the courts to figure out."

They'd gone so far ahead of what Avery's mind could process she could hardly keep up. "But the building, and the business, isn't worth as much as I paid for it. Even if I sell it, how can I give them back a million dollars if I haven't got a million dollars?"

Renay looked at her with an expression of pure sympathy, which made Avery feel even worse. "You would still owe them the money, honey. But you just hang in there. It'll get sorted out eventually, and you'll be okay, one way or another. That's just the way the world works."

# CHAPTER 17

*A*s soon as Liam bowed out, he went over to the stands and sat down for a minute. He was utterly gassed. It had been a long time since he'd worked out this hard, and it felt good, even though he smelled absolutely disgusting. Somewhere in there was a paradox about how feeling weak can make you strong, but his brain was too tired to work it out.

The dojo's lead sensei had done him in. The fourth-degree black belt looked a little short, a little round, and unendingly cheerful. He had watched Liam during the workout and for forty-five minutes of sparring with the other black belts. They were eager to feel him out, find his weaknesses, and steal a few secrets. That's the way it was when you went to a new place, especially since his training was Brazilian jiu jitsu, not kenpo karate, as it was in this dojo.

But Sensei had stayed on his feet and made the strikes, more than Liam could count and most straight to his face. Over and over. Just hard enough to hurt. Taking him down was like wrestling a greased pig, and then the strikes got borderline dirty. Claws, blades, extended knuckle punch to the temple.

Through it all, Sensei had grinned, even when Liam had made his mark.

Sensei Sam found him on the stands and sat next to him for a good five minutes without saying a word. Liam was just glad to see the man was breathing hard.

Sensei broke the silence first. "You don't want to compete, do you?"

"No." Liam had visited a couple dojos, different disciplines, since coming back to Montana. Everyone had been excited to train him, to get him competing.

"And you don't want to switch to Karate."

"No, Sensei. Jiu-Jitsu has been good for me."

"Hmm. Maybe. So what was this about?" the man asked, gesturing toward the dojo floor.

Liam met his eye. He had no idea what he meant. "Did I do something wrong? I didn't mean to be disrespectful."

"You weren't. In fact, I saw you pull a few punches. More than I might have. You care about letting the other person save face, at least most of the time. And yet you were clearly here to make a point. So I'm just curious, who are you trying to make a point to?"

As Liam tried to wrap his tired mind around that, Sensei stood. "Don't worry about it now. But if you come back, I'd be happy to talk. When you are happy to talk."

Liam hauled his gear to the FJ Cruiser and started the long drive back from the east side of Billings to the mountains of Moose Hollow. He had just wanted a workout, and to keep his reflexes sharp. Liam knew he was good—only a brown belt in his dojo but far ahead of most black belts. And no, he didn't want to compete. He'd never liked getting the crap beat out of him, and that's precisely why he'd chosen jiu-jitsu.

But maybe he *had* tried to make a point or two. He was just letting off steam. He'd gotten annoyed by the sneer from the tall blond black belt who'd said he had studied BJJ and found it lacking.

But in truth, Liam had been irked before arriving at the dojo. He'd spent hours trying to make sense of a couple of journal articles. He'd read the same lines over and over again, his own distracted mind wasting his time.

No, he'd been mad before that. Because of the fight with Cash. Not that Cash and he every really fought, but his uncle had gotten a few snide comments in and taken off. Cash had been teasing him about "his new girlfriend, Avery." He wouldn't let it drop, which made Liam wonder if Cash himself had his endlessly roving eye on her. Then it had escalated when he insisted Liam was hooked and would never be leaving Moose Hollow again. Liam had blown up.

After Cash left, Liam had spit curses at all the employers he'd called this week who wanted absolutely nothing to do with him. He'd more than proved he could do the work, yet they'd turned him down because no one rejects their own intern unless something is really wrong with him. They'd all assumed he had done something illegal. When Ackerman, Jones & Fetterman hired him, they were under no legal responsibility to sign off on his CPA requirements at the end of the internship. Getting turned down at the end of the year was the stuff of urban legends.

The only option left was staying in Montana and relying on the small circle of friends his parents had gained through years of kindness, hard work, and honest dealings. Maybe one of them would take a chance on him. He'd run home to his mom and dad, just like Griff had said.

Cash was right. He might never get out of here.

He slammed his right fist into the passenger seat, which didn't make him or the Cruiser feel any better.

And an hour before the fight with Cash, Liam had watched Avery's dreams die. He'd never seen anyone look so shell-shocked. She'd insisted on going back to work, although she'd almost walked right by her own front door. He'd felt so bad about leaving her alone that he'd asked if she wanted to go to the branding in a couple weeks, saying some nonsense about having friends there, that it would be good for her to get away for a bit, blah blah blah. She'd said yes. In hindsight, he wasn't sure she'd known what she'd said yes to.

And before that. Liam had been mad before that.

Before that was Elijah Canten.

Her fiancé had been Elijah Canten. Avery had been engaged to Elijah, Griff's best friend. The same man—or was it boy, then?—who had seen Liam kissing Lynn during the school dance and had run to tell Griff.

Liam moaned out loud at the ridiculous drama. Griff had just dumped Lynn. And who cared? It was high school. Dumping happened all the time. Girls cried, guys tried to act like it didn't matter, and in a week everyone had a new boyfriend or girlfriend to dump at will. It wasn't supposed to be life and death.

Later Griff must have sent Eli to find him, which he did, lingering in the hall outside the commons where the dance was winding down. Eli had told him Griff wanted to make peace. He'd been so convincing, the way he'd talked about the importance of forgiveness. Liam was scared of Griff. He had just wanted to go home. But his car was at school, and he'd been worried Griff would vandalize it if Liam left it there. All along, they had waited beside the parking lot. Elijah Canten, Chris Parks, and Griff Hallowell.

Liam had known instantly he was in danger. He couldn't outrun them all, especially Elijah. He'd told himself he'd take a few hits, play dead, and it would soon be over. But it hadn't stopped. And he hadn't passed out. He'd seen fight after fight on TV where one direct hit turned out the lights. Why hadn't he passed out?

Liam opened all the windows and let the cold air blast the

memory away, then he turned up the radio to some ridiculous thump-thump song. It sounded like a twelve-year-old girl was singing. He thought about moving. Thought about anything, and everything, until all he felt was tired again.

He parked at the back of the hotel parking lot and hauled his workout bag and all the weapons in it onto his shoulder. He would need to air out all the sweat. He threaded his way through the cars and used his key to open the back door. It was quiet in the hall, and he tried not to disturb anyone. But as he got closer, he realized there was something different about his door. It was ajar.

He knew his dad didn't like to do work in the room at night, and his mom wouldn't be inside. She was respectful of his privacy. More so than he deserved, of course.

The door was open, but the lights were off. Liam was aware of a strange smell—solvent, maybe. But no one with access to the room would have left the door open. He set down the bag and shoved the door open with his fingertips, staying to the side of the open doorway. It was silent. And something was scattered on the floor in the short hallway between the bathroom and bed. He waited, listening, smelling. There was nothing more. He walked in slowly and flipped the switch.

His room had been tossed.

His clothes were everywhere. As his gaze lifted, it got worse. Furniture overturned. Sofa cushions turned inside out, ripped and destroyed. Shelves from the antique dresser thrown on the floor. He cautiously turned the corner to see the bed. The mattress was overturned and all his books and journals spread out over the slats of the bed frame. And above it all, written in red spray paint across the new wallpaper, a message.

*Die, Thief.*

# CHAPTER 18

*H*e'd had a few hours of sleep, sort of. Liam had drifted in and out of images and thoughts—some real, and some imagined, and none of them good.

The sleeping arrangements didn't help. His parents' new sofa was better suited to looking sleek and modern than serving as a bed. Their suite had one bedroom, and all the rest was a single spacious room with high ceilings and tall windows, and equally sleek and modern curtains that let in the light from every passing car. When sirens went off and the lights swirled past the windows, any chance of sleep was gone for good. The lights didn't go far down the road, and for a moment Liam worried about Avery, then the futility of that struck him and he pushed any thought of her out of his mind.

There were plenty of other things to think about.

His mother had flat-out refused to let him stay in the trashed room. And although there were probably a couple empty rooms in the place since it wasn't the weekend, she'd insisted it was too much trouble to get him a new room so late at night. His dad shrugged at Liam. They both knew the damage to the room had rattled her. She wanted her chick tucked safely under her wing, no matter how old that chick had grown, and the men who loved her would agree to it. At least for one night.

The police had asked the same questions over and over, and all the while he'd gotten overly attentive looks from his parents. It was all too familiar. Do you know who would do this? Do you know what this means? No, he'd answered. And just like before, he wasn't telling the whole truth. But it was closer to the truth this time. He didn't really know who, or how, or even why his room had been destroyed. But he suspected who was behind it.

When Officer Everett left, and his mother went to put sheets on her couch, Dad lingered behind to ask if Griff Hallowell was involved. That surprised Liam. Years ago his parents had never mentioned Griff by name, and Griff's name had never crossed Liam's lips. But of course they'd known. Liam had been a young teenager living in a small town, and naive and foolish enough to think he was safe if he never said Griff's name out loud. He was old enough now to know they must have suspected. Everyone had suspected. Even Officer Mike had questioned him once, though he was highway patrol back then and his jurisdiction didn't extend to beatings in the high school auxiliary parking lot.

"No," he'd told his dad about the trashed room. "I just saw Griff by the real estate office on my way back."

"Could he have come by earlier?"

The look on his father's face chafed him. So protective, so certain his son would be willing to cover for that piece of work...again. "No. He was an ass. And staggering drunk." His father looked unconvinced. "And I haven't stolen anything from him."

Anson Gunnerson was no fool. He'd caught the qualifier, of course. From *him*. "Whoever it was did a lot of damage without a lot of noise," his father reiterated, as if the obvious mess and the third-degree from the cops hadn't made that clear. "We want you to be safe. And the rest of our guests. If there is anything you think we should know, I hope you'll share it."

In the faint morning light, just thinking about his father's words made Liam's heart sink, as if it poured down through his spine and into the not-so-soft cushions of the new couch.

Liam paraphrased his father's words in his mind. What did you do wrong? And what can we do to protect you and everyone else from your mistake? So much work down the drain. Not just the job or the license, but the training and prayer and daily rebuilding of a mind that had been small. Trapped. Suffocating. And after all that, he'd ended up back here. Same cops, mostly. Same parents and their unbearable patience.

And what could he say to them? He didn't know who did it, or why. He wanted to believe it was a question of mistaken identity because he wasn't a threat to anyone. He'd laid low all these months, hadn't he? He hadn't even challenged Ackerman, Jones & Fetterman's refusal to accept his year of apprenticeship. Although the commission would have almost certainly upheld his dismissal, he could have raised a stink. How could it possibly be them? They were an accounting firm, not the mob.

*We want you to talk to us, son. We know you're not ready. We just want you to know that we're ready whenever you are, and nothing you can say will change how much we love you. We're a family. We go through these things together.* Well, there was some grace in the fact that he hadn't had to hear that soliloquy again.

His phone vibrated, buzzing on the coffee table just out of reach. It was a text from Cash.

*Office broken into. Alarm chased them off.*

He had a minute to digest that before the next text arrived.

*Didn't want you to worry.*

So Cash hadn't heard about the vandalism in the hotel yet. When he did, the whole town would know, and wouldn't tongues be wagging then? The common denominator for both break-ins was clear.

As the sky began to lighten and the stars faded in the small hours of the morning, Liam realized that no matter how many excuses he made, no matter how hard he'd worked or what he'd accomplished, he was an unemployed adult son living on his mom's couch. And there was a small but real chance that he was a danger to his family. It was time to go. He didn't have anything useful to contribute to anyone in Moose Hollow anymore.

By six-thirty he had the Cruiser packed, and he'd had breakfast with his parents. He broached the subject of moving on. They ignored him. He ignored them ignoring him. Then he went to the office.

Cash's desk was a disaster. Papers had been tossed everywhere, drawers jerked out and their contents dumped. The big wooden filing cabinets must have been next, but just the top drawers were open, half their contents scattered on the floor.

No spray paint. A small blessing.

He looked around. Most everything else was the same. His little desk in the back was untouched, but there hadn't been anything on it or in it, except pencils and an address book. It looked like no one worked there. But that was no surprise. Anyone who might have observed the office would have assumed that the big desk by the window belonged to him since that's where he spent most of his time. He went to the old metal filing cabinets in the back and pulled one bottom drawer out as far as it would go. He got down on his knees and reached an arm in and around, under the drawer, and felt for the thick envelope. It was still there. Still sealed.

Then he looked at Cash's desk and felt his stomach churn. First his parents, now Cash. He didn't have any right to put them in danger.

He pulled out his phone and dialed.

"Oh sure. You say you're gonna stay in touch. Then months go by. Months, dude."

"One month. Did you find someone to sublet?"

"Nope. I'm living happily off the remainder of your lease money. Just joking, Gunnerson, I found someone. And she's a hell of a lot prettier than you."

"I hope she knows what a horrible slob you are." Liam walked back toward Cash's desk. In truth, Mac was as good a roommate as anyone could hope for, and it was a relief to banter with him again.

"Are you kidding? I'm the man of her dreams," Maccus said flatly. "So what have you been doing out in the boondocks, Gunnerson?"

"Taxes."

"Ah, yes. Mind-numbing misery. Good for you."

"I didn't thank you for mailing that envelope, Mac."

There was a pause on the line. "No problem. Hey, back to the roommate situation. I've gotta tell you a funny story. Before I settled on my lovely new roomie this week, I had a guy answer the ad. He showed up with a friend, and as he asked about a thousand pointless questions, the friend gave himself a tour of the apartment. And by apartment, I mean your room. In the closet. And under the bed."

"That's weird," Liam mumbled.

"I thought so too, so I played along for a bit and then bolted in there. He was trying to pry the air vent off. Said he was worried about his friend being exposed to mold."

Liam's mouth tightened into a thin line.

"On another subject, I'm glad those comic books arrived safely." Mac was smart enough to have guessed what was in the manila envelope, and he certainly didn't think it was comic books. He continued before Liam could respond. "If you've been talking about those comic books online or anywhere else, you might want to quit it. I think they might have gotten someone's attention. You know what freaks those Comicon collectors can be."

"You know how I am about my hobbies," Liam said. "I like to keep them to myself."

"Good. Well, maybe the guy was just worried about mold like he said."

Liam doubted that. He couldn't think of anything to say. Was Mac talking this way because he thought the line might be bugged? Did things like that really happen?

"It was good to hear from you, Gunnerson. Remember our deal. If you decide to set up shop in Montana, you have to hire me."

"It's cold."

"You lie. You Montanans just say that because you want to keep it to yourself."

Liam chuckled. "Right. Thanks, Mac."

"Stay well," Maccus said, saying it as if he meant it. Then the phone disconnected.

An hour of cleaning did a world of good for the office, but it didn't do much to sort out the thoughts in Liam's mind. Why him, and why here? Were the trashed hotel room and office connected, or was he missing something? He had a hard time thinking he was worth this kind of trouble. He couldn't imagine how they could have found out about the envelope, but what else could they have been looking for? He was in the middle of nowhere, doing nothing at all. Wasn't that enough for them?

His phone vibrated. He ignored it. There wasn't anyone he wanted to talk to. He finished filing the papers and started moving boxes and furniture. If he was going to leave Moose Hollow now, he was going to leave Cash's office looking like the million-dollar business it was.

He lost track of time until the downstairs door opened and he heard heavy steps on the stairwell. When he turned to give the obligatory statement about how Cash wasn't in because he was out helping tenants, he saw Officer Mike in his black uniform.

"I called first, son," Mike said in a low, melodic drawl. "I think your phone might be broken."

"I have the ringer turned down."

"That explains it." He looked at the office. "Did you clean all this up? Cash is pretty lucky to have you around. So what do you think, did Cash finally make someone mad enough to pitch a fit?"

"Who knows?"

"You, maybe." Officer Mike gestured to the chairs that sat in front of Cash's desk. "As long as I'm here and so are you, how about we go over a few things?"

Officer Mike sprawled comfortably in one of the chairs. Liam would have preferred to stand, but he followed Mike's lead.

"So here's my conundrum. All kinds of crazy happened last night, and maybe it's my suspicious mind, but I have a hard time believing these two break-ins are a coincidence."

Liam gave him the same noncommittal "I'm listening" expression he tried to give rambling clients.

"First your room at the hotel is vandalized. Then the office you share with your uncle is vandalized."

Liam said nothing.

"And all this after you and Griff Hallowell had a tussle out on the street."

*Small-town life strikes again.* Liam exhaled. He couldn't think of anything useful to say, let alone something that wasn't incriminating.

"What do you make of that?" Mike prodded. He waited, looking as relaxed and comfortable as a person has ever been with an uncomfortable silence.

"I don't know what to make of it," Liam finally said. And that was the truth.

"Did you steal something?"

Liam was more irritated by the question than anything else. He glared at the officer.

After a while, Mike flicked one eyebrow up and said, "Well, then." He moved as if he was going to stand up but then leaned back again. "Oh, I almost forgot. I got a call this morning from a representative of Ackerman, Jones & Fetterman. I take it you used to work there?"

"I did." He knew Mike was stringing him along, but he couldn't help but ask, "What did they say?"

"They said you were let go because of some questionable ethical something-or-others you did. They said they were calling as a public service. They were concerned you were working as a CPA when you aren't licensed to do that."

"I'm not."

"They said they've filed a complaint with some bean-counter association. You know anything about that?"

"No." Liam wasn't surprised. It was a preemptive strike. But he hadn't decided to pursue them. He hadn't made a single move in that direction. Why go to so much trouble to ruin him?

Unless they were in trouble themselves.

What if they were in trouble? A lot of it? What if he was their loose end? What did that mean for him?

"Are you in trouble, son?"

"I'm fine."

Officer Mike nodded and stood up slowly. At the top of the stairs he turned around and said, "I don't know what it is about you Gunnerson boys that makes you so prone to messes, but in my experience, your stubbornness isn't much of an asset. Asset. You hear that? It's an accounting joke. I bet you didn't know I knew that word. In fact, I'd be willing to bet that you don't think a small-town cop like me knows much about the kind of trouble you might get in with a big company and, say, something of theirs they don't want you to have. But maybe I've just been reading too many thrillers, right?"

"I haven't done anything wrong," Liam said. He immediately regretted letting the words slip out.

"And I would be inclined to believe you, Liam. But from where I'm standing, you look about neck deep in a really big mess. And if you wait until you're nose deep, it'll be too late to ask for help." He ambled down the stairs, his heavy work boots loud on the steps. "I saw you packed your car." *Clomp.* "Don't leave town just yet, son." *Clomp.* "Not until I get a better handle on this." *Clomp, clomp.* The door creaked open. "Or I'll call you in for questioning. See you soon, Liam."

*You can't do that to me,* Liam wanted to yell. But he didn't say anything. He needed time to think, to make a plan. And to find a safe place to land.

# CHAPTER 19

*M*ara was sitting at the checkout desk with her feet up, wearing black Doc Martens with hand-painted red roses she said she'd found on eBay. Avery could see why she had a hard time getting a job. Unconventional, pregnant teenage girls weren't usually the first to get hired.

"Dying of boredom?" Avery asked.

"No, actually, it's nice," Mara said. "You need a new stereo system, though, if you want me to cover for you anymore. And please hook it up to the Internet. The eighties' tape you've got looped is driving me insane."

"Fair enough."

"I did get a few things sold. Not much, though." She spun the laptop around for Avery to see. "Is that okay?"

Avery peered at the screen and scowled. "How do you do that? You've been here for two hours. I haven't sold that much in a whole day."

Mara shrugged. "I love it. It's like forensic science."

Avery considered that. "Okay. I'll bite. Why is it like forensic science?"

"Well, you've got this dead body." She gestured to the out of date inventory. "And you have to psychoanalyze the customers that come in. Like, what's the connection between them and the dead body? And which dead body? You look for clues. Do they like certain colors? Something warm? Do they have a thing for paisley? And you ask a few questions. But you have to make it seem like you're not interrogating them because they'll clam up. And if you do it right, they take responsibility for the dead body. Sure, it's dead, but they take it anyway because it suits them. And I haven't even mentioned how you can mess with potential shoplifters."

Avery thought about that for a moment and said, "I like you, Mara."

"Thanks. I'm going now. Zane's going to finish work soon, and if I'm not home, he gets lonely. And if he gets lonely, he starts projects around the house we haven't got money to finish."

"Understood. Hey, I owe you wages."

"Nah. I stole a pair of black yoga pants, and they're in my bag," Mara called, and she disappeared out the door.

Avery laughed. She was still smiling when she heard the bell on the door ring again. "Hey—" she began, but it wasn't Mara returning. It was Griffin, looking sharp in a suit and tie and freshly clipped hair. For some reason, it made her think of Liam's slightly shaggy hair. The two men didn't have anything in common. No wonder they rubbed each other the wrong way.

"How are you doing, beautiful?" Griffin said as he smiled at her.

"Pretty good. And you're in a good mood."

"Indeed. Actually, after today's closing, I'm close to a promotion. Senior is talking about letting me head up the Bozeman office. Goodbye small town, hello higher property values. There's a ton of money to be had. Plus skiing. Hot Springs. Wanna go with me?"

She smirked. "I'm happy where I am. Well, pretty much."

"Why, Aves? What's up with you?" He looked concerned. "You worried about business? I know it looks like it's been a little slow, but you're still okay, right?"

"Yeah. Well, things might have gotten more complicated."

He put an elbow down on the desk. "Is it something I can help with?"

"No. It just turns out that I owe someone. A company. Some money. Maybe a lot of it." She knew she should tell him, but she just couldn't go through it again. Not now, at least. She promised herself she would say to him later.

Griff looked concerned. "This is new?"

"It's new to me. I thought something was taken care of, but it wasn't."

"This doesn't have to do with Liam Gunnerson, does it? Sorry, I was in the front office when he dropped you off. I'm not the kind to tell someone what to do, but..." He shook his head and sighed. "He's just trouble. Did you hear about the break-ins? Two in one night. If I were his parents I'd be scared to death, and if I was Cash...well. I just can't stand thinking about you getting mixed up with that guy. It just isn't safe. He didn't buy into the building, did he?"

She blinked. "No. I'm not in business with him at all."

Griffin looked relieved. "Good. You know Cash tried to buy your building, right? I figured he still wants it. And now that Liam's working with Cash...well, if you say so. But Liam is one bad decision after another. Trouble just follows him. And it usually lands on the people around him. I know he's a friend—he's a friend, right?—but I don't want him to hurt you. I really like you, Avery. You add a touch of class to this place. In fact, I'm meeting friends right now, want to come by? I sure would like it if you'd celebrate with me, just for a few minutes."

She wanted to say no, but she didn't. And when six o'clock rolled around, she headed up the street to the Lantern Bar. When she walked in, a few people actually called out a hello, and Griffin stood, gestured to the bartender, and came over to her. He gave her a half-hug and a kiss on the cheek, which was a bit excessive, but he was apparently still in a good mood. The bartender handed Griffin two flutes of champagne, and Griffin put one in her hand.

"Cheers! Here, let me introduce you. You know John from the office." She didn't, but she nodded. "This is...Bob, right? And Al?" They smirked at the name as if it was a joke between them. "And this," he said, gesturing to the woman sitting beside his empty chair, "is Lynn."

Avery smiled, and a few drinks were lifted in salute. Avery decided that Bob and Al, if those were their names, were to be avoided. And Lynn...had she been to the store? She looked familiar. Griffin pulled up another chair, and Avery found herself seated at his right hand, with Lynn at his left, which felt utterly weird. Was Lynn his girlfriend?

Then it hit her. The red streaks in her hair, the long red nails flashing in the streetlight as they tangled in Liam's hair.

Avery plastered a smile on her face and took a sip of the sweet champagne. She had to come up with a good reason to leave. Now. She wished her mom would call, or a brother or two. Anyone.

Lynn tossed her glossy hair. "Do you work with Griff?"

"No," Avery said. "I just work next door." She tried to come up with some way of indicating they were just friends, but "we hardly ever hang out" sounded insulting to Griffin. He was celebrating, and she didn't want to put a damper on that.

"We've known each other forever," Lynn said, directing a sideways smile toward Griffin.

Avery would have guessed she was Griffin's co-worker. She had the same professional but slick style that Griffin had. Legs for miles, too. If Avery had been wearing the woman's short skirt, it would have hit her below the knees. In fact, Avery probably couldn't have slipped it on over her hips at all.

Then Al—or was it Bob?—leaned over and held out his hand for her to shake. "Any friend of Griff's is a friend of mine." She had the impression of a hot, meaty hand, and a sports cap too low over his eyes. And he had about a week's worth of facial hair spotting his face. "New to town?"

"Pretty much."

"Be careful who you keep company with," he said, clasping her hand but not shaking it. "And whose secrets you keep."

It was a weird thing to say, said in a weird way, but she just smiled, shrugged, retrieved her hand, and turned her attention back to Lynn. But then Griffin leaned over and whispered in her ear. "I just can't stop worrying about that loan trouble you were talking about. Are you sure you're okay?"

She wiped her hand on her skirt and pulled back so his face wasn't quite so close to hers. "I'm fine." She caught Lynn watching as he leaned in again, her smile narrow and tense.

"Mind if we talk outside for a sec?" Griffin said. Without waiting for an answer, he stood up and held out his hand for her. Avery set down her glass, fumbled with her purse to avoid holding his hand, and followed him outside, but she stood right in front of the window in plain view. She didn't want to cause any trouble with Lynn. Although if Lynn was dating both Liam and Griffin, she was going to create plenty of trouble on her own.

Griffin put a hand on her shoulder. "I gotta tell you. I've noticed you've been looking a lot more tired lately, and it just bugs me. Now if there's money trouble…" he shook his head. "I don't like to pry. But I know you've got to be strapped just keeping that big old building from falling down around your head. So I just want you to know, if you need a fresh start, I can help. I know more than you'd believe about good places for business. I could get you a place that would have half the overhead you have right now. Imagine the profit you'd make."

Behind Griffin, either Bob or Al—she still didn't know who was who—came out to light a cigarette.

"I know you're making a good go of it, but if you ever think you need a fresh start, I'm your man," Griffin said. "If you need to sell, Avery, do it before things get bad. Because time equals money in this business. If you have to sell fast, you won't get as much. And I like you." He rubbed his fingers across his forehead, and his tone of voice changed. "I like you a lot, actually. And I know a little bit about wanting a fresh start. So if you want one, I hope you'll let me help."

"Thanks, Griffin. That's a lot to think about. And I think that's what I'm going to go do. Do you mind if I skip out on your celebration?"

"No," he said, but his expression said otherwise. "I understand. We can talk later."

"Thanks. And congratulations." It occurred to her as she walked away that she wasn't sure what she had congratulated him about. *Falling down around your head*, he'd said. That was just the kind of thing she'd end up thinking about all night.

# CHAPTER 20

$\mathcal{H}$alf blinded by the morning sunlight, Avery ran straight into someone and did precisely what she was trying not to do, which was to drop the foil-wrapped breakfast burrito on the sidewalk as she tucked her wallet back in her purse. And when both of them bent to reach for the burrito, she came within inches of bonking heads with him. She finally looked up, eye to eye as they crouched on the sidewalk.

It was Liam.

"I'm sorry," he said, quietly because his face was so close to hers.

Her first thought was that he had gotten a lot better looking over the last couple weeks. Which was ridiculous, of course. He'd always been good looking. And unreliable. After taking her to see Renay, the insurance lady, and sending her a text message with the name of a lawyer, he'd avoided her like crazy. "You're actually out," she said. "On the street. In public."

He gave her a wry smile. "I am."

She snatched the burrito from his hand. As they stood, she eyed his ankle. "I don't see one."

"See what?"

"Rumor has it you have an ankle bracelet, and you're under house arrest."

"You're just making that up," Liam said.

"Nope. And that's not even my favorite rumor."

"I don't need to know."

"Oh, sure you do," Avery said. "It's that you aren't actually you."

He took a deep breath and shoved his hands into the pocket of his jeans. He was actually wearing jeans. Nice, dark, crisp looking ones, but jeans nonetheless. "Okay, tell me."

"The guy creeping in and out of the office is an undercover cop, and you are actually in the witness protection program because you stole emeralds from the Chicago mafia."

"Okay, why would the mafia have emeralds?"

Avery shrugged. "I made the emerald part up. Just saying 'stole something from the mafia' sounded too vague to me. Emeralds give it mystique."

He crossed his arms across his chest and nodded slowly. "I can't argue with that." He was smiling, sort of, and it looked terrific on him. Whatever the cause of his exile, he still looked fine.

"I know you've been staying out at Colton's ranch. Poppy told me. I haven't shared that with anyone, though, because I find the rumors pretty entertaining. Well, most of them. And I get the feeling that where you're staying is something of a secret, which is weird, but you are kind of strange sometimes."

"I am not," he said, but the smile lingered.

"Yes, you are. You're the kind of guy that when someone says hey, you wouldn't believe who found a way to hack into Fort Knox and steal all the gold, I'd guess it was you."

"Hack? Like with an ax?"

Avery rolled her eyes.

"Besides, there's no gold at Fort Knox," he said.

"You do realize you're proving my point. You know things."

There was just a flicker, a shadow across his eyes. He *did* know something. She'd hit closer to the truth than she'd ever intended to. She spoke quickly to cover it up. "I'm sorry about the hotel. And Cash's office."

"Thank you." He looked as if he might say more, but didn't. "Any word from the insurance company?"

Avery shook her head.

"Did you meet with Connor, the lawyer I told you about?"

"No." Avery crossed her arms. "Wait, you want to talk about that? That's not how it goes. Friends share information. Both of them."

He looked her in the eye so long she felt uncomfortable. "Were you on your way back to work just now?"

Liam had changed the subject. Avery rolled her eyes. "No, actually, I have a couple hours off. Mara's holding down the fort. I think she's got a bad case of cabin fever, being out at the ranch without any women around. And the baby isn't due for weeks yet."

"How about I take you on a drive past the old mines? They haven't cleared the snow from the pass yet, so I can't take you there. It's just a quick sightseeing trip. Friends do that sort of thing, you know."

*No, no, and no.* Liam was really handsome today, and no matter how absurd the rumors were, he was definitely trouble. It was a bad combination. She could feel it in her bones. "Sure."

She walked with him to where his Cruiser was parked and remembered what Griffin said about him spending all night in his car in her alley. He opened the door for her, and they both realized that there was a big duffel bag in the passenger seat. "Sorry, let me get that—" he said as she reached for it, but she'd gotten there first. She lifted the handles. It clanged but didn't budge. She let go and took a step back, and he said, "Just a little exercise equipment."

*Right.* "It sounds like guns and bayonets."

"Um. No." He lifted the bag like it was nothing and tossed it into the back with another loud clang. "Don't let me keep you from eating your lunch," he said as he came back around to close the door for her.

He drove straight east out of town, and the first amazing view was looking back over Moose Hollow with a snowy mountain range rising impossibly high above it. She rolled down her window and, since it was the warmest day she'd seen yet in Montana, kept it down. Liam did the same, and he pointed out things here and there, mostly the ruins of mining equipment. They rode up and up the valley, the road flirting with a whitewater creek, until he pulled over at a historical marker. It told the story of a mining accident that signaled the end of the coal mine that sat across the valley. But all signs of disaster were lost under green grass and tall stalks of new lavender-colored blossoms, and the old wooden ruins looked mysterious and romantic, not industrial and sad. He drove on.

Finally they crested a ridge, and the scenery changed, turning drier and less green, and definitely flatter. He pulled up to a big, old building that looked like a renovated barn. It had a neon beer sign in the front and one gas pump on the side. "Want a soda?"

"Water sounds good," she said, and she stepped down out of the Cruiser before she realized he was coming around to open the door for her again. She wasn't used to that, and she wasn't sure she liked it, so she hurried out and walked in the front door ahead of him.

It was a bar, mostly, and she felt out of place. She felt Liam touch the back of her elbow, and walked with him a few steps to where a refrigerated case of drinks stood. He pulled out two water bottles and paid at the bar. Avery looked around without trying to appear too touristy, but the sheer number of animal heads on the walls was enough to get anyone's attention. She was happy to leave. "I can't believe how different it looks here," she said as they climbed in the Cruiser again. "It's like we drove through Ireland and landed in Nevada."

He laughed out loud, which made her grin. It was fun to make him laugh.

"I'll take you back to Ireland, then. We passed a good view about three miles back."

He pulled off on an overgrown two-track and drove right over a tiny bridge that seemed to have been made from rotting railroad ties and not strong enough to hold them. Then it was straight up the hillside. Avery found a good grip on the door handle. Just about the time she was debating walking back down on her own, they crested onto a grassy plateau, and he stopped.

The view was breathtaking. Snow-white mountains with blue-black patches of pine rose high above the valley, with tiny white clouds forming airy mountain peaks of their own. Avery sighed. Liam got out and stood with his back to her, feet spread, arms crossed, contemplating something. "Not a lot of views like this in Chicago," he finally said.

"Did you miss this when you lived there?"

He looked over his shoulder at her, then came closer, resting his elbows on the open window frame. "I didn't think I did. But spending time at the ranch..." he shook his head. "I don't know. If I could go back, I don't know if I would. I'd go someplace else, maybe. Someplace with mountains."

"I thought you'd be gone by now," she said. If he was offended by her words, he didn't show it.

"Yeah, me too."

"What happened?"

He gave such a long sigh she regretted asking. "No one will hire me."

When she asked, he told her that the person who'd fired him had refused to sign off on the internship. She was surprised to find out that meant he had to start all over again with someone new. She had thought he just had a little time left. She asked about legal recourse, asked about why people were reluctant to hire him, and he answered all of her questions with a practiced sort of patience. But when she asked why his mentor had done that to him, the answer didn't come fast.

"It's like I said before. He did something that I didn't think was right." That told her nothing at all, except he didn't want to talk about it.

"Did you steal something?"

He frowned. "Why does everyone assume I did?"

"Duh. 'I'm going to kill you, Thief.'"

"Actually, the message wasn't that threatening," Liam said.

"What did they write?"

"Die, Thief."

"Oh," she said. "So maybe they only hoped you would die of natural causes after a long, happy life?"

He fixed her with a blank stare. "You're funny. And I didn't steal any emeralds. And as long as we're talking like friends now, why didn't you go talk to Connor?"

"I don't need a lawyer. The insurance company hasn't written to me, no one has called, nothing. There's no reason to think I have a problem at all."

He gave her that look, the one that had irritated her from the very first night she met him. Like she was foolish. Like he couldn't believe how gullible she was. "Okay."

She crossed her arms. "What are you not saying?"

"I talked to Connor myself."

Avery's brow drew in. And it struck her how weird it was to have this handsome young man leaning in a window, all his attention on her, the glory of creation in the background, and the scent of new grass and budding flowers flowing by, and here she was feeling mad. But Liam wasn't interested in her that way, he was just meddling. And she wasn't interested in anyone and wouldn't be. Ever. "Fine. What did he say?"

"He said you should call some of Eli's climbing friends and see if the insurance company had contacted them and get a feeling for what is going on. Then you should go talk to Connor yourself."

"I can't afford a lawyer."

"You can afford Connor."

"Why, did you do him a favor too? And what happens when you get a job and get the heck out of here, and there aren't any more favors for me to cash in on? I bet I get a bill then."

He frowned right back at her, his dark eyes piercing. She wanted to look away, but she eyed him right back, hoping to look calm and confident. "I won't let that happen," he said. "I won't let you fight this alone."

He said it like he meant it. A shiver went down Avery's spine. "Why?" The word came out before she had the good sense to swallow it.

"I don't know," he said. He looked back at the mountains, then opened the door and got in. With a shrug, he added, "That's what friends do, I guess."

# CHAPTER 21

"*Y*ou look way too nice to go down in the basement."

"I'm not going down there, you are," Avery said.

With that quirky smile and her arms crossed like an annoyed librarian, Liam could see this wasn't going to go the way he'd thought.

"So you called me over here on a Sunday afternoon to explore your basement by myself?"

"You said you were curious, and I'm not. Well, I am, but not the kind of curious that would make me go down there. Just the kind that makes me want to know if there are any pools of murky water, crumbling foundations, or dead bodies."

"Dead bodies?"

"Mice. Or any other kind. And I called you over here because this is the one time that it's daylight and the store is closed. And I'm doing you a favor."

"Favor? Oh. Satisfying my curiosity."

"Exactly."

"How kind of you."

"Did I interrupt something? Someplace else you'd rather be? Got a big date? Did they take the ankle monitor off?"

Liam chuckled. "Yeah, no." She actually rolled her eyes at him, as if he had any sort of social life. "My only date was with a bale handler that needs greasing."

Liam half expected her to ask what a bale handler was, but instead, she muttered, "Bale handlers are easy. Try fixing a baler instead. There's grease and cow poop and little bits of straw everywhere. And chopped up dead mice." She shivered. "Am I going to have to pay you to do this?"

It took a split second to respond as his brain processed a few unexpected pieces of information from her. "No. And you're right, I am curious."

"I never imagined you owned a sweatshirt."

He gave her a sideways glance as he put on the tool belt he'd brought. He had no idea if she was serious or if she was teasing him.

"And what's with the tool belt?"

"Okay. I'm going into your basement now. If you want to keep supervising, you need to put on a pair of jeans and boots and meet me down there."

She shook her head quickly and tucked her arms around her stomach.

He went out the way he'd come in, which was through the back door. He trotted down the steps and to the low doorway that had been hidden by the pallets weeks before to find his first obstacle. It made sense that it would be locked from the outside since it would be the best way to access utilities beneath. He ducked down to get a better look, holding on to the padlock for leverage, and it popped open in his hand. It wasn't locked. That wasn't good. Better than getting the bolt cutters out, but not good for Avery.

"What's wrong?" she called from the doorway above him. She looked too scared to even peek out the door. No problem—everyone had their fears, and this didn't happen to be one of his.

"Nothing." He pushed the door open. Before he even had a chance to turn on the flashlight, he saw it. She wasn't going to like this. "Uh-oh," he muttered.

"What's wrong?"

How had she heard him? "No supervising," he called back.

The basement room was in good shape. There was a dirty floor that seemed to have some sort of stone underneath. The ceiling looked to be nothing but the joists and subfloor for the first floor above. Liam ran the light up and down each joist and around the massive stone wall that was the building's foundation. No dead mice. In fact, everything looked fine. Good, even. The ceiling was a little higher than most, and so it would be easy to work in. To his right was a boiler that looked clean and reasonably modern. He'd have to get his dad in here to take a look at it just to be sure. Anson Gunnerson knew a lot about keeping the guts of old buildings functioning.

The back wall was a bit of a conundrum. But before Liam got to that, there was the matter of the old stairway to nowhere.

He'd told her there might be another entrance to the basement. And it had made her mad. But along the south wall, directly underneath the stairway that led from the main floor to the second floor, was another wooden stairway. There were turned spindles and wooden treads, and he walked to the bottom of it to shine a light up to the top. It ended in a small landing above him that had no apparent doorway. Maybe it had been closed off. He tried to remember. Didn't the stairway above have built-in shelves and drawers beneath it? They could be hiding the place this stairway emerged. He took a step up, pointing the light down on the steps to see if they were solid, and froze. And scuffed his boot on the tread and examined it again. He compared that to the thick dust at the edges of the step.

This stairway had been used a lot, and not too long ago. This was how the people who stayed in the flophouse had gotten into the building. There had probably been a path through the middle of that pile of pallets to this open door. Liam sighed. Avery couldn't catch a break.

He still had one more wall to investigate. He couldn't imagine that the basement ended fifteen feet from the back wall, and the wood floor of the Moose on the Loose didn't feel or sound like it was laid on solid stone or concrete. There were more shelves here, as if the rest of the basement had been closed off, but he was suspicious of those shelves. He didn't know what he was looking for until he found it: a double row of wooden supports and a strange gap. He pulled on the shelf, braced himself, and then tried pushing. The shelf not only moved, it pivoted inward. He pointed the flashlight in through the small opening, and his heart started pounding in his chest.

He couldn't go in alone. It just wouldn't be fair.

Liam came back out through the alleyway door, closing but not bothering to lock it. When he looked up, he found Avery with her arms tightly wrapped around herself, chewing her lower lip, chocolate-brown eyes wide. "Is it bad?"

"It's definitely different," he said. "Nothing's falling down, and there's no flooding and no dead bodies. But I need you to change clothes."

"I did. I put boots on."

Sure enough. Now she was wearing muck boots with her lace skirt. Only Avery would manage to make that cute.

"Do I have to go down there?"

"I don't think so," he said, and he walked past her into the back room, eying the built-in cabinets and tiny apothecary drawers. He opened a couple. There were bits and pieces in them, something like wool in one, and a mess of dried leaves in the other.

As he reached for the next drawer, she called out, "No, not that one!"

It had a dead mouse in it. And she knew it. He turned around to face her.

"Don't look at me that way."

"What way?" he asked, confused.

"Like I'm just a stupid girl who can't handle a mouse."

"I don't think that," he said. But he was confused. If Avery could, and had, handled pieces of a mouse ground up in a baler, why had she left the mouse here? And why was she so obviously bothered by it?

"I was going to get rid of it. But then I'd have to go through all the drawers, and I don't even know what is in the others. What if it's poison or heroin or whatever? And how am I supposed to clean dead mouse goo out of a wooden drawer?"

There was an edge to her voice he hadn't heard before. Or maybe he just hadn't noticed. This was why she'd kicked him out when he'd suggested there was another entrance to the basement weeks ago: she was overwhelmed. He'd felt that way in high school, when the thought of just going into a public bathroom or an empty classroom had filled him with paralyzing fear. How would she react when he showed her the rest of it?

*I should let it go*, he thought. But he wanted to show her the basement so much that the idea of turning away made him want to scream in frustration. Would she see what he saw? Would she see mystery and treasure, or would it be just one more worry, one more burden?

"I can handle it," she said flippantly.

She meant the mouse. But Liam took her words as more than that and went back to searching. Yes, the drawers weren't as deep here, just a few inches. He looked for, and found, the same double wall construction, and pushed. And then he pulled, and it moved. Silently.

"What is going on?" Avery asked softly.

"This is your other entrance to the basement," he said. He handed her the larger of the two flashlights in his tool belt.

"It's a secret passageway."

"Yes."

"Why is there a secret passageway?"

He couldn't keep the smile from his face. "That's what I want to show you. I haven't really looked inside, but I saw enough. You have to see this, Avery. It's amazing."

"You haven't been in there? What if there's something awful?"

"I'll check for mice, then follow me," he said, and he ducked through. He made himself count to ten. "It's clear. Come on in." He took her down the stairs and to the false back wall, then slipped through the second hidden door.

The next room was nothing like the basement they had come from. Gone was the dirty flooring. Beneath a thick coat of dust and dirt, the floor looked something like marble in a black and white pattern. The walls were wood panels, the ceiling plaster. There were square columns that spread out onto the ceiling above, giving the impression of arches. And all around the floor were objects covered in canvas cloths.

"What is this place?" Avery said from the doorway.

"I have an idea. But we'll have to look around. And we should start with...this." He chose one of the shrouded objects, then folded and rolled the canvas back and off it. It was a tall table in the shape of a semicircle. "Recognize this?"

"Yes."

He was surprised, again.

"I grew up in Iowa," Avery said. "Riverboat casinos are a big thing. It's a poker table." She reached out to touch the top. It was in good shape, but it was small and didn't look new by any means. He pulled the sheets off one more, then found a third. Chairs were stacked against one wall. And near them, something big leaned against the wall. Lifting the edges of a dirty cloth and cobwebs, he uncovered a mirror in an ornate frame. Beyond it were more frames and what looked like paintings.

All the while Avery followed close behind him, shining the flashlight wherever he looked. "How do we find out who this belongs to?" she asked.

"It all belongs to you," Liam said.

"What?"

"I read the contract, remember? It was actually part of their liability clause. Anything left inside the building is yours. I imagine they thought they were protecting themselves, but it turns out they protected you."

She frowned at the stack of wall hangings, then she moved on, her flashlight sweeping across the whole room. One corner had a raised platform with a turned spindle railing. It was some sort of performance stage, Liam guessed. Next to it, nearly the whole wall was covered in a light cloth and spiderwebs. He took hold of a clean-looking spot. "You'd better step back."

She did as he asked.

Liam tugged, then moved to the side and pulled the cloth off in one big swoosh. Through the dust that it raised, he saw the ornate carving, the old mirrored backing, the nooks and crannies, and the wide serving area in front of it.

"It's a bar," she muttered.

"It wouldn't be a speakeasy without a bar."

Liam dove right in, ducking behind the bar where the bartender would have stood. He knocked here and there, and then slid some sort of door aside. "Wow," he said, and he came up with two bottles, each of which had traces of something remaining in the bottom. "Genuine hooch, and we'll throw botulism in for free."

She eyed the bottles without humor.

But Liam's attention shifted. There was another door. A red painted door on the wall facing the front of the building. "I knew it was here."

Across the room, underneath the front of the building, there was no plastered rocky foundation. Instead, there was the red door and two paned windows facing nothing but blackness. The door was angled into the left, canted just like the building above. And all around the elaborately carved doorway was a stone arch. It was the secret passageway he'd always known existed.

# CHAPTER 22

"There are windows and a door to nowhere," Avery said. "This is so creepy."

"Not nowhere," Liam said. "A sidewalk vault." And it wasn't creepy, it was fascinating. "It's probably connected to other buildings. If you count the one in front of the hotel, there could be three full blocks—"

"What is a sidewalk vault? Some kind of burial?"

"No, nothing like that. These old buildings ran on coal, and coal was messy. In a lot of towns and cities, they dug out access through the sidewalk directly to the basement. Wagons would pull up to the front of a building, open a hatch in the sidewalk, then dump the coal into a chute. That way the coal got close to the burner without getting anything upstairs dirty. When the coal burners went away, some of these spaces were filled in, some converted, and many were forgotten. In some towns, they were used to install utilities like sewer and water, because the tunnels were already dug."

He tugged at the door and it pulled open a bit at a time, making creaking noises as it did. "I heard a rumor that one stretch of this road used to have a boardwalk underground, but

I could never confirm it." The beam of his flashlight found the wooden boards, coated in decades of dirt and dust. "And there it is." He blew out his breath. He was right. He was more right than he'd ever imagined. He'd found buried treasure. Liam stepped out onto the boardwalk. To his left, the vault stopped, but it was walled off with piled up stone, nothing like the foundation of the building. He was sure the vault continued on the other side of that wall.

And to his right was the Hallowell Realty building. The old wooden boardwalk went right past it and into the darkness. He walked forward and found yet another storefront next door. Once upon a time, the Hallowell building had been part of this basement "shopping mall." He examined the beautifully painted woodwork of the underground storefront. The windows were filthy, but he could see through the cracked glass on the door. Inside the basement, his flashlight landed on stacks of colorful plastic tubs. New plastic tubs.

They used the room as storage. Hallowell had known there was a door here. When they stacked the bins, they must have seen the windows and the sidewalk vault beyond them. "He knew all along it was here." Liam was so amazed by what he was seeing that he wasn't angry. He wasn't even disappointed. The Hallowells were who they were, and now at least one of their dirty little secrets would come out.

"What is this?" Avery asked from behind him. He walked back to where her flashlight was illuminating the sidewalk above her.

"It's concrete and steel. That's actually the sidewalk in front of your store. They must have put this concrete in after they stopped using coal, because I don't see a hole for a coal chute. They were round with metal lids. In some towns you can still see them. They look like small manholes in the sidewalk."

"That's enough to hold up the whole sidewalk?"

"Well, yeah. I don't know if I'd drive a moving truck onto this sidewalk, but it works."

The beam of the flashlight dropped to the boardwalk. "It's not safe," she said.

"No, it is. Maybe it needs a little reinforcing, but maybe not. This one is probably recent, not more than a hundred years old."

"Oh?"

He heard the edge to her voice, but with the flashlight shining down, her expression was shadowed. "It looks good to me," Liam said. "Some people fill these in with concrete, but that's really expensive, and it ruins the historical value. You really have a treasure here."

There was silence for a few beats before she spoke again. "If this collapses, whose responsibility is this?"

Liam froze. "Well, insurance—"

"I have to tell my insurance company about this, don't I? Or I'd be lying. What if they cancel my policy?"

Liam felt his heart sinking. How could he have been so stupid? Why hadn't he thought of this? When he was a young man, and Griff's dad had insisted there was no sidewalk vault in his building, he'd thought only about the mystery that was lost to him. But he wasn't that young anymore, and if anyone knew anything about risk and business management, it was him. He should have been the first person to think about what a discovery like this would mean for Avery's liability and exposure. And now, for heaven's sake. Now when she was most vulnerable, personally and financially.

He couldn't even speak. There was no excuse, no apology. The truth was he hadn't wanted to see what this would mean for Avery. He'd been so wrapped up in his childhood fantasies he'd just blocked it out of his mind. He wanted to say he was sorry, but those words sounded so inadequate in his mind.

Avery turned around and walked back into the speakeasy. He looked over his shoulder, just for a second, at the dark tunnel that extended who knew how far to who knew where. Perhaps all the way to the Third Street Inn, undiscovered for generations. And then he followed after her. "Avery, please give me a chance to talk to you about this."

She was moving fast, already passing through the door to the boiler room. *What an idiot.* His head burned with frustration with himself. He'd promised her he was going to watch out for her.

He jogged up the stairs, but she was gone. Then he heard footsteps above him, and he hurried out to see her walking up toward her apartment. "Lock up behind you," she said.

And he did. He took his locker-room lock out of his martial arts bag and put it on the small, outdoor basement door, leaving a note for Avery taped to the inside of the back door so she would know the combination. He took his tool belt out to the car. But then he came back and stood at the bottom of the stairs. He knew he should go. He had no doubt about it at all. Instead, he called out. "Avery, I need to talk to you for a second."

She didn't answer.

"Avery?" Still no answer. Now he felt a chord of fear strike inside his chest. Was she okay? "I'm coming up." Still no answer. He started up the stairs. "Are you okay?"

He looked up to where the sunlight was glinting off an old chandelier, and then made it to the top where he looked down the long hallway toward the angled windows at the front of her building. All he could think about was watching her from across the street that awful night when she had been grieving Elijah. Elijah Canten of all people. But she loved him. And she'd been curled up on the floor crying, and he hadn't helped her. He'd trusted God to take care of her then. But this was different, wasn't it? He was the one who had hurt her. The very least he owed her was an apology. And then he had to try to find a way to make it right. "Avery?"

The door to her room was open. But she wasn't crying on the floor. She was standing by the window.

The room shocked him. He hadn't seen it for a long time. The windows were draped in a silky peach-colored fabric, the plaster walls were a pale grayish color. The trim was painted white, and there was a large white chandelier with old-style bulbs in it. The golden light through the window bathed the whole room, from the fluffy and lacy bed at the other end to Avery herself.

It was disorienting. Liam thought of her as the feisty girl who worked in the overstuffed old outdoor shop below. But this was someone else. This was a woman surrounded by feminine things. Old dress forms were lined up against the brick wall, including one that looked like the one his Grandma Emily used to use. And they were all covered in dresses, frilly things, things nothing at all like anything in his own life.

And Avery. Everything about her was soft and curved and flowing, light and airy. Even the black muck boots looked sweet and endearing on her. He felt like he'd stumbled into yet another secret room, more mysterious than the speakeasy, more impenetrable than any dark passageway. He stopped at the doorway. Even if he hadn't been taught to do so, there was no way he could break the invisible barrier that stood there. "Avery."

She turned and looked at him.

Why hadn't he seen it before? She wasn't cute. Or quirky. She was absolutely lovely.

"I'm not mad at you," she said.

That stung. "You should be. I was a selfish idiot." Liam had cultivated the ability to endure and wait out silences. But this one he couldn't. "I'm sorry," he said, and he turned to go away.

"You aren't even going to come in here and talk to me face to face?"

"I can't. Mom's rule. And most certainly Dad's rule. Never go into a girl's bedroom unless you're married to her." He pushed away from the door frame and headed down the hall, his shadow long in the afternoon sunlight.

He heard footsteps behind him. "Really? You can't even face me?" There was an edge to her voice. She'd said she wasn't mad, and he believed her—she was furious. He could hear her coming down the hall after him. He hoped she would stop. And he hoped she wouldn't, because he couldn't stand the thought of her being so mad at him. Not that he had any idea what to say to her to make her anger go away.

He stopped and spun around, and she stopped suddenly and backpedaled, barely avoiding running into him. He hadn't even noticed she'd reached out to touch him, but there it was, her hand resting on his shoulder. "I can't believe you," she said, but she faltered when she said it. "You said you were going to help."

There it was, the worst thing she could have said to him. And he had it coming. Standing next to her felt like being wrapped in barbed wire—awful and impossible to escape. He breathed out. "I'm so sorry, Avery. There's no excuse for not thinking this through. But if there's any way…" A strand of hair had fallen out of her bun and slipped across her left eye, and he reached up to brush it aside. "If there's any way I can fix this, I swear I will."

His fingers still touched her cheek. Her skin looked pale, almost translucent, and there were faint freckles across her nose and cheek. That same pink gloss was on her lips, light but unmistakable. Her lips parted as if she was going to say something, but she didn't.

He wanted to kiss her. And he almost tried. But he knew that would have been the most selfish mistake he'd ever made. Without a word he turned, walked away, and headed down the steps, locking the door behind him. What was wrong with him? He climbed into the Cruiser. He couldn't get away soon enough. *God*, he prayed, *please don't let her realize what I almost did.*

# CHAPTER 23

*A*very moaned out loud, her embarrassment was so sharp. She gripped the steering wheel tighter. She had almost kissed him. What was wrong with her?

It had been almost a week since the ill-fated tour of her basement, and still, the thought of it made her face and neck feel hot. She squirmed in her car seat. Seriously? How insane was that? She was mad at him, and then he was all sorry and sweet, and he was looking at her like he really, really cared, and then he said something—she didn't even remember what it was—something about making everything all right. She couldn't even find words for how it made her feel, all wrapped up and warm and safe. And he was looking at her so intently. Was it regret or, worse, pity he was feeling for her? That's what it must have been. At the moment it had felt like something else. And she'd leaned up into him and...

He'd turned and walked away.

She'd spent that night reliving Eli's death. Her never-to-be father-in-law holding his wife as she cried. Hours holding Eli's limp hand, not even knowing what to pray for as the news came back worse and worse. Internal injuries. Brain hemorrhage.

Spinal damage. No response. She deserved to relive it, because she had forgotten Eli while looking at Liam. Eli had lost the beautiful, wild life he was meant to have. She only had this one thing to do to make up for it, this dream of a shop in the town he'd loved. And she was messing that up, too.

She groaned again. She never should have agreed to come here today, but Poppy had been so insistent. She left the closed sign on the door, and now she could only hope Liam wouldn't be there. He didn't seem like the branding type, anyway. He was a lot more white collar than that.

When she crested a small hill on the Gunnerson ranch "driveway," she saw Poppy standing outside a beat-up old pickup, leaning back against the door. She waved as Avery approached, and Avery pulled up beside her and got out. "Is something wrong?"

"Nope. Just waiting for Colton. I'm not allowed in."

"You're not allowed in the house?"

Poppy waved a hand as if to erase her last words. "Actually, I'm allowed to go anywhere, but Liam is at the house, and Colton's errand took a little longer than he thought it would."

"Is that a problem?"

"No, but I can't be alone with Liam."

Avery bit her lip. Her mind tried to come up with a good, sensible reason for that, and couldn't.

"Well, I blew that, didn't I?" Poppy went on. "It's not a secret, I suppose. And it's actually the other way around. Liam isn't supposed to be alone at the house with me. Last time I popped over here unexpectedly, Liam said hello, walked out the door, and drove off. He was in the middle of eating lunch. I felt terrible."

"Oka-ay," Avery said. She was still trying to sort out any way that this didn't either make Colton a control freak or Liam just a freak.

"Let me try this one more time. Liam wanted to stay out

here until he figures out what's going on with those two break-ins. Colton told Liam he trusts him to take care of himself, but he thought it was too dangerous for him to try to protect me at the same time. So if I'm here with Liam, Colton wants to be here, too. I guess that way they could both protect me. Which is funny, because you can see anyone coming a long way off, and I'm pretty sure I'm a better shot than either of them."

Somehow that didn't surprise Avery.

"So that's why. And I can see Colton's truck now. Let's get you parked at the house, and I'll drive you out to the corrals."

Avery tried to park out of the way and opposite from where Liam's FJ Cruiser was parked. After seeing how muddy the roads were, she dumped her sneakers and pulled muck boots up over her jeans. And grabbed a hat. She had been learning the hard way how much fiercer the sun could be at this elevation. "Nice boots," Poppy said. "I keep forgetting you grew up on a ranch."

She climbed into Poppy's truck. "A farm, actually, and not a very big one. Dad leases out some of our land, and he makes most of his money haying for other people's ranches. They're on the first cutting right now, so they're busy."

"Well, it's all new to me," Poppy said. It didn't look new to Avery at all. It looked comfortable. Poppy drove out toward the barn and backed the big truck in neatly between two others. "You going to wrestle a few steers?" Poppy grinned.

"Nope. I'm here for the burgers. And the new recipe you promised me."

"Southwestern cilantro salad. I'm trying to expand Colton's tastes. He said cilantro tastes like crabgrass."

"He might be right," Avery teased.

"You northerners."

A dually truck towing a long horse trailer pulled up in the tall grass across from where they were parked. "Pretty stiff competition for horseback jobs today," Poppy said. "Between

Colton and Travis's friends, there are a lot of ropers around. I think all the younger guys will be stuck on the ground. Look at them." She pointed to where a group of young men were standing, joking and jostling each other around. "They're here to impress Colton."

"You said he used to rodeo, right?"

"That's a bit of an understatement. And that," she said, "is my sister."

Avery looked where Poppy directed and saw a tall woman with long legs, a sleeveless green tee, and the most amazing, wavy, and long mass of copper-colored hair she had ever seen. She looked back at Poppy.

"Yeah, I know. Not a lot of family resemblance."

Actually, they were both tall and thin and not much for makeup, but that was where the resemblance stopped. Poppy's sister walked past the group of young men with a smile and a peace sign, and they practically fell over themselves trying to fall in behind her. Poppy's sister laughed.

"Flirts more than you," Avery said.

"Flirts more than anyone."

"Well, heck. Look at her. She doesn't exactly fade into the crowd."

Poppy took a deep breath. "Yeah. But it would probably be better for her if she did, at least once in a while. Anyway, Sierra will be staying here this weekend while Cash gets some water damage fixed from my neighbor's drunk bathing incident."

The red-haired sister was staying with Liam. That really bugged her. She was just Liam's type. A supermodel, like Lynn.

"I stayed with Mara and Zane last night, and I gotta tell you, that's no fun for anyone. If she doesn't have that baby soon...I don't know."

"Getting cranky?"

"Oh, my word. That girl. And I don't know what it is about her, but if she says jump, everyone jumps. We can't help it. But she's not feeling very good today, so she won't make the branding. Okay, enough, you're all caught up. Oh, see that older guy on the buckskin horse? That's Peter somebody. Colton said Liam wanted you to meet him, so don't let me forget. You can stay with me by the irons or just hang out by the corrals. In fact, you can chase those young cowboys around if you want. Or..." she looked around. "Oh look, there's Colton and Liam, finally."

They were walking up the road together. Liam's jeans had made a comeback, along with a pair of worn boots and a dusty straw cowboy hat. He was wearing a blue and white plaid shirt. Plaid. She never would have guessed he owned one, except that it fit him perfectly, like all of his clothes. As the two men walked, Avery could see the family resemblance—in the long stride and the smiles at least. Just looking at him made her face burn with embarrassment over the stupid, inexplicable way she'd acted the other night. She was determined to stay as far away from him as possible.

Poppy jumped out of the truck. "I'd better move it. There's water, soda, and beer in the cooler." And she jogged away. Since Avery didn't want to be stuck with Liam walking right by her, she walked over to the corral rails.

It was hot. There were flies, some of them huge, and the air smelled of leather and horse sweat. She also caught traces of sage, alfalfa, grass, and cologne in the air. There were lots of men. And a couple impressive and wildly focused dogs. She would have loved to call one over and scratch its furry ears, but they were all business and didn't have time for the likes of her. Poppy was standing by an oil drum that had been turned into a grill of some sort, complete with propane and a fan. It was 90 degrees on this overly warm May day, and though Poppy was standing by a blazing fire, she looked comfortable. Happy, even.

Avery finally spotted a group of women. They were stationed farther down the corral, dressed in their finest cowgirl chic, with sloppy hats and perfect hair. And between them and Avery, Sierra was standing alone near Poppy's forge. She had one boot on the lower rail, leaning into a stretch in a way that showed off her long limbs without looking as if that's what she was trying to do. She had a smattering of freckles that, instead of making her look young or unrefined, made her look exotic. But most of all there was her hair, red and wavy, glinting in the unrelenting sunlight like copper and gold and everything lovely and precious. She was really, really something. And more than one cowboy had his eye on her. It really wasn't fair to the younger women, who had obviously put some effort into getting attention of their own. Sure enough, one member of that pack shot Sierra a nasty look over her shoulder. Maybe that was what Poppy meant by wishing Sierra didn't always stand out in a crowd.

The cowboys and horses were something to look at, too. Poppy's fiancé, Colton, was there, next to Mara's husband, Zane, who was tall and boyish and a little too thin. They were cousins for sure, standing in almost exactly the same position as they spoke to each other. There were a few older men around, too, ones with fancy saddles and hats, wearing long-sleeved shirts despite the heat. The horses looked clean and combed and wore bridles with braided horsehair and tiny conchos. It seemed to Avery as if everyone had put on their best work clothes and brought their best horse.

Then there was Liam. It shouldn't have surprised her that he would be here. After all, he was Zane's older brother and Colton's cousin. He must have been around cattle at least a few times.

He looked Colton's age, too young to fit into the group of older men in the saddle and just a little too old to be one of the young men in the corral. He didn't fit in the same way Sierra didn't. Avery sighed. That was none of her concern.

"Avery!" Poppy gestured to her to come closer with one

gloved hand while holding a long iron rod in the fire with the other.

"This is my sister, Sierra. Sierra, this is Avery."

Sierra turned and gave her a brilliant smile, showing two rows of neat white teeth, except for one that seemed a little twisted. Without it, her smile might have looked fake, capped, and bleached.

"Nice to meet you," Avery said. Sierra smelled of an earthy, exotic perfume, and the heat didn't seem to bother her any more than it bothered Poppy.

"I hear you own the Moose on the Loose."

"I do," Avery said, plastering a smile on her face. It didn't feel like ownership right now. She felt owned by it.

"Are you hiring?"

In her peripheral vision, Avery caught Poppy's quick turn and the frown on her face. "Mara fills in a couple hours here and there, but I can't really afford to hire someone yet," Avery answered.

Sierra shrugged. "Well, I have a ton of experience with managing stores a lot like yours. Big ones, little ones. Worked as a buyer, too. Even worked at a distributor once, but that was lonely work. I missed the people."

Side-eye from Poppy again.

"Do you love working there?" Sierra asked. "Moose Hollow is adorable. And since it's a ski town, there are always new people to meet, right?"

Avery had no idea how to respond to that. She struggled for a moment. "My customers are nice," she said. Usually.

"I know, right? That's probably because people who shop at a store like yours are planning to go on an adventure. Skiing, hiking, whatever. What's not to love?" Sierra said.

Avery nodded. But she had never once thought of it that way.

"But that's a lot to handle by yourself."

"Sometimes." *Always.*

"Have you got all your summer stock in?"

And order stock with what? The tiny amount of money she still had left? Which would she do, skip paying utilities or forgo groceries? She hated swiping her debit card, waiting for the day they shut down her account and seized her funds. Their funds, actually. "Not all of it." Not any of it. She hadn't placed a single order.

"I sure would love it if you let me take a look at your catalogs. Not for pay, of course, just as a favor. On the ranch, it's been cow this, cow that. I'm going to need a break." Sierra's smile was infectious.

"Sure," Avery said.

"Brilliant. Are you working on Monday? I can come by bright and early, to avoid the rush."

There was no rush, of course. "Great," Avery said.

On the other side of the metal rails, Colton strode up behind Poppy, brushed a strand of hair aside, and kissed her on the side of her neck. She laughed and swatted him away with her leather-gloved hands. "I'm ready to go," she said. "Are we ever going to get some real work done?"

"I see how you are," he said with a grin. He turned toward the six men on horseback and called, "Let's go."

In the swirl of horses and men and dust, Avery had a hard time sorting out what happened next. All the men, on foot and on horseback, went out into the larger corral where the cows and calves were. Men moved through the smaller corral on horseback, ropes flew, and then the first calves were dragged out by their feet into yet another pen. That was when two young men took over, flipping the calf over and stretching it out. Colton gave each calf some sort of medicine, then Poppy handed him a red-hot brand from the fire and a cloud of white smoke rose from the calf.

Avery bit her lip. It had been a long time since she'd seen

something like this. It was a *branding*. Poppy had said it was a branding. But she'd made it sound like a social event, not a time for medieval animal torture.

Then things got even more confused, with multiple calves being moved and teams jumping into action. And it was dirty work in more ways than one. She'd never realized just how much poop could stick to the back end of a cow. And then there was the dirt, sweat, flies, and heaven knew what else. She ducked through the rails and stood near Poppy. "I have no idea what's going on."

"These guys are separating the cows and calves," she said, waving one of the glowing red branding irons toward the riders. Ropes whistled through the air into the melee of crowded cattle and seemed to find the right target every time. Poppy had been right about the ropers being good. "They drag them over to where the wrestlers can take the calf down. They vaccinate and worm, and if it's a bull calf, castrate. Then they brand them. Watch Zane and Liam—they know what they're doing. That's a big one, it might be one of mine."

Poppy owned her own cattle? Avery never would have pegged her for it.

Poppy was busy switching irons with Colton. As she did, Sierra came back over to stand next to Avery. "Poppy has cattle?"

"Girl's got mad investing skills."

When Poppy returned, Avery just had to ask. "Why brand them?"

"That's what I wanted to know," Poppy said. "There's a lot of land out here, and thieves, too. A brand is still the best way to identify cattle and prove ownership. Nothing else works the same way legally, or on the range. Someday, maybe."

Avery found Liam in the cloud of dust. A roper had brought him and Zane a large calf, and Zane was struggling to lift and drop the calf on his side. Finally the calf went down, Liam said something she couldn't hear, and the two brothers laughed loudly.

*He looks so different*, Avery thought, marveling at his broad, toothy smile. He'd never once smiled like that around her. Except for the other night in the basement, and what a mess she'd made of that.

He didn't smile because he was around her, of course. There was nothing to laugh about there. Just her stupid self making stupid decisions and spending her time either whining or arguing. Whining, mostly. It had been a horrible few months in Moose Hollow, but that was her own fault. In fact, it was shocking to take a moment and think about how much time she'd spent in a dreary stupor lately. Here, out in the sun in the middle of miles of green grass banded by blue mountains, it seemed so wrong. She looked at the smile on Liam's face as he was nearly flat on his back trying to keep hold of the calf's head. *I wish he didn't see me that way.*

She got a bottle of water out of the cooler and listened as Poppy explained more than she'd ever expected to learn about cow parasites, freeze branding, and more. And she tried not to notice Liam, until she saw him land a calf right in front of her. Zane had the head, Liam had the heels, and they stretched the calf out.

And right then, the back end of the calf exploded all over Liam. Sierra gasped, Avery gasped, and Poppy let out a low chuckle. "That was a nice shirt, too," she said.

Liam didn't let go. The roper was laughing, and so was Zane, and as he came over, Colton looked as if he was trying to be sympathetic but failing miserably. Still, Liam held on until it was time to let the calf up and find its way back to its waiting mother. When Liam stood, the damage was clear. Slimy greenish poo covered him from his belt to just below his collar. He plucked his shirt away from his skin. Poppy hurried over to hand him a plastic bottle of water, but faced with how pathetic a solution it was to such a cleaning nightmare, she started laughing too.

Liam unbuttoned the shirt, which brought a few snarky catcalls from his coworkers and a few comments about the blinding light reflected off his Chicago tan. But the jokes stopped when he got the shirt off. He looked like a model from one of those overpriced jean companies, the kind that only took black and white photos. Shirt on, he looked like a medium-height, medium-age, medium-good-looking guy. Shirt off, he was a fitness icon.

"I love Montana," Sierra said reverently.

Avery felt her face flush.

# CHAPTER 24

own the fence, a couple of the younger women whistled, and the rest jostled them for their misbehavior. If Liam heard them, he gave no sign.

"Give it over," the roper said, an older man on a beautiful, buttermilk-colored horse. "I'll run it under the pump." And he rode away holding the shirt out like a dead skunk.

Avery tried not to stare. But Liam turned away from the corral—which meant turning her way—and opened the bottle of water. He dumped it over his arms and splashed it across his chest. He reminded her of a horrible, boring movie she saw once starring Bruce Lee, which she had watched because he was one of Eli's heroes. The movie was bad, but Bruce Lee had a whole new level of movement, speed, and sharpness. Liam looked like that: tight, like every muscle had been stretched just a little too far. And the impromptu shower was just too much to ignore.

"Is he yours?" Sierra said.

Avery looked at her in confusion and saw Sierra's long, narrow hand gesture toward Liam. "You two an item?"

"Oh, God no," Avery said. She winced. She wasn't one to take

God's name lightly, because she'd always had a sneaking suspicion he paid attention when she called him, and because the times she said his name weren't usually the times she wanted him paying attention to her. But embarrassment wrung it out of her. She'd been caught looking in a way that made a complete stranger think he was hers.

The action started up again, but Zane left and started walking across the pasture. "Where is he going?" Avery asked.

"Probably checking on Mara. The bunkhouse is back that way. Which means Liam is without a partner. Wanna go give it a try?"

Her new friend Poppy had a very dry sense of humor. In fact, she still wondered sometimes when she was joking. "No, thank you."

The clump of young women was moving amoeba-like toward the coolers, which were conveniently close to where Liam was standing. One had the audacity to snap a picture of him with her cell phone. Sierra checked the propane levels for Poppy, which left Avery to stand around feeling useless. That was when the older man rode back with Liam's dripping shirt. Liam wrung it out and put it back on, stained but obviously cleaner. The wet shirt wasn't a whole lot less distracting than no shirt, and another young woman snapped a pic. The older man got off his horse, Liam protested, and then the older man tipped his hat and walked her way.

Liam was going to try roping. She felt sorry for him since just about everyone was watching him, and all the ropers had been excellent. But he waited his turn, trotted the beautiful horse up smoothly, and *ss-ssp*. The rope zipped through the air and neatly caught two back legs. How did he do that? How did any of them catch the legs at the exact moment they were off the ground? Liam tied off before she knew it and tugged the calf to the next team of wrestlers.

Cowboy accountant. Who knew there was such a thing?

The man who'd given up his horse came over to chat with Poppy and added Avery to the conversation. "I hear you've been making big changes over at the Moose on the Loose, Ms. Maier." He held out his hand. "Peter Henderson." Avery realized he was the man that Poppy had mentioned before. Why would Liam or Colton want her to meet him?

Whoever he was, he was easy to talk to. He mentioned working in the banking industry, although he said he had a few other hobbies as well. Roping included. Before she knew it, she was talking Iowa with him, then haying operations, then Poppy's wedding dress, which he said he'd heard so much about. She was sure he was just being polite. He seemed good at that. He even noticed the shirt she was wearing, which she'd designed. He said he was sure his daughter would love one if she ever made another, and Avery admitted she had a fair amount of inventory from her failed attempt at the art fair circuit, and that his daughter could drop by to look anytime.

He asked her a few questions about her failed business, what she'd learned from it, and what she thought about her new store. He was an attentive listener, and Avery answered as best she could until she became a little self-conscious about how much she'd monopolized the conversation.

In a while, he was commandeered by a couple older men debating his horse's bloodlines. He seemed like a nice enough guy, and he reminded Avery of her dad in some ways.

Then the sight of someone running caught everyone's attention. Liam had just released a calf, so he rode through the cattle to meet his brother Zane as he came across the pasture. Avery saw him fish for something in his pocket and throw it to Zane, and then Mara's husband went running back the way he'd come.

Everyone's eyes were on Liam as he returned. "Mara's in labor," he announced with wide eyes.

"You guys can go—we've got this," Peter Henderson said.

Avery saw the conflicted look on Colton's face. The whole

crowd was here to help work his cattle for free. Standing next to Poppy, Sierra softly said, "I can do this." After a moment's hesitation, Poppy handed her gloves over to her sister. Then she hurried over and put a hand on Colton's horse. "Stay here. I'll let you know what's going on when we get there, okay?"

He nodded, looking relieved, and Poppy headed for the truck.

Avery had no idea what to do. She wanted to be with Mara, or at least in the next room, but she didn't think it was her place. As much as she liked Mara, she didn't know her that well, and the thought of spending time in a hospital waiting room again made her stomach turn.

She hovered by Sierra, who was happily playing with nearly molten iron. With Poppy gone, there was nothing for her to do here but watch Liam like one of those lovestruck teenagers. And right on cue, Liam rode up to the rails near where she was standing. "I hate to hand him back," he said to Henderson, "but I think I should go to the hospital."

"I understand. And it's about time I got some exercise," Henderson replied. They switched places across the fence.

"Thanks again," Liam said.

"That horse is really something. Colton's buddy Travis is a miracle worker."

"No, I meant for washing my shirt," Liam smiled, and Henderson laughed. "Now I just need to find a working truck."

Sierra didn't miss a beat. "I'm sure someone can give you a ride."

He looked at Sierra, then his gaze landed on Avery. "Avery, would you mind? Zane's car wouldn't start, so I gave him my keys."

"No problem," she said. Except for having to make conversation with him all the way to Billings while trying not to die of embarrassment, of course.

They walked quickly and silently back to the house, and

Liam ran inside to change into a clean shirt and jeans while Avery switched shoes. He jogged back out in a couple minutes and said, "Mara wasn't due for another week and a half. Do you think this is bad for the baby?"

Avery was surprised to hear the worry in his voice. "No, I think she and the baby will be fine." As soon as the words were out, she felt her own loss. Her own baby wasn't fine.

*If you even had one*, she thought. It was as if she didn't really have a right to grieve. But she *did* mourn the loss. Something truly was missing—Eli and the future she was supposed to have with him.

"Isn't the baby premature?" Liam asked.

"I don't think so," Avery said.

"I sound like an idiot, don't I?" he said.

"No. You sound like you're going to be a great uncle."

He stared out the windshield, knee bouncing. And then he glanced at Avery's speedometer, probably wishing she'd go faster. "I really hope they don't really name him or her Pistachio," he said.

That made her laugh, and he smiled. She got him to list all the names he remembered them using during the pregnancy, and she could feel some of his tension ease as he smirked over which was the worst.

When she pulled into the parking lot, she felt as if she was finally home free. "Thank you," Liam said.

She shrugged. It had been nice.

"Are you sure you don't want to come in?"

"I don't really think I belong."

Liam gave her a searching look. "You know, Mara pretty much lost every friend she had over the last couple months. She hasn't had much time to make new ones. And she speaks highly of you."

"I don't know her that well."

He leaned his head to the side a little. "But you make people feel...I don't know. Just good."

She wished he wasn't looking at her that way. It was enough to make her imagine he wasn't just talking about Mara.

Liam's phone buzzed, and he looked at the screen. "Poppy says the baby's coming fast. Let's go," Liam said, and she couldn't say no.

The hospital smelled the same. It was a thousand miles away, but it could have been the same hospital as the one where Eli had died. It brought back memories with perfect clarity, but she felt a strange distance from that time when Eli was hospitalized. So much had changed. It hadn't been very long, though. The distance she felt made her feel guilty.

After checking into the maternity ward, they still had to wait outside the security doors. Avery was the odd person out, and she knew it. Liam's father, Anson, was there. She'd met him when he'd mysteriously appeared to check out the boiler in her newly discovered basement. He'd done some maintenance and refused payment. She had a little trouble imagining that tall man in grease-stained jeans and a T-shirt as the owner of a fancy hotel, but looking at him now in clean jeans, a button-down shirt, and a stern expression, he seemed as intimidating as he'd looked friendly before. He was telling Colton that they'd been on their way to the branding when they'd heard the news. From the way he put his arm around the middle-aged woman beside him, Avery guessed she was Liam's mother.

She felt a touch on her shoulder. "Come meet my parents," Liam said.

That was the last thing she wanted to do. The last time she'd met parents, they'd spent the whole time saying she wasn't ready to marry their son, and that he wasn't prepared to marry her. But this was nothing like that, she told herself. She really couldn't care less what they thought of her. All they had in common was Liam, and since he was leaving town as soon as he could, that wasn't much.

But as soon as Liam mentioned that Avery was designing Poppy's wedding dress, his mother was interested. "Poppy said you were almost done," Julia said.

"That might be a little exaggerated," Avery smiled.

"She said something about velvet ribbons and silk organza and floral lace, and I just couldn't picture it."

Avery was trying to figure out how to respond without giving too much away when Liam broke in. "Avery's designs use a lot of different fabrics, but they all come together in a way that makes sense. She designed the shirt she's wearing—see what I mean?"

"So, you're a fashion critic now?" Anson said to his son in an utterly deadpan voice.

Liam rolled his eyes. His mother came to his rescue by changing the subject. "That's really beautiful, Avery, and it looks comfortable. Do you ever make something similar, but a little more forgiving through the waist?"

Avery immediately thought of a basic empire shirt pattern she'd made, but before she could speak, Poppy came through the security doors. "Look out. There's a new Gunnerson in the world. Wash your hands, give her twenty minutes, and you can come in." And she disappeared again.

They did as Poppy asked, and the seconds ticked slowly by. Avery could hardly breathe. She didn't want to be here. She didn't want to spend another minute thinking, *What if this had been me?* Would her parents have been able to make it in time? She was just like Mara. She'd lost all her friends too, but it was because she'd abandoned them to schoolwork and weekends following Eli around the country. If it were her in that room, would she have been alone?

Not alone. Avery would have had a child. And the thought of that left her feeling so conflicted she felt like she could hardly breathe. Was it wrong to grieve a child she might never have had? Or was it wrong to feel relieved that she didn't have another life to be dragged through the mess she'd made of things? Both. She knew it. She was wrong either way.

She could hear Colton's running steps before he arrived. He was out of breath. Anson announced, "It's been twenty minutes," and pushed open the door. For a second Avery thought she might pass out. The others went through, but then there was a touch at her elbow. It brought her back to the moment. Liam was standing behind her. "Are you okay?" he murmured. She nodded and walked down the hall.

Mara handed the baby to Julia first. Avery stayed back, still uncertain. She couldn't see the baby, but she could see Mara, and she looked like a different person. Her hair was back in a ponytail, most of her makeup was gone, and she had an unabashed smile on her face. Mara looked lovely. Julia turned to show the baby to Anson, and Colton stepped right in. "Mara, you did good. Now cough it up. What's the name?"

"First I'll tell you his middle name. It's Sam, for Emmaline Samantha, his great-great-grandma. And his first name is—drumroll—Paul. He's my favorite superhero, you know. He murders people, gets knocked off his horse, goes blind, and then saves the world. He's the smartest guy ever, too."

"Not smarter than John," Zane said. "Or Solomon."

"Meh," she said, flipping her hand at him. "I mean street smarts."

"I can't argue with that," Zane conceded with a smile.

Avery wasn't sure about the horse or the murders, but she thought Mara might be talking about Paul from the Bible. He was one of the disciples, or not. She couldn't remember. Either way, she hadn't pegged Mara as that sort of girl.

"Now make Liam hold the baby, he's hiding back there," Mara ordered.

Liam stepped forward, and his mother handed the baby over

to him. Avery could see Paul's head then, impossibly tiny and covered with a swirl of black hair. Liam hunched over the baby and moved very slowly, as if he was afraid Paul might break.

"He's named for you too, Liam Paul Gunnerson," Zane said.

"Really?" The look of awe on his face made Avery's eyes sting with tears. She blinked them away as best she could.

"Smart name, you got a two-for," Colton said, and Mara laughed. Then winced. "Ouch. No laughing for a while. Okay, that's long enough. Hand him over. Everyone can go update your social media, I've got a baby to feed. And you, Avery. Come here." Mara surprised her by pulling her down for a hug, a gentle one right over the sleepy baby. "Thanks for coming. Don't forget you promised me some nonmaternity clothes, okay?"

"I remember." Her gaze lingered on the baby, and Mara waited with a smile. "He's beautiful, Mara," Avery said.

"I know," Mara said softly. "He's proof God's got a plan. I thought God was all about just knocking me off my horse when I got pregnant, but look at the beautiful thing he had in mind all along."

# CHAPTER 25

*L*iam was still on a high when he made it back to the office to close up for Cash, who was still back at the hospital. The influx of Gunnersons and Gunnerson affiliates meant there was a steady stream of visitors and an impromptu tailgate party in the parking lot. He was pretty sure the hospital didn't like that, but that's just the way it was. Mara and Zane would be bringing Paul home in the morning. *Paul.*

He imagined his brother pointing to him, talking to a ten-year-old, saying, "We named him for you." And then he had to sit down. What would be on the other end of that pointing finger? Who would he be in ten years? Maybe just another schmuck working at the big-box tax store. What would the boy think? Would he think he had been named for a nobody?

Liam wanted to be successful in that boy's eyes. And polite. And funny. And have presents with him, all the time. And drive a cool car the kid loved to ride in. And buy the kid a cool car. Have him spend a few weeks in whatever city he was living in and take him to see all the sites. He wanted to be the cool uncle.

Or would he be a stranger?

What about brandings and the Christmas Strolls and the

first day of school, or the first time a teenager named Paul
wanted to talk to someone about the trouble he was in and how
to tell his dad about it. He couldn't be that guy if he was living in
Portland or Seattle or anyplace so far away.

He wondered when he'd decided he didn't want kids of his
own. He hadn't, at least not consciously. He'd always thought he
would have kids. He thought of them as something that was
bound to come along eventually. But the life he envisioned for
himself didn't have kids in it. A wife maybe, someone professional and as busy as he was. Someone who wouldn't miss him
and resent his work schedule, like the girls in Chicago had.
Which meant he probably wouldn't miss her either, he realized.
And that left no room for kids. Besides, there wouldn't be dirt
or horses or snowballs or sledding hills, at least not like in
Montana. Or moose on the high school football field. Or a
whole hospital parking lot full of people ready to love on his
kids just because his last name was Gunnerson.

Because the Gunnersons had been spreading kindness, in
their own little way, for generations. Enough so that people
thought well of them despite Cash's skirt chasing and Colton's
out-of-control years. And Liam's everything, he supposed. They
granted favors, big and little. And they showed up.

He didn't want to raise kids without a front yard or without
a backyard a thousand acres big and full of mountains and
unexplored places. He wanted everyone in town to know his
kid's name so that when that kid was seen trying to get in trouble, they called Liam before they called the police. There was so
much grace in a small town. So much gossip and double-
crossing and general silliness to be sure, but so much grace to
cover all of it.

He couldn't have the life he'd had in Chicago and give his
kids the life he wanted for them. They were two different lives.

He spun around. He hadn't even realized he was sitting in
Cash's chair again. And as he watched the sun reflect off Avery's

windows, he decided that more than anything else, he wanted to be the kind of man who kept his promises. He closed everything up, set the alarm, and went across the street. The door was locked, and he checked his watch. Just after five. But she opened the door for him. "Hello, Uncle Liam."

He chuckled as he followed her inside. "I like the sound of that. What are you working on?"

"Just checking online orders and getting tomorrow's shipments ready."

She said that with so much more confidence than she would have months ago. She was a quick learner. "How's the main store doing?"

"Leveling off, unfortunately. I need new stuff in the store if I want to keep things moving. I'll make a decision about that tomorrow."

"Why, what's tomorrow?"

"Tomorrow I open the letter I got from the insurance company yesterday."

Liam considered that for a long time, trying to understand. "Isn't it killing you not knowing what the letter says?"

"Maybe."

"You didn't tell me you got a letter." She hadn't even talked to him until he asked for a ride, actually.

"It's my problem. I'll figure it out in my time."

That rankled him. It certainly was his problem too. He'd said it was. *And Avery had agreed*, he thought. "I think you and I need to have a talk here."

"Oh, now you've graduated from being an uncle to dad," she said with a not-too-friendly smirk.

"No, I want to be your friend. You know that."

A few different expressions crossed her face, none of which he could read clearly. He was pretty sure she'd read his intentions the other night, the night he'd come far too close to kissing her and ruining their friendship. And probably getting slapped. But he didn't want to think about that now. This was about fulfilling his promises and being the kind of man he wanted to be. He waited her out. And after a while, she sat down behind the checkout desk. Liam sat down across from her. "You have options, Avery. Even if it's bad news, it isn't a death sentence, not for the business and definitely not for you."

She sat still, arms crossed, a fierce expression on her face. Liam had absolutely no idea what she was thinking. He felt that way a lot around her. It made him so uncomfortable he kept rambling on.

"I have ideas to get you out of this bind. And I know some guys who are a lot smarter than me that will probably have ideas, too. The lawyer I recommended is one. And your ideas count the most because you know what you want more than the rest of us."

Another shift in her expression, darker now. "I don't think wanting something is going to make it come true, Liam."

"Okay. But you don't know for certain. I'm here now, so just open the letter."

"Liam, I don't want—" she didn't finish. He waited her out again, this time managing to keep his mouth shut. And after ignoring him for a while, she reached under the counter, pulled out an overnight mail envelope, and slammed it on the counter. "You read it."

Suddenly Liam dreaded opening it. He got a small taste of what she had to be feeling. He tried to act as if it was nothing, opened a letter four pages long, and read the opening line. Not good.

Avery must have seen it in his face. She stood up and walked a few steps away, arms wrapped across her ribs, shaking her head. "Great. Well, now I know to tell Sierra not to come tomorrow. Thanks for your help."

He hurried over to stand in front of her, but she turned

away. "This isn't the end. All that letter does is tell us where the starting line is. Are you crying?"

Her tears turned to anger faster than he ever would have imagined. "This is why I didn't want to open it while you were here."

He was confused. "Because I might see you cry?"

She glared at him.

"That's stupid," he said.

Her jaw dropped.

"Come on. Sit back down, we'll go over it together. And get some paper, we need to start writing ideas down." He sat down and shuffled papers, trying to look productive, ignoring the doubt he was feeling, and hoping against hope she wouldn't kick him out. *Let her be mad, God*, he prayed. It was better than seeing her so depressed. When she came back to the desk, he said a silent thank you and got to work.

Even with takeout ordered, it was hard work. Liam had to explain the concept of different income centers and the pros and cons of separate businesses from a tax standpoint. She worked hard, asked questions, and took notes. She said she thought renting out additional space was good, said she understood the idea of a mix of private equity and loans, percentages versus a fixed rate, all of it. But her heart wasn't in it.

He couldn't get a grip on what was going on with her. He wrote it off to grief, to exhaustion or confusion, whatever popped in his mind, but when he asked questions, she ignored him or changed the subject. She just wanted to know what was expected of her. She didn't blink at the thought of raising a million dollars and then carrying that debt entirely on her own shoulders. She didn't blink at anything or smile at anything. He'd lost her.

And maybe that was realistic. Maybe by trying to help Avery hold on to her dream, he was only delaying the inevitable. Or making things worse.

That was when he realized he'd been alone with her, in public view, for hours. He didn't know why he hadn't thought of it before. His only comfort was that if anyone were watching him, it would be obvious this was business and not pleasure. He wasn't about to bring her into the dark cloud that was following him around. He said his goodbyes abruptly, shook her hand for good measure, and left. And just in case anyone had wondered if their talk had been about business, he went back to Cash's office. He turned on the light and did some filing in the cabinets closest to the window. Then when it felt like he'd done enough, he turned off the lights and took a last glance out at the road to see if anyone was watching.

Someone was in Avery's store, standing close to her. He could barely make it out. Liam ducked out of sight and watched. Was she in danger? Should he intervene?

Yes. And no. Avery appeared to be crying, her hands over her face, when the man—it was apparent it was a man—took her in his arms. And Liam knew who it was, who it had to be. He sat down in Cash's chair and swore out loud.

# CHAPTER 26

*A*very couldn't believe what a blubbering idiot she was being. All Griffin had said was she looked tired. But then the tears had started. He'd put his arms around her and swayed gently, cooing about everything being all right, and she had soaked it up as if she'd been starving for it. And as the first rush of emotion started to fade, she thought about how glad she was that she hadn't lost it around Liam. That would have just been too much to bear.

"Okay, I want to hear all about it," Griffin said. "But first, let me get you something to eat. You look like you're starving."

She wasn't, but she was willing to agree just to have a few moments alone to get herself back together. And to figure out what to say to Griffin that would satisfy his desire to help without making her look even more the fool than she already felt.

She'd barely had time to dry her eyes when he was back with a wrapped plate of cheese and crackers, a bottle of wine, and two wine glasses. "Where's your living room?" he asked.

She explained that she didn't have one, and no, she didn't have a couch at all, and Griffin took a patterned fleece blanket off the shelf and spread it over the floor. Then he added a couple packable rain jackets for pillows. He was so proud of himself it made Avery laugh, and she sat down with him.

Griffin handed her a glass of wine. "It's a guy, isn't it?"

"No." *Eli*, she thought. But this wasn't about grief. It was about fear as much as anything else. And before she could stop herself, she blurted out, "I feel like my life is over."

It all spilled out after that. Avery told him about the insurance company and that she could have the building, her business, and money she hadn't even dreamed of making all foreclosed upon. And she didn't stop there. She told him that she'd just discovered there was a basement in her building, although she didn't tell him about the speakeasy. She told Griffin that the entrance in the alley had been unlocked all along, and there were nights she thought she'd heard someone moving around downstairs and all she could do was hope it was the creaking of the old, creepy building. And now the best she had to hope for was to rent out more rooms, bring in more strangers to live in her home, and just try to pay it all off before she died.

Griffin shook his head and made sympathetic noises, never once taking his eyes off her. He was a good listener. He didn't tell her she was stupid for crying, either. He just watched her and waited until she was through.

"Was Liam Gunnerson the one who found your basement?"

She could have groaned. What was it between the two of them? "He wanted his dad to check out the boiler to make sure it was okay." She wasn't sure why she stopped there, but she didn't want to stoke the flames between them.

"I bet," Griffin growled. "I hope you didn't leave him alone down there. He's always trying to find secret passageways. And there might be some, who knows. But why would someone work so hard to see them if they didn't want to use them? He's a thief, Avery. He stole stuff in high school, although everyone thought his family was so upright there was no way it could be him. That was before Colton turned into a drunk and a woman beater, of course. Judging by what happened to his room in mommy and daddy's hotel, Liam is still a thief. Don't give him access. I know you like him, but I'm telling you, don't give him a key.

Avery didn't say that the lock on the basement was Liam's.

"Did he tell you about the coal mining they did under the city and that they haven't even found all the shafts?"

She groaned again. "I don't want to know about more secret tunnels of any kind. I just want…" She had no idea what she wanted. Anything she might wish for sounded about as ridiculous as asking for a flying unicorn.

"Well, I might have something for you. I wasn't going to tell you—"

"What?" She knew she sounded frustrated, but she didn't need any more surprises.

"I asked Dad a few questions, and I was pretty surprised by what I found out. I told you he looked into this building when Tabitha put it up for sale, right? And he decided there was no way he'd pay what she was asking. But over the last couple months, he's been working the numbers on buying a new, bigger place, and he keeps getting stuck on all the marketing problems associated with changing the address. I told him about all the work you'd done here. And even though there are still problems—big, expensive problems—even with that, he thinks he might not lose too much money if he bought the place. And he wouldn't have to move everyone out of the office while renovations were being done, so if it takes two or three years to make it safe, so be it."

"Wait, he wants to buy the Moose on the Loose?"

"Not yet. And not the store. Just the building, maybe. But like I said, I could help you relocate the store, although I'm going to have to insist you check out a couple properties in

Bozeman for your own good. The economics are just so much better there."

He poured a little more wine into her glass, even though she was far from done with it. "I can't believe how much you have on your shoulders. And I haven't even seen the building inspection."

"There wasn't one," she breathed.

Griffin's expression went from concerned to dire. "So there's probably more that you don't know about."

"Probably."

"If I can make all this trouble go away for you, Avery, I will. Just give me the word, and I'll start trying to convince Dad. And if it works, no more creepy, dangerous building for you. No more looking at a lifetime of debt. You'd be free, Avery."

# CHAPTER 27

*L*iam was late, which was rude. Sensei knew it, and he let Liam stand at attention on the edge of the dojo floor a good long time before acknowledging him and calling him onto the floor. And when everyone else was sparring or working on new techniques, Liam was given a verbal list: five hundred crunches, five hundred pushups, one hundred side thrust kicks, one hundred roundhouse kicks. As soon as Liam was done with one, the list grew. After an hour, the formal class was closed and everyone who wanted to was allowed to stay and spar or work on forms, but Liam had squats to do. The crowd dwindled, and the work switched to weight-bearing stretches. He was drenched in sweat. Three trips to refill his bottle at the drinking fountain hardly put a dent in his thirst. When Sensei became absorbed in conversation with the last student, Liam lay spread-eagle on the floor. He knew he should just get up and leave. But he couldn't move.

He closed his eyes for a moment, and when he opened them, Sensei appeared above him, foot poised above his face. "Always on guard," he chided.

Liam bit back a complaint and stood up. He was surprised to

find he was a little taller than the instructor. When they sparred, it seemed like the opposite was true. "There," Sensei said, pointing to a bench. "Sit. If you're still here, you're probably ready to talk."

Talking was not Liam's friend right now. He considered what he would say. He even tried out a few things in his mind, but all he had were complaints. Complaints didn't have any place in a dojo, and Liam wasn't fond of them anyway.

Sensei spoke first. "You passed by the front door three times before parking. Last night you passed by twice before leaving. Who do you think is following you?"

"I don't know if anyone is."

"But someone has reason to follow you."

Liam considered that. Maybe whoever was after him had already spoken to Sensei. Or perhaps he was getting paranoid. Either way, he had nothing to lose by speaking the truth, at least part of it. "I have information about someone. I took it as a kind of insurance, but they probably saw it as a threat. Now they've threatened back. I think they expect me to either use it or give it back to them."

"And are you planning to use it?"

"No."

"Why not?" Sensei asked.

Liam blinked. And then ran through the options in his mind. "I can't win." Liam leaned his head back against the wall.

"And if you don't return it to them, they may never stop following you."

"I can't return it. I got rid of it."

Sensei chuckled. "You think I might be a spy. Good. A man in your position shouldn't trust anyone, but if someone threatened me, the last thing I would do is get rid of the one piece of insurance I had. So. You said you can't win. Is that all you want to do, win?"

"I just don't want to fight."

Sensei laughed loudly for entirely too long. "Right. That's why you came in here, fists clenched, red in the face. You were so hunched up you looked like Yosemite Sam. And for the record, no one in your state of mind is allowed to spar in my dojo."

That got Liam's ire up. "I don't play dirty."

"You don't get to play at all unless you play by my rules."

Liam took a deep breath and let it out. "Yes, Sensei."

Sensei waited. He was just as good at that game as Liam, which was annoying. But his next question took Liam off guard.

"What does winning look like to you?"

He was too tired to come up with a smart way to say it, so Liam just said, "Everyone I know is safe. And so am I."

"Then you're right. You'll never win."

Liam endured another full minute of silence before the man continued.

"Besides, this sounds like half of your story. It doesn't explain why you are so angry tonight in particular. Although I will tell you, this kind of angry usually involves a woman."

Liam only made it a few seconds before he jumped up, paid his respects, grabbed his bag, and left. *I'll probably never return*, he thought. And that was fine. He wasn't in the market for psychoanalysis.

As he drove past the dojo the second time, Sensei was in the open doorway. Waving.

It was nearly eleven by the time he approached Moose Hollow. He knew he should go home, shower, and settle into the couch in Colton's living room, but nervous energy coursed through him, leaving painful little trails like miniature lightning strikes. He had to get out and walk it off. He pulled over and ditched his gi pants for jeans and running shoes, put a fleece jacket on over his damp T-shirt, and drove into town.

He convinced himself this was a good idea, that it would calm him down. And as he pulled into Moose Hollow, he dropped in for a particular brand of ginger candy they sold at the gas station. But after he got that, there was no real reason to drive into town. So he walked instead. Walking was always a good idea. And the closer he got to Moose on the Loose, the more he reasoned with himself. He didn't want to see Avery or check to see if Griff was still at her place. He just wanted to tell her not to give up on her dream. But they were not good enough friends for a late-night conversation like that. And he still had a target on his back. He promised himself he would walk right by, get being near her out of his system, and then go home. And hope Colton let him sleep in.

It was a cold night, and beautiful, with a breeze and a clear black sky filled with stars and galaxies. And going up and down the streets that he found so familiar, he still felt lost in the middle of it all. It was a Saturday night, and a few people strolled the sidewalks or sat talking on the sidewalk benches. The light was on in Avery's upstairs hallway, but the curtains were drawn in her bedroom. Maybe she was still awake. But that wasn't any of his business. He kept walking, over the hollow sidewalks and past empty stores and the neon-lit bars.

"Liam." It was a woman's voice. A familiar one. He didn't want to see anyone he knew, he just wanted to walk off these nerves and then sleep the world away. But he stopped, and behind him he found Lynn waving and smiling. "I knew that was you!" she called. She hurried over to him, hugging her arms around herself against the cold. "How funny you're here. I was in town with the reunion committee. If I thought you were interested in that sort of thing, I would have invited you. Come on in, everyone would love to see you."

It took him a moment to realize she was talking about a high school reunion. "We have a reunion coming up?"

She laughed and flipped her hair back over her shoulder. "There's an all-class reunion every year, Liam. Which you miss every year. You should give it a try."

"Thanks for coming out to say hi, but I'm just out for a walk. Have fun, Lynn."

He was about to go when she grabbed hold of his arm. "Come in," she said, smiling. "Just for a minute. Let me buy you a drink. Everyone is by the pool tables, but you don't have to go back there if you don't feel like chatting. Come on inside. I'm freezing to death, so don't make me keep asking."

It wasn't until he passed the giant moose carved out of a tree trunk inside the bar that he realized he was at the Lantern Bar, Griff's favorite haunt. He scanned the crowd. No sign of him, thankfully. Besides, he couldn't imagine why Lynn would want to be here if Griff was here. Lynn leaned her elbows on the bar and blinked huge eyes at him. "What can I get you?"

"Water would be good," he said.

"Two glasses of red wine," she told the bartender, and she winked at Liam. *It could have been worse*, he thought. It dawned on him that it had been awhile since he'd been in a place that had red, white, or pink as the extent of its wine list. But this wasn't a good place for him to be now, or ever. He needed to chat for a bit and make his exit. The deafening nineties' music wasn't making him feel any better, and neither was the fact that Lynn sat down and patted the seat of the stool next to her as if he were a toddler who needed to be coaxed. "Just a sip or two," she said, reading his mood well enough. "What's got you all growly tonight?"

"Just tired. It's been a long day." *I'm an uncle. And I already stink at it.*

She laughed. "Well, you came to the right place for not sleeping."

She tugged at one of the scarlet strands of her silky hair. She looked away, toward the pool tables in the back, and waved at someone there. A few people waved back. Their faces were familiar, but their names would take time to conjure. Moose Hollow was a small town, but he didn't move in those circles.

He didn't belong in those circles. And just like that, in the distant presence of classmates, it was there again. The feeling that he was less than them. That there was something critical lacking in him.

He just needed sleep, some rational part of his brain decided.

Lynn looked him in the eye again, settled one manicured hand on his knee, and leaned in a little closer. "I'd rather be with you." Her breath smelled of wine, though she hadn't had a drink from her glass yet. And she was giving him such a studied, wide-eyed look. It didn't feel natural at all. Still, he was sure it worked for her, most of the time.

He used reaching for his glass of wine as an excuse to shift his knee away from her, took a drink, and tried to come up with the perfect thing to say. "I think I should go."

Before he could say another word, he saw her blink. No, wince. That kind of reaction from just saying he wanted to go? He'd underestimated how fragile she was. Again. "I have an early morning tomorrow," he added.

"With that new girl in town?"

He frowned. "Who?"

"Avery. The cute short girl."

She wasn't short. Then again, most girls probably seemed short to Lynn. He played dumb. "Avery who owns Moose on the Loose?"

"That's the one. I met her. I thought she seemed nice enough." Lynn swirled the wine in her glass and took a sip.

"No, not her. She is a client, but I don't have an appointment with her."

"You like her too," Lynn said. "Throw a little fresh meat in the water, and all the boys circle like sharks. That's the problem with you men."

He noticed it now, the slight slurring of certain words. This wasn't anywhere near Lynn's first glass of wine. And this wasn't a version of Lynn he particularly liked.

"You always want the newest model," she continued. "You can't see what's been right in front of you right from the beginning." Her gaze shot past Liam, and she raised her glass as if giving a toast. "And here's the proof right now."

Every hair on the back of Liam's neck prickled. He didn't have to turn around to know that Griff was walking in the door. Call it instinct or just adding up the clues, either way, he knew it. So instead of turning around, he listened. He put his feet on the ground and pushed himself a little bit away from the bar to give himself room to maneuver. Griff walked right up to them and gave Lynn a kiss on the cheek.

*What on earth?* Liam's alarm ratcheted up a little. Why were those two still friends? Griff raised a hand to the bartender. "Bubba. Champagne over here, ASAP."

Then he faced Liam. "Well hey there, Liam. You look like hell. And smell like it too. What happened?"

Liam smiled at him and slowly took a sip of wine. Griff appeared to be alone, but there was no telling what allies he had in the drunken crowd.

Lynn gestured toward the champagne bottle that the bartender thumped down in front of them. "What are you celebrating?" The bartender ripped off the foil, and Liam decided the chances that his name was Bubba were slim to none. But as much money as Griff spent at the place, he could probably call him anything he wanted.

"It's what *we're* celebrating," Griff said. "We're celebrating me."

Lynn leveled a flat stare at him. For the life of him, Liam couldn't get a bead on her, or Griff, at all. But she didn't seem afraid or uncomfortable. And that meant there was no reason Liam had to stay. "Great. Here, Griff, I was just leaving. You're welcome to my seat."

"No, don't," Lynn said, reaching out for his arm again.

He didn't have any trouble at all reading Griff's gaze as it shifted from her hand to Liam's face. And it didn't match the smile on his face. "No, don't," he parroted. "Besides. I have you to thank for this celebration, at least a little bit. You see, I am officially one deal away from Daddy handing me the keys to the new Bozeman office. More money, more fun, and less of Daddy's supervision."

Liam didn't take the bait. "Glad to help."

The way Griff shifted his position was subtle but effective. He put one meaty hand on Lynn's shoulder, jostling her slightly as he spoke. The rest of his attention was focused on Liam, who he blocked from leaving the bar—unless he was willing to vault the stool. If Liam stood and tried to push past him now, there was going to be a confrontation. Wryly, Liam wished it had happened a few pushups and front kicks ago.

"Where have you been, anyway?" Lynn asked, shrugging off his hand. "You said you were going to be here hours ago."

"Funny you should ask. I was at Avery Maier's place. Liam scared the living hell out of her, and she's ready to sell. I'm going to make a deal that my dad couldn't even make, and for less money. Let's just say that Dad didn't put the quality time into Tabitha that I've put into Avery."

Liam rose to his feet, and Griffin looked straight down his nose at him. All Liam could think was one short, sharp jab to the solar plexus and Griffin would fold. That would be instantly followed by one kick to the groin, and he'd catch him with a knee to the face on the way down.

*No one in your state of mind is allowed to spar in my dojo.*

*I don't play dirty.*

He needed to leave. "Goodbye," Liam said. He rubbed his own forehead, a subtle way to get his hand up and ready to block a head shot.

Griff smiled. In a quiet growl, he said, "You have to come through me first."

"Liam, don't," Lynn said. He glanced at her. She was telling *him* to stop?

It was enough to distract him. Griff got the first shot in, point blank to the gut. It was a stupid punch to a stupid target since two inches higher would have floored him. Griff didn't even have time to pull his fist back before Liam punched him twice, once in the solar plexus and then quickly in the jaw. He hit him hard enough to hurt, and nothing more. He could control his anger.

Griff fell back onto the floor. "What the hell was that for?" Griffin yelled. Loudly. And theatrically.

"I'm calling the cops," the bartender said behind him. Beside him, Lynn was sitting still, eyes wide, hands over her mouth as she turned away from Liam. And in front of him, Griff kept up the act, demanding to know why Liam had hit him. As someone helped him to his feet, Griff started laughing. "Is there a bruise? I hope there's a bruise. Women love that, don't they, Liam?"

He'd been had. Brilliantly. Liam walked out, knowing this wasn't the end of it. He made it just past Avery's store and Hallowell Realty when the police cruiser drove up the road. Then blue and red lights rotated his own shadow around and around the nearly empty main street, marking him with spotlights that would be the talk of the town by noon tomorrow.

The window on the police car rolled down. "Get in," Mike said.

# CHAPTER 28

*L*iam's head was pounding with memories, frustration, and guilt. He walked to the back door, but Mike shook his head. "Not there," he said, and with a thumb, he gestured to the passenger seat. "Put your seat belt on."

Confused, Liam walked around and climbed in. Mike turned right, and then right again. "My car is at the gas station," Liam said.

Mike chuckled. "I don't think so, son." He reached up to one shoulder and said, "326."

"Go ahead, 326," a woman's voice said over the radio.

"I have the suspect detained, please have 344 interview the complainant at the Lantern Bar."

"Ten-four."

"Detained," Liam said.

"Not arrested." Then he read Liam his rights. It was so surreal and so unbearable that Liam found himself fighting the urge to laugh at the lunacy of it all. Griff had outsmarted him. Liam thought himself so clever, so self-controlled. And that lying hunk of meat had played him.

They pulled up to the police station, and Mike led him into his office and closed the door without a single word. With a long sigh, he settled in behind the desk. "You are causing me trouble again."

Liam stared at his own interlaced hands. This was just another race, he assured himself. Maybe a short one, perhaps a marathon, but this would all sort itself out. He just had to stay cool and keep putting one foot in front of the other.

"I can see you're eager to talk," Mike said.

Liam glanced up. "Am I supposed to be?"

Mike shook his head. "I don't think it's wise to be difficult with me right now, son."

"What do you want me to say?"

Mike leaned back. "You really asking?"

"Yes."

"I'm glad you're really asking because I know exactly what I want you to say." Mike's drawl was slow as molasses, as if he enjoyed baiting Liam.

"Go ahead," Liam said.

"Before I do, I want to tell you something interesting."

Liam rolled his eyes. He knew it was rude, but he just couldn't stop himself.

"Yesterday an apartment was broken into," Mike said. "Not much was taken. The place was tossed pretty good. But there were some odd things about it. Electronics were left behind, but the pantry was dumped out onto the kitchen floor. Vents were ripped out. The stove hood was even torn apart. Does that seem normal to you?"

"You think I broke into some apartment?" Liam said. He tried to sound smooth and unflustered, but next to Mike's perfect drawl he probably sounded like Kermit the Frog.

"Nope. Because you were in Moose Hollow. And the apartment isn't." Mike lifted a sheet of paper off his desk and read the address aloud. He added "Chicago" at the end, probably for effect, but Liam had no trouble recognizing the apartment where he'd lived with Maccus for a year.

Liam sat up. "Was Mack okay?"

"Mack?"

"Maccus Fortner. And he had a new roommate, a girl I think. Are they okay?"

"Yup. All okay. No one was home."

Liam tried to sort it out. Why hadn't Maccus told him? And why did Mike know? "How did you find out?"

"I asked someone there to let me know if anything unusual happened with your associates. Those Chicago folks are helpful sometimes. I'd like to repay the favor by catching the guy who broke into that apartment." He leaned forward, the bulletproof vest under his uniform shirt sliding up a little as he did. "Here's what I want you to say, Liam. For starters, I want you to tell me what happened tonight. The whole thing. Preferably in chronological order. Because right now one of my officers is getting a statement from, I assume, Griffin Hallowell. And I can be pretty certain he's going to have a lot to say about you."

Liam stared at his hands again. The inside of his brain felt like a war zone. Every single word he might say could and would be used against him, just like Mike had said in the car. That was pitted against the patient look in Mike's eyes. But that was his job, to trick people into saying something incriminating. Yet he had a reputation as a fair man. One who cared about justice.

But the fact that Liam was "detained" was proof that there wasn't going to be any justice here. Besides, he'd already lost. It was the price he had to pay for being played.

If Mike was getting impatient, he gave no sign of it.

Then Liam started talking. He told Mike about being restless, driving into town, and going for a walk. Then meeting Lynn, her buying wine, and Griff's arrival. His posturing and unspoken threat. The first punch, and Liam's two, and the words spoken afterward. The whole thing just made him feel more stupid the more he talked.

Mike listened. "I have a few questions," he finally said. He asked about the walk, driving into town, and where he'd been before, who could vouch for him, and how much he'd had to drink. The thought of Mike calling Sensei was just one more dose of humiliation.

"Why did you walk into town again?" Mike asked.

Liam stared at him and his pleasantly neutral face. "It really isn't any of your business."

"See, now, why be like that? I thought we were making real progress."

"Fine. I had someone on my mind. I couldn't sleep. The drive didn't work, so I thought walking might."

"Thinking about Griff?"

"No."

"Lynn?"

"Neither of them. This person wasn't there. They wouldn't be at a bar. But they don't have anything to do with this. Or me. In general."

"They. Okay. We'll leave this girl out of it, for now. So let me ask you this, do you think Griff has anything to do with the break-ins?"

"What? No. Griff's just a local thug."

"Hmm. Speaking of Chicago."

Liam sighed. "Can we just talk about it later? I want to go home."

"You know Griff is going to have a barroom full of witnesses talking about how you assaulted him. I have to wait to hear what my officer finds out, and then I have to make a decision, and I'm pretty sure it's not going to go well for you. Actions have consequences. So while you're waiting, what information did you steal from Ackerman, Jones & Fetterman? And why don't you just give it back? If it's extortion you're going for, you just might have gotten yourself in over your head."

Liam had never told Mike that he had taken anything from his former employer. "I'm not blackmailing anyone."

"Hmm." Mike tapped his pen against the desk. "Do you know a guy named Arthur Smith? How about William Sartie? William goes by Billy. Both are from Chicago. Thought you might know them."

"It's a big city," Liam said. Mike's ramblings were driving him insane.

"Small world, though. I just thought maybe Moose Hollow had some sort of booster out there in Illinois. First you come back, then two complete strangers from Chicago show up. I find that interesting. Although you guys may not have crossed paths since you aren't in the same line of work. They're in public relations."

"For who?" Liam asked, playing along. Maybe if he cooperated Mike would let him go.

"Well, that's just it. Arthur and Billie work for a holding company run out of a warehouse. My new buddy in Chicago seemed to find that a little unusual. Of course, he'd never even heard of Moose Hollow."

"Maybe they're on vacation," Liam said. His buzzing brain was just now beginning to get what Mike was driving at. "Where are they staying?"

"Vacations, plural. And they don't spend much time here when they come. Must be staying with friends. Word is they like to hang out at the Lantern when they're in town. Which they aren't, right now. Maybe you should keep an eye out for them, say hi if you spot them someone wearing a Bears cap, I suppose. Everyone from Chicago does, right? Oh look, there's Officer Haynes. You stay right here while I go have a chat with him."

Liam felt his world spinning out of control. Mike was warning him. Why was this mess still haunting him? He hadn't made a move on the information he held, but neither had he given it back. What he'd meant as an insurance policy had turned out to be just the opposite. When he first copied the documents, he considered taking them straight to the authorities. But it hadn't taken him long to realize no one would believe him. *Maybe Mike would,* he thought, *whatever good that would do.* Liam was surprised to find that Mike had been investigating Arthur and Billy. The man knew more about the break-ins at Cash's office and the hotel than he was letting on.

The officer had always been that way. He knew about Griff and Eli and Chris. He'd probably known all along, but Liam hadn't given him the information he'd needed to prosecute. Looking back now, knowing the power the Hallowells held, Liam wasn't sure that it hadn't been the right idea to keep their identities secret. Griff's dad would have spent years trying to get back at Liam and his parents. He was just that sort of guy. But Mike had been mad, too—in a quiet way. Liam could still picture Mike's expression: anger with a heaping dose of disappointment.

Maybe Mike was someone he could trust. Maybe he needed to tell him everything.

The door behind him opened and Mike entered. "Liam, the investigating officer has decided to forward your case to the city attorney, and he very well may press charges." The officer rubbed the back of his hand against his forehead.

"What? Are you serious?"

"You should know that the officer, despite consistent witness testimony against you, has serious concerns about their testimony being compromised."

Liam processed that. One more black mark against him, one more dead end.

"You are free to go for now. Unless you would like to talk, we could go—"

"I'd better save my voice for the city attorney, right?"

"Liam, I think my officer has chosen a wise—"

"Am I free to go? Like, out of Montana?"

"It might not be the best decision. But yes, legally, at this time you are."

Liam stormed past him. He didn't have anything left to tell him. Or anyone.

# CHAPTER 29

*Please let her like it,* Avery prayed into the silence around her. She was standing in the hallway outside her closed bedroom door as anxiety flooded her heart once again. *Not for my sake. Do it for her. And I promise I'll never put someone at risk like this again.* There was no answer but the soft whir of the fan in the window.

"I finished changing. You need to come in here," Poppy called.

When she opened the door, Poppy was standing with her arms open wide and tears in her eyes. "I am so ready to get married now."

A laugh escaped Avery's lips. Then she got herself back under control. Nothing was ever perfect, especially after just one other fitting, and so much of the overskirt was new. "Let me see." She closed the tiny buttons Poppy couldn't reach and eyed the seams. She checked the length. Looked for gaps at the cap sleeves, lumps and bumps, anything at all to make the dress look less than perfect. But it looked exactly the way she had imagined it. She wasn't sure that had ever happened before.

"We're coming!" Mara finally made it down the hall and

around the corner, dumping a bag in the doorway. If Paul was disturbed by having his mommy run in high heels, he gave no sign of it. Then again, she had her hands pressed to either side of his head to keep him from flopping around. "What did I miss? Oh. Oh!"

Mara came closer. Four-inch heels, Avery guessed. And looking awfully fit. Maybe that was the benefit of wearing high heels and a baby carrier all day.

"Oh, my gosh, Poppy. Look at you." She circled her slowly as Paul cooed. "Look at your butt. Seriously, girl."

Poppy laughed. "I hardly even have a rear end."

"You do in this dress." She finished her circle. "This is so you." Then she said to Avery, "This is so her."

Avery tried to be professional, but she felt like cheering. Things had never gone like this for her, ever. Especially that summer she'd spent trying to hawk her goods at climbing hot spots and desert festival sites for the endless parade of nice, broke, and slightly wild girls who just didn't have the money for a handmade dress. Especially since the ones shipped in from overseas sweatshops only cost fifteen dollars.

"I forgot to show you," Avery said. She came over and undid the four hidden buttons that were roughly knee-length in the back. Their placement and how it affected the design had been one of her biggest concerns. Once they were let down, the dress had a small train. That brought a few more tears to Poppy's eyes, which seemed to be contagious. At least until Paul started hiccupping impossibly tiny little hiccups, which made everyone laugh.

"Wait, you need a veil," Mara said.

"I'm not wearing one."

"Whatever. Avery, any ideas?"

Of course she had an idea. But Avery was even less sure about the veil than she had been about the dress. "I might have something." She went over to her sewing table and lifted the scrap of fabric that was hiding her idea for a veil. "It's a little different." She unwrapped the veil from around the comb. "I was picturing you wearing your hair back, but not too tight."

"Exactly. Natural, but not messy," Mara concurred. Poppy listened without comment.

"So assuming you have some sort of fancy bun or something at the base of your neck—"

"Ooh, I can do that," Mara said, and she pulled a comb out of her purse. When she started teasing Poppy's hair, Poppy swatted at her hand, but it didn't slow her down. Paul made a soft gurgling sound as Mara bunched Poppy's pale, almost white hair into a ponytail. "Now what?"

Avery did a half-hearted job of hiding the veil as she came around the back of her friend. "This goes here," she said, pushing the comb into the top of the bun. "So this has pearls and silk baby's breath, so I figured you would put real baby's breath in all around here, like a tiara, and it would blend in with the veil."

"What is this made of? It's incredible."

It was silk tulle, but Avery didn't say because Poppy might realize it would have been tremendously expensive to purchase, and probably impossible to find in just the right shade of creamy white. In reality, the fabric was yet another thrift store treasure. Luckily, the ruined part of the fabric could be easily cut out and the rest trimmed in lace to match the dress.

"Does the bride get to see?" Poppy asked pointedly.

"Not yet," Mara said. "Got any more of the little fake flowers?"

Avery nodded and pulled some from a drawer, slipping them into Poppy's hair like a natural crown. Then she stood back and sighed. The veil was perfect. So much better than when she'd tried it on herself, just to see how it fit and if the comb would hold.

They finally let Poppy go back to the full-length mirror. She looked at it from all angles and used the hand mirror to see it from behind. Then she said, "You're right. I'm wearing a veil."

Mara cheered, which set off Paul. "He's hungry, again. Avery, do you mind?"

"Not at all." At the sound of the baby's soft voice, Avery felt the ache of loss again, but it was okay. She'd made it all this time this morning with Mara without feeling any pain at all. Eventually, it would get better. "You can sit on my bed. Do you need anything?"

"Nope, we're good." Mara picked up the bag she had dropped on the way in the door and settled in, looking awfully comfortable for a new mother. Avery thought she never could have been so confident. Or peaceful. *It was just as well I didn't have a baby*, she thought for the thousandth time. And even better that Paul would grow up with a mom and a dad who loved him.

Poppy was still looking at the mirror. "Why aren't you doing this for a living?" she asked.

It took Avery a moment to realize the question was directed at her. "I don't know what you mean."

"You have that whole back room. Once you mentioned something about renting it out. So why not rent it out to yourself?"

"That wouldn't work," she said. Both of the other women looked at her as if she was crazy. "It would make a lot more sense to let a successful business rent out that spot instead."

"So why haven't you done that?" Poppy asked, direct as always.

Avery shrugged and rearranged a few things on her sewing table. She kept it up as long as she felt was necessary, but when she finally looked up, she realized both women had been staring at her the whole time.

"What's going on, Avery?" Mara asked.

Poppy studied her so hard Avery could have crawled right out of her skin. "Are you giving up?" Poppy asked.

*Giving up.* Avery's mood plummeted as quickly as it had soared. "I'm not giving up. I'm broke." She sighed, then laughed. "And this is not the time to talk about it, with you all beautiful in your wedding dress and Mara and Paul over there."

"I'll get out of the dress. Then we talk," Poppy informed her.

Avery knew that tone of voice. She took the veil from Poppy's hair and undid some of the tiny velvet-covered buttons, and Poppy slipped into the bathroom to change. When she returned, there was a moment of grace as Paul fell asleep on a blanket Mara spread out on Avery's bed. Then both women faced Avery, arms crossed, mirroring each other like mismatched twins. "Talk," Mara said firmly.

Avery talked. She told them about the insurance money. And Griffin's sale offer, which he said he was still negotiating with his father, but should arrive any day. Then because everything was already out, she told them about the basement and the noises at night and how she knew it was crazy, but it scared her to death. And she told them about last night, when she'd heard knocking on the pipes and what sounded like banging on the floor of the store below. "Sometimes I feel like I'm losing my mind," she managed to say without crying.

They both listened intently, making sympathetic noises here and there just when she needed it. When she was done, no one spoke for a while.

"I'd be freaked out too," Poppy finally said. Her mouth drew tight and her eyebrows pinched downward. "I'm trying to find the right way to say this."

"That'd be a first," Mara said.

"I have a gut feeling. I'm not saying you shouldn't sell. I'm not saying you should ever spend the night here alone again, either. It's just this feeling that you're under so much pressure that this can't be the right time to make such a big decision. Is the insurance company going to give you any time at all to repay? Can you hold off a little longer?"

"The lawyer thought they might give us a month to reach an agreement. It's been a couple weeks since he said that." And she hadn't heard a thing from him...or Liam, who had once been her go-between.

"Avery, I know Griffin is your friend, but it just seems like having him advise you on selling to his father is a conflict of interest. I wish you had more time to think, and to get good counsel." Poppy put her fingertips to her mouth. "I'll be right back," she said, and she left the room without explanation.

Mara watched her go, then fixed her gaze on Avery. "How much of this leaving business has to do with Liam almost getting arrested a few weeks ago?"

Avery shook her head quickly. "It doesn't. It's not like that. We aren't dating or anything. Besides, I found out about the insurance in April." Unhappy with how she had rolled the veil, she looked for a place to hang it up properly.

"You know they haven't even pressed charges."

"It really isn't any of my business, Mara. I haven't spoken to Liam in weeks." She'd heard more than she wanted to know about the fight with Griffin, if it could be called a fight. It sounded more like Liam had attacked Griffin for no reason. She'd waited to hear from him, at first, but Liam evidently didn't want to talk to her. His silence spoke volumes. "It's not like we're close."

"He didn't talk to me, either." Mara's expression made it clear how much that irritated her. "So I went and talked to the police."

"What?"

"Actually, I talked to the chief of police. Officer Mike. Well, Chief Mike now. We go way back, to when he was Highway Patrol. He cited me for careless driving when I rolled my car."

"You what? Oh my gosh."

"Don't worry, we were all okay. It could have been a lot worse." She glanced over to where Paul was sleeping. "Especially for you, peanut. Anyway, Chief Mike is trickier than you'd think. I went in there all mad because of the history between Griff and Liam. I mean Liam almost died, for heaven's sake, and no one got charged, but now they want to charge Liam for Griff being Griff? Really?"

Mara put her fists on her hips. "Anyone who knows anything can see Liam could go all Krav Maga on Griff and rip out his larynx with one eagle-dragon-claw-whatever strike if he wanted. Besides, why would he go to the Lantern if he wanted to start a fight? Anyway, I gave Chief a piece of my mind, and he did that super cool cowboy thing he does, and the next thing I know we're talking due process. Somewhere along the way I figure out that no matter what he says, Chief doesn't think Liam did anything wrong. But the witnesses are supporting Griff's story, which is no surprise at all. Chief says it would just take one conflicting account to make the charges go away if the right person was in the right place to have seen everything, and it dawns on me, someone must have been there. Someone saw the whole thing. And Liam might know who that someone was, if he would just stinking talk to me. But you know him. Stubborn."

Avery blinked, finally. She tried to process what Mara had said, and the first thing that came out of her mouth was, "He almost died?"

"Oh yeah. Not that he ever talked about it to me. But the story was online. I bet he never told you, either. Wait, Griff didn't tell you about it, did he?"

"What does Griff have to do with anything?"

"If he ever tells you, you go straight to Chief, okay?"

Frustrated, Avery asked, "Tell me what?"

Poppy's voice interrupted them, coming closer down the hallway. "Why? Because I am the bride. The. Bride. I get to make demands on you because I want everything perfect and I'm busy...yes." She turned the corner into the bedroom, her phone still pressed to her ear. "Don't mess this up. I want to see results today. Bye."

Mara made a face. "You've gone bridezilla."

Poppy considered that. "Hmm. Power really does corrupt. Oh well. Whatever it takes." She turned to Avery. "So Sierra was coming in today, right? Good. Mara can answer whatever questions she has. I have an errand for you."

# CHAPTER 30

*S*he went straight for the puppies, and that wasn't going to work.

It had been a horrible plan from the start, but Poppy was unusually adamant, and he couldn't say no to her. Besides the fact that Colton would kill him, he was becoming fond of her. There was something light and welcoming about her that made him feel like she'd been family for a long, long time. But that didn't make what she asked of him any less ridiculous.

Poppy had called to tell him Avery needed a dog. Today. It had to be a good, strong dog, one who would make her feel safe. The moment he heard the word "safe," he remembered what Griff had said about him scaring Avery, and he felt awful. And responsible. But judging by the look on Avery's face, Poppy hadn't bothered to tell Avery she was getting a dog. Neither had she mentioned that she'd ordered Liam to rush over and drive her to the closest animal shelter, which was in Billings. Poppy had just shooed her into his car and told her Liam would explain on the way.

Avery didn't have much to say about their mission. She listened, probably, as she looked out the window and away from him. He didn't like it when she did that. And then she told him she'd go to the shelter to please Bridezilla, but they better be back before noon. And after about ten more miles of silence, she added, "The last thing I need is a dog."

She didn't have anything more to say. Liam decided that was for the best, since the next logical thing for her to mention was the fact that her boyfriend had accused Liam of assault. If she had half a brain, and she most certainly did, she'd think it was true. And in the twenty-something miles that passed in silence, he spent a lot of time coming to two realizations. First, avoiding Avery hadn't made anything any better. And second, a dog was a brilliant idea.

So when they walked into the shelter and Avery went straight for the little enclosure in the lobby, which was over-flowing with chubby puppies, he tried to get things back on track.

"Hello," he said with a smile to the woman at the front desk. She glanced up without interrupting the scrolling she was doing on the computer. "We'd like to see the dogs you have for adoption."

The woman reached with her free hand and handed a clip-board to him. "Please fill out the application first. Are you two married?"

"No," Avery said clearly. Well, at least she'd been paying attention.

"Then we need to know who the primary owner will be."

Avery came over then, and she checked through the applica-tion. "Yes, I own my home. For now. Indoor, definitely. Who leaves their dog out at night?" she muttered as she checked the boxes. "There are bears and moose. Nope, no fence."

That statement made the woman's head pop up again. "You don't have a fence?"

"I don't have a yard to put a fence around."

"Well, just fill out the rest of the application, and we'll give you a call."

Avery glanced at Liam, and he spoke up. "We haven't even looked at the dogs yet."

"We'll let you know."

"Let us know what?" he asked evenly. "If we're allowed to look at the dogs you have up for adoption?"

"We'll let you know, but a home without a fence is just too dangerous for a dog." The judgment in her voice was unmistakable.

Avery didn't say anything. She took her application off the clipboard and walked out the door.

Liam wanted to make it right. He stood there for a minute, trying to think of something to say, then he gave up and followed Avery. By the time he made it out into the sunshine, she was already in the car. He saw her through the windshield, already looking out the passenger window again. Only this time, she swiped a knuckle across the side of one eye. He'd made her cry. He resisted the urge to go back inside and cause a scene. It wouldn't make her feel better, but it might have made him feel less useless. Instead, he got inside and drove toward home. But he was so distracted he took a wrong turn, and it took a few minutes for him to realize it. That was when Avery finally spoke up. "You know, I've had a dog almost my whole life. Usually a couple at a time."

"Really?" Liam was so relieved to hear her speak that the word came out a little too loud and fast.

"I almost didn't go to college because every place I wanted to go wanted me to spend the first year in the dorm. No dogs allowed. I couldn't even imagine how I was going to sleep without a dog at the end of my bed."

Liam waited to be sure she was finished before saying, "We allow dogs in some rooms. My dad was worried their dogs would get in a fight with our dogs and we'd have trouble. Or maybe it was just one more thing they'd have to worry about."

"That's so sad," she said.

That wasn't the response he'd expected. "Did you have a favorite?"

"Yup." She turned away again. "All of them. But my dad was right. It wasn't fair to have a dog when I didn't have a home. Just like you need a home if you have a kid, right?"

There was something about the tone of her voice that made her sound heartbroken, but he felt lost in the conversation. He waited, but she didn't say anything more. Frustrated by one more street that dead-ended at the railroad tracks, he pulled over and grabbed his phone. If she hadn't been in the car, he wouldn't have pulled over. But it was the law. And he needed to not cause any more trouble for her, or him.

He tapped on the map, trying not to let her see because it would tell her that he had no idea where he was or what he was doing. But Liam knew which street he was on, and if he knew how far he was from the shelter, he'd know whether or not to turn around. "Animal adoption," he typed, trying to remember the official name of the shelter.

The result his phone gave him wasn't very close to where he was. He stared at it. Yellowstone Animal Shelter. That wasn't where they had just been. He silently debated with himself, and then he memorized where the cross streets were. He flipped the phone over, out of sight, and without asking her, he drove toward the other shelter.

When he pulled into the parking lot, she shot him a nasty look and said, "You don't listen very well, do you?"

Nope. Not when he didn't want to. "Maybe I want a dog," Liam said.

She huffed.

He left the car running and went in.

This shelter was nothing like the other one. It was a relatively small building in an industrial area, and there was no cute, comfortable, puppy-filled waiting room. It smelled like wet dogs, not cherries and artificial flowers. The woman at the front desk was wearing scrubs and looked absolutely swamped. She glanced up and said, "Can I help you?"

He didn't know what to say.

She put down an armful of pill bottles, picked up two leashes, and then she seemed to realize he wasn't talking. She stopped still and made eye contact. "You okay?"

"Can I have about one minute to talk?"

She tipped her head sideways, then nodded. "Shoot."

"I have a friend in the car. She needs a dog. She's always been around dogs, until she went to college, but she lives in this big building in Moose Hollow, and works there too, and I think the nights get to her. And that's my fault, because she didn't even know there was a basement." Precious seconds were ticking by as he rambled like an idiot. He had to get to the point. "The other shelter wouldn't even talk to her because she hasn't got a fence, and she hasn't got a fence because she hasn't got a yard, she's got an alley and a busy street. But she also has tons of room in her apartment rooms and lots of customers coming in and out of her shop down-stairs, and she likes to walk. And she's nice. And not just to the people she likes, but to the real jerks too, you know? So you can imagine how she'd be with a dog. So I just need to know one thing. If I drag her in here—because she doesn't even want to get out of the car—but if I drag her in here, just for a look, are you going to kick her out because she hasn't got a fence?"

The woman eyed him and looked him up and down. Then she looked out the window where his Toyota sat running. "It depends on the dog," she said.

Relief flooded through him, mostly that she'd managed to look past the nonsense he'd just been spewing. He opened the

door and jogged over to the car to turn it off. "Come on," he said
to Avery.

She glared at him.

"We are only looking. Okay? Please. Just come in so you and
I can both tell Poppy that you actually met a dog."

She sighed and followed him in.

The woman was sitting at the front desk now, sorting
through an enormous pile of mail. "Go on back," she said with a
tip of her head. "Dogs are on the right. Let me know if you want
to meet anyone in there, and I'll bring them out to the backyard
for you."

The animals were in chain-link kennels, most with a blanket
and a toy, and all of them on damp concrete that smelled of
disinfectant. The barking started the second the door opened,
and it was deafening.

Avery crept up the first aisle, her head swiveling as she
looked on both sides at the dogs in cages, one after another.
Beagles, a terrier, a pit bull, a blue heeler, a tan-colored mutt, a
dog that looked like a short, fat border collie. He only made it
halfway down the aisle before he wanted to leave. Every single
dog. If he'd been a kid, he would have wanted all of them. No
matter about the missing fur, the cropped tail, the crazy barking. He would have happily made a life with any of them. Or all
of them. Now he could hardly stand to be around them because
he knew not all of these dogs would be going home to a boy
who would love them no matter what.

Avery was hugging her arms around her ribs. Liam understood how she felt. She kept walking, eyeing every single dog.
They reached the end of the aisle, and she dutifully turned and
walked down the next one, too. This time she didn't even look
at the cages. And when she reached the end of that aisle, she
spent a little too much time reading the notices pinned on the
bulletin board.

But there was one more aisle, this one facing a cinder block wall. Here the dogs were noticeably more nervous and agitated. Probably they were here so that they didn't have to face open cages full of other dogs. At the next to the last cage, Liam saw a dark dog. His first thought was that it looked a lot like a German shepherd, which would make it good for protecting Avery, but it was curled up in the back corner of its cage, turned away from him. The dog opened his eyes, stared at Liam, and curled even farther away.

No wonder he was here. He looked scary. He had the dark shepherd face, but his eyes were milky white, and dark smudges around his eyes gave him a fierce expression. *This dog will never find a home*, he thought.

He heard Avery approaching. She walked right by without looking. But as she did, the dog looked up and then suddenly came to the gate of the cage, tail at half mast, almost as if he recognized her. He watched Avery walk away. Then he looked up at Liam, looked once more to where Avery had disappeared around the corner, and then lowered his head.

He stepped slowly back to his corner and curled into a tiny ball with a sigh Liam heard over the barking.

He could be reading too much into it. It was a dog, not a person. But Liam felt as if the dog had made his feelings more than clear, and that watching Avery walk away had just broken whatever little pieces were left of his heart.

Liam jogged back down the aisle, getting to the door just as Avery reached for it. She was going to make a break for the car again, he knew it.

"Did you want to meet anyone?" the woman asked.

"Yes," Liam said firmly. Avery turned around with a frown, and what might have been tears in her eyes. He really couldn't make more of a mess of this if he tried. "The German shepherd with the white eyes."

The woman looked at him with a frown. "Sinatra?"

"I'm sorry, I didn't catch the name."

The woman leaned back and put both hands over her mouth, and then she stared at nothing on the desk and rocked back and forth. He'd said something wrong, and he had no idea what it was.

"He has to have a fence, doesn't he?"

She shook her head. Then she removed her hands to say, "I don't know what he needs. He's been adopted twice and returned both times. He just doesn't connect with anyone. The second adopter gave him two weeks, but all he would do is sit in the corner of the kitchen. I just…" The hands came back again. Then through them, she said, "I just don't think it's worth getting his hopes up again. I don't know the whole story on that dog, but I just don't think he's going to work out. Not yet."

# CHAPTER 31

*A*very was done. She walked toward the door.

"Five minutes in the yard," Liam said too loudly. "That's all I'm asking."

Avery turned just in time to see the woman smirk and hear her say, "I've already seen how long your minutes are." But she stood up and put a hand on the door that led to the loud, dismal, awful place. "Go out front, turn left, and go through the gate. Close it behind you, and I'll meet you out there."

"What are you doing?" Avery asked Liam.

"Just meeting one dog," Liam said, palms in the air as if he was surrendering.

"You do that. I'll be in the car."

"Come on. This way you can tell Poppy you tried."

"Tried what? Being yet another person to turn this dog down, proving he has no hope of ever having a family? How does that help anyone, including the dog?" Avery had tried, and she had more than fulfilled any obligation she had to the bride. She was just ready for this torture to be over. But when Liam held the door open for her, she reluctantly walked back on the overgrown sidewalk to the tall chain-link gate. Then she stood there in the sun, on the only patch of grass visible anywhere on the property. It was more than she wanted to know about the life these animals lived. "Why don't they fix this place up?"

"This is a no-kill shelter, so I have a pretty good idea why," Liam said. "You probably do, too."

Of course. Because landscaping and fresh paint didn't mean much when the funds could go to rescuing another animal instead. And if some of the animals were like Sinatra, this might be the only life they would ever have.

She wondered which dog was Sinatra. None of them had stood out to her. She couldn't remember seeing a dog with white eyes, whatever that meant anyway. And why was Liam pushing so hard? And why was Poppy? Maybe the wedding stress was getting to her. Avery found herself just wishing the wedding was over. Then what? Then she would sell the building and try to rebuild her life.

Another gate opened, admitting the woman from the front desk first, and several feet of a leash stretched taut behind her. She pulled gently, and reluctantly a dog followed. He was dark, and his large ears looked like low-set radar dishes. Then his brilliant blue-white eyes settled on Avery. His ears lifted. Then his tail went up a little, and he walked quickly over to her. At first she was a little frightened. He looked like a German shepherd—an angry one with dark smudges like war paint around his eyes and fierce blue eyes. But she also recognized the slow, low wag, so she stood her ground. He circled quickly behind her and settled into a seated position, one foot on the toe of her left shoe, and looked up at her. And then he smiled.

He looked right at her and opened his mouth into a wide, toothy smile, with his cheeks all bunched up at the edges. A woman had told her once that dogs didn't smile. She still thought the woman was singularly unobservant. What else could this be but a smile?

Avery leaned over and scratched Sinatra gently under his

chin, and in return, he leaned so hard into her he nearly knocked her over. She had to widen her stance. "He hasn't got white eyes, they're glacier blue," she said. The smile changed the angles on all the black smudges of his face, and he looked as sweet as the day is long. "He doesn't seem very antisocial to me."

She glanced up and caught a look and some silent gestures passing between Liam and the shelter woman.

"I'm not adopting him," Avery said quickly, in case they'd gotten the wrong idea.

"Mind if I ask why?" the woman said.

"I don't have a fence. Or a yard. My dogs at home always had acres and acres to run."

"We have a hard time getting him to leave the doorway when we let him out into the yard," the woman said. "I don't even know if he likes yards."

Liam pulled out his phone. "If you don't mind, I have a few questions."

The woman crossed her arms. "Go for it, Internet trainer."

Liam's mouth quirked at being caught, and Avery might have smiled if this whole outing wasn't so depressing. "Does this dog have a history of aggressive behavior?" he asked

"Not that I know of. In fact, he's had hardly any behavior at all. He was found in the middle of a ranch tied to a rock. He'd been there for at least a few days without food or water. The place was abandoned and had been for sale for years. In other words, someone left him there to die."

"Or to be rescued," Avery said. She couldn't even stand the thought of it.

"And that's what happened. Someone saw him twice, and the second time she cut him free and brought him here."

Avery looked at the dog with concern, and in return, he looked back at her with the same smile and blinking eyes. If she moved her left foot, she was sure he'd fall over sideways trying to stay close to her.

"Okay," Liam said. He sounded a little angry. Avery didn't blame him. "Food aggression?"

"Nope. He doesn't care much when I bring food to him or when I take it away. That explains the ribs sticking out."

Liam consulted his phone. "Startle response?"

"Got any keys? Toss them across the enclosure."

Liam did as she suggested, and they made a loud noise as they collided with the fence and landed on the gravel that bordered the run. The dog came to attention immediately and stepped in front of Avery. He stared for a moment, then circled Avery again, sat, and leaned. After that, everyone stared at Avery. Including the dog.

"I must remind him of someone," Avery said.

"Maybe. Probably. But that doesn't mean he's mistaking you for someone else," the woman said. "Dogs are too smart for that. You sure you don't want to adopt?"

She shook her head. "My life is up in the air."

"You rent, then?"

"She owns her house. And works there too. She owns the Moose on the Loose in Moose Hollow. It's a huge building, and the dog would hardly ever be alone. And there would be customers to interact with, too." If Avery had been holding keys, she would have thrown them at him just to get him to shut up.

"Hmm," the woman said. "You know, these questions you've been asking bring up a good point. Part of the problem we've had with adopting this dog out is that we don't really know what kind of home would be good for him. I wanted to place him with a foster parent until we get a feeling for the kind of home where he'd thrive, but no one has been available to take him on yet."

Liam chimed right in. "But he's pretty comfortable with Avery. So if she spent some time with him, you'd know a lot more. And be able to find him just the right home."

Avery smirked. "Subtle, Liam."

He gave her a bashful look.

"It's true, though," the woman said. "I haven't seen this dog act like this before now, with anyone. Even just a couple days with him would help me out. A couple weeks would be even better. Would you be willing to foster him for a little while? As long as you want. And when your life gets crazy, you can send him back to me."

"You said you didn't think it was a good idea to have him be adopted out and returned again," Avery said.

"Yes. Well." She put her hands on her hips. "I'm trusting you to get to know him well enough that it won't be the same the next time someone wants to bring him home."

"But I don't have dog things. I don't even have a leash."

"We could get one on the way back," Liam said. "Then we could…donate it here when you bring him back. That would be good, right?"

"That would be good," the woman said, nodding at Liam.

The dog looked up at Avery. "This stinks," Avery whispered.

He wagged.

# CHAPTER 32

*L*iam said hello to Sierra, barely. He was far too excited by the extravagant toys and trinkets he'd bought at the pet store, most of which he was carrying—along with a large bag of food and a couple bags of treats. Avery followed with the dog and the bed. Who knew they made $120 dog beds? Did her own mattress even cost that much?

As soon as she saw the dog, Sierra stopped what she was doing and hurried over. She grabbed him by the head, flopped his ears, and kissed him right on the forehead, and Avery froze. "I don't know this dog very well, you might want to—"

"Smooch him," Sierra said. The dog hardly moved at all. When she let go, he glanced at Avery, wagged once, then slipped around the other side of her and out of Sierra's reach.

*Not too bad*, she thought. If the dog was going to spend time at the store, he was bound to have some admirers, especially with those icy blue eyes. He was handling this well for his first time.

"What's his name?" Sierra asked.

"Sinatra," Liam said. He was standing at the door to the back room, and he sounded impatient.

"Absolutely not," Avery said. "His name is Glacier."

"Hello, Glacier," Sierra said.

Avery headed back toward the stairs, and Glacier walked right with her. She wondered if the stairs would spook him, but the dog trotted all the way up beside her like a pro.

"What's wrong with Sinatra?" Liam asked. "He's Ol' Blue Eyes. Get it?"

Avery shook her head. "That's not his name."

"Fine. But now that you've named him, you'll have to keep him."

"Don't push it, Gunnerson," she said, giving him a backward glance as she walked through her bedroom door. He flashed her a smile so brilliant she had to look away to avoid smiling right back at him. A few steps in she realized he wasn't following her, and she looked back. He was setting everything down in her bedroom doorway. "You can come in, you know," she said.

He shook his head. "Nope."

She pointed at Glacier. "I have a chaperone."

"True, and I hope he'd bite anyone who laid a hand on you. But I'll just put the bowls and food in the kitchen."

She took the leash off Glacier's new collar. It was a nice thought that the dog would defend her. She followed Liam to the kitchen and Glacier slowly, methodically checked inside the bathroom and then met her in the kitchen.

Avery had been wanting to do some investigating herself, and now seemed as good a time as any. "So are you going to tell me what happened with Griffin?" she asked Liam.

He hesitated, just for a second, before filling one of the bowls with water. "Nope."

"Why?"

"I'm sure you heard it all from Griff."

He was so frustrating sometimes. "I thought you might have a different point of view."

Liam set down the water and crouched down to read the

food bag. "I forgot to ask how much he weighs, so I don't know how much to feed him."

"A lot. He's skinny. And if you won't tell me about that, why don't you tell me what the issue is between you and Griff?"

Liam looked up at her, took a deep breath, and shook his head slightly. "It doesn't matter anymore, Avery. I'm interviewing at a firm in Helena on Monday. I'll be out of his life."

"What?" Avery felt like she'd been the one punched, not Griff. It took her breath away. And then it made her fighting mad. He'd dragged her around town, forced this dog on her, and now he was leaving?

"I need to get in with a reputable company," he said. "Then just maybe they'll take me on for a CPA internship. I'm not going to get that year back. I just need to move on, to Helena, Portland, Boston, don't know. Just somewhere."

"Just somewhere," she echoed. She was actually shaking. Glacier paced circles around her legs. "Anywhere is better than here, right?" She saw thoughts crossing his face, but she couldn't make sense of the expressions there.

"Yeah. In a way it is."

"What about Glacier?"

"He'll do good," he said softly and stood up. "I think he's going to be a good friend."

"Right," she said. "Unless he runs away."

Liam stared at her, then nodded. "I think I've overstayed my welcome."

"I think so," she said, and he walked past her and down the hall. She stood in that same spot until her legs felt strong enough to move. Then she looked down at Glacier.

"We can do this, right?" she asked. Glacier glanced at her, but he was watching the door as if he was waiting for Liam to come back, wagging a hopeful, slow wag every few seconds when he heard a noise from the floor below. Liam was letting him down, too. That was all she needed to know about Liam Gunnerson.

# CHAPTER 33

*A*very woke to the smell of pancakes. She opened her eyes and felt clearer than she had for months, even without coffee. She had slept straight through the night. *Parents always do chase away the monsters*, she thought wryly.

Her mom had called from somewhere in South Dakota the same night Avery brought Glacier home. Little brother Daniel had come home for a week to take care of the farm and Garrett, her littlest brother. The plan was for her parents to take a long-overdue break. But instead of going someplace vacationy and relaxing, they had come to Montana to see Avery's store. They'd arrived the night before, bearing leftovers, an inflatable bed, and bedding. Mom had said she didn't want to be a burden.

She hadn't even had time to tell them about Glacier. But as soon as he'd seen them at the door, the dog had started his slow, thoughtful wag. They were okay in his mind, more or less. By bedtime he'd discovered that Avery's dad was a treat-sneaking ally.

Avery smelled coffee. That meant Dad was up as well. She pulled on comfortable clothes, grateful it was a Sunday and the shop was closed.

As soon as she walked into the kitchen/living/whatever-it-was room, her mom said, "What time is your church service? Are we late?"

She'd made it through the night without any uncomfortable questions being asked. In fact, most of the talk had been about the farm and her brothers. But that was over now.

"I haven't been going to church," she said.

Dad, who had been pouring a cup of coffee, looked at her over the rim of his glasses. "What's up, Avery?"

"I haven't had much time."

A beat passed. Then Mom said brightly, "Where do your best friends go?"

"A couple different places, I think," Avery said.

"Pick one."

"Um…" Poppy had mentioned a place, and she said the name of the church as best as she could remember it. "Next week I'll—"

"Donald, do you mind?"

*Uh-oh*, Avery thought. Donald instead of Don. Things had gotten serious.

"On it, Jenny," Dad answered, and he pulled out his phone. Avery only had time to pour a cup of coffee and sit at the tiny kitchen table she'd found in someone else's dumpster before Dad said, "Ten o'clock. Is that possible, having a service that late?"

"I think that's to get millennials to come, Donald. And it gives us enough time for pancakes," Mom said. "Does it look like a dress-up church or a jeans-and-sandals church, honey?"

"They have a lot of pictures of kids on their website. Camping and such."

"Jeans and sandals it is. I might be a little overdressed, but that's just how I do it. Avery, do you think your sweats will be dressy enough?"

Avery got the hint. "I'll be right back," she said, and she went to her room to change.

She had a serious talk with Glacier about behaving while she was gone, and then she and her parents walked the six blocks to church. She hadn't realized it was so close, and she was grateful her parents didn't make a single comment about how little effort it would have taken to at least try it out.

Mom had nailed the dress code. It was a jeans church, even a shorts church. It was in a small, old building with a steeple and bell. And even better, there were just enough skirts in attendance to make Mom fit in.

Avery busied herself with her parents. She didn't want to talk to anyone, in case they might expect her to keep coming to the church. People found her anyway. She waved and said hellos to many familiar faces and hurried inside.

"Up front, honey," her mom said. "Your father can't hear very well anymore." Avery moved up as far as she could, but there was a crowd in the center aisle blocking her way. Then from the middle of it, she heard her own name, and Poppy emerged to give her a hug. "Good morning! I promise not to give you grief about taking so long to try our church out."

Avery had to laugh. Poppy was direct as always. "Poppy, this is Jenny and Don, my mom and dad."

Poppy introduced herself, and then Colton as he came over to join her.

"Oh! You're the bride," Avery's mom said.

"Yes. That's why there's such a crowd," Poppy said quietly. She jabbed a thumb at Colton. "This guy is famous." Colton rolled his eyes. "Everyone is just trying to get an invitation to our wedding. But you are invited. And I mean to the wedding, not just the reception, which is getting out of hand."

"That's how things go," Colton said. "Once you get too many Gunnersons in one place, it turns into a party."

Music started up, and her parents sat down in the nearest pew. Her dad mumbled something about being glad there were padded cushions, and Mom shushed him. Avery sat next to them, and to her surprise, Poppy sat down next to her, and then Colton squeezed his tall frame past them all to sit on Poppy's other side.

The first song was "Amazing Grace," with a modern chorus added in. The next song was new to her, and then there was a third song, and she could feel her father getting restless. It was amazing he'd ever made it through a church service of any kind. *If he could have a hammer or a wrench in hand, he'd be here all day,* she thought. She could picture that—pews alternating with tables filled with tools, motors, and all things broken. All the men in town would be saved.

The assistant pastor made his welcome and announcements, including the fact that they, and everyone else in Moose Hollow, were invited to Colton and Poppy's wedding reception. Avery's eyes went wide, and Poppy leaned over and whispered, "They were going to come anyway."

"The reception will take place after a small ceremony for close friends and family," the pastor announced. "Let me repeat that. You go to the party after the small ceremony for close friends and immediate family. Please feel free to share that distinction with everyone you know. In fact, share it with a few people you don't know." Like everyone else, Avery laughed.

Then there was more music. Despite her dad's discomfort and her mom's preference for hymns, Avery enjoyed the next two songs, worship tunes she knew from the radio. She wondered when she'd stopped listening to that kind of station. Or music at all, now that she thought of it. She'd even turned off the eighties tape that had come with the building.

Finally, everyone settled into their seats for the sermon. Her mom nudged her with her elbow. "Jeans and sandals," she said, and sure enough, that was exactly what the pastor was wearing. Avery bit her lip to hide her smile. He looked young and tan, but his hair was gray. His clothes were casual, as was his sense of humor, but it didn't take long for him to dive deep into a long passage of Scripture.

He was talking about forgiveness. The concepts weren't new to Avery, although some of the ways he approached it were different. God is holy, he said, and he cannot be in the presence of sin. She got that. God was always some sort of above-it-all, unfathomable thing to her.

Then he really got her attention. "As much as people try to hide it or medicate it," he said, "we all have the feeling in our guts that we've blown it. That we are condemned. Everyone has that feeling. Believers, atheists, everyone."

Avery had it. But she really was condemned.

She sat very still. She tried not to look away, not to cry, not to feel anything at all. But she felt like everyone could see it in her. Adulterer, sinner.

*Murderer.*

She had doubted her decision to marry Eli, and that was why she had pushed him into a physical union. She had wanted to create a spark that wasn't there. And then he had died.

Then she thought she was pregnant and single and she didn't want to be. Sure, there were moments the idea of having Eli's child was sweet and filled her with optimism, but just as often she hadn't wanted that burden. And now that child was dead too.

"So you try to do better. To make up for all the things you've done. And maybe you feel better for a while, but it doesn't work, does it? You feel like an imposter. And in your heart you're thinking, God knows the truth about how awful I am."

Her head hurt so bad it tingled. She tried to steady her breath. She actually worried she might pass out. What kind of scene would that make? She was surrounded by church people. She had to leave, but walking past them all during the sermon was too terrible to imagine.

*Wham.* The pastor's palm smacked the podium. "You are a

sinner. So is everyone in this church. If you think you're the worst of all sinners, I suggest you spend a little time with the heroes of the Bible. How about Abraham, like we talked about last month, sending his beloved, beautiful wife to marry someone else to save his own hide. God has seen it before."

*But some sins can't be forgiven*, she thought.

"And here's where someone always asks me about the unfor-givable sin," the pastor said. She looked down at her neatly crossed hands in case he looked her way. "Apostasy, the willful, consistent, knowing rejection of a God you know. One you *know*. Here's how I think of it, although there is plenty of room for debate. I think to commit apostasy you have to have complete faith in God and then reject him. Knowingly. Have you done that? Well, if you're worried about being forgiven, you haven't rejected God. By definition."

Avery glanced up, relieved to find him looking somewhere else. "So two days ago while my wife was out getting groceries, my daughter got into her mom's secret stash of cookies. I found out. Four-year-olds are terrible at covering up their crimes, right? But she denied it. As I was presenting her with the evidence, I told her, 'your mom *really* wanted those cookies.'"

There was a rumble of laughter. "Yeah, I know, there are days with toddlers that a cookie might be the best thing a mom has going on, right? So my daughter just sort of melts right in front of me, and she says how sorry she is, and parents, what do you say? You say 'I forgive you,' because you want your kids to learn what they need to learn, and then come back together as a family. And just when I'm thinking I've got this parenting thing down, my daughter says, "Mom won't love me anymore."

He held his hand to his heart. "It hurts, doesn't it? This isn't what you want your four-year-old to think. Because our love is so much greater than that. Her mom and I love her more than life. I don't want her to doubt that. And yet that's nothing, abso-lutely nothing, compared to the love God feels for my little girl.

And that's what he feels for you. Overwhelming, eternal, sacrificial love.

"We are stained by sin. But being forgiven doesn't depend upon how good you are at being good. It depends on how good God is, and how perfect Jesus' sacrifice was. And is."

It occurred to her that it might not be a coincidence that she was here today. But her brain was buzzing with words and memories, and it was too tangled for her to make sense of any of it. She felt like something important was just out of her grasp. When the sermon was over, all she could do was shuffle through the crowd and out into the sunshine like everyone else. That's when Poppy caught her by the arm. "I didn't realize your parents were in town."

Avery took a deep breath and tried to push away the tangle of emotions. "It was a surprise visit."

"I know you said you'd bring out those safety pins and the Christmas lights for me, but forget about that," Poppy said. "Just have fun."

"Safety pins?" Avery's mom said.

"Just trying to get the decorations up. They probably wouldn't work, anyway. Decorating the hayloft is turning out to be more difficult than I expected."

"What's the problem?" her dad asked, and that was it.

Avery knew it immediately. Colton gave him the details, and soon he and her father were brainstorming. And her mom wasn't far behind, asking about how Poppy planned on getting enough cake made for all those people and how to make sure it didn't melt in the heat—and did she have a cellar? The overwhelmed look on Poppy's face was enough to turn Avery's mom into a one-woman cavalry. In a matter of minutes, her parents had assembled a list of items to retrieve and promised to head out to the ranch as soon as they could change clothes and go shopping.

"Excuse me, Avery?" a woman asked.

Avery didn't recognize the woman who had touched her arm. She was about her mother's age and, as her mom would say, "well kept." She wasn't overdone, but her hair and nails were perfect, and of course Avery noticed her pretty clothes.

"Hello, my name is Naomi. I believe you met my husband, Peter Henderson." The woman, who must have seen the blank expression on her face, added, "He was one of the ropers at Colton's branding last month."

"Yes, of course," Avery said, and took the woman's outstretched hand. The handshake was firmer than she'd expected. "He was very kind, and when Mara went into labor, he took charge of everything."

"He's good at that," Naomi said. "He mentioned you to me, and he did such a good job of it that I recognized you from this outfit you're wearing. I like the combination. You definitely have a good sense of style."

"That's a very nice thing to say," Avery said.

"And you designed Poppy's wedding dress, is that right?"

Avery nodded, and the weight of that responsibility dropped right back down on her shoulders.

"Excellent. We can't wait to see that dress. At the reception, of course," she said with a grin. "It was a pleasure, Avery. See you soon." And the woman disappeared into the crowd.

"Was that Naomi Henderson?" said a voice. It was a quiet voice, but it was situated directly above her head. She whirled around to look up at Colton. "Yesss," he whispered.

She had no idea what he was talking about. "What?"

"Oh, nothing. Hey, where did Liam go?"

She looked down, her face heating as she did. She hadn't even imagined he would be here. And she really, really didn't want to talk to him. She resisted the urge to search the crowd to see if he was there, and all the while Colton was speaking to her dad, planning what was probably going to be the least vacationy, most enjoyable vacation her parents had taken in ages.

# CHAPTER 34

*L*iam felt strange coming up the steps to the house where he'd been living for more than a month. He'd moved his things out last night. Every time he moved he got rid of a few more belongings, and now everything he owned barely filled the back of his FJ Cruiser. He was happy for the new life Colton and Poppy were about to start in the old house. And it would be easy to move on, if only he knew where to go. The Bozeman firm still hadn't called. He wondered how far they were willing to go to investigate his background. He hadn't been dishonest, but he also hadn't offered up more than he'd needed to. Like the fact that at any moment the city attorney for Moose Hollow could file charges against him.

He didn't really think that moving now would put his troubles in the rearview mirror. But at least the people he cared about most wouldn't be dragged through his messes anymore.

He heard the tone of conversation change as he walked up the steps, and he moved slowly, giving the women time to adjust. Avery's mom answered the door. It was easy to identify her, even from the first time he'd seen her six days ago. She looked like a wiry, slightly shorter version of Avery. And she was brandishing a frosting-covered spoon. "No boys allowed," she said with a smirk.

So that was where Avery got her smirk. And now he knew that twenty-something years from now it would still look cute on her.

"I know, I'm not coming in. I have a message from Colton. He wants Poppy to meet him at the back door. He's walking over from the bunkhouse now."

Half a dozen female voices rose at once, and Liam had to speak up to be heard.

"He's not going to see her. He just wants her to open up the back door for a second and take his hand. Okay?"

Liam didn't come across the threshold. "I know I can't come in," he said. His breath caught just a little when he saw Avery, and he hoped no one else noticed. "You look lovely," he said.

"Woo-oo," Mara said. She was lounging on the couch in her bridesmaid dress, playing on her phone. "He li-ikes you."

"I was talking about Glacier," Liam said, giving Avery a shy grin.

"So was I," Mara said, not missing a beat. Avery smirked and shook her head. Then she turned her back on him, as she had every single time he'd seen her since he left her with Glacier at the Moose on the Loose.

Poppy trotted down the stairs. For some reason, seeing his cousin's girlfriend in a wedding dress brought home how much things were about to change. "Should I change out of the dress?" Poppy asked.

"Absolutely not," Julia said. "When he gets here I'll be your gatekeeper."

"Any minute now," Liam said hopefully.

Poppy was pacing. And as she passed by Glacier, she said, "Glacier's a handsome boy." He wagged at her.

"You found his Kryptonite," Avery said.

"He likes being called a handsome stud better," Mara said.

She set her phone down for a moment. "Who's the handsome stud, Glacier?" Glacier got up and went over to lean against the couch and surrender his forehead to Mara's scratching.

"I stand corrected," Poppy laughed.

"He's just excited because he's the only guy allowed in the ranch house today," Jenny said, giving Liam a pointed look.

"Well," Avery said, "I'm just excited Dad gave Glacier a bath. But if he sheds on this veil, I'm going to shave him."

That raised an uproar, and Avery had to promise not to mess with his locks now that he smelled of lavender and lemon and, Liam's mom said, looked like fluffy royalty. Poppy handed Liam's mom a baby carrot, and she gave it to Glacier. Liam smiled. The dog had so ingratiated himself into the Gunnerson household that he figured Avery would have a heck of a time letting him go. Unless she sold the business and moved. No, not unless. Until.

And she'd been so upset when he'd said he was moving. He'd gone over it and over it, and that never made any more sense to him. He was beginning to think he'd missed something, but he was tired of trying to figure it out.

He heard the rustling grass and looked to his left. "Okay, he's almost here. I'll see you ladies in about an hour." He gave one last hopeful look at Glacier, who stared intently at him, and nothing more. The dog's growing tolerance for attention didn't extend to him. *Hey, buddy, I'm the one who got you here*, he thought. Glacier didn't blink. Liam closed the door and walked around to the side of the house and nodded to Colton. Then he waited.

He could hear what happened, but he couldn't see it. There was a flurry of conversation when they opened the French doors at the back of the house. Somehow they got everyone situated with Colton on one side of the wall and Poppy on the other, hand in hand through the doorway, but out of sight of each other. That was when Colton started to pray.

He thanked God for bringing Poppy into his life. He thanked Jesus for the changes he'd made in his own life. Liam heard the crack in his voice, knowing that for everything that Colton had been through, he'd never heard him sound so emotional as now. Colton asked to be a blessing in Poppy's life and for their marriage to be a blessing to others. It was as honest and selfless a prayer as Liam had ever heard, and it was one of those times when it felt like God was bending low to listen to every word.

Then the prayer was over, and a few sniffles were heard here and there. Liam turned the corner and saw the doors close. Were those tears in Colton's eyes? It was hard to believe. Liam couldn't have admired Colton more than he did then. As a young man he'd looked up to the rodeo star, but that was nothing compared to the humble, loyal man he saw now.

They were only a few years apart. But just as when he'd been the shy, hiding boy in Colton's larger-than-life shadow, he knew there was a huge distance between them now.

Colton must have seen it in his eyes. "What? Is something wrong?"

Liam shook his head. "I'm proud of you," he said.

Colton smiled, then bowed his head and rubbed at the back of his neck. "You know you're my brother."

"Actually, we're cousins."

"Ha ha," Colton said.

"I know what you mean, Colton. I feel the same way."

"I want this for you," Colton said, jabbing a thumb back toward the house. "All that craziness."

Liam nodded. He wanted that too.

"But I don't see you making choices that'll make that happen."

That hit Liam right in the gut. He wasn't uncle of the year. And he wasn't Avery's steadfast friend. He waited for Colton to point out his flaws, but he didn't. "Liam, you need to stand up to whoever is bullying you."

Liam was so shocked he took a step back.

"I don't know what's going on with you, but it's pretty obvious you're in trouble. From where I stand, you look like you've gotten stuck. I know a lot about how that feels, but you haven't talked to me about it. I'm guessing you haven't told anyone else, either. Sometimes you just need to face things head on, and trust that the people who love you will stand by you. No matter what."

Liam didn't know what to say. He just stood there staring at Colton's boots. He felt like a failure. "We should go," he said.

Colton nodded. "Yeah."

# CHAPTER 35

*A*very sat near the back, next to her mom and dad, and took a moment to admire how the hayloft in Colton's old barn had been transformed. Dad called it a Gothic arch barn, and said there were just a few left in the part of the country where she grew up. Bent timbers curved upward to a pointed roof with no cross members, so the entire space was open for hay. Or in this case, a wedding that fit Poppy and Colton just right.

Someone had hung a big, white chandelier from the center of the barn and wrapped it in soft white string lights. Four simple swaths of white lace draped down from the peak to the walls, and nestled in them were more tiny white lights. A simple wooden cross was at the end of the building, over the open hayloft doors, and on either side of that were antique-looking candelabras and old gas lanterns, all lit with fairy lights. White rose petals had been scattered down the center aisle.

Avery didn't know the person who stood up to play the flute, but she looked too young to play such pure, steady notes. The song seemed familiar, but she couldn't place it. All around her people were gazing and admiring, and smiling at one another. And Avery knew so many of them. She hadn't expected that.

The only way up to the hayloft was a half stairway, half ladder, but one by one everyone had navigated it. And it helped that all the groomsmen and bridesmaids wore cowboy boots. The men wore suits, and the bridesmaids were wearing knee-length dresses. It made Avery glad she'd taken Poppy's advice and worn boots as well, a pair of vintage Frye boots that were another thrift-store find. With the lace skirt she had made and a tailored silk shirt, she was about as cowboy as she got.

Shortly after the music began, the pastor and Colton came down the aisle. Avery gave the groom an encouraging smile, and he smiled back, but he looked so pale she wondered if he was going to pass out.

Drew was the first groomsman, walking along with his bridesmaid wife, Lindy. Avery didn't know them well since they'd only arrived yesterday, but Liam's oldest brother seemed nice. His wife had her hands full with energetic Max and his precocious sister, Sam, so they barely even got to talk. Yesterday Drew had almost looked out of place, but with boots and a black cowboy hat on, he fit right in with the other Gunnerson men.

Liam was next, walking with Sierra. They made an absolutely stunning couple. Then again, either one of them with just about any other human being would have made a stunning couple. Liam looked nervous. Sierra, on the other hand, seemed absolutely ecstatic.

The last couple was Mara and Zane, who looked lost in some shared memory for a moment, then seemed to realize it was their turn to walk and hurried down the aisle. Following hot on their heels were Max and Sam, the ring bearer and flower girl, who jostled and finally raced each other down the aisle. Drew cut them a warning look, and they settled down in their front row seats.

Then Julia and Anson came in and sat on one side of the front row. Julia was holding baby Paul in her arms, and he seemed to be sleeping peacefully. Avery knew they weren't actually Colton's parents, but Colton's mother had passed and his father wasn't here—and no one seemed eager to talk about him. She'd heard that he had been a rodeo star, too, and that was all she knew.

Julia was already tearing up. Tears spread like wildfire at weddings, and Avery had to blink a few times to make sure she didn't catch them. That was when she realized Julia and Anson were sitting on the bride's side. Avery's estimation of Anson and Julia Gunnerson ratcheted up a notch. She'd seen Julia interact with Poppy a lot over the last few days, and she knew they were close. Poppy's parents were alive, but there was a disconnect of some sort there. It was hard to imagine how or why, since Poppy was so welcoming. Avery was happy to see Zane, and Liam's parents step into the gap.

Avery glanced at her own parents, who were holding hands and beaming. They were still in love. She was blessed to have them. She thought of everything Colton had said in his prayer an hour ago, while all the women in the house listened, nodded, and teared up. Except for herself. Avery felt as if she was listening to Eli's heartfelt words again on the day he asked her to marry him. She'd never felt the passion he felt, and she wished she could have, for his sake. Colton's words just made her feel lost.

A moment later, everyone stood and turned around. Poppy trotted right up the steps, a huge smile on her face, and she moved the beautiful bouquet of yellow roses and forget-me-nots to one hand so she could wave at everyone. Avery had to giggle at that. She looked absolutely stunning. But then again, Poppy would have looked stunning in a paper bag, she was so happy. Every step she took toward Colton made him smile more, and finally, a little color returned to his face.

The ceremony was the only thing truly traditional about the wedding. There was something beautiful in hearing such familiar words. It made Avery think about all the marriages that had come before this one through the generations. The ceremony was short, heartfelt, and sweet, almost as sweet as the tender kiss Colton gave his bride at the end. And that was when baby Paul decided to comment with a gurgle of his own.

Poppy was married. Avery felt grateful to have been counted as part of the small circle of friends and family who had witnessed it. But the final offer to buy her building was in her car, and signing it would change everything. Griff had dropped it off for her last night. He'd wanted to talk, again, but again Avery had said she didn't want to take time away from being with her parents. So there it sat, ominously waiting for her, like some sort of final judgment.

Lately, the thought of selling and moving hadn't felt much like a burden being lifted. It felt like a loss, one that made Avery's heart hurt. And there was Liam, smiling and laughing with Sierra. He didn't seem to mind leaving—why should she?

Rather than rushing off, the bride and groom stopped at every row and hugged and shook hands, thanking everyone for coming. Finally, all the members of the bridal party were whisked away by the photographer, a young woman with gray eyes and jet-black hair, who had done an excellent job of capturing the ceremony without interrupting.

They had a half hour, maybe more, before other guests would begin to arrive. In the sudden absence of direction, Avery's mom took over. All the young men were recruited to move food from the ranch house to the tables outside the barn. The older men were told to make sure people followed the signs and didn't drive up to the house, and that the young men didn't eat all the food. The young women were told how to rearrange the hayloft, and the older women were given more specific tasks. It was a classic Jenny Maier moment, and as usual, everyone was charmed by her sweet smile and motivated by her fierce look. Except for Avery.

For the very first time, she wasn't given a task. "You go make sure my granddog is okay," her mom said. She sounded worried. Avery bit her lip and nodded. Now wasn't the time to argue that Glacier was definitely not her mother's granddog. He was a foster dog, and he would go back to the shelter soon.

But on the way back to the house, just the thought of her mother saying that made her grin. Then she realized, and sorrow poured through her veins. Her mother had missed out on a baby, a real grandchild. It stopped her in her tracks. She breathed. She reminded herself it would get better, that it was getting better.

Then she remembered Glacier, and somehow knowing he needed her was enough to get her moving again.

# CHAPTER 36

*I*t was weird, watching Griff and Avery chat together. It was evening, and he'd hoped Griff would be at the bar by now. She had danced with him once, during an energetic rock song, and he'd left her in his dust. She looked uncomfortable. Griff didn't notice because, as usual, he was the star of his own show. Then Glacier, who had been hiding out under one of the food tables, came out and wound his way around Avery's legs until he nearly tripped her. She laughed and left the dance floor. She didn't notice that behind her, Griff didn't look amused. The whole thing seemed so wrong to Liam. But she stuck by Griff and talked to him all the way through the next song.

Liam knew he shouldn't be so fixated on them, but he also knew that there was no way someone like Avery could date someone like Griff and come away unscathed. Something bad was going to happen. The best he could do was hope he was there at the right time, in the right place, to stop it.

If not him, then Glacier. He hadn't seen a single trace of aggression in the dog, but one could hope he'd bite Griff if he deserved it. He'd read that dogs can smell all sorts of human emotions. He wondered if Glacier could catch the scent of Griff's general thuggery, and if he was planning on biting him anytime soon. He'd buy Glacier half the doggy store if he did.

Mara came up next to him. "Hey, you might want to check that," she said.

"What?"

"Your obsession is showing."

He sighed and looked at her. He hated it when she was wise. As much as he loved her, it could be so annoying.

"And I'm not just talking about Griff."

So it was psychoanalyze Liam night. "Yes. I like Avery. A lot."

"I've heard admitting you have a problem is the first step toward healing," she said. "You know what the second step is?"

He rolled his eyes. "What?"

"Asking her out."

He shook his head. "That ship has sailed."

"Oh, really?" Mara said, making it clear by her tone of voice that she didn't agree. She looked up toward the roof. "They did such a great job in here."

"They did." He looked up as well. "This hayloft was always one of my favorite places as a kid," Liam said. "The roof is so high, and the curved beams cause a kind of optical illusion. It's like you can't tell how high it is. If you come up here when it's windy, the whole place creaks and leans and it feels like you're going to fly right up into the air. Other times, it felt like a hidden forest. The beams were the trees, and you could see sunlight peeking through here and there like the sun through the leaves."

"There's more sunlight peeking through these days," she said. "Colton wants to put a metal roof on to protect the beams."

"I know. Colton said he's going to make a profit this year. I'm planning on donating my portion back to the barn. But that's easy to say. I made money in Chicago, and I lived with a roommate in a rent-controlled apartment. No one else in the family is in that situation."

"You're unemployed, though. If you keep that up, you should be broke in no time, just like the rest of us."

Liam chuckled.

"And now you're upset because Griff is hitting on your girl-friend in your special place."

"Yeah." He nodded slowly. "That pretty much sums it up."

Mara looked him in the eye. "Whaddya gonna do about Avery?"

"Nothing." He hoped the Helena firm would be calling soon, and then he'd be gone.

She smiled. "You aren't the brightest bulb on the Christmas tree, brother-in-law." She took her plastic glass of water and clinked it against Liam's beer bottle. Then she headed off to analyze someone else.

So Liam debated. He shouldn't be showing interest in anyone until the threats that were hanging over him went away. He was leaving town. And she was angry at him. Words bounced around in his head for what seemed like ages, and he tried not to glance Avery's way, but he did. Mara was right, he was acting like a fool. Worse, he was acting like a high schooler. And then the next time he looked across the hayloft, Avery was talking to Griff and her parents, and Liam realized a slow song was starting. And if she danced it with Griff while her parents smiled at them, Liam thought he would explode. He walked straight across what had become the upper dance floor.

"Would you like to dance?"

Avery nodded. There was the slightest flicker of her gaze toward Griff, but she didn't exactly look to him for approval. She clasped her hands together and walked out onto the dance floor.

And then there he was, in the middle, in front of God and everybody. And other couples weren't exactly rushing to dance to this tune, either, so they were out in the open. He took her hand the way his mother had taught him, placed his hand on her back—she was warm to the touch—and they started dancing. Swaying, really. He wasn't much of a dancer, and all the steps his mom had taught him years ago were long gone.

Avery was looking at a spot somewhere on his right shoulder, and he hoped he wasn't sweating too terribly. He'd taken off the jacket, but he should have shed the tie as well, he soon realized. *Not the brightest bulb on the Christmas tree.*

"It's turned out to be a nice party, hasn't it?" Avery said.

He tried to think of something to say, but everything that popped into his head sounded imbecilic. And when enough time had passed without him responding, things got uncomfortable. Then Liam just said, "Do you mind if we don't talk?"

She blinked. Her hand suddenly felt so tense it was like holding a warm rock. He tried to think of a way to explain why he'd just said that, something witty and disarming, but his mind was entirely empty. Other dancers finally came out onto the floor. But he was waiting for the inevitable moment she would let go and walk away.

Then she looked up at him. Oh, those eyes. They were absolutely bottomless. And when moments passed and she didn't look away, he felt his heart beating loud in his chest. And just then he saw it, at the spot at the base of her throat. The hollow where her collarbones nearly joined. There was a quick rise and fall. She was breathing fast, and the thought that she might be feeling the same thing he felt sent electricity through him. He tightened his hold on her hand, and when she did the same, he thought he would never make it through the rest of the song. He couldn't speak. He could hardly think. So he pulled her closer, just a little bit, and bowed his head so that her hair pressed against his cheek. She didn't pull away.

That was when Glacier came out from under a table filled with the crumbled remains of wedding cake. He circled their legs and laid down beside them in the middle of the dance floor. Liam closed his eyes and wished the song would never end.

# CHAPTER 37

he DJ, who was downstairs in the heart of the
deafening lower dance floor, couldn't have picked a
song more opposite to the one she and Liam had just shared.
Avery pulled away, laughing nervously and saying something
about skipping the next dance. But it felt strange to just walk
away, and stranger still to go back to Griffin's side. But that's
where her parents were, waiting for her. And now her parents
were probably wondering what the heck was going on since a
few minutes ago Griffin had sounded, for all the world, like her
boyfriend. He'd told them, "Avery and I hit it off right away."
And "I'm worried about Avery staying in that big, creepy
building all alone." And the worst: "Has Avery told you we're
talking about moving to Bozeman?"

Then this. This weirdness with Liam. When she told him she
wasn't going to dance the next song, he'd said, "Sure. Okay." And
suddenly, again, his face had become a closed door. He'd shoved
his hands in his pockets, turned on his heel, and gone the opposite direction.

Griffin was talking to her parents. They looked intrigued by
what he was saying. She wondered what other misconceptions

she'd be cleaning up tonight, their last night before driving home tomorrow morning. It was late, and it had been a long day. She needed to go before anyone asked her what on earth she was doing dancing with Liam like that.

She couldn't think about it, either, because it made her stomach go queasy and her heart race.

"Mom, Dad, I think I'm turning into a pumpkin."

Mom jumped right on that. "I'm so glad you said that, honey, I was just thinking the same thing."

"Turning into a pumpkin?" Griffin said.

"You know, like in Cinderella."

"The carriage turned into a pumpkin, not Cinderella," he said. "I can't believe you don't know that. Cinderella has to be your thing."

He said it a little too loudly. And he made a sweeping gesture that nearly splashed beer out of his red plastic cup. Avery had seen him like this before, usually after a few hours spent at the Lantern. It wasn't going to get better from here on out. "I know, it's silly. It just means we're tired." He protested, but her mom wasn't having any of it.

"Donald, will you help me get down those steps? Hurry up and say your goodbyes and thank-yous, Avery. It's time for me to go."

As soon as they started down the steps, Griffin said, "Why don't I just take you home later?" He looked down at Glacier. "Your parents could take your dog."

There were many reasons not to stay with Griffin, not the least of which was that she wasn't sure he was in any condition to drive. Driving the long ranch roads was nothing like driving home from the Lantern. "Thanks, but this is my last night with my mom and dad. I'm going to enjoy every moment."

Griffin laughed, and it was a bitter sound. "The way you talk about them makes you sound like a little kid. Then again, my parents sucked long before I grew up."

She'd heard bits and pieces about that before, enough so that she believed him. Comments about bruises, affairs, arguments, and long vacations with nothing but a maid to check in on him once a day to make sure he made it to school. He'd said he was only eight the first time it happened.

"I wish things were different for you, Griffin."

"Yeah." He scanned the crowd over her head. She was pretty sure he'd missed Liam sneaking out right after her parents left, but she hadn't. "Let's go out tomorrow night, okay?" he said. "I'll take you somewhere nice since I didn't get to take you and your parents out."

"We were busy."

"I know. You said so. But at least I can take you out tomorrow. See you at closing time, okay?"

She smiled and nodded. And she reminded herself that Griffin was Eli's friend. But she knew right then that she wasn't going to go out to eat with Griffin tomorrow or any night. He was getting the wrong idea. She would meet him tomorrow at lunchtime and tell him she was grateful for all his help, but...

But she didn't have those feelings for him.

Her heart ached. Thinking of it brought her too close to thoughts of Eli, and the weight of the guilt that hung on her.

Avery found Colton and Poppy, and after a silly group hug, they let her go. Then she started the long trek to her car, where her parents would be waiting by now. They had insisted she park far away, to make room for the guests, as if they weren't guests. They'd put so much time and love into the wedding, and they still acted as if they were lucky to be there at all. She breathed the cool night air, scented with alfalfa and carrying the low calls of cattle and grass rustling. The noise of the dance party receded with every step, and she felt her mind clearing.

But there were three shadows by her car. Someone was talking to her parents, and she knew from the silhouette it was Liam. Now he was facing her way. It was too late to turn around. She saw the dome light as her parents climbed into the car, and saw the car doors close as Liam walked toward her. "I was just thanking your parents," he said. "I really enjoyed working with your dad."

Inside her car, the dome light faded and turned off. Glacier's ears were pricked, facing farther out in the pasture where someone had started a bonfire. "I know he really enjoyed—"

Liam's phone rang. He was distracted but ignored it. It rang again. "I'm sorry." He glanced at his phone, his face lit with blue light. It took all his attention.

"Go ahead. I need to get my parents home," she said.

"No, please don't go. This call...I just need to..."

Was it Lynn? She shouldn't care. She *didn't* care.

"It's the firm in Helena. They told me they'd call this weekend, but I didn't expect a call now. I told them I'd be at the wedding."

He tapped the phone, and she saw his eyes dart as he read the screen. Then his face went blank. He glanced over his shoulder toward the ranch house, then back at the phone.

"I need to go, Liam."

"No," he insisted again. He started to speak, then stopped, staring at her in a way she hadn't been stared at since...since the dance floor a few minutes ago. "I'm not going to Helena."

She tensed. So he hadn't gotten the job. That didn't really change anything. "So where do you think you will go?"

"I'll stay here. Probably have to go back east for a while to tie up some loose ends first. It's confusing."

What was he trying to say to her? Why was he even talking to her? She'd been happy to close the door on him and wave goodbye, and now they were having this confusing conversation. So he didn't have any other jobs lined up and he didn't know where he was going to live. There was nothing new here. "Liam, I'm sorry you didn't get the job but—"

"I got the job, Avery. I'm not taking it. And I need to tell you something. Please just give me one minute."

"Fine." One minute, then she was gone.

"I'm in trouble."

More than she already knew about? She felt dread weighing her down to the spot where she stood.

"I didn't do anything wrong—well, kind of, but it was for the right reasons. I don't know if I'll be able to sort it all out. And if I can get it fixed, it'll take time. In the meantime, some people are pretty angry with me, and they might want to…"

She saw him struggle for words, and she thought, *hurt you.* She didn't want to hear him say it. "Stop you?"

"Yes. Stop me. And I don't want to make anyone near me a target." Liam shook his head. "I just want you to understand that I'm not going to talk to you for a while or be seen with you, or anything like that. It was wrong to dance with you back there. So wrong. I haven't got the right to put you in any kind of danger."

*Danger.* He'd said it. She wanted to ask what was going on, but she could see by his expression she wasn't going to get an answer. "Is that why you wanted me to get Glacier?"

"That was part of it." His shoulders slumped. "Mostly I didn't want you to feel so alone."

She swallowed. What do you say when someone says your saddest secret out loud? She felt pathetic. And some tiny part of her felt relieved. But she didn't want to admit it out loud, so she just stood there, saying nothing.

"Avery, I just wanted to tell you that I'm not going anywhere. And if all this shakes out, I'd like to have the chance to stay here and get to know you better. That is, if you decide to stay."

She knew a statement like that demanded a response, but her mind was too busy spinning to make sense of it, so she said, "Okay." Just okay. Anything, absolutely anything, would have been better than that.

"Good night, Avery," he said, and he left. She watched him walk away. It felt like she was drowning, like she should be thrashing or screaming or something, but there was nothing to do. She was thinking about Griffin and what she had to tell him tomorrow. And Liam and his mysterious trouble, and how the thought of him wanting to get to know her better—whatever that meant—made her heart beat all the way up into her throat. She didn't want to feel anything for him.

What she had wanted, desperately, was to feel something for Eli. For kind, enthusiastic, handsome Eli. And she had never felt that way about him. What was wrong with her? She had felt doubts about living her life with him, doubts about what she was or wasn't supposed to feel for the man she was going to marry. She had thought maybe the decision to remain pure before marriage, to save what Eli called "out-of-control awesomeness" for their wedding night, had turned off a switch in her. But the truth was she'd been scared that something was missing. So she had pushed. She'd arranged their night alone. She'd orchestrated the whole evening.

Why hadn't it been enough for her just to be loved?

The car door behind her opened and her father stepped out. "Avery, are you all right?"

She shook her head as she faced him in the dark. "No."

"What's wrong?" he asked gently.

"Me," she said.

Her father crossed his arms. "Well then, little girl, does this mean you're ready to tell us what's going on?"

# CHAPTER 38

The store was closed, but Avery had plenty of online work to do. But instead of staring at her laptop, her eyes were drawn to the three-page chart of Sierra's recommendations based on three different budgets. She had listed items and recommended sizes and quantities, and included thumbnail images of each piece. She had mixed high-quality manufacturers with smaller, more unusual vendors. They ranged from custom knitters to makers of handmade, tailored clothes in extended sizes. Avery shook her head as she looked at it. Even she wanted to buy these items. Sierra had done an incredible job.

She'd asked Sierra where she'd found some of the more unique vendors.

Poppy's sister had just shrugged. "I've done a lot of traveling. I keep my eyes open for things I like."

"You want to open your own store?"

"No, oh my gosh no. Too much pressure."

Avery wasn't sure she believed her. Sierra had been so excited about ordering. And instead of telling her the truth, that she was broke, Avery said she wanted to think about it. Avery just couldn't bring herself to say it, especially after all the work Sierra had put into her research. But as soon as she got the okay from her lawyer to sell the property, the Moose on the Loose would become part of the Hallowell empire.

And now Griffin Hallowell was walking by the store window.

Avery winced. She really should have moved upstairs. She went over to unlock the door, her furry, blue-eyed shadow beside her all the way. Griff was wearing a suit and tie. "I got your text message, but I've been too busy to talk until now." He glanced down at her scarf and T-shirt with a confused expression. "You ready to go?"

Glacier rubbed against her legs, doing a full circle that no doubt left a trail of fur on her suede booties, and probably on her bare legs as well. She slipped back behind the checkout desk. "I wanted to talk to you," she said.

Griffin leaned one elbow on the desk. "I wanted to talk to you too," he said with a raised eyebrow and a smile. He glanced down at where his elbow was, looked at the sale papers, and then looked at the order list that Sierra had made. "Planning your new store, Ave?"

"No, I'm not. I don't think I'm going to start a new store, Griffin."

"Sure you are. You're just feeling a little down right now, but when we find the right place for you to lease in Bozeman, you'll get excited again, I promise."

When had he become so certain she was moving to Bozeman? Had she said something wrong? "I'm probably moving back to Iowa." The moment the words were out of her mouth, she wondered if they were true. She was still surprised her parents hadn't seemed eager to have her return. In fact, her father had told her she should consider staying. That had brought tears to her mother's eyes, but she hadn't disagreed.

*This door may be closing, but the whole world is open for you, Avery,* she'd said.

The smile was frozen on Griffin's face. "Wait, are you serious?"

She nodded.

Griffin tilted his head sideways as his smile melted away. "What's going on, Avery?"

"What's going on is that I'm going to spend the next few decades of my life trying to pay off what I owe the insurance company. I don't really know where or how I'm going to do that. I won't have money to buy inventory or pay for the lease. And I don't even know if a store is the right thing for me. Not anymore."

She thought about the place she had been this morning, having a church service of sorts in the misty Beartooth Mountains. She had stopped at the top of the world, eye to eye with snowy mountain peaks, and surrounded by tiny wildflowers on the low grass. Beyond that, the ground gave way to black chasms below, and between the peaks and canyons, she had seen the winding black line of the Beartooth Highway. It was as close as she could get to heaven. She'd gone to say goodbye to Eli and her baby.

She couldn't quite trust that God had forgiven her, not just yet. But she could trust that Eli and the baby were together, and that they were in God's hands. It had been bittersweet. She hadn't expected the sweetness.

The memory made the conversation she was having with Griffin seem distant. Or maybe it was unimportant. She certainly wasn't close enough to tell him what she had been doing.

Griffin shook his head slowly. He pressed his palms against the edge of the desk and leaned back. "This is about Liam Gunnerson, isn't it?"

"No," she said. She was surprised by the jealous tone in his voice.

"I was right there when you were dancing with him, Avery."

"And dancing was all we were doing."

"You met with him later."

Had he followed her, then? That made her feel uncomfortable. Glacier stopped his leaning and stood, ears pricked, staring at the shelves below her as if he could see right through the desk to where Griffin stood. "Yes, I did. And we decided it was best if we didn't see each other anymore."

"So you *have* been dating."

Avery sighed. "No, we never dated."

"Just 'seeing each other.'"

"Griffin, he's a friend. Or he was a friend. Sometimes. But even that was up and down, and now it's just over."

"Then what does that make me?" Griffin asked.

"You're my friend," she said, although the tone of this conversation was beginning to make her doubt that. "And you're Eli's friend. That matters to me."

He looked at her for a couple of beats, and then his expression suddenly brightened. "That's right. And as your friend, I want to remind you that my father's offer to buy expires tonight at midnight. So let's put all this behind us, go to dinner, and I'll answer any questions you have."

What had Poppy said? *Having him advise you on selling to his father is a conflict of interest.* Her father had said precisely the same thing. For the first time, she was beginning to agree. "I know you worked hard to get your father to give me the best possible offer. And I know that if I don't accept it now, he may not be willing to make the same offer again. But after talking to my parents, I think I want to have someone else look over the offer, just to be sure."

"Sure of what?" Griffin asked.

"Sure it's the right decision for all of us."

"Do you think other offers are going to be rushing in, Avery? We could be talking years here. And you haven't got that kind of time. I'm sure your dad knows farming, but I know real estate, especially in this town. You've got a buyer who wants this building, warts and all, for more than a fair price. I can't believe your dad would want you to miss out on that. And I can't believe you'd want to endanger them, either."

"What do you mean?"

"If you can't sell, there will be legal action from the insurance company. And I'm sure your family would want to protect you. Do you really want them to mortgage their farm to pay your debts?"

Her heart rate went up. They had mentioned getting money together to help. Glacier did a loop around her legs, distracting her for a moment. *It can't be the right time to make such a big decision,* Poppy had said. Making a decision under pressure was what Avery had done to get into this mess in the first place. She didn't know if there were other sellers. She didn't know what she was going to do once the building was sold. She hadn't even heard from the lawyer about the insurance company's settlement. She had to have faith.

*I'm sorry you ran out of faith,* her mother had said to her last night. Instead of comforting her, it had wounded her to the core.

"I can't," Avery said. "I can't do it right now. I think it would be wrong. I'm sorry, Griffin."

His lower eyelids twitched up into a glare, then the moment was gone. "Dad will just have to wait, then. Let's forget all of this for a while and go have a good time. You deserve it, after having all this worry on your shoulders. You haven't had any more weird noises from the basement, have you? Because if you have, my offer is still open to help you find another place to stay while you check out your options."

"I don't want to go out to dinner tonight, Griffin." She didn't want to say those words. She could feel her heart racing faster and faster, and at her feet Glacier made a thin whining sound, the first sound he had made since she'd started fostering him.

"Aw, come on," Griffin said. "We're friends, remember?"

"We are." But as she watched his eyes turn icy again, she doubted it. "But just that, Griffin. We aren't dating."

"Just like you're not dating Liam?" His tone was sarcastic. He laughed softly, then he was all smiles again. "I know you're having a hard time, Avery. I think you need a good night's sleep and everything will seem clearer then. I'll check in with you tomorrow."

She didn't know what to say to that. She couldn't tell him not to drop in on her. The store would be open.

He smacked the counter with his palm. "Missing a good dinner, too." He winked at her and strode out, adjusting his suit jacket as he did.

Avery waited a little while before locking the door. Then she fed Glacier, changed into shorts and sneakers, and took him for a walk up to the trail a couple blocks away. As she had been for days, she was rewarded with sunshine and a bag of dog poo to carry back home. But today the sunlight had a strange orange color, which was both beautiful and unnerving. One of her customers had told her it was smoke moving in from the fires in California and northwestern Montana. She couldn't smell the smoke, but the air felt thick in a way that made her nose stuffy. Still, she didn't cut the walk short. The walk wasn't about her, anyway.

At the top, she caught her breath and looked out over Moose Hollow. It was cuter than it had any right to be. Tall, narrow Victorian houses in postcard-worthy colors, the castle playground, the narrow streets where people strolled along and cars crawled even slower than the people. And right in the middle of it was her building. Not the biggest, fanciest, or oldest...but there it was, in the center of things. She had paid too much, that was true. But it was a bad decision she could have made right, if the insurance money had actually been hers to keep.

And there on the top of the ridge, she changed her mind about something else. Maybe looking into Liam's past wasn't the worst thing she could do. In fact, it was only fair. If it was in the public database, didn't she have a right to know? So she pulled out her phone and typed in "Liam Gunnerson Moose Hollow police." And there it was, in the archives of the *Moose Hollow Herald*. "Liam Gunnerson still recovering. If you have any information call the Moose Hollow Police at..."

She clicked back to the previous article. It cost her three dollars to access more archived articles, which irked her, but not enough to let it go.

"Moose Hollow Teen in Serious but Stable Condition."

The article had precious little to say, except that he had been attacked on school grounds and beaten. The first article was three days earlier than this one. He'd been in the hospital at least that long. Now that she knew Julia, Avery could just begin to grasp the pain she must have felt, wondering if her son would recover. She reread both articles and tried to find more information, but there were no answers. He'd been beaten. No reason why, no arrests, nothing. Yet Mara thought there was a connection to Griffin. How could any student in a school so small not know what happened? She tried to remember something, anything, either Liam or Griffin had said that would give her a hint of what had happened. But she couldn't think of a thing.

She could imagine Liam, stubborn as anything, keeping his mouth shut. Then again, he'd been a high school student, and he'd been hurt badly. Maybe he'd just been afraid to tell what had happened. But something surprised her. Griffin had never said a word about the incident. *Trouble just follows him*, he'd said about Liam. He seemed happy to share bad news about Liam.

Was it strange that he hadn't ever mentioned something so dramatic and awful?

Unless he'd been involved. What had Mara said? *Griff didn't tell you, did he? If he ever tells you, you go straight to Chief, okay?*

No, she had a hard time believing that. Yet the strangest, most unbelievable connection started to form in her mind. She pushed it away. It was too crazy, and had too many coincidences across too much time and distance.

She scratched Glacier on the top of his head, and he smiled at her. Tonight she still lived in Moose Hollow, Glacier was still her foster dog, and it was time to go home. For now, that was all she needed to know.

# CHAPTER 39

*L*iam had a message to give to the two Chicago thugs that had ransacked his parents' hotel room and his uncle's office. But how could he send it?

He could go to the FBI. Or the Securities and Exchange Commission. Or one of the many other agencies that would want in on a scandal like this, if they knew it existed. But the truth was that he didn't have enough proof. He had documents, but his accounting firm probably had their own documents, whitewashed clean of the evidence that Solarthea, its number two client, was nothing but a shell of a company, and it was ready to collapse under its own weight. The only reason the doors were still open was that Ackerman, Jones & Fetterman had falsified their financials.

He wondered how an established company could have taken such a risk. Maybe they believed Solarthea was going to turn around. But once that first lie was down on paper, it must have seemed easier to continue lying than admit the truth.

Liam wondered what it was like to try to sleep at night with those lies hovering over your life. But Liam was no threat, unless someone else had information that would support Liam's documents.

What if Liam could find his own corroborating information, anything to back up the documents he already had? He'd spent every moment since church thinking about it. He couldn't get it directly from Ackerman, Jones & Fetterman. They were smart enough not to talk to him. They would circle the wagons like the team they were.

*You're just not a team player, are you?* his former boss had said when he fired Liam.

But the thugs that had tossed his room and Cash's office were linked to his former employers. If he could contact them, they might give something away.

Mike seemed to think those thugs were also connected to Griff in some way. If that was true, Liam could get some juicy piece of information to Griff, and he might pass it on. But Liam wasn't allowed in the Lantern, so he couldn't talk to Griff there. And showing up at Hallowell Realty could very well get him arrested.

Suddenly Liam knew who could get a message to Griff, and if Liam made it juicy enough, it would be passed on to Arthur and Billy as well. He pulled out his phone. He knew which number was hers because at one time he'd thought it ironic that the last digits were 99, Griff's old jersey number. Now he didn't think it was ironic at all. He wouldn't have been surprised to learn she had chosen it. Liam dialed. His call went to a voice message, a cheerful one that didn't quite sound like her. "Hi, this is Lynn. Please leave me a message."

He hung up.

He didn't know what he'd say if she called back. And she probably wouldn't. He'd have to call her several times over the next week, he guessed. Maybe even send a card, but what would it say? I forgive you for not telling the truth, and for backing up your abusive ex-boyfriend, which leaves me open to criminal charges and a lawsuit, and—

The phone rang. It was Lynn.

With nothing better to say, Liam took a stab in the dark. "Can we meet?" he said.

"Yes," Lynn said.

That was a surprise. "Tonight?"

"I can meet you at Annie's at six."

That was even more of a surprise. "I was kind of hoping to meet in Billings. I'm not very popular around here right now."

"I'm going to be in Moose Hollow later tonight. I'm meeting some friends. And I don't want to be seen in a restaurant where my friends go. So it's Annie's or nothing."

Liam put his forehead in his hand. He could try for another night, and she might just balk. "I'll meet you then."

At ten minutes before six, Liam stood outside the door to Annie's and tried to look, and feel, relaxed. He didn't know what he'd do if Lynn stood him up. But she showed up on time, wearing a professional jacket and short skirt along with stilettos that were clearly not work shoes. She looked vaguely guilty when she saw him…or maybe he was just imagining it. He gave her a brief hug and escorted her inside the restaurant.

There was no mistaking the look he got from Annie when he came in. Rather than saying hello, she handed off the menus in her hand to another server, then pointed to a small table in the back, jammed in next to the kitchen. Other tables were open, but they had been banished to Annie Purgatory. He wasn't sure which transgression had landed him in her dog house. Maybe it was the fight with Griff or the fact that he hadn't visited in ages. Maybe it was Lynn, since Annie had seemed instantly fond of Avery. Lynn didn't seem to notice anything was wrong, and Liam didn't point it out to her.

"This place is weirder than I remembered," Lynn said as she looked at the menu.

Liam didn't want anything. His stomach was doing flips. Should he record the conversation? He had no idea what to say. He pressed the hidden button on the side of his new pen and tucked it in his shirt pocket, for practice, if nothing else.

"Are you doing okay?" he asked. He truly was worried about her, maybe even more than he was angry with her.

She sighed. "It's been a tough few weeks for me."

He blinked. She had watched Griffin punch Liam, then told a police officer she hadn't seen a thing, and it had been a tough few weeks for her? He pulled himself together. "I'm sorry to hear that, Lynn."

She nodded and set her menu down. "Thank you."

Liam tried to see things from her point of view. "Have you got someone you trust to help you? Or just to listen?"

"My life coach. We're up to two meetings a week."

"What does your life coach say?"

"He says I need to work on my mantras. To realize I am beautiful, I am worth loving, and I am perfect just as I am."

Liam nodded slowly. *Every stinking word of that is part truth, part lie*, he thought. Who cared if she was beautiful on the outside? She spent so much time trying to look beautiful that it was hard to see the real, and truly beautiful, Lynn beneath the veneer. Was she worth loving? Everyone is. And everyone isn't. Because no one is perfect. Love is a gift, not something you should feel like you have to earn. And telling yourself you're perfect is the best possible way to get stuck and make sure you never seek forgiveness. And without forgiveness...

The waiter came and Lynn ordered a pasta dish and a glass of wine. He asked to have what she was having. And Annie walked by with her nose in the air.

"Lynn, I'm going to tell you something I haven't told many people, okay?"

She looked at him with skepticism.

"I know the exact moment my life turned around and everything went from mostly bad to mostly okay, which was a big change for me."

"Was it when you were in the hospital?"

He was a little surprised she brought that up. He shook his head. "No. It was a few years later. I was in college, honor roll, lifting weights and some other stuff about four hours a day. A lot had changed. But I didn't feel any better at all."

Lynn frowned at him. "Why?"

"Because I was still me."

She took a deep breath and crossed her arm over her ribcage. "You didn't love yourself."

"Actually, I was pretty enamored with myself. I felt accomplished. And strong. But I was miserable."

Lynn nodded slowly. "Did you get a life counselor?"

He had to smile, a little. "Yeah. His name is Jesus. I figured the guy who created the universe was probably the one best equipped to help me navigate through it."

Lynn leaned back. "I know a lot of people choose a spiritual path. I'm happy it worked for you."

She didn't want to listen to what he had to say. But he was going to finish anyway, because this was more important than his mission to find the Chicago thugs. "I was worthless." *Worse, a coward*, he thought. "But I was still created by God. He actually made me the way I am. So I finally realized he must have something planned for my life, and after. Something better and more important than I could've accomplished on my own. I'd heard all that before, growing up in the church, but I didn't get it. It sounded like…like a mantra. I memorized the words, but I still felt like I was the exception to the rule. Until I asked to be forgiven."

"Forgiven for what? If God made you, he made you, you have nothing to feel bad about. You just need to learn to feel good about yourself."

He'd figured out a long time ago that some people got the

"wretch" part of "Amazing Grace" and others were too afraid to face it. For him, nothing was more comforting than knowing he wasn't the first wretch God had to deal with, and wouldn't be the last. "It's like a Kata," he said. "You know anything about martial arts?"

She shook her head.

"A Kata is a long form, a series of attacks and defenses. Some are very long and complicated. And when you learn one, you know that you'll never have two, or forty, people attack you with exactly those moves, in order."

He was rambling. How could he explain? "But when you spar, every moment is something that's never happened before. You're creating something new. That's why they call it an art. And that's what living is like. God gives you the Kata—that's the Bible. But you get to help create your life. God's seen it all before, but he takes pleasure in seeing me try, no matter how awful I am or how many tantrums I throw. That's love and forgiveness all wrapped up in one."

She took the glass of wine the waiter brought and took a long drink. "It's pretty when you say it like that," she said. And she looked around as if she was hoping to find a more interesting conversation at another table.

Again he had to smile. A few years ago he would have felt the same way. It was past time to change the topic. "I stole something from the company where I used to work," he said.

He had her attention now. He had no doubt that she knew exactly what he was talking about. "Oh?" she said. "I didn't know that."

"I took it as a sort of insurance policy. But I think I made a mistake, and now I need to find a way to get it back to the people I took it from."

"Why don't you just send it to them?"

"Because I want to talk to them first and make sure that if I give it to them, they'll leave me alone. Not press charges. Or worse."

Lynn tilted her head sideways. "Why are you telling me?"

"You know business, Lynn. I just thought you might have some advice. Have you ever gotten in trouble with an employer? Do you think I'm doing the right thing?"

She shrugged, "No, not really. But maybe. Let me think about it."

He nodded. Mission accomplished. "Enough about me. Tell me about your rough few weeks, Lynn." And she did. He heard about a back-stabbing co-worker, being asked to go out to dinner with her mother when she was clearly so busy, and that no one on the class reunion committee appreciated her. She talked until the pasta arrived and he'd eaten more than he could stand to eat, which wasn't much. That was when Annie yelled from the kitchen, "Avery! I have your calzone ready. And a little something extra for your new doggy."

Avery was standing in the open doorway of the restaurant. She waved. And she gave him a perfectly fake smile. Then to make things worse, Glacier caught sight of him and tugged at the leash. His ears bent down a little, and he wagged. A real wag. And all Liam did was wave and then turn back to Lynn.

He felt lower than dirt. But he held his position and gave Lynn all his attention. "Nice dog," he mumbled.

"He looks like a demon dog with those white eyes," she said.

He wanted to correct her. They were, in fact, glacier blue, and that to get a wag and a smile from Glacier was like the heavens opening and angels singing. Yet he'd just turned his back on the dog, like so many people had done before. He could imagine what Avery was thinking of him now, dining with another woman, acting as if Avery was just another person at a busy restaurant with just another dog. She was anything but that. Would it matter that he'd told her he couldn't be around anyone he cared about? *God, please let her trust me. And let me be worthy of that trust.*

"I thought you guys were an item," Lynn said.

He shook his head. "No, she's not even my client anymore." He shrugged and tried to look uninterested.

"Griff told me she has too much baggage," Lynn said. "You know they had a big date planned tonight, and she canceled? He just texted me about it on the way here. He said she was being extra flaky. She's nice enough, but a bit of a drama queen, you know?"

Liam didn't say a word. He thought about what Avery was dealing with in her life and weighed it against snotty co-workers, a lonely mother, and the same high school drama that had been going on for as long as high school had existed.

He bit his tongue. No matter what he thought of Lynn, she was struggling. He didn't know how difficult or how insurmountable her problems might seem to her. He took a deep breath and tried to look interested in his pasta, but what he had eaten already felt like a bowling ball in his stomach.

Lynn cut a glance toward the doorway. "So he's going out with her tomorrow night instead. I guess he has something planned for just the two of them. He won't tell me what, and he tells me everything, so it must be really special."

Liam didn't have the nerve to look at Avery. He watched Annie go by with a paper bag, and he tried not to think about the way Avery savored Thai pizza or wonder if Glacier was still looking at him. "I thought you and Griffin might still be dating," he said.

She drew herself up, smiled, and said words that sounded as if they'd been practiced often. "He's not ready for me. Yet."

Liam had no idea how to respond to that. He wished for her sake that Griff would never be ready for her.

# CHAPTER 40

She had just reached the top of the steps when she heard the rattle. Glacier spun to head back downstairs, but she grabbed his collar. She held still, and then she heard a creak and the bell on the front door clanged. Avery set the bag from Annie's Asian Ciao down on the step and crept down. Glacier crept along with her like a wolf stalking prey, his paws hardly making a sound on the shabby carpet of her stairs. When she reached the bottom, she hardly knew what to do. She went to the back door, ready to run. "Who's there?" she called.

No answer.

"Who is there?" she said, louder this time.

She thought she heard something. It sounded like a curse. Then, "Who else would I be?"

Avery breathed again. Mel. She hadn't been here in so long Avery had almost forgotten the woman had a set of keys. She wondered who else might have a key to the front door. Well, when she left, it wouldn't be her problem anymore.

"Mel, what are you doing here?" she said as Glacier tugged her through the doorway to the main store.

The old woman's eyes grew wide when she saw the dog. "Why is that wolf here? Is it living here now?"

In the time since she had seen her, the woman's appearance had declined. Gone was her overdone but meticulous makeup. Her hair looked dirty and stringy and was pulled back into a narrow ponytail. And if it was possible, she looked thinner. "Mel, are you okay?"

"No! No, I am not. Look what you've done. You changed all the locks in the back. Where will he go? Where is he supposed to go? I would have cleaned for you. Just like I did for Tabitha. Cleaned her home, even showered her when her mind failed her. Every day. I brought her flowers. I told her stories about our lives and only the good ones. Who is going to tell him stories? How will he find his way home now? What if he waits outside and no one lets him in?"

The woman was getting more agitated by the second, and her eyes filled with tears. At a complete loss, Avery dropped her hold on Glacier's collar and took the old woman in her arms. She barely resisted. Then Mel cried. She cried so long and so hard Avery wondered if her frail body could even take it. As the sobs subsided, Mel just stood there, head bowed.

"They told me he might be dead," she said softly. "But they couldn't be sure. How could they tell him from the other gritters? They don't know him. They don't know the curve of his earlobes. Or the freckles he gets from the sun. Only I know these things, and I never saw him. They burn them in heaps, you know. I never went there. I promised him I would never go back to California and I kept my promise. Why would he have gone there? I kept my promise. He'll keep his. He said he'd come home."

Avery gently led the woman the few steps to the front of the store, where the low wall between the window display and the store made for a good, solid bench. After sitting for a moment, Mel's gaze finally met Avery's.

"Send the wolf away. Please. Take the lock off the basement door. This is the only place he felt comfortable. He told me so. He could bring his friends here. Tabitha let them sleep here until their minds were bright again. Then if something went wrong, he wouldn't be alone." Her voice caught again. "I watched him sleep once. He looked like a child again. So clear. All calm and smooth. So very clear, even his skin, like he was healing right in front of my eyes."

This time the silence stretched on for a very long time. It must have been longer than an hour, and the sunlight through the window behind them was dimming. Avery kept her arm around the woman. She noticed the stained clothes, the odor of mildew on her raincoat. Then suddenly Mel stood and announced, with authority, "I quit. I'm far too busy to dust floors, don't you think? I'm going home."

"Please let me go with you," Avery said. "I can help settle you in for the night."

"No. Thank you."

Avery felt like her heart was breaking, and she didn't even know why. So she said the only thing that came to her mind. "He knows where you live, right?"

Mel's chin went up. "Of course he does. I am his mother."

She was talking about her son. Avery had already guessed that. "Then he can find you."

The old woman flipped her words away with the flight of her bony hand. "Of course he can, child." She reached into her pocket and pulled out a set of keys, then she dropped them into Avery's lap. "You'll just have to replace me."

"I'd feel so much better if you let me walk you home."

Mel gave Avery one backward look. "And chase the memories away from there, too? Sweep away your own ghosts, young woman. I'm comfortable living with mine."

She walked out the front door. Avery had no idea what to do, but she felt as if she needed to do something. It was a small town, so someone would know Mel and where she lived, someone would know how to help. In the meantime, Avery just sat on the wall and let the connections drift around in her mind. The flophouse. The smell. The alley light that unscrewed itself. The basement entrance unlocked and hidden by pallets, and the stairs that led to the moving bookcase. Had Mel lost her son to the needles Avery had seen upstairs? It scared her. And it made her feel incredibly sad. Death. Loss. And forgiveness. She sat still and let the thoughts chase around her brain.

Until Glacier growled. The sound startled her so badly she hurried to lock the front door. Glacier was looking out the front window, though his piercing eyes drifted from place to place as if he was listening for something.

She heard it. A scrape on the floor. The hair on the back of her neck stood on end. *Thump.* She stared at the middle of the half-lit floor of the store where the sound seemed to be coming from. A soft scrape, then a quiet sound like a small drum. So faint. Then another, coming nearer. She stood and backed toward the door, and the old wooden floor creaked as she moved. Glacier circled her legs again and again.

It came closer. So soft...*scrape. Thud.* She stared at the floor. Glacier stepped forward, staring at the same spot where she had heard the sound. He dug his nose into the old wooden planks and snuffled. Then suddenly he started out across the floor, nose still down. He was leaving her. Scared and upset, she followed him. He went across the floor, turning circles here and there. She heard it behind her, louder this time.

"Glacier," she called, her voice thin and wavering.

But he was moving again, even farther away from her. He followed his own winding path through the doorway to the back room. Then he trotted straight to the secret bookshelf door and growled.

That was enough for Avery. She ran up a couple steps to grab the leash from where she'd dropped it. Glacier was bright and attentive as she clipped the leash to his collar as if nothing had happened. But she was so scared she could hardly stand to lock the door behind her before she hurried away. Glacier thought they were just going for another walk. It comforted her that he wasn't growling anymore, but not enough to go back inside.

She thought about calling the police. But what would she say?

There was no such thing as ghosts. But Avery was picturing ghostly men with needles stuck in their arms, coming after her and her "wolf." She kept heading south, uphill, toward the mountains, her heart racing and her head aching, looking behind her again and again. Then she remembered the apartment where Poppy had been staying. Maybe that was where Sierra was now. She circled around and backtracked, desperate to see a familiar face and have a normal conversation and somehow get her feet planted back on the ground. She ran up the steps and knocked, hoping she had chosen the right door.

But it was Liam who answered. He took one look at her, frowned, then pulled her inside. He scanned the view outside, looking for something. *Lynn*, she thought. How would she explain being there to Liam?

Then he shut the door, put both arms around her, and held her tight.

She was shaking. She hadn't even realized it until she was pressed against his unmoving form. She closed her eyes and soaked it in for a moment, just a moment. She heard the sound of dog paws retreating, then a soft thump behind her. She felt as much as heard Liam chuckle. Was he laughing at her? His hand came up to stroke her hair once, then he wrapped her tight in his arms again.

She would have to pull away. And to explain somehow. But she just breathed in the scent of his shirt, so much like the cashmere sweater next to her pillow. And why was he so quiet? Why didn't he demand an explanation?

She had stopped shaking. And the whole scraping sound thing at the store suddenly seemed like a fabrication of her mind. But Glacier had heard it too. Maybe she wasn't crazy. It was a rat, perhaps—or a raccoon. Finally she straightened and pulled back, but she couldn't bear to look him in the eye.

"Mind if I make us some tea?" he said.

She nodded. That was when she noticed Glacier curled up in the middle of the futon couch. That was what Liam had chuckled at—how quickly Glacier had made himself at home.

"Bad dog on the furniture," she said softly. Glacier only blinked contentedly. So Liam had the same effect on the dog as he had on her. No matter how much she didn't belong here, she felt safe. She went to sit next to the dog. *This is bad*, she thought. Being here was bad for many reasons. But when Liam joined her, bringing with him two mugs with tea bags, he didn't act as if anything was wrong. He didn't ask her a single thing. She could smell chamomile and honey. "I thought maybe Sierra was staying in this apartment," she said.

"Nope. Just me." And he let the silence drift on while she gathered her thoughts. He sat down on the other side of the dog and turned to face her, his gaze on the mug in his hands, and waited. After a while, she couldn't help but start talking. And as soon as she started, his eyes were trained on her, and he listened. She told him about Mel's visit first, then the sound, like a ghost dragging itself across her floor. Later she admitted her less-than-graceful exit. He nodded and gave her concerned looks, but he didn't say a word. She could see the wheels turning in his mind, but she had no idea what he was thinking.

When she was done, she finally took a sip of her tea and waited for his response.

"That's really creepy," Liam said.

She frowned. "You're supposed to give me a perfectly logical explanation for what I heard."

"Yeah, well...I actually have several possible explanations. But I won't know for certain until I get a good look at the place. The problem is, I can't be seen doing that. And you can't stay here, and I don't want you to go home. I don't have any reason to think you are in danger, but it's pretty clear someone is trying to send you a message."

Liam pulled his phone out of his pocket and tapped the screen. After a moment he said, "Dad. I need a favor."

# CHAPTER 41

*A*nson Gunnerson came in her back door, which she had propped open, and into the main part of the store. "Your furnace looks good," he said, wiping a blue cloth against his blackened hands.

He looked every bit like a handyman, although since he was well over six feet tall, she wondered how he got into some of the tight places a handyman had to go. He had the blackened hands, the dirty shirt, jeans, and tools. But then there was the stern, almost regal expression and the perfectly enunciated words that didn't quite fit the handyman vibe. He was a conundrum. And he made her feel more than a little nervous.

"I appreciate this so much," she said.

First Liam had turned off all the lights, then loudly and openly headed toward downtown. Then, as he'd asked, she'd waited ten minutes to sneak down to where Anson was waiting and follow him down the back alleys to a service entrance at the Third Street Inn. Julia had met her there with clean pajamas, toiletries, dog food, and bowls. They had put her in a small room on the third floor where, to her surprise, she'd slept perfectly all night long.

Julia had woken her with coffee and breakfast in her room and told her Anson would be up to take her back to her building. Then Anson had led her by another roundabout route back to her home. While they'd walked, she'd apologized multiple times. Anson had assured her it was okay at least a handful of those times, and after that, he took to shaking his head without a word. But he had tossed her a smile that made him go from okay to startlingly handsome in one move. And that was the first time Avery had seen the family resemblance between Liam and Anson. It was the smile.

When Anson had said the alley was clear, they'd sneaked in the back door. He'd insisted on checking the upstairs first. Liam had done the same that night he'd attacked Mel, she remembered. It felt so very long ago. Then Anson had checked the main floor. Then, under the guise of checking her "malfunctioning" furnace, he'd gone down to the basement. Of course, the furnace hadn't needed to run for two weeks, the weather was so pleasant.

And now he was here, sticking to the furnace-checking story because there were customers in the store. And as soon as they left, he went from slouchy repairman to business owner. And Glacier, who had been resting at her feet, came out to sniff his legs.

"That's quite a treasure you have down there," he said. "I bet Liam just about flipped his lid when he saw that. You know he's always been fascinated by this sort of thing. I'm surprised he didn't tell me about it."

She bit her lip. She didn't say it, but she knew why Liam hadn't talked about the speakeasy or the sidewalk vault. It was because she was terrified of the ceiling collapsing and bankrupting her. So he had kept her secret. But that was before she'd gone bankrupt anyway. It was ironic in a sad, stupid way.

"There's a great deal of dust built up," Anson continued. "As funny as it sounds, it's even on the ceiling. I was able to see marks on the ceiling, although they're difficult to spot. The dents are easier to see, rounded ones, something like the butt end of a pool cue. Let's see…" he looked around the room. "There's a line of dents and marks from about here"—he pointed to the middle of the room where she and Glacier had first heard the scraping sound—"and it stretches out to about here. Then there's a big scrape near the door."

She had chills run down her back. "What could make those marks?"

"People," he said smoothly. "No sign of animals. Lots of footprints in the dust, probably some the police could use." He must have seen the look on her face, because he added, "After all, ghosts don't usually use sticks to go bump in the night. The question is, how did people get into your basement?"

She told him she suspected Mel of opening the basement as a flophouse because she was hoping someone in particular would come back. Anson's eyebrows raised. "Maybe. But they were going upstairs, right? I thought that was where all the damage was. I would expect more disturbance in other areas of the speakeasy if—"

The door creaked. The bell clanged.

Without moving a muscle, Anson said, "I know it's warm right now, but the nights don't stay warm. So as soon as you need to start the furnace up again, let me know if you have any trouble. If you sense weird smells or sounds, just turn it off. And I'll try to get information on how to order that part I told you about. Hopefully, I can get that today and call you a little later on."

It was Lynn coming in the door. Of all people. She was checking out the crates against the wall with her back to Avery, but the perfect, shiny black hair with its asymmetrical red streaks was unmistakable. And the expensive suit. The shoes. And the model's body. Why was she here?

"But call me if something feels wrong," he said, his gaze

locked on her. "Don't mess around with this sort of thing. The firemen are five blocks away. I'm only three blocks away and a hell of a lot faster."

"Thank you, Anson." Avery could barely talk. But she was conscious of Lynn listening, so she added, "I still feel like I should pay you."

He grinned again. Just like Liam. "Business owners need to stick together. What goes around comes around, right? But I should get back to my own job. Mind if I let myself out the back door?"

She shook her head. "Not at all. Thank you."

He strode out, never once turning around to see who had walked in. Avery wondered if he knew somehow. She was pretty sure Anson Gunnerson was not someone to be underestimated.

And now there was Lynn to deal with. Avery tried to be sneaky too. She tipped her head sideways and said, "Lynn, is that you?"

Lynn pivoted. "Hi, Avery. I've been meaning to come and see your new store."

"I'm so glad you did," she lied. "Are you looking for anything in particular?" In her mind she saw Liam leaning over the tiny table in the back of the restaurant, his face close to Lynn's, smiling. Enjoying her company. Enjoying her everything, this woman who physically, and probably in every way, was Avery's exact opposite.

Lynn walked over on her high heels and skinny legs, all topped by that hair. How did hair become that shiny? Avery resisted the urge to ask her about it. Instead, she just stood there —not tall, with a messy bun, in a barely-had-time-to-change-clothes outfit with a stupid smile on her face.

"So I hear you and Griff have a big night planned," Lynn said with a sly smile.

Avery opened her mouth, but nothing came out. There was

nothing planned. He'd said he was going to drop by. What had he told Lynn, and why?

"I'm sorry, I can see I overstepped," Lynn said smoothly. "Don't mind me. Griff and I go way back. Second grade, actually. We know a lot about each other. In fact, you could say we know each other inside out." She smiled a big, toothpaste-commercial smile. "I'm happy for him."

Happy for him? For what? Avery had nothing to say. "I didn't know you've been friends so long. That's nice." Nice? She was such a hopeless derp. "I guess that's the best part of living in a small town, right?"

"It has its ups and downs." Lynn looked around the store, and then her large eyes settled on Avery once more. "I saw you last night, right? At Annie's?"

"Yeah." This morning was taking a fast-and-hard nosedive. "I couldn't come in, though, with the dog. I guess they don't appreciate fur on their food." She laughed at her own feeble joke.

"Probably not," Lynn said with a toss of her head. "I just want to make sure I'm not stepping on your toes, Avery. You and Liam seem to have spent a lot of time together. Liam and I go way back too. Way back. But if there's some unfinished business there—"

"No," Avery said with a quick shake of her head. "Liam helped me out with financial advice. We were friends, kind of." She saw Lynn's eyes narrow just a touch. "He's really not my type." *Yeah*, she thought. *Who likes handsome, kind, and smart guys?*

"I heard you guys got pretty cozy at the wedding. That you had quite the romantic dance."

Avery shook her head. "Hardly. We just got stuck with a slow song. It was pretty awkward, really. He even apologized for it later." *That was a nice touch*, she thought. And it was half-true. She looked at sleek, stylish Lynn, and added, "He's not mine, and I'm not his." Did Lynn believe her? Avery gave a dramatic shrug. "Actually, I think he's pretty darn lucky to be dating you. I kind of pictured you with someone else."

"Like who?"

*Anyone other than Liam.* "I don't know. Someone rich. Powerful."

"Liam's more powerful than people think."

Either Lynn was baiting her or Avery was just plain awful at lying. And Avery was awful...except when it came to lies of omission. She'd gotten way too good at those lately. "I'm sorry. I don't mean to say anything bad about your boyfriend. He's a nice guy. I will say that you two make the best-looking couple I've seen in ages."

Lynn smiled. "That's nice of you to say." She tucked a perfect lock of hair behind her ear. "I do have to admit he hasn't got the kind of presence that Griff has. Griff just owns a room when he walks in, doesn't he?"

*Yeah, something like that.* She had the feeling, again, that Lynn had more than friendly feelings for Griffin.

"So you really aren't seeing Liam?"

This woman was hard to convince. And why did her opinion matter so much? Could she have seen her at Liam's apartment, and now she was jealous? Avery couldn't be sure. On the way back from the hotel, Anson had told her to act as if she'd spent the night at home. So she did. "No." She wrinkled her nose for good measure.

Was Liam dating Lynn? But he had said he wanted to get to know Avery better. Just the thought of it gave her a jolt that couldn't compare to her coffee. Or a couple pots of coffee. And what had she said to him? Nothing. Yeah, he wasn't her type. That's why she'd been sleeping with his sweater like it was some sort of stuffing-less stuffed animal, until the scent of it that she'd found so intoxicating was gone, like the memory of a good dream she couldn't quite remember except for the feeling of something good, something peaceful.

And how long had she been standing here, silent, like an idiot?

"Sorry, I just remembered I had something to get back to Liam."

"Really? What?"

She was ready for Lynn to leave. This whole conversation was exhausting. "A package." It would be a package after she de-furred the sweater and wrapped it up in a plastic bag. She really couldn't blame Glacier for stealing it from her. But did he like her scent on it, or Liam's?

"A package?"

Lynn really was pushy. "Yeah, a package of...papers. Work stuff. I just need to get it back to him."

Lynn's eyes narrowed again. "You have some papers of his that you need to get back to him?"

"Yeah." Had she said something wrong?

Lynn's gaze drifted over the checkout desk as if the imaginary papers might be there somewhere. Then she tossed her hair back and said, "I can get them to him."

Well, this was awkward. "The package is a little hard to get to right now. I had it tucked away for safekeeping." Actually, the sweater was sitting on her bed, since Glacier liked to drag it off the bedside table when she wasn't looking. It had become the world's most expensive doggy blanket. "I'll get it out after work and give it to him then."

"I can help you out with that. If you could get it ready during lunchtime, I can get it to Liam," Lynn said. "Besides, you're going out with Griff. It's not my place to say this, but I don't think he'd be thrilled if you take a side trip to visit Liam."

"That's really nice of you," Avery said. *Absolutely not*, she thought. "I'll let you know. But I don't know your number."

Lynn pulled a card out of her purse. "You can call me on my cell." She was a banker, then. That figured. Avery didn't like bankers very much right now. "I'll be around. I have work to do in Moose Hollow." She looked around the store again. "Isn't it weird to be here all by yourself? Old buildings give me the creeps. Do you sleep okay?"

There it was. The question Liam had told her to look for, just before he left and sent her to the hotel with his father. He said to be very suspicious of anyone asking about her being scared. But why would Lynn sneak into her basement? It had to be a coincidence. Nevertheless, Avery gave the answer Liam had said she should give. "Nah. Old buildings make the weirdest sounds, so I just lock up the dog and use industrial strength earplugs. I sleep like a baby."

# CHAPTER 42

The call had come at ten minutes past six o'clock. Cash had left long ago, and Liam had the office to himself. The number calling him was blocked. Liam set the phone to record before he answered.

"Hello, thief," a voice said.

"Who is this?" He knew who it was. It was one of the Chicago thugs, either Billy or Arthur. It didn't matter which one.

"We want what you stole."

"I didn't steal anything." Liam tried to sound anxious, and it wasn't very hard to do. "I just want you guys off my back. If I give you the papers, how will I know you'll leave me alone? How do I know the company won't press charges?"

"You have the papers on you?"

"I have them right now, in my hands." *Come and find out, jerks.*

There was a pause. "Go to 2750 Marquis Road in Billings. Park in the main parking lot. Be there at nine o'clock. No phone, no weapons, don't be stupid."

"Wait a second—"

"At eleven o'clock get out of your car with the papers. Wait fifteen minutes. Do not get back in the car. Then walk three blocks south to Essex Car Repair. Go in the side door. If you don't follow instructions, I'll be gone. And you will have missed the only chance you're going to get."

"I need to know you guys are gonna leave me alone. How can I—"

The phone went dead. It was interesting that they'd asked for papers, specifically. It was interesting that they wanted him to go someplace they could observe him for two hours. And the timing was interesting, too, coming so soon after his conversation with Lynn. But it was a circumstantial link between Griff and the Ackerman, Jones & Fetterman hired hands.

He was pretty sure the location they directed him to was in an old industrial district of Billings, about a mile from the dojo. There were a lot of abandoned buildings there, along with the old rail lines that had once been their lifeblood. There was one main road, and other than that, almost no traffic. There was little chance of being seen or heard. So what were they planning? An honest trade? He doubted it. Not after going to all that trouble.

So what did they want?

They wanted the papers. And they wanted to scare Liam into absolute silence. Liam thought about how he would accomplish such a thing in their place. And no matter how many times he mulled over it, he couldn't see what they had to gain by risking a meeting. Just calling was a risk, but anything more was ridiculous. Why would they get him to follow these convoluted steps when every move could make them vulnerable? He knew he shouldn't go. But without some recorded information, something substantial to implicate Arthur and Billy, his chance of nailing Ackerman, Jones & Fetterman was slim.

What had the pastor said about making decisions yesterday? He had trouble remembering, but he had no problem at all recalling how much time he'd spent scanning the crowd from his seat in the back, looking for some sign of Avery. She hadn't been there. But what difference did it make? He would have cut out early to avoid her anyway, just like he had the week before.

Frustrated, he wandered over to the windows and gazed down at Broadway, the main street of Moose Hollow. It was midsummer, and the place was in bloom with fragrant flowers —and tourists in a riot of cheerful colors, wearing T-shirts with questionable sayings.

Below him, someone was looking in the door of Moose on the Loose. He was a burly man, definitely not Avery's usual clientele. Something about his carriage and clothing marked him as one of the out-of-towners. Was this one of the thugs?

Liam was acting paranoid. It was a tourist town, full of strangers. He could drive himself crazy this way.

That's what the pastor had said, that prayer shouldn't be an afterthought. He hadn't prayed about this path he was on. When Liam was stressed, he sometimes held on to things so tightly and worked so hard to fix things, he acted as if the whole universe was up to him. Reluctantly, he closed his eyes to the world and prayed.

It turned out he didn't have much to say. So he listened instead.

And after time slipped by minute by minute, something occurred to Liam. Maybe things had changed. Maybe someone had already gotten information on Ackerman, Jones & Fetterman, and that's why they were willing to draw him out, even though they could be recognized or caught. His eyes opened. He could be near the end of this mess. The documents he had, plus the phone call and whatever someone else might have, could add up.

But if the firm was in trouble, he was too. If an investigation was underway, his testimony could be significant. Maybe the thugs didn't want the papers so much as they wanted to do whatever it would take to shut him up.

Liam knew his next move was a risk. There was a chance the computer was bugged in some way. But the phone felt like even more of a threat right now. He pulled out his wallet and drew out the business card Mike had given him. There was an email address on the card. Liam dug a little deeper in the wallet and retrieved the tiny chip, then put it in the chip reader of Cash's over-teched, overpriced computer. He couldn't go any further alone. He had to trust God would put all the pieces into place.

He hit send. In the meantime, things were about to hit the fan. Liam turned off the computer and swiveled the seat to take in the view outside, wondering which part of his life might blow up first.

The answer came fast. Griff Hallowell was knocking on the door of the Moose on the Loose.

# CHAPTER 43

 very's phone rang, a quiet bird-like tone she had chosen so it wouldn't disrupt customers. But she wasn't at work now, she was at play, sewing the first seam on a new pattern based on something Julia Gunnerson had said. She focused on the project though she had several messages to return, including one from Anson and one from Connor, her lawyer.

She'd been ignoring those messages because she could barely stand the thought of taking the very call she'd just received. She'd been dreading it, and until it was over, she couldn't face the others. Her phone stopped ringing, and then a message scrolled across her screen: "On my way."

She considered hiding in her room. She looked at Glacier, who was sleeping next to her sewing desk, on his back on the pricey dog bed Liam had bought him. That was his day bed, of course. At night he liked to sneak up onto her bed. Last night at the hotel she'd tried to get him to sleep on the floor instead of the antique-looking quilt, but she'd learned that with Glacier, some habits were harder to break than others.

"Let's get this over with, Glacier," she said, and he flopped over onto his belly. "You'll help, right?"

Glacier wagged. He always wagged now, every single time she talked to him. And it made Avery smile, every time.

He was knocking at the door. She could hear it all the way upstairs. She marched down the long hall, down the stairs, and across the wide back room.

It really could be a good place for a custom clothing shop. The bookshelves, the apothecary drawers, the exposed brick. With a new coat of paint, it could really be something. She set her phone down in the back room, tucked out of sight so he wouldn't see she'd been avoiding his calls on purpose.

Griffin was waiting at the door in a black suit with a pinstripe black and silver tie and a shiny dark purple shirt. Slick. And here she was in what amounted to repurposed rags and thrift-store boots with the tops cut off and folded over because she didn't like the original design.

What had Griffin seen in her?

She unlocked the door and smiled. "You look handsome," she said.

"Thank you." He didn't come in very far. "Bring that contract, okay? We're going to Jet. The owner hired a new chef. Tables are hard to find, but I pulled some strings."

Glacier stood next to her, staring at Griffin's feet. "Griffin, you are kind for wanting to take me there. But I'm not going out with you."

He looked at her completely without expression. "You're still on that?"

"I'm not going to go out with you, Griffin."

"I had to convince my father to give up his reservation and give it to me. He doesn't do that sort of thing, Avery. He's got to be the first, always."

"I'm sorry. But I didn't say I was going to go anywhere with you."

"No," he said, his voice raising a little. "No, you didn't. But I also thought you were a little better mannered, recognizing maybe if someone does you a favor, you don't throw it back in his face."

Avery tried not to show how startled she was. "I'm sorry you feel that way. But I'm not going to date you, and I'm not going to do anything that could be mistaken for a date, either."

"Until the next time you need free help from someone, right? Accounting help, furnace repair, real estate? Do you only use men, or are you an equal opportunity user?"

"You can leave now," she said. She stood up as tall as she could, and as still as she could, but her legs quivered. Beside her, she heard a short, low hum. Glacier was growling. She was certain Griffin hadn't recognized the sound yet.

"I'm sorry," he said. "I don't know why I said that." He ran his hand back through his hair. "I can't tell you how much stress I've been under. My dad is talking about taking Bozeman away from me. I know that's not your fault, Avery, you've been nothing but classy. I had no right to say those things. But I'm in trouble—real trouble. You really need to come with me tonight. Just let my dad know we went out together, then he'll know you're still considering his offer. That's it. No date, no expectations."

"I can't."

"You don't understand. Things are going down tonight. You can't be here."

"Griffin, you need to leave now."

"What the hell?" he shouted. "Do you really not understand, or do you just not give a damn? What is wrong with you? I'm trying to help you. I'm the only one trying to help you."

The growl was unmistakable now, but Griffin didn't seem to notice. She reached down for Glacier's collar and stepped back, and that's when she saw Glacier bare his teeth.

"What the hell?" Griffin repeated. He looked from the dog to her. "Really? Do you know who I am? Do you know who my family is? There isn't a person in this town that doesn't owe us something. You had my support. You will burn without my help."

"Leave now," she said, keeping the words short and firm to hide the shaking.

Griffin reached over the dog as if he was going to point a finger right into her face, and Glacier leaped up with a flurry of barks. She dropped her phone to grab hold with both hands. She heard the dog's teeth snap as Griffin jumped back, and she was nearly pulled off her feet. She backpedaled and struggled to hold on to the dog's collar.

Griffin straightened his tie and pointed at her. "That moment when you figure it out, remember I tried to help you. And you threw it in my face." He finally opened the door, slamming it so hard behind him that she was afraid the glass had broken, but she didn't see any cracks. She let go of Glacier, who trotted along the front windows, growling and following Griffin as long as he could see him.

Avery stood in that same spot for the longest time. How had she been so wrong about him?

"Glacier," she called, and he came to her, a smile on his face. He was perfectly happy, as if nothing had happened. "Tomorrow we're going to the shelter, buddy," she said. "You're not my foster dog anymore. I think I owe them some adoption fees."

# CHAPTER 44

*E*very light in the office was off, and Liam was watching, debating his next move and changing his mind over and over again. He'd almost run over to Avery's store when he'd heard Glacier bark, but shortly after that Griff had left her place with a door slam that half the town probably heard. The way he straightened his jacket, trying to look cool and collected, made it clear he was anything but.

And Glacier didn't bark anymore. He saw Avery briefly when she locked the door, then she and a wagging dog disappeared into the shadows.

Go or not? Should he risk it or trust she was okay? But she wasn't okay. He should call his dad and have him drop by. Or maybe someone else. Anyone.

But it should be him.

It should be him, and it wasn't because of the choices he'd made. Colton was right. He had to stand up to the bullies, and that had very little to do with Griff. The email to Mike was just the first step in a marathon he had to run.

To Liam's right, Griff swaggered up the street, even stopping half a block away to loudly salute a friend and laugh at whoever it was. They were all attempts to save face. Liam's eyes moved from Griff to the Moose on the Loose, but there was nothing to be seen there. Back to Griff. *There wouldn't be much to see there, either, just Griff on his way to the Lantern*, Liam thought.

But Griff was jerking his arm away from someone. Had he started a fight already? Griff was just over a block away, far enough that Liam had trouble seeing what was going on. But the person he was facing wasn't moving. Griff waved his hands in the air and strode into the Lantern. The other person ambled closer, bit by bit looking all around as if to see who had been watching. He sipped something from a paper coffee cup. He kept walking, eyes down, navy blue baseball cap obscuring his face.

It was a Chicago Bears cap.

Seriously? Was Mike being literal when he'd said to watch out for someone wearing a Bears cap? And as the man came closer, Liam was sure it was the same person he'd seen earlier looking through the door of the Moose on the Loose. He wasn't paranoid. They were hanging out across the street to make sure Liam left as planned. After all, Liam couldn't think of any reason they would want to watch Avery.

He made his decision. Liam locked up and climbed into the Cruiser parked in the alley behind Cash's building. He pulled a U-turn in the narrow street and headed north, toward Billings.

# CHAPTER 45

*G*lacier did a funny little dance with his paws when she put the leash on. She wished she could do better for him than a short stroll through the alleyway in search of anything that resembled grass just so he could do his business. But now the sun was down, and she didn't want to walk all the way up to the trailhead. If she was staying, she would have reclaimed one of the awkward parking spaces behind the building and found a way to grow grass there instead. She turned the doorknob on the back door.

She hardly had time to breathe, let alone think, when a body shoved through the door. A hand clamped down over her mouth.

"Shhh," he said.

Eyes wide open, her brain recognized Liam, but the scream was already on her lips. He pressed harder and shook his head. With his other hand, he very slowly and carefully closed the door.

Had all the people in Moose Hollow gone insane at the same time? And why wasn't Glacier ripping Liam's head off?

Liam released his hold, and she said in a low voice, "Leave. Now."

And that was when she heard a sound at the front door. Liam grabbed her around the waist and pulled her over to the secret door in the bookcase. She wanted to yell. But there was something in his expression that stopped her. He didn't look angry. He looked scared.

He opened the bookcase door and pulled her onto the small landing at the top of the secret steps, tugged Glacier inside, and shut the bookcase door behind them.

And instantly it was completely dark. Now Avery was scared too.

"There are two men," he whispered. "One at the front door, one at the back. I can't get you out either door safely. Come on."

"Who's here?" she whispered back, but he pulled her down the steps so fast she stumbled. He steadied her at the bottom, and that's when Glacier hummed quietly into the darkness.

"Gunnerson!" someone called from inside the store.

Liam's forehead touched hers in the dark. He was breathing fast, as if he'd been running. "Stay here," he whispered. "Hide in the speakeasy if you can."

"Liam, what's going on?"

"You have to stay here. The guy in the back might've seen me. If they know I'm here, they'll keep looking for me. But they don't know you're here. They aren't after you. You have to stay here, out of sight."

"Glacier can help you, he—"

"Hold on to him. I need you safe, Avery," he said. There was something in his tone of voice that stopped her from saying another word. "Stay here with the dog."

He let go. She heard the sound of quick, quiet steps on the stairs and then nothing. The door opened, there was a moment of light, and then it was dark again.

"Hey, you," Liam called. "The store is closed."

Someone answered. It was a low voice, farther away, and Avery couldn't make sense of it.

But she could hear Liam's response. "What are you doing? Hey. You don't need a gun. If you want money, you can have it."

*Gun.* She heard the back door open and the sound of footsteps right overhead. Glacier hummed, and she tapped him on the top of his head. He stopped. Both men were in the store now, and at least one had a gun. And she was stuck in a basement with no way out. Just the thought of it made awful images pour into her head, as if the basement were full of ghosts reaching for her from every direction. She could feel tears stinging her eyes, and Glacier made a quiet whining sound.

She froze. If she lost it now, Glacier would react, and someone could hear him. She had to hold it together.

"You're supposed to be in Billings, Gunnerson."

"It's you," Liam said. "You're the guy who called me."

"Take your phone out of your pocket and drop it now," a different voice said. "We want the package."

"I want my license reinstated. Then you'll get the documents."

"We're taking them now."

There was a pause, and then some shuffling on the floor above her head. "Fine. I just want this over with. The package you're looking for is across the street."

The man closest to the back door let out a short, bitter laugh. "We know it's upstairs. We found out, Gunnerson. Your girlfriend was hiding it for you right under the frat boy's nose all this time. She said she was going to give it to you tonight, but she never did. So here we are, your courier service. And where is she?"

"She's out looking for Griff. I hoped she would be here, but she wasn't. And I don't know what you're talking about. The papers are in the office across the street. There's nothing here."

Stars sparked at the edges of her vision, and Avery sat down on the damp, dirty floor. Liam had said he was in trouble. He'd said the name of a company. Was it the one that had fired him? And what about these papers? That's what she had told Lynn. All those strange, pointed questions Lynn had been asking. Lynn had been so determined to get her hands on the sweater, which Avery had said was papers. Had Lynn thought Avery's package was the documents these men were after? Lynn was Griff's friend, and probably something more than that. Then there were the two creepy men who had been in the Lantern with Lynn and Griff. What had one of them said? *Be careful who you keep company with. And whose secrets you keep.* Could he have been one of the men who now threatened Liam?

It all seemed outrageous. Was she crazy for thinking Lynn, Griffin, and Liam were all mixed up in something dangerous? But nothing she could imagine was crazier than two men with a gun standing on the floor above her head.

Liam was in danger, and so was she. That much was certain.

Three sets of footsteps started up the stairs to her apartment, spaced well apart. There they would find a sweater wrapped in a plastic bag sitting in the middle of her bed, instead of whatever documents they wanted. And when they did, Liam would be in even more danger than he was already facing. She stood up and felt her way over to the utility entrance. It moved, then stopped. The padlock still held. She held back a sob.

In the slightest hint of light from the edges of the utility door, she turned and reached out, walking forward to the second secret door in her building, the one that led to the old speakeasy. In her head, she heard the thump and scrape from the night before. She dreaded the sound of a gunshot and the touch of a ghost, each seeming just as surreal and inevitable as the other. Her hands touched something thick with slimy dirt. Tears sprang to her wide open, unseeing eyes, and she grabbed hold and pulled.

The secret door scraped along the stone floor. Avery

stopped, barely breathing. Had they heard her? She held Glacier's leash tight. His low, humming growl filled the darkness and sent chills up her spine. She had to close the door in case they came looking for her. She pulled it slowly, wincing at the sounds it made until she was sure it was closed.

That left her in the speakeasy, in complete darkness. She blinked again and again, as if the blackness could be washed from her eyes, but the darkness never shifted. It was the same in every direction. She was safer here, she tried to convince herself.

But Liam wasn't safe at all.

# CHAPTER 46

*A*s he climbed the stairs to Avery's apartment, what Liam was seeing and what he had seen in the past superimposed in his mind. He saw the first night he'd been here, and the indescribable mess he'd found then. And the time he'd come up after Avery, feeling guilty about his search for secret passageways and hidden treasure when it had meant nothing but trouble for her. And now he saw his reality, with one captor ahead of him and one behind, each keeping a safe distance.

He passed the spot where he'd almost kissed Avery. *God, I wish I had.*

He had to find a way to get closer to the men. He had practiced disarming maneuvers in the dojo, but these men were smart enough to stay triangulated and well out of reach, and their focus didn't waver. The man in the navy blue cap walked in front of him, backward down the dark hall and then through Avery's bedroom door. It was surreal to walk through that door now, when he remembered so well standing in the doorway and refusing to come in. He'd said it was because he was taught to be polite. But he'd also done it because she flustered him and confused him and he said things he should never say in her presence. *Please keep her safe*, he prayed. By the time Liam made it through her doorway, the man in the cap was already off to the side, gun pointed at him. It was a comfortable, confident grip, and the aim never wavered.

"Open it," the man said, lifting his chin toward the bed.

There was something there, wrapped in a plastic bag. Liam could tell by the feel of it that it wasn't papers. He opened the bag and drew out a sweater.

His sweater. And it smelled of flowers, old-fashioned, fresh. It smelled like Avery.

He eyed the man behind him. "I told you the documents are in my office."

"It's not there," said the other man, the one who had followed him up the stairs.

"I bet you always lost at hide-and-seek," Liam said. Then to the man in the cap he added, "I'll tell you where it is."

"No. You'll take me there." His eyes shifted to his partner. "Give the frat boy what he wants, and make it big. He deserves a little bonus after sending us on this goose chase." The other man went out of the room ahead of them, and to Liam he said, "You, back downstairs. We're going on a little field trip."

Give the frat boy what he wants? Griff, no doubt, but what did he want? What possible interest did he have in any of this, other than happily throwing Liam under the bus?

"You should know I'm a good shot," the man said. "So here's how we're going to do this. I'm going to open the front door. You're going to walk straight across the street and unlock the door to your office. And I'm going to follow you. If you walk a different way, if you talk or look at anyone, if you run, I will shoot you. Then I will shoot your mom, shoot your dad, and disappear into thin air like I always do. Do you understand?"

Liam understood two things. First, that going across the street was his best chance to make a clean break. There would be lots of witnesses, and he'd been taught more than one technique to get a gun out of a man's hands. And the second thing was that he still had a chance to get more information out of him. He had to make a decision.

But what if this wasn't a strong-arm maneuver? What if the man had actually been sent to kill him, not just to get the papers? Even now, with a gun pointed at his chest, Liam found that hard to believe. He worked for an accounting firm, not the mob.

The man in the cap unlocked the front door of the Moose on the Loose. Liam had to get away, and now.

But if he went across the street, the men would go with him. Avery would be safe.

Liam walked through the door and across the street, and punched the combination into the new lock. As soon as the door opened, he felt the presence behind him. "It's up here," Liam said. He had the heavy, horrible feeling he'd made the wrong choice.

# CHAPTER 47

*A*very walked forward, taking no more than five steps before her foot hit something. It made a loud, scraping sound. A chair leg? She froze, listening hard. There were still no sounds on the floor above her. *Please, God, let Liam be safe.*

She blinked back tears. "Please, God, help me too," she whispered.

Maybe this was it, just what God had planned for her. Maybe she'd failed again. She had failed Eli, and her baby. She had failed her one chance to make it all right, to open the store Eli had wanted.

*So you think God's calling was for you to sell pricey outdoorsy clothes to ski bums and vacationers?*

The thought was like a knife in her head, severing all other thoughts.

In a world with thugs and guns and ghosts, nothing seemed impossible. So she answered out loud.

"Yes."

Silence. Okay, it sounded ridiculous, when it was put that way.

"Yes, I thought I was called here," she whispered.

No other thoughts went ripping through her mind.

Maybe she was called here.

Maybe it wasn't for penance. Perhaps it was for something else.

"But I screwed up," she whispered, partly to herself, partly to God, and partly to Eli. "I really screwed up. I ruined Eli."

*Ruined.* Avery thought of all the energetic, happy hippie evangelizing Eli had done. *We're never too far from God,* he had said. He'd said it over and over. Had she ever really listened to him? In some ways, she had just humored him. He'd been a new believer, and she'd thought he would cool down after a little time passed.

"I am the worst of sinners. So are you. Isn't that amazing?" He'd say it with a smile on his face.

Avery pressed her hand to her heart. "But I killed Eli," she said. And when she said it out loud for the very first time, she knew it wasn't true. So she tried again, digging more deeply into the well of guilt she carried around. "I killed my baby."

*They were loved.*

She sobbed so loudly she had to press her hands to her mouth. It took her a moment to be able to speak the words out loud. "I did love them," she whispered into the dark. Maybe not the way she should have, but she did love them. "Have you got them, God? Are they safe?" And one more hard question. "Have they forgiven me for failing them?"

There was no answer. *Love never fails,* Eli had told her. She had seen his face the morning after they'd made love. He hadn't looked scared, sad, or anything. He'd just looked at her with that funny grin of his. *Sometimes we aren't strong. That's what forgiveness is for,* he'd said. *We'll make this right.* She'd thought he'd meant the two of them. She wondered now if he'd meant God would make it right too.

It was what the pastor had said. And what her parents had

said. What if it was the truth? What if God was more real than she'd imagined, and he was waiting for her to trust him?

"I'm so sorry," she whispered.

There were footsteps overhead, and a low murmur. Were the men leaving?

"Remember, one wrong move and I shoot." She heard that clearly enough. Then she heard a familiar click and the clang of a bell against the door.

She unhooked Glacier's leash so it wouldn't drag and make noise, and then grabbed the dog's collar. "That way," she whispered. She tried to picture the speakeasy in her mind, but she couldn't remember it well enough. But Glacier moved, and she followed. He knew how to make it through the dark. Maybe he saw something, maybe his whiskers felt it, but he knew how to make it through. She put both hands on his collar and fell in behind him. And when he stopped, she stepped forward, arms out.

She felt carved wood, not a wall. The door to the store slammed directly over her head, nearly making her jump out of her skin. Glacier had led her to the door that led to the sidewalk vault.

She pushed and turned the knob, but nothing happened. Then she pulled and it opened with hardly a sound. She walked out into another place she had never wanted to be, and in that moldy, damp secret passage that threatened to bring the street down on her head, she saw a light.

She could see light.

She put her hands out and moved to her right. Faint light was coming through the tiny blocks of glass in the concrete above her. But there was more. A greenish light. She wouldn't have seen it if she'd had a flashlight in her hand. She went farther forward with Glacier pressed against her left leg, matching her every step. She could make out the outline of another door. The door to the basement of Hallowell Realty.

And through the window, she could see an open pathway, and somewhere beyond, a green sign: EXIT.

*Thump, slide*, she heard in her mind.

Griffin had access to her basement.

Griffin had reason to scare her enough to make her want to sell.

She swore, and beside her, Glacier hummed in response. She turned the knob to Hallowell Realty's basement, and the door creaked open. "You should have locked it, idiot," she muttered. Then, to Glacier, she said, "Come on. We're getting out of here."

She jogged up the steep steps to the door, then through another door. The entrance to the basement was concealed in the back of a closet. Once she made it out, she was in another world, clean and spacious, lit by windows full of the streetlights and neon signs of Moose Hollow's main street.

Then the alarms went off. Avery jumped, but a second later she realized what the sound was. "Thank you," she whispered. *Bring the police. Bring everyone.*

The front door was locked. But there was a chair nearby, and Avery wasn't going to wait a moment longer to get out of Hallowell Realty.

## CHAPTER 48

*I*t wasn't easy to get to the underside of the filing cabinet, but Liam did, cutting his hand along the way. He hardly felt it, but he noticed the dark red streak on the manila envelope as he drew it out.

He had to get the man to talk. "You swear to me that this is the end of it and you won't bother me anymore?"

The man in the cap smiled. "Oh yeah. This is the end of it."

Fear fired every nerve in his body. Was he hearing him right? He had to think fast. "Do you think Ackerman, Jones & Fetterman is going to pay you for what you're doing? You realize what all this is about, don't you? You realize they're bankrupt."

The man didn't so much as blink. *Just talk,* he wished and prayed. *If this is the end, don't let it be for nothing.* "Who promised you money? Wilkins? No. Dermott, the CFO. Of course, he's the one who would do time. At first they just wanted you to scare me. But things changed, right? If he's this desperate, it's because they're investigating. And if they're investigating, they will have already shut down his accounts."

Still nothing.

"You'll never get paid," Liam said, pressing on.

"You talk too much."

The door below opened, and the other man jogged up the steps. "We're done," he said.

It registered in Liam's mind that the man had left the door open at the bottom of the steps, making it easier to get out. He just had to find a way past them both.

That was when Liam saw the lights. He started forward, but the movement of the gun halted him. A strange light reflected on the ceiling—there was a fire across the street. "What did you do?" Liam said.

"Frat boy wanted to torch your girlfriend's place, thief," the man with the cap said. "Well done, Arthur."

"You can't—" Liam edged forward, and the gun reached closer to him. "She's in there. You have to let me go. I'm the only one who knows how to get into the basement. Please, she didn't have anything to do with any of this."

An alarm went off.

"That was fast," Arthur said.

"Small town," the man with the cap said. "Be patient. We need more noise."

Liam stood still, watching, waiting for his chance. And they stood still as well. The man with the cap backed away and looked over his shoulder as sirens grew louder.

"The cops made it first," he said. "They're only a couple blocks away. It will take a little longer for the hick firemen to get it together." His gaze bored through Liam.

"This should cover the sound of the gunshot," the man with the cap said. "Head down the fire escape, and get across the street with the crowd. You know where to meet me. Too bad we won't have time to say goodbye to the frat boy. I would have liked to have given him a parting gift."

"Stop!" Liam held up his hand as if it would make a difference. He had to think. "Arthur Smith," Liam said, and both men froze. "That makes you Billy Sartie." Liam tore his gaze away from the flickering in the front window of the Moose on the Loose. He couldn't panic now. "The police told me your names. That means the Feds know. If they find me dead—"

"Then it won't be a moment too soon," Billy said, and he cocked his head to aim straight down his arm, right at Liam's chest.

Liam dodged hard to the left, toward Arthur, and that was when he heard a roaring sound like a freight train blasting up the stairs.

He was watching the aim of the gun as it moved through the air, almost in slow motion, swinging with a perfect arc as Liam's shoulder hit the floor. He couldn't make sense of the shadow that hurtled in front of him. But he heard the pistol blast.

And then he heard a scream—his name. Had he been hit?

His body finished the move, kicked through Arthur's head, and reached out to pull him down into a hold, fast and hard. There was the crack of breaking bone and a cry. Liam heard a spitting, snarling sound where Billy stood. He was already moving, half running and half crawling, hurtling toward Billy. And he wasn't the only one.

Just as he lunged for the takedown, he saw Glacier tearing at the man's arm. At the end of that arm was the gun, twisting to take a shot at the dog. Liam hit Billy in the face with the heel of his palm. Then a strike to the hand—he heard the gun hit the floor. But the man was still fighting.

Glacier snarled and shook, tearing flesh, and the man growled nearly as loud. Liam was on him now. Full mount. Arm bar. He heard the sucking noise and felt the joint give way and the collarbone snap. The man screamed out. Liam let go—and then gave him one straight punch to the temple.

The man went limp.

He heard some shouting below, but he ignored it, searching

for the gun to secure it instead. He thought it might have gone through the railing and down the stairs.

"Police! Nobody move!"

"There's a fire," Liam called. "Avery's in the basement, you've got to save her. He tried to stand up and realized he could hardly breathe.

"Police! Show me your hands!"

"She's in the basement!"

"Show me your hands!"

Liam raised his hands, but the officer wasn't talking to him. There was a beam of light illuminating where Arthur was writhing on the floor. "He can't do that right now," Liam said.

"Liam?" Mike's voice. "We have Avery. She's safe."

How could that be? Liam felt relief like he'd never felt before in his life.

Glacier had stopped snarling at the unconscious Billy, but he wouldn't let go. "Good boy," Liam said. He took hold of the dog's collar. "Let go. You did good."

His hand was wet. He stared at both palms, and a flashlight beam swept him as he did. His right hand was covered in blood. He had absolutely no idea where it was coming from. Was it from the cut?

"Are you safe, Liam?"

"I'm good, Mike."

Liam heard Mike's footsteps coming the rest of the way up the stairs. The flashlight swept across the room and back to Liam. That was when Liam saw there was a gun just below the flashlight.

"Step away, son," Mike said. He was all late-night DJ again, Marvin Gaye smooth. It actually made Liam smile.

"You have a hell of a voice, Mike."

"So I've been told." Then, louder, "Haynes, let him up."

Anson Gunnerson took the stairs in three steps. Liam only had time to step free of Billy's legs before his father had him, wrapping his son in his arms so tight Liam's feet barely touched the ground. For a moment he felt like a child again. "Whatever is going on, we'll get through this," his father said.

He always said that. And for the first time, Liam really understood how much he meant it. So he let his father hold him, just for a moment, and soaked up the same sense of safety and protection the man had given him all his life—until he'd grown too foolish to accept it. "I'm okay, Dad."

Anson drew back and looked at every part of his son. "Did you get hurt? Did you get shot?"

The blood. It finally made sense.

Liam fell to his knees, reaching for Glacier, shoving past Mike, who was next to him putting handcuffs on a dazed Billy. Liam felt around the dog's neck for his collar. It was hot and wet. "He shot him."

"Shot who, son?" Mike asked.

"Mike, he shot my dog." Liam gave Mike a desperate look. "Glacier saved my life."

Mike pressed a black box on his shoulder and spoke into it. "All clear. Come inside. And call the vet."

Liam felt around. He wanted to stop the bleeding, but he couldn't figure out where it was coming from. Glacier was breathing too hard, and his eyes looked strange.

"I'm sorry, did you say vet?" The woman's voice buzzed over Mike's radio.

"Veterinarian," Mike said. Then with more force, "Make it happen."

"Yes, sir."

Liam looked up at his father. "What am I going to tell Avery?"

## CHAPTER 49

*A*very made Glacier stay back, then with a clear view of Griffin Hallowell in her mind, she tossed the chair through the glass door. It crackled into a million pieces but held intact. So she picked up the chair again and swept it through the glittering green shards and it rained down like sleet over the floor.

Not so great for dog paws, she realized. She turned back to find something to cover the glass, but Glacier just leaped through the doorway and onto the sidewalk. So she did the same.

The alarm had drawn a crowd. People were staring at her. Even though it was a Monday night, they were all around, lured by the alarm. But they were looking another direction, too. Avery took a few steps along the sidewalk and saw the flames inside her building, and the black smoke that boiled up to the ceiling. She ran for the door, but it was locked. Could Liam still be inside? Where were her keys?

Someone grabbed hold of her, but she pulled away. She would break this window too, and—

Whoever had grabbed her arm turned her around. It was Anson. "You're not going in there," he said.

That was when she heard the hum. But Glacier wasn't looking at Anson, he was looking across the street. She heard someone shout, "Stop!"

It was Liam's voice.

Glacier must have known it too. He bolted straight across the street, oblivious to people and cars. Red and blue lights flashed as the dog disappeared into Liam's building.

Then a gun went off.

"Liam!" she screamed.

Anson was gone in a second, running the same way the dog had, but two officers stopped him at the door. Avery stared up at the windows where the office was, but she couldn't see anything but flashing lights reflecting from the glass. The police started to shout and ducked behind their cars. She could hear Anson's voice over the sirens. She tried to get closer and found her legs were shaking so hard she had to hold on to a parked car to stand upright.

An awful sound behind her returned her attention to the Moose on the Loose. It took her a second to realize that the sprinklers had come on. Everything inside turned to smoke, then went dark. She looked back toward Cash's office. There had been a gunshot. And there was no sign of Liam. Or Glacier.

She couldn't even think. She ignored the sound of fire trucks pulling up, adding more chaos to the street. What if he wasn't okay? She wasn't sure she could bear it. It didn't matter that Liam wasn't her fiancé, that he wasn't anything to her. The thought of losing him meant everything. He meant everything. She stared at the open doorway, willing Liam to walk out.

And she waited.

Then Liam did come, materializing as if she'd wished him into existence. He looked disheveled and dirty, but he was there. And so was Anson, with Glacier in his arms, holding him like a lamb. She searched Liam, looking for some sign of injury, but he was walking toward her, faster and faster until he embraced her.

"I'm so sorry," he said, stroking her hair. "I'm so sorry I put you through all of this."

She couldn't answer him. All she could think was, *I thought you left me.* She thought it over and over until somehow the words slipped out between sobs. He only held her closer.

"Not going anywhere," he said, his voice warm and quiet against her ear. But then he leaned back, just far enough to look her in the eye. "Glacier saved my life."

She blinked. Then she looked down at where Anson had set Glacier down. She saw the wide, dilated eyes, not quite focused on her. Shaking legs. And blood. "Oh no."

She reached down for the dog, and as she did, he lay down, right in the middle of the street.

"Is this the dog?"

It was a woman's voice. She got down on her knees and lifted Glacier's head, looking him in the face, lifting a lip. "I know you, buddy. You're Sinatra, aren't you?"

"Glacier," Avery and Liam said at the same time.

"That's his name now," Avery added.

"That's a good name for you, handsome boy," the woman said. She held a stethoscope to the dog's rib cage. Pinched his paws. And did a few other things between petting him. "Such a good boy. So he was shot?" Her voice never changed as she asked the question, and for a moment Avery couldn't be sure she was asking a question at all.

"I think so," Liam said.

"Caliber? A pellet or a bullet? Aw, you're doing so good, Glacier." It registered in Avery's mind that the woman was wearing a tight red dress and high heels and that Avery had no idea who she was.

"Bullet. Nine millimeter or something similar." Liam's answer sunk Avery's heart even farther into her stomach.

The woman was feeling all around the dog's neck and face. "Through and through. Time to go for a ride, Glacier. I need oxygen and IV immediately. Help me get him in the front seat of my truck. No crying, no freaking out. Right, Glacier? If you can do it, so can they."

Then a different person spoke. "Who are you?"

Avery looked up to see an officer questioning the woman. He didn't look happy. "Where is Dr. Daughtry?"

"Grace Wright. And Mexico. Permanently. And if you want to make yourself useful, you can get the blanket out from behind the driver's seat and spread it on the passenger side of my truck seat."

No one moved.

"Now," she said, only slightly more firmly than the "dog voice" she'd been using.

And the officer moved.

"You boys," she said, glancing at Anson and Liam, "work as a team. Lift on three." She eyed Avery. "Stay next to him, he's focused on you. Calm, right? One. Two. Three."

The vet led them to a white pickup parked in the midst of the police cars. It had a built-in structure in the truck bed. She recognized it; their large animal vet back home called it a "vet box." The officer was spreading the blanket on the seat, and he got out of their way.

"2900 Beartooth Circle," she said. "Meet me there." She closed the door, got in the other side, and then drove away, leaving the four of them staring after her.

"She took my dog," Avery said, feeling stunned.

## CHAPTER 50

"I thought it was your dog," Mike said to Liam.

"It's complicated," Liam said.

"Of course it is. That's how things go for you Gunnerson boys. Listen, I need you guys to tell me what happened. I'll drive you both over to the clinic to get the dog settled, but then you have some things to explain."

Mike frowned and looked at Liam. Then he looked between them, where their hands were interlaced. Liam didn't remember when he'd reached for her hand. Then something completely different caught Mike's attention, and he stood up straight. "Nice of you to show up, Alexander."

"Is this him?" a man asked, jabbing a thumb at Liam.

Liam took in the suit and tie and knew this was a Fed. "I was just telling someone about you," he said.

Mike cut a warning glance at Liam, then addressed the man in the suit. "I'd like to introduce Liam Gunnerson. And this is Avery Maier."

Alexander, whether that was his first or last name, turned to Liam and said, "You need to come with me now."

"Hold on there," Mike said.

"This is a federal case."

"Not entirely. We have assault, possibly a strong-arm robbery, arson. So much excitement to be spread around. And not all of it federal jurisdiction. And there's one more thing. If you want to talk to Gunnerson right away, you'll have to wait until he gets checked out by the paramedics. Then I suppose you could have your interview at the vet's office."

The man eyed Mike. "The vet's? What would he have to do with this?"

"You're assuming the vet is a man?"

Liam smirked, since Mike had been so quick to assume that the woman in the red dress wasn't a vet.

Mike continued. "As you know, he's already decided to cooperate. He's not going anywhere, Alexander. And since I doubt you have any reason to take him into custody right this moment, give them a minute to tend to their dog. After all, things are obviously more complicated than either you or I realized."

The man looked around the street at the tangle of first-responder vehicles. "Complicated. Maybe that's because you run such a smooth operation here," he said sarcastically.

Mike grinned. "We're a little rusty on the simultaneous break-in, arson, kidnapping, attempted-murder thing. Tell me, what's the normal response time in New York? Never mind, I'm sure it's excellent. You're going to 2900 Beartooth Circle. I'd be happy to give you a ride."

"We should be going to the police station, Captain."

"That dog saved his life, Alexander."

"What the hell?" a man screamed. Liam turned to see Griff standing in front of the Moose on the Loose, rushing from side to side among the firemen and hoses. Someone tried to direct him away, but he was apoplectic. "What happened? What the hell? Did the fire spread next door?" He swore again and again. "Did you have to use a hose? Oh my God, it's broken. It's broken! What is wrong with you? What are you doing? You have to save the building next door, not this hellhole!" He spun around, and his eyes settled on Avery.

"Avery." He stared at her as if she were a ghost.

She let go of Liam's hand and walked up to Griff. And she slapped him so hard across his face that even with all the commotion, every single person in the street turned her way. Mike must have seen trouble coming because he immediately arrived beside her to pull her away. That was when Griff's eyes darted to Liam. "You," he mouthed.

Mike said something. And other officers were coming too. But Griff was faster, and so was Liam, and they ran straight at one another. Griff went for a strong left hook.

Liam saw it coming in slow motion and dodged it. He landed a left punch to Griff's right temple, followed instantly by a right elbow to his left temple. Griff was out before he hit the ground.

And everyone around them stopped still. Even the officers looked a little startled. Liam turned to face them all. He marched up to Alexander. Liam pulled his new pen out of his pocket, pressed the hidden button on the side, and handed it to the man. "You and Mike will be needing this. Now we're going to the vet."

# CHAPTER 51

*L*iam's phone had survived the fire sprinklers, but it had also been taken into evidence. It had been a long time until he'd been able to call and find out that Avery was fine, Glacier was improving, and that the filthy black sprinkler water had destroyed every bit of clothing in the store. His family had promised to help her, and he had felt better knowing they would.

He'd never had the chance to say goodbye to Avery. He'd left her at the veterinary clinic. Mike had let him use his phone to book Avery's parents on the fastest flight to Montana. Then Alexander had started turning the screws, and after a long night at the station, the Feds had given him ten minutes to pack his bag.

The way Liam saw it, Griff had saved them. Griff had given it away by talking to Billy out on the street. Billy had been focused on Avery's building, and that was how Liam had known Avery was in danger. So he'd left town as if he was following their instructions, but then he'd stopped at the gas station, gone out the back door, and run like a madman to the alley behind the Moose on the Loose. It was a miracle Avery had opened the door at that moment. But one of the thugs, or maybe it was Griff, must have seen him come back.

It didn't matter who it had been. He couldn't thank God enough that they never realized Avery was there. That she'd made it out on her own. That Glacier had saved his life—and then the vet, who had been dining only a block away, had saved Glacier's. That the arson fire hadn't spread, that his whole family had rallied around him. There were so many things to be thankful for.

And now his two weeks of "detained, not under arrest" in New York were over. The various agencies involved had realized he was there to help, not get away with something. Of course he had handed them a slam dunk with the recordings of his interactions with the thugs on the cheesy "James Bond Pen Recorder" he'd bought online. And he'd recorded Lynn, too, during their dinner at Annie's. He didn't know how that would play out in her life, nor did he care much. Since Griff was up on assault, kidnapping, and arson charges, he guessed things wouldn't go well for her, either.

The worst memory of all was when he had pulled Avery down into the basement. Leaving her there had felt like having his heart ripped out. Having a room full of strangers listen to him tell her he needed her to be safe was as exposed as he ever remembered feeling. He'd had to listen to that three times, so far. Maybe they could skip that part in court. But probably not.

He hated how desperate he sounded in that recording. And how desperately, clearly, and obviously he was in love with her. The whole world must have realized it before he had, including Avery.

But she didn't act like a woman who loved him back.

She had called him, eventually. She used Poppy's phone since hers was destroyed in the fire, and they had given each other some of the missing pieces as they'd talked. He had apologized until she made him promise to stop. She'd said Glacier's progress was better than even the vet could have hoped for. But when he had asked about her and her plans, Avery insisted she was busy and they'd talk when he returned to Moose Hollow. To Liam, it had sounded like she was delaying passing on bad news.

Avery had never once asked him what his plans were. But for the first time in months, he actually had plans. The Feds had talked to the CPA licensing board's governing committee, and an agreement was reached. With one more month of service under a CPA in good standing, they would count his time at Ackerman, Jones & Fetterman as completed. Starting Monday, he would be working in Billings with a friend of a friend of his dad's. The wages were terrible, but it was only temporary, and Liam would make his family proud. Then, when the month was over, Liam would be free to open his own company. Maybe even in Moose Hollow.

But where would Avery be?

When he arrived home again, Broadway was full of tourists. He avoided the crowds and drove the back road to park behind Cash's office and then walked to Avery's. The first thing he saw when he came around the corner was a sign that read "Grand Reopening" over the windows of the Moose on the Loose.

He stood and stared at it.

He wished she had told him what the heck was going on. He was standing there with a red face and thumping heart, wondering what bone-crushing news he was about to face. And this, he realized, was why she hadn't opened the overnight letter from the insurance company. He really got it now.

Cars had stopped both ways, waiting for him to cross, even though he wasn't at an intersection. Liam forced himself to move and reached for the door, but it opened of its own accord.

"Oh, hey," Mara said. "It's about time you got here."

It was about as matter-of-fact as a welcome could be. Then again, Liam hadn't been gone long, although it felt like a lifetime to him. But that thought slipped his mind as he looked around the Moose on the Loose. It looked spacious. And clean. And the checkout desk was new. Behind it, slabs of barn wood decorated the wall. Anson stood up from behind the desk and patted the top of it. "What do you think?"

Liam had no answer. He was too busy trying to figure out what was going on. What were Mara and Dad doing here?

"Oh, the wood hides the fire damage. But we decided to keep the smoke scars on the old ceiling tins," he said, pointing straight up.

Mara came up behind him. "Adds character," she said. "A little element of danger." She shrugged. "Hopefully people spend more for ambiance. Sierra says they will."

"Sierra?" Liam repeated, completely confused. Mara pointed to his left and he looked that way. Sierra was there unpacking boxes. "Hi," she said, barely looking up from what she was doing. "I think Poppy had something for you to do in the back."

He hadn't been expecting a parade or anything, but this was weird. And awkward. He walked across the floor, which had a new coat of varnish on it, and stepped into the back room. No one was there. And everything was different.

The built-in shelves and stairway looked freshly oiled, and all but the brick wall had been painted a midnight blue, with some sort of shimmery wash here and there. "Like the faux finish?"

He followed the sound of the voice up to find Poppy on a ladder, hand-painting the edge between the walls and a ceiling that had been painted black. "Just think how great the fairy lights are going to look when we string them up," she said.

"What?"

"Fairy lights," she said, as if that explained everything. It didn't. By the door, he saw clothing stands and hooks piled up. So the Moose on the Loose was expanding into the back room.

While that sank in, he heard barking, followed by something like "*wuh-woo-woo.*" He turned in time to see Glacier barreling down the stairs. He crouched down, but Glacier met him midair, a giant wagging, wooing, furry missile. Liam fell backward, and Glacier continued his assault, wooing and licking his face relentlessly.

Yeah, that was the kind of welcome he'd been wanting. He saw Avery then, standing at the top of the stairs with her hands on her hips. She was cuter, sexier, prettier, smirkier, and more of everything than he had remembered. He didn't know what to say. "Glacier, he's—"

"Talking," she supplied. "Yeah, he started doing that when he was discharged from the vet. And he does it a lot."

Glacier talked again, and Liam got to his feet. "I can't believe it."

"I need your help moving something," Avery said, and she walked down the upstairs hallway and out of sight.

So much for the warm welcome. Liam followed the dog up the stairs and found Avery near her room, pointing at a dismantled bed. "This has to go in the last room," she said, gesturing toward the back of the building.

He did as she asked. He walked past closed doors and retrieved the mattress, carrying it down to the smallest bedroom, the one with the fire escape. When he opened the door, he was stunned.

He propped the mattress against the wall and took it all in. It had been repainted. No, more than that. It was small and rustic looking. The trim was painted a coffee color, and the walls were denim blue. And the ceiling had been covered in wooden slats, too. A small chandelier hung from the ceiling. And the floor, which had looked beyond salvaging, looked amazing with a shiny coat of black paint. "I know," Avery said. "You're not supposed to paint small rooms dark colors. But I wanted this to be my quiet place. And I love it."

He thought he heard someone coming up the steps behind her, but then he realized she'd said "my." My quiet place.

"You're staying."

She nodded. "Yup."

Why? And did it matter to her that he wanted to stay too? Was she counting on him leaving? Too many questions raced through his mind, so he started with, "How?"

"Well, there's the insurance policy on the Moose on the Loose, although it's Griff's insurance that'll be paying for the renovations and all the ruined clothes. Ironic, right? And I got money from Eli's dad."

"What?"

"My dad talked to him," Avery continued. "Heaven only knows what he said, but I know Dad told him about you. And it turns out he knew about what Eli and Griff and that other guy did to you in high school. Eli told his father about it years ago. He had wanted to apologize to you in person, Liam. He just ran out of time. Mr. Canten said he even drove out here once to talk to you, but you'd moved to Chicago."

Liam tried to process that. "You found out about all of that."

"I wish you'd told me."

The silence dragged on as Liam tried to make sense of what he was hearing and how he felt about it. He hadn't wanted her to know about the assault. But whatever he'd been afraid of seemed to fade away, until all he felt was relief.

"Mr. Canten said it was a God thing that you were in my life, and he was really sorry about opening the insurance investigation. He'd thought Eli's insurance policy was some sort of scam I was running. I understand that, it was out of character for Eli to get life insurance at all. His dad said he wished he'd left it alone, and that Eli was right to try to protect me. And Mr. Canten wanted me to have the money he got from his own family policy, one he'd had since Eli was born. It's not a million-dollar policy of course, but it was so kind of him. I just wanted you to know, I think you're the real reason he gave me that money. Dad was under the impression that you and I were a couple." She looked down, her lashes shielding her eyes. "So that's what he told Eli's dad. And that made Mr. Canten happy."

The silence stretched on while Avery hugged her arms across her stomach and tapped at something invisible on the floor with her shoe. Then she took a deep breath. "Actually, this is all about the plan you laid out for the lawyer."

Liam had to think hard to pull that information back out. It seemed so long ago, vanished in the losses that had happened since then. "The plan?"

"But we're actually doing five profit centers, not four like you suggested." She held up one finger. "First the Moose on the Loose. Sierra is going to manage that. The online store makes it two," she said, splaying two fingers. "Three is the residential rental. It's really me paying me to live here, but the banker said it still counts."

"The banker?"

"Sure. Peter Henderson. Part-time cowboy. He was at the branding, remember? Colton was trying to fix us up. In a business sense, I mean. Anyway, it turns out that his wife is a pretty big fan of Poppy's wedding dress. And Stevie Nicks, for whatever that's worth. So she dabbles in investing, and therefore…" She lifted another finger. "Four is just downstairs. It's called Avery Designs. I know, it's a boring name."

"You're staying," he repeated.

She smirked. "You're missing something," she said, and looked at her own hand, with just four fingers held up. "And I don't even count the civil suit. I didn't want to file one, but it's free. Did you know the lawyer you recommended has had trouble with the Hallowells, and he's happy to work on the suit for free? It's a long story. So guess what five is."

Liam shook his head.

"Do you know George Deeds? He's a local historian. He also

does hay rides, by the way. Glacier really likes him, probably because he smells like horses. Anyway, he's going to be giving tours Wednesday night through the sidewalk vault tunnels, ending up in the speakeasy downstairs. As soon as we knock down that last wall. The tour starts at the Third Street Inn. They go through the vaults, past a couple old storefronts as he tells scary stories, and then they come upstairs through the secret entrance and end up in Avery Designs. I'll serve wine and appetizers from the Third Street Inn restaurant. Your mom is going to help me get furniture that—"

"You're staying."

She smirked at him again. He ignored the sound of a door closing down the hall and waited for an answer.

"I am," she said. "Are you?" Her eyes narrowed. "Or are you going to Portland?"

He didn't know what she hoped to hear. But his decision was made. "I'm staying," he said. And there it was, the slight quirk at the corner of her pretty mouth, the crinkle just at the corner of her eyes—all signs of the smile she was hiding.

That was all he needed to know. He walked over to Avery and closed the door behind her. Then they were alone in the room so that whatever was going on in the hall wouldn't intrude. Liam took her hands in his own. And she looked up at him, brown eyes full of everything he wanted to see. He brushed back a strand of silky hair and drew her closer. He was caught up in the look of her lips, shining and pink, just like the cold morning she'd come storming into Cash's office. And when those lips parted, he kissed her.

*Some things*, he thought, *are better than a person could ever imagine.*

"Woo-oo," Glacier said just outside the door, and Avery giggled.

"He's saying I shouldn't be in here," Liam said. "And he's right."

"The mattress is in the hall, so it's not my bedroom yet. Are you going to keep this up?"

He nodded. "Yup. Unless...if you decided...if our relationship was more permanent...not that I'm assuming." The more he stumbled, the bigger her smile got. He cleared his throat. "It'll stay this way until our relationship status changes."

She put a hand over his heart. "Good," she said softly. "I like that."

"Ah-woo-woo," Glacier said more insistently.

She reached for the door. "You should see what your cousin did," she said, taking off down the hallway. He had to jog to catch up to her. When they turned the corner into what used to be her bedroom, she pointed to the back wall. There was a gaping hole. "What happened?" he asked.

"Well, we're going to open a wide door between the living room and kitchen. Poppy's idea, of course. She's brilliant at these things. Colton wanted to see what was inside the wall to get an idea how hard it would be, and a couple sledgehammer hits later, this is what I got. Check it out."

Liam walked over to the hole, but the rustling inside gave it away. He didn't know what to expect when he stepped through the wall into the kitchen/whatever room, but he knew it would be something.

It was his family, and his friends, and a huge and badly handmade sign that read, "Welcome Home Liam." There was a homemade cake to match the sign, and taped up all along the wall, copies of the newspaper articles on the investigation of Solarthea and Ackerman, Jones, & Fetterman. And there were cheers and applause, and all the warm welcomes he'd been denied downstairs.

"Did we fool you?" Mara said.

"Yes," he said. She wrinkled her nose at him. She wasn't buying it.

Everyone was talking at once, but all that mattered was the

way Avery slipped her hand into his, interlacing their fingers. It was everything he wanted in the world. And it was just the beginning.


The End


I hope you enjoyed Bright Montana Home, book 2 in the Moose Hollow series. While it's still fresh in your mind, I hope you'll consider writing a review on Amazon. Book reviews help match the right readers with the right books.

In other words, reviews are the Stevie Nicks to an author's Fleetwood Mac, the Thai peanut sauce on her pizza, and the wagging tail on her furry best friend. Thank you!


For news about special offers, new books, and to download a *free* short story, visit cynthiabruner.com.

Made in the USA
Coppell, TX
15 October 2022

84667763R00194